300 Days of Sun

ALSO BY DEBORAH LAWRENSON

The Lantern

The Sea Garden

300 Days of Sun

Deborah Lawrenson

HARPER LUXE

An Imprint of HarperCollins*Publishers*

300 DAYS OF SUN. Copyright © 2016 by Deborah Lawrenson. All rights reserved. Printed in the United States of America. No part of this book may be used or reproduced in any manner whatsoever without written permission except in the case of brief quotations embodied in critical articles and reviews. For information address HarperCollins Publishers, 195 Broadway, New York, NY 10007.

HarperCollins books may be purchased for educational, business, or sales promotional use. For information please e-mail the Special Markets Department at SPsales@harpercollins.com.

FIRST HARPERLUXE EDITION

ISBN: 978-0-06-244032-7

HarperLuxe™ is a trademark of HarperCollins Publishers.

Library of Congress Cataloging-in-Publication Data is available upon request.

16 17 18 19 20 ID/RRD 10 9 8 7 6 5 4 3 2 1

Prologue

A few careless minutes, and the boy was gone.

Violet shadows stretched from the rocks, clock hands over the sand. She shouldn't have allowed herself to linger, but the sea and sky had merged into a shimmering mirror of copper and red; it was hard to tell if she was floating above the water, or standing on air. Waves beat time on the shore then reached out to caress her feet.

She could hear the children shrieking with pleasure. A short distance away, the path threaded up through the rocks to the garden of pine trees and gold coin daisies: Horta das Rochas, the "garden of rocks" near the edge of the world, where famous explorers and navigators once set sail for unknown continents.

Her eyes were still on the dissolving horizon when she called the children. A scampering on the wet sand brought a small hand to her leg. She glanced down.

"Look!" said the girl.

Her daughter pointed to a flock of birds flying in silhouette against a blood-orange cloud. They watched for a moment.

"Time to go back," she said.

The boy, older by a year, spent hours by the rock pool, staring at the stirrings of sea life in miniature. It was no more than a few steps from where she was standing. "Tico!" she called, using his baby name.

No answer.

The rock pool was deserted.

"Where's Tico?"

"Gone," said the girl.

"He's hiding! Come on."

She took the girl's hand and they ran to the wind-carved cave. "Tico!"

"Tico!" echoed the girl.

The opening in the rocks was in deep shadow, cold and dark. The girl clutched tighter. They both called again. No answer. They felt along the damp creased walls, for a warm, giggling mass balled up on the ground. The cave was empty. Outside the sunset deepened. They were alone on the beach.

All the way up the path, they called to him. No answer.

The onset of panic froze her in the heat. Why had she not felt the prickle of danger, sensed the change? When she first arrived in this curious country, she had used her skills constantly: patience and observation, subtlety and guile. She needed them, they all had. Vigilance was vital.

She should never have forgotten that the sardine fishermen pulled their boats up from the beach and into the streets for safety when they felt the first intimations of storm swell. The change in atmospheric pressure registered on their skin and in their bones. They trusted their senses and protected themselves because the water could surge right over the walls of the old town fortifications and knock on the door of the cafés.

They knew these seas and storms destroyed houses: waves reached inside and snatched a lifetime's work, floating precious contents out to sea. Boats were smashed into driftwood. Channels vanished; islands were submerged. New inlets were gouged by the wind and the wild rain, redrawing the coastline, making maps obsolete.

But quiet forces were equally destructive. She should never have let down her guard, never forgotten the old threat that remained unseen and insidious.

She began to run.

PART ONE
Faro

i

I met Nathan Emberlin in Faro, southern Portugal, in August 2014.

At first, I thought he was just another adventurous young man, engaging but slightly immature. His beautiful sculpted face held a hint of vulnerability, but that ready smile and exuberant cheekiness eased his way, as did the radiant generosity of his spirit, so that it wasn't only women who smiled back; people of all ages warmed to Nathan, even the cross old man who guarded the stork's nest on the lamppost outside the tobacconist's shop.

Yes, he appeared from nowhere—but then, so did we all. I didn't go to Faro to get a story. That summer I was on the run, or so it felt; I was trying to consign an awkward episode to my own past, not to get entangled in someone else's. Besides, a lot of people I met in Faro were in the process of change, of expanding their horizons and aiming for a better life. The town was full of strangers and constant movement: planes overhead, roaring in and out of the airport across the shore; boats puttering in and out of the harbour; trains sliding between the road and the sea; buses and cars; pedestrians bobbing up and down over the undulating cobblestones.

The café, at least, was still. On the way to the language school, it had the presence and quiet grace of an ancient oak, rooted to its spot in the Rua Dr. Francisco Gomes. The columns and balustrades of its once-grand fin de siècle façade had an air of forgotten romance that was hard to resist. I pushed against its old-style revolving door that first morning simply because I was curious to see inside.

True to its promise, the interior was cavernous, the ceiling high and elegantly proportioned. But the plaster on the walls was cratered, and mould speckled the cornicing. The tables and chairs were plastic garden furniture, set out haphazardly on a coral-and-white-checkerboard floor; few of them were taken. I went up to the main counter, into an aromatic cloud of strong coffee, where a group of men knotted over an open newspaper. The barman, wiping his hands on an apron that was none too clean, seemed to be engaged in voicing his opinion and was in no hurry to serve me.

Photographs of old Faro were set into wooden panelling: black-and-white scenes of a fishing community, of empty roads and dusty churches. The argument at the bar counter intensified, or that's what it sounded like. It's not always possible to tell in a foreign language. It might just be excitability. But some words were easy to understand. *Contra a natureza. Anorma. Devastador.*

"*Bom dia?*" The barman had noticed me at last. There was a sense of a question about his greeting. Or perhaps it was supposed to double for "What would you like?" Four days into *Portuguese for Beginners*, and I could manage to order a cup of coffee. There didn't seem to be anything more substantial for breakfast on display and there were no menus.

The barman pressed some buttons on a brute of a machine, which released a dribble of muddy liquid.

"*Bica,*" he said, pushing it towards me in a tiny chipped cup along with a bowl of sugar cubes.

The bill came to pennies. I didn't know this was the Café Aliança.

No, I didn't meet Nathan at the café. At that stage he didn't know any more about the place than I did.

It **was** gone nine o'clock by the time I started the short walk to the language centre. The *calçada* pavement was a mosaic of cobblestones studded with images of fish and wave patterns. It was so uneven that, several times, as I looked up to admire white Moorish-style buildings against an unbroken blue sky, I experienced a disconcerting drop as the ground fell away beneath me.

I plunged north into a labyrinth of pedestrian streets, away from the tang of salt and boats at anchor. This was always the quietest time of the day. Few shops were open and most people were only slowly coming round. Nights were late and lively in the town. Faro, like the café, had the air of a once-grand old lady fallen on hard times; too many shops had closed down, empty boxes tied up with ribbons of bill stickers and notices of liquidation. Peeling walls were embossed with election posters from which bland, toothsome faces stared out and made promises on behalf of the Workers' Party and the Communists, and the Man Who Believes in Better for Faro.

The language centre was on the Praça da Liberdade, next to a pharmacy. An illuminated green cross flashed "Go, go, go!" above a small crowd of men and women dressed for business but going nowhere on the pavement outside the entrance to the Centro de Linguas. They watched the closed door with palpable impatience; the lateness with which the morning lessons habitually began was already an issue, particularly with the Swiss and German students, for whom nine o'clock meant nine o'clock.

"*Bom dia,* Joanna," said one of them now, an IT specialist from Berne.

"*Bom dia,* Tomas."

He looked at his substantial watch and rolled his eyes.

I shrugged. Actually, I was finding the relaxed approach quite restful. The teachers seemed to work hard and offered equal slippage at the end of the day, so nothing was lost.

The door opened at twenty-five past and we filed up the stairs: two Swiss men, two Germans (a man and a woman), a Belgian woman, a Dutch woman, an Italian man, an Irish man, and me, all professionals and businesspeople eager to learn Portuguese. They talked about giving themselves the edge in emerging markets, by which they meant Brazil. Most of them would have gone straight to Rio de Janeiro to learn the language had they been able to afford it. Portugal was cheap, there were three hundred days of sunshine a year, but it was no place to be working unless there was a specific deal to be made.

The owner of the language centre, Senhora Davim, greeted us cheerfully outside the open door of her office. She was a fleshy middle-aged woman with pencilled brows and immaculate red lipstick applied over thick foundation. Despite the August heat, she was packed into a dark suit, from which a froth of silky blouse burst when she undid the front buttons.

We took our places in the classroom.

My first few days in the country, I was astonished by how many Russian tourists there were here, chattering in the shops and streets. Then I realised: to the uninitiated, Portuguese sounds like Russian. The language is nothing like the soft singsong of Spanish or Italian. The sounds shush and slip around like the shining, sliding cobblestones under your feet.

"*Baleia cachalote morta,*" said Caterina, the teacher who took the first morning lesson each day. She was fairly young, though perhaps it was only the untamed frizzy hair that made me think that, along with the large round eyes. Those eyes peered out of her overgrown fringe like a startled lemur's through foliage.

She spoke only in Portuguese, which meant we had to concentrate hard.

She held up a newspaper and pointed to the main photograph. It looked like the page the men in the café had been arguing over, and this time I could see what it was: a whale, washed up on a beach. *"A causa da morte da baleia ainda não foi descoberta."* Caterina enunciated slowly and carefully. *"Remoção da carcaça . . . município é responsável."* Cause of death not yet discovered. Removal of the carcass. The municipality was responsible. Caterina pointed to the whale's head. The chain-saw teeth were huge cones, she mimed, each the length of her dark-haired forearm.

The door opened and in sauntered Nathan, wearing ripped jeans. He'd gone native within the first few days as far as timekeeping was concerned. He gave Caterina a salute and flopped into the nearest seat, letting his tatty rucksack drop on the floor.

"Bom dia, Nathan."

"E aí, tudo bom?"

Caterina's face always looked tired and her smile rarely lit up her eyes. But she made an exception for Nathan and his slangy greeting ("Hey there—all good?"), especially when he had plenty to say about the beached whale, all in nonstop Portuguese. There had been a terrible storm, or that's what I thought he said, something about devastation on the islands. His conversation might not have been grammatically perfect (I suspected it wasn't) but there was no doubt he was a natural linguist. He was the only other British student and, at twenty-four, the youngest among us.

We moved on to question-and-answer exercises taken from a book. After an hour of stilted interrogation about names and jobs and methods of transport ("My name is Enzo; I am from Italy; I work as a company manager; my company makes shoes; I travelled to Faro in a plane.") we broke for morning coffee in a bar down the road.

Enzo was quite jolly, actually, and wanted to speak English whenever possible. ("Fuck shoes. I want stop shoes. But shoes good for Rio de Janeiro.") He was in his mid-forties, corpulent, hair quite possibly dyed but plenty of it. I sat between him and Nathan and had another tiny coffee along with an almond pastry I justified as a late breakfast.

"You speak Portuguese very good," Enzo told Nathan.

"Not really, but you've got to have a go, haven't you."

"Where did you get to last night?" I asked him.

It was fast becoming a standing joke that Nathan's nights were spent drinking and making new friends (we knew he meant girls) at the clubs and bars.

"After O Castelo? The Millennium in Rua do Prior. I met this mad local who said he was a bus driver. I thought he might be good for some free rides. He wanted me to teach him racist abuse in English. I only told him because I'd necked at least six mojitos. I felt awful afterwards."

Nathan had only been in Faro for a week and he already had a diverse collection of acquaintances. In addition to his encounters with women, he had befriended an Ecuadorian who believed in voodoo and evil spirits and a Spaniard whose idea of punctuality was being only three hours late. Then there were the girls in his lodging house who constantly knocked on his door and had silly, shouty conversations outside in the corridor to make him come out.

He was tanned and rail thin, as if he hardly ate, or rather had got used to not eating if circumstances didn't allow. His cheekbones were sharp, catching the fall of long dark hair and giving a masculine cut to features that might otherwise have been too prettily girlish. He claimed to have flunked normal school somewhere in South London, but he had guts and drive and had travelled around Spain and Portugal, staying three weeks here, one week there. He pronounced the names of the places he has passed through with absolute linguistic accuracy. The course would have been a lot duller without him.

"Nice clean T-shirt," I said, then turned to Enzo. "His landlady is doing his washing for him, free of charge."

"Couldn't stop her! I feel like I've been adopted. Friendly lot here, aren't they. Credit where it's due."

"That is because you are friendly," said Enzo.

"Got to be, haven't you? You should come out one evening, mate. We'll have a laugh."

Another couple of hours in the plain white rooms of the language centre with its purposeful staff of women. Lunch. Three more hours of listening and trying to speak in response. It was hard work.

Senhora Davim's secretary, a young girl with dyed red hair and a tattoo of a butterfly on her leg, came out of her cubbyhole office as we left to wish us a good evening, shyly, in English. She caught Nathan's eye and looked away quickly when he winked at her. "Cheers, Lía."

"You coming to O Castelo this evening?" he asked me as we walked out onto the street. This was the cocktail bar and nightspot on the Old Town wall we'd all been to the first night of the course, when everyone was being sociable. It would be packed on a Friday night.

"Not tonight."

"What are you up to then?"

"Not much. I'm shattered."

"See you tomorrow, then. Eleven o'clock at the ferry. You are still going, aren't you? I've asked the others, though I'm not sure how many of them will actually do it."

"Yes. I'll see you there."

The studio apartment I had rented on Rua da Misericórdia for the six weeks' duration of the language course was on the second floor above a boutique selling hats and beachwear. Across the road stood a fine sixteenth-century church and, only a few paces away, the Arco da Vila, the arched gateway into the Old Town. I didn't need to use my key to open the faded red entrance door to the side of the shop—someone had forgotten to close it properly, again. I checked the post box numbered 7. Empty. As I climbed the stone staircase lined with patterned ceramic tiles, my footsteps echoed.

Apart from an air-conditioning unit that was losing its battle against the heat, the studio was perfect. It wasn't huge, but not too small either. I've never minded being on my own. In fact, I had been longing to be alone, for these weeks away from Brussels, from Marc and all the complications, while I made up my mind what to do.

From the window was a view of the formal garden behind the marina, the Jardim Manuel Bivar, where old men sat under palm and jacaranda trees in clothes that were too dark, too thick; at the end of the day, elderly women would proceed slowly as the incoming tide to fetch them.

I took a shower to put off the moment I would have to look at my mobile. When I did, there were two missed calls and three texts, tone increasingly angry. With no Wi-Fi in the building, I couldn't access any emails. Of course, I could have connected at the language school to download them, but I'd decided to give myself a break.

By eight o'clock the air was soft and tinged with pink from the falling sun. I pulled on jeans, flip-flops, and a floaty top and took my iPad off to a bar where I could access the Internet and read some news of the world beyond southern Portugal.

The first evening I was here, I started to notice how most of the streetlamps were tufted with dried grasses and twigs. Then I saw more ragged wigs on church porches and high ledges. I assumed it was yet more evidence of neglect, that weeds had seeded and been left to grow in sandy crevices, but as I began to study them more carefully, I figured it out. They were birds' nests. There was one high on the stone pediment of the gatehouse to the Old Town, a great wheel of grasses, big as a tractor tyre. I looked up as I passed.

I was lucky. I caught a movement inside the wheel, then a powerful white wing extended and then folded in on itself. These weren't just any birds' nests: they were storks' nests, and I was absurdly relieved to see the great creature settling down safely for the night. During the past week there had been unpleasant incidents of storks being found poisoned. Then, a corpse was left on the steps of the town hall. It was a substantial creature. Its wings were broken and spread. Blood matted the white feathers. The outrage had provoked a spontaneous protest, though whether that was against the stork killers or current town hall policies it was impossible to say. Various noisy marches had clogged the town in recent days; these seemed to be political, ahead of a local election, and the word for corruption— corrupção—was hard to mistake.

A line of stalls was starting to open in the public garden. Vendors had filled them with traditional cakes and desserts to offer the crowds coming for the nightly Folk Faro concert on the waterfront, which already seemed like contrived joviality, as authentic as cheap plastic dolls in national costume.

Outside the grand café in Rua Dr. Francisco Gomes, posters were propped up on easels. One was for a candidate in the forthcoming election, another for a talk about Old Faro. A group of men and a few women stood outside talking animatedly. The place still intrigued me but I went on past this time, down the street to the bar-bakery where they were happy for me to sit at a table outside with just a drink at a time when most of the tourists were looking for somewhere to eat dinner.

In reply to the last of Marc's emails, I spent twenty minutes writing and rewriting, trying to find the right words to explain how I felt. In the end I deleted it all and wrote: "Please do not come. I need time on my own." A gulp of wine, and I pressed Send.

ii

I was certain it would be a long wait for Nathan the next morning but he loped up almost on time, wearing knee-length shorts, a red T-shirt, Converse sneakers, and his rucksack over one shoulder.

"No one else coming?" he asked, looking around.

"Not yet. We're the first."

Beyond the jetty where ferries left for the island beaches, the sea was a wide expanse of harsh glitter. Boats scored dark scratches over the silver as they puttered in and out of the harbour and towards the waterways of the lagoon. The salt marshes lurked green and alien on the entrance to the ocean.

We sat on the grass at the foot of the old city walls, watching a man and a woman as they crossed the railway tracks to fish; they sat side by side, hunched over their rods. We waited for twenty minutes but none of the others turned up. It was a relief to be able to speak normally in our own language; even when we spoke English to our fellow students, we had to water down our expressions and choose our words carefully. Nathan chatted easily about nothing in particular (fish dishes he had tried, the covered market, how to dig for clams) as beach trippers trooped onto the open-sided double-decker ferry to Praia de Faro, filling it almost to capacity.

"Come on, let's go," he said. "We don't want to have to wait for the next one. If any of them was coming, they'd be here by now."

We were the last aboard. The steel gate on deck clanged shut behind us, the engine thrummed, and the ferry moved away from the quay while we were still climbing the steps to the top deck. We managed to squeeze into a space on a bench seat.

"You know the ferry boats have no insurance—or so the rumour goes."

"Well thanks, Nathan. You might have saved those comforting words until we actually arrived."

"If the worst comes to the worst, it can't be that deep."

The ferry took a channel through the marshes. On either side of this sea road, green fields sprang up from narrow mud beaches.

"Did you see this from the air when your plane came in?" I asked. "I couldn't think what it was at first." The interlocking islands of the marshes formed miles of green lace on the water, like a wide frill that hung from the edge of the mainland.

"No. I came on the bus."

At sea level, this delicate lace-land was unexpectedly solid. Storks and other large birds pranced regally over the grass, stopping to delve for food. After a while, we began to see low, whitewashed houses that gave the lie to the impermanence of these narrow strips of sea marsh.

"They look as if they've been there for centuries," I said, not bothering to explain my train of thought. "But over there, the buildings look as if they're sinking." Two stone cottages, pockmarked and desolate, seemed to be straining to keep their windows above watery ground.

"I'd have my house on the other side."

On the south-facing bank, a row of wooden cabins suggested a ramshackle, shantytown scene: old car tyres were piled up to protect a row of saplings; a palm grew at an angle in front of one dwelling on a front stoop; tarpaulin flapped in the wind, slowly being shredded by the gusts. Small rowing boats rested at anchor close by, along with fishing lines and rusting buckets.

"A boat, a wooden house . . . clam digging," said Nathan. "Sorted."

Two men and a woman were bent double, brown legs planted in triangles, as they chopped at the mud with axe-like tools with one hand and grubbed in the soil with the other. Plastic buckets stood close by.

"Hard work," I said.

"But worth it. Best clams in Portugal."

I smiled but said nothing. It was refreshing, being with someone who soaked up so much information and pumped it back so guilelessly. I wondered about his bullshit filter at times, but as mine seemed stuck on maximum cynicism, I reckoned that between us we struck some kind of balance. I certainly didn't buy the idea of Nathan as a clam fisherman.

Faro beach is long and sandy. That Saturday it was also crowded. We took our shoes off and walked along the edge of the water for a while. A carpet of grasses floated on the surface, broken up by the waves that flung it onto the sand.

"I wasn't expecting quite such a green furry sea."

"It's not always like this," said Nathan. "The marsh got ripped up by the storm the other night. Bits and pieces are still being brought in by the tides."

We stopped when we found some sunbeds under straw parasols for hire. Nathan would just have flopped down on the beach where we stood, unwilling to pay the ten-euro fee; I insisted on paying, on the basis that I was the fair-skinned softie who needed some shade and comfort.

I had hardly put down my bag when he pulled off his shirt and ran down to a patch of grass-thatched sand where the shore shelved, paused a second, then pitched forward to dive into a breaking wave. His head popped up and he slicked the long hair back off his face, seal-like. He turned and waved, gesturing me to join him. In many ways, he reminded me of my younger brother, the same cocksure bravado alternating with naivety. I was nearly six years older: thirty next birthday. I felt a twinge of self-consciousness, but quickly got over it. All Nathan wanted was easy company in the hours before he could go off again into the nightclubs to find some action.

I shrugged myself out of my dress and ran to the sea.

"If a stork builds a nest on the roof of your house, people here say you have received a blessing: you will live long and be wealthy, and you will be lucky in love," said Nathan. "That's what the old bloke outside the tobacconist's says, and that's why he's guarding the one on the lamppost. Sits all day on the bench next to it shaking his stick at anyone who gets too close. But why would anyone want to attack the storks?"

"Do we know it's deliberate? I mean, the poison could be in some new crop spray, or—?"

"They all think it's deliberate."

"But who would do that—and why?"

"Who knows? Horrible, either way. And it's bad luck if a storks' nest comes down, or a bird dies."

I peeled a strip of grass off my wet arm. Our swim had felt a lot more pleasant than it looked. The temperature of the water was blissfully cool and the long rollers that folded against the shore were invigorating.

"They can last for decades, storks' nests," Nathan continued. "The birds return to the same nest and the same mate each year. The old bloke asked me how long I thought the record was, for a nest to be used. I said fifty years and he shook his head. Wrong—it's centuries! And there are records to prove it, he reckons."

He lay back on his sunbed, hands behind his head. The sun sent a searchlight through the gaps in our straw parasol and picked out the brown muscles and ridges of his chest. I forced myself to look away to where a doughnut vendor trudged up the beach, calling out the words emblazoned in red on the white box he carried: *Bolas de Berlim.*

"Are you hungry?" I asked.

"Always. Those doughnuts are good."

"I brought a picnic, actually. Nothing very exciting, just from the supermarket—some bread and cheese and fruit, and some little custard tarts. I wasn't sure what we'd find for lunch here."

He fell on what I brought out of my bag with child-like appreciation. There was only mineral water to drink but he gulped it down with as much enjoyment as if it had been cold beer, all the while offering comments and observations.

"Portuguese girls . . . are very attractive, but don't they just know it. A bit too pleased with themselves for my taste. But that might just be because I haven't got lucky yet." He winked as if to imply it was only a matter of time.

"I thought you had—down at the clubs."

"No. I met a nice Spanish girl the other night—and an Irish girl. They're everywhere, Irish girls. It's all the Ryanair flights. Mind you, half of them think they're landing a bit closer to Lisbon than it turns out. This girl, right, she says to her mate," he put on a passable Irish accent, "'Didya not read the small print, Siobhan? It's de small print where dey tell you where de floight for fifty pee is *really* going!'"

We both laughed hard. As I said, Nathan was the easiest of companions. I didn't regard any of his questions as intrusive, because he was so happy to answer mine. So when he asked me, "Is your bloke coming to see you, then?" I gave him an honest answer.

"I hope not."

"Why's that then?"

"I'm running away from him."

"Like that, is it? How long you been together?"

"A couple of years."

Nathan reached for his cigarettes, not offering me one. I don't smoke, and he knew that by then. He took a drag and sucked the smoke into his lungs like nourishment before exhaling. "What did he do wrong?"

"Long story."

"Aren't they all."

I said nothing.

"What can you do, except be as kind as possible?" said Nathan.

He was a sweet boy. For a minute I did wonder about telling him a bit about Marc and how he still wanted it to work out between us, whilst I had never intended our arrangement to be permanent. I'd seen the light at the end of the tunnel, and was racing to meet it.

"That's all you can do," I agreed.

The trouble was, I had tried being kind, but that meant staying to listen to all the arguments to stay. And even if I did capitulate, our relationship was not the only thing that wasn't for me anymore.

"Is he a journalist, too?"

"No."

I was quite surprised Nathan remembered what I did for a living. It hadn't been mentioned since that first evening at the cocktail bar with the rest of the language course students when we all threw chunks of biography at one another. I certainly hadn't brought it up, mainly because it wasn't strictly true anymore. Learning some Portuguese was my way of treading water while I worked out what to do next.

"Must be interesting, though, being a journalist," said Nathan. "Bet you enjoy it."

"I do," I said, truthfully.

"You work for a newspaper, right?"

I hesitated.

"Only, I wanted to ask you—"

"Actually, I'm here because . . . I was recently made redundant."

"Shit. That's tough."

"Yes, well. Onwards and upwards."

"What're you going to do? You can get another job, yeah?"

"With any luck. Newspapers are like every other business in these tricky times: cutting down on margins, and that means staff. It's not so bad. If I don't get another job straightaway, I can always free-lance."

"Course you can. You must have loads of experience. I mean, journalists know how to find out anything, don't they—so all you need to do is find out where the work is and go for it." He nodded encouragingly.

I had to smile. "Something like that."

We lay back after eating and dozed. "I'm going to burn if I stay here much longer," I said after a while.

"We could walk from here to see the whale, if you want," said Nathan. "The one that was in the papers."

I hadn't realised this was where it was.

We smelled the dead whale before we saw it. Newspaper reports couldn't convey the rank, cloying nature of rotting fish and sweet putrefaction that reached up the beach and pulled crowds of the curious towards its source. Sightseers were held back by a rope circle staked in the sand. The jawbone was the size of a tree trunk. One side of the whale was cruelly exposed, like the open engine of a broken-down bus, trailing viscous organs in the wet sand.

"Was that what killed it, or did that happen after it died?" asked Nathan, holding his nose as he leaned closer.

"Hard to say."

"Poor thing."

It was high tide and waves nudged gently at the body. The skin of the great mammal was being cured to leather with every new day it was exposed to sun and wind and salt water. I wondered whether it was shrinking, whether it would eventually shrivel to a gigantic black sac. What with the dying storks and now this, it was hard not to feel that nature was struggling.

Nathan interrupted my thoughts.

"When you said, earlier, about finding out things. How do you start?"

"Sorry?"

"How do you find out about something that happened years and years ago. How do you prove it's true?"

I turned to look at him. He was staring out to sea, eyes unreadable.

"That's a 'how long is a piece of string?' question."

"Seriously."

"Well . . . you'd start with what you know is fact, and work from there. There are records that can be checked, and people who can provide answers, and one fact leads to the next until you start to build up a picture that can be verified."

"Even if it was quite a long time ago?"

"It can be done. How easy it is depends on how long ago it happened. Whether people are still alive to tell what they know. Whether there exists any evidence that can be traced. Anything is possible, though that doesn't mean you can get a story to stand up every time. Are you interested in journalism?"

"Might be."

I assumed that was why he was asking, and it struck me that he had many of the qualities that made a good reporter, even if they were currently undeveloped. We wandered back along the shore, musing about the whale and the story it had brought to the town. It had to do with a human need for answers and a desire for the world to make sense. Some of the more lurid representations—there was a national colour magazine that had run a six-page spread complete with photoshopped blood—pointed to a less attractive need to be entertained by misfortune.

It was only as we were boarding the ferry that Nathan got to the point and I realised how badly I had misunderstood him.

"Jo?"

"Yes?"

"If I asked you to help me with something, would you?"

"Probably—depends what it is. I draw the line at drug running and bank robberies."

He gave a thin laugh that betrayed a nervousness he hadn't allowed himself to show before. "Well that's that, then."

"Go on. What's on your mind?"

We shuffled forward and had no choice but to climb the stairs to the upper deck. We took seats in the rear corner where we could see each other's faces and didn't have to talk too loudly.

Nathan was serious. "I need to find out some stuff."

"Ri—ight. What kind of stuff?"

"I need to know about the big tourist developments down here—and the criminal connections the developers had in the 1980s and '90s."

That took me aback.

"I mean, how can I get started? You can't just walk into one of these places and book a lesson on the golf driving range—though, believe me, I've thought about it—and start firing off questions, can you? They'd march you straight out again. So, what I was thinking was, there's a story I want to find out, and who knows how to find out? And that's when it came to me: that's what you do, isn't it?"

"I don't have any contacts here," I said.

"But you'd know how to get started, at least?"

"Nathan, I'm not an investigative reporter. I'm a politics and economics specialist."

"It's important."

He looked about sixteen, hungry, and desperate. I responded as anyone with a heart would. "I can't promise anything."

Silence, except for the call of a gull.

"You'll have to tell me exactly what you want to know with as many details as you have. Names. Places. Dates as near as you can get. It might also be worth telling me why you need to know."

He shot an anxious look around. On one side a gaggle of teenagers, boys and girls, were oblivious to anything but their own noisy flirtations; the young couple on the other side were speaking together in French, discussing whether it was worth hiring a car.

"There are two places. One is called Horta das Rochas near Albufeira. It's a resort on the coast, with a golf course and spa. The other is Vale Navio. Its reputation isn't great. It's changed hands several times, sometimes for dirty money—Portuguese, and British, too. The name of the man I want to find out about is Terry Jackson."

"Pick an easy subject, why don't you?" I kept my voice down. "I'm not sure either of us should get involved in anything like this."

"I'm not saying I want to get involved. There's no getting involved—it all happened a long time ago. I just want to find out if there's anything on record about it."

His eyes were locked onto mine.

"Well, OK. I take it you've done the obvious Google search?"

"As I said, this was early 1990s. There's not a lot that goes that far back online, certainly not that I can find in English. That's what I mean—if you had to write a newspaper story about this, how would you get started?"

The wind blew my hair back from my face and I could taste the salt in the air. I watched the boats rocking at anchor in the channel and a plastic jerry can float by.

"If I was at work, I'd probably call the local English language newspaper. Ask one of the journalists there if they could help with some research, sweeten the request with the implication they'd be giving their career a little boost, or at the very least their bank account."

"Would you be up for that?"

"Well, obviously I'm not at work."

"You could have a go, though, eh?"

"You still haven't told me why this is so important."

"I will do. Just not here. But trust me, it is."

"Give me a bit more to go on," I said.

Nathan rubbed his hands over his face. I waited, and he seemed to reach a decision.

"You know the little girl who disappeared in Praia da Falesia years ago—the famous case, parents both lawyers who did everything they could to keep the case in the news?"

Tilly Stern. A three-year-old at the time she was snatched from a holiday apartment in the middle of the night while her parents slept in the next room. It would have been around 2006, because I'd landed my first job on a financial magazine after Oxford and, even there, it was one of those stories no one could avoid. I nodded.

"I think there could have been others. Going back a lot longer."

The engine of the ferry started up. Vibrations overrode the slight tremble in my limbs. Some of my best stories had started this way, the shot of adrenaline confirming the strength of my instincts.

"Connected to the resort developments you mentioned?"

"It's a possibility."

I didn't know what to say. I hadn't seen any of this conversation coming.

"Terry Jackson," I managed, eventually.

"Horta das Rochas. Vale Navio."

Neither of us said anything more. He watched Faro's apartment blocks appear over the water, an unlovely jumble of utilitarian concrete, their uniform balconies serving as shutters pulled down over the western side of Faro. Overhead, planes screamed in and out of the airport. I gazed out across the marshes at the glimpses of the lighthouse on the rim of an outer island. It wasn't until the ferry bumped the jetty outside the fortified walls of the Old Town back where we had started that it occurred to me.

"You didn't ask any of the others to come today, did you?"

"No."

"And to be straight about other matters as well—you know all this, how? Have you got into something over your head?"

"Not me. But Terry Jackson obviously did."

We disembarked and joined the file of wind-blown beach trippers flip-flopping past the old-fashioned seafood restaurant and the Bombeiros Voluntarios, the fire station.

"So tell me what you know about this Terry Jackson, then." To be honest, I was starting to feel irritated by Nathan's methods, and his patchy approach to detail. "Where are we most likely to find him?"

"Don't know exactly. Vale Navio. Albufeira . . . could be anywhere along the coast here."

"And you think he was involved in the abduction of children?" I hardly knew where to begin. "And he was, what? Actually taking them, organising some pae- dophile ring?"

"I don't know. Maybe."

"So what's Terry to you, Nathan?"

"A family friend."

"But you don't have an address or phone number."

"He wasn't that much of a friend, as it turned out."

"Doesn't sound like it."

We walked slowly and sun-drunk to the edge of the Jardim Manuel Bivar. He didn't add anything more. I gave him a quick hug as we parted. His shoulder bones were light and angular as a bunch of twigs.

I don't know where he went that evening. I didn't ask.

I'd told Nathan I was running away, but it really wasn't that exciting. It made a good headline for a dull story, that's all. Marc was a forty-year-old European banking lobbyist (keep awake at the back). Never married. Dual nationality, thanks to a Belgian mother (a French-speaker, known as a Walloon) and a British father. Undeniably handsome and diploma-clever, with a fondness for bureaucratic in-jokes that weren't funny at all, but once in a while he pointed me in the direction of a bloody good story. I never should have moved in with him, but I was swayed by his sheer persistence, and some surprisingly great sex. I never saw it lasting, but it seems he did.

Hard to believe that only a week previously I was still in Brussels, cold cloudy home of transactions and transitions. Marc and I sat morosely in the Grand Place, with its gilded mercantile houses that seemed to glow as the grey sky darkened, and hammered out our own deal. He called it a trial separation and I called it an escape, though not to his face. I watched men and women in suits scuttle into the surrounding streets of restaurants where bureaucrats go to stuff their faces, and played it the Brussels way, hedging my bets and lying if necessary to get what I needed. It seemed a world and a lifetime away.

It's astonishing how quickly the mind adapts to new surroundings and stimuli. A week before, I had never been to Faro and knew no one here. Now, it was expanding around me in unexpected directions, displacing the old preoccupations. Nathan was clever, I'll give him that—perceptive, too. His hunch about a journalist's nose for an intriguing story was bang on the money. I was never going to pass on this. By the time Monday morning came around I had a list of English-speaking publications, websites, and societies all along the Algarve coast and had already emailed the most likely sources of information. The Internet didn't close down for the weekend like libraries and records offices. There were plenty of Terry Jacksons online but no sign of the right one in Portugal, criminal or otherwise. That didn't really surprise me. As Nathan said, not everything that happened in the eighties and nineties is accessible on the Web. If it were, he wouldn't have needed my help.

The *Algarve Daily News* had a lengthy archive on Vale Navio. It was the first time-share resort in Portugal, I learned, comprising a hundred villas and three hundred apartments on a scrubby expanse of coastal hillside. It had been designed in the 1970s to what, at the time, were enlightened environmental ideals. Only three pine trees had been cleared to make way for its construction. But with its success had come rapid expansion. Ideals had been jettisoned in favour of fast profits. By the late 1980s there were repeated allegations of corruption involving planning permissions granted by the local municipal authorities, and criminal prosecutions of aggressive touts.

Portugal Today also covered Vale Navio's decline. Neither had much on Horta das Rochas beyond a few mentions of it in general terms. It was a much more upmarket resort the other side of Albufeira from Vale Navio, and looked to be a well-maintained and fairly expensive option, with appreciative reviews.

For anything more penetrating, I was going to have to wait for a response to one of my queries. I didn't see why a local journalist wouldn't want to speak to me but, even so, I'd fudged the issue of my current employment status.

My mobile rang as I was walking to the language school. I fished it out of my bag and was surprised to see it wasn't Marc calling for once. I didn't recognise the number.

"Yes?" I said.

"Joanna Millard?"

"It is."

"Ian Rylands."

I hesitated, unable to place the name; so many new ones had passed across my consciousness in the previous twenty-four hours.

"You left me a message."

"Sorry, I—"

"The Anglo-Algarve Association."

"Of course! Thank you so much for calling back. I wasn't expecting such a quick response."

It had been a very long shot. I hadn't expected anything to come of it, far less for this to be the first bite.

"You were asking about Vale Navio and Horta das Rochas. I might be able to help."

"That would be great. I was wondering—"

"Where are you? Might be better to meet."

"I'm in Faro."

"That's fine for me. When are you free?"

There seemed no reason to delay. "How about early evening today?"

"All right, then. I will be at the marina bandstand at six."

"I'll see you then—and thank you very much."

Nathan managed a lop-sided smile when I saw him in class, but he looked dreadful. He hadn't bothered to shave and his complexion was so pallid it lent his tan a sallow orange tinge.

"Hungover," he grimaced when I asked the obvious. "I haven't slept since . . . Friday night."

"Good weekend, then."

"Not really."

"What's wrong?"

"Nothing I can't handle."

I stared at him, expectantly.

"The girls at my house . . ."

Part of me didn't want to know but I waited for him to go on.

". . . they said that some bloke had been round asking about me. Then I got beaten up on Saturday night. Nice."

"You've hit on someone's girlfriend?"

"Didn't think so."

"Where did this happen—at the house?"

He shook his head. "Nightclub."

"Are you badly hurt?"

"Not really. Few bruises." He rubbed his chest. "At least no one can see them."

"It might not have been connected," I said, trying to be dispassionate. "You're sure you're all right? Did anyone see—did you report it to the police?"

"I'm a bit shaken, to tell the truth, but all right. No one saw. And no, I didn't tell the police. What's the point?"

"Well . . ."

"No police."

I shrugged, to show I didn't agree but that it was up to him. I didn't tell him about Ian Rylands. I was going to, but was wary of saying anything that the others might overhear. Besides, Nathan wasn't in any state for serious conversation. He was uncharacteristically quiet all morning, and bunked off after lunch.

By the end of the day only one other reply to my request had come in, from a woman who ran an expat information website based in Vilamoura. The message was friendly enough but offered little in the way of information.

iii

At ten to six I was walking slowly through the public garden towards the bandstand at the far end. I was curious. What kind of man would arrange to meet an unknown woman at a bandstand these days? One who ran an expat association, I supposed.

It was a circular Victorian relic, insignificant and neglected in comparison to the steel scaffolds and lighting rigs of the temporary stage across the road where, later, the Folk Faro festival would showcase singing and dancing from around the world. That night, according to the sound checks and flashing signs, there would be performances from Guatemala, Romania, Spain, and India. I had been giving it a wide berth, though I had gone down to listen to a local *fado* singer the previous night; her mournful wails had called to a weakening of my determination to stay strong.

"Joanna?"

I turned around.

The man was elderly, in his early seventies, perhaps. He was white-haired, tall and broad-shouldered but perhaps not as substantial as he had once been. The cotton drill jacket hung loosely, bulging with whatever he had crammed into the pockets.

"Ian Rylands?"

"At your service."

We shook hands and he accepted my offer to buy him a drink. I allowed him to lead the way into the familiar cobbled pedestrian streets. We stopped outside the grand old café that had seen better days.

"The Café Aliança," he said. "The perfect spot for an interesting conversation." He gave a little chuckle. "It's not really a café, you know. Not any longer. It closed down a few years back, but now it's been re-opened for a few months in the run-up to the elections. It's being used as a political meeting place. A spot of damage limitation conceded by the authorities. Things have been getting rather ugly, what with the protests and other—unpleasantness."

"The storks, you mean?"

"Ah, you know about that. Nasty business. Some say it was done by a far-right group, but that's what the far-left activists always claim. Both sides shouting equally loudly, neither with any workable answers and ignorant at all times of human nature. After you."

Ian Rylands stood back, upright in a military stance, as he allowed me to take the revolving door first.

We took a table by one of the high arched windows. A huge potted plant gave us the illusion of privacy, dispelled as soon as we sat down by the barman coming over and addressing him as Senhor Rylands and staying to chat in Portuguese, very little of which I understood.

A small carafe of Vinho Verde was brought swiftly, along with a plate of cubed cheese and olives.

"Your Portuguese sounds excellent," I said. "How long have you been here?"

His forehead and cheeks were sun damaged; deep creases surrounded his mouth. It was a fair bet that he had been living abroad for quite a while.

"Retired down here seven years ago."

"What did you retire from?"

"The civil service. Couldn't get out quickly enough."

"What made you choose Portugal?"

"Had some good holidays here. The sun. My wife and I enjoyed a game of golf."

"Enjoyed?"

"She passed away two years after we got here."

"I'm sorry."

He waved a hand as if to indicate he accepted my sympathies but wanted to move on. "It was after that I started the Association as a way to meet other people. There was only so much drinking on my own I could do."

I acknowledged that with a sympathetic nod.

"On the whole, the expats down here are pretty congenial. A few petty-minded individuals, of course, like anywhere. You learn to avoid them."

He took a contemplative sip of his wine. The backs of his hands were mottled. On one, a mole had flowered into a black rose, ridged and ominous. If I hadn't only just met him, I might have urged him to show it to a doctor. "You said you wanted to know about Vale Navio and Horta das Rochas. And you're a journalist? Remind me who you write for."

I heeded a warning against glib half-truths. He was sizing me up intently, and I recognised him as someone who might well have had experience of dealing with newspapers. I should have asked him what exactly he'd done before he retired.

"The *Independent*—or rather, I used to. I've just left after six years. Made redundant," I said. So much for thinking I could bluff it out.

"Did you specialise?"

I was right to be wary. "Economics, mainly. Latterly on the European desk in Brussels."

"Tough business."

"Every newspaper I know has been cutting its staff."

Milky blue eyes stared intently at me over his raised glass. "Do you know Will Venning?"

"I do, yes." Will was one of the nice guys, a feature writer at the *Indy* with a wife and five kids, still hanging on grimly to his job.

"I've met him," said Rylands. "Well, I say met . . . not quite. We've spoken."

"When was that?"

"A couple of years ago. I helped him out with some information he needed."

I nodded, expecting he would enjoy telling me what that was, but he sat back in his chair and made an expansive gesture with one arm. "This, this space we're in, this room with the high windows and panelling . . . this is Portugal's modern history. And," he smiled, revealing uneven teeth, tending to brown, "for various reasons it has plenty to do with Horta das Rochas and even Vale Navio, if you can bear with."

"Tell me."

"The Aliança is one of the oldest cafés in Portugal, or it was until it got closed down due to safety and environmental health issues. The building was in a state of near collapse. They say they've shored it up, but—well, let's not count on that. Be ready to run if you hear an ominous creak. As I say, a deal's been done to open the place again for political meetings, concerts, and poetry readings. Bright idea by one of the socialist candidates who said he'd rather pay for the reopening than for billboards. Gives everyone a chance to reconnect with a part of Faro's history. Have you seen the Hall of Fame at the back?"

"Not yet."

"The pictures on the wall are famous visitors. Amália Rodrigues. José Afonso. António Ramos Rosa. Marguerite Yourcenar."

"I'm going to have to look them up."

"Amália Rodrigues was a very famous, much loved singer of *fado*. You know about *fado*?"

I nodded. "The mournful songs."

"José Afonso, also a singer and poet, symbol of the Portuguese revolution. António Ramos Rosa, influential writer, likewise Yourcenar. Simone de Beauvoir— she came here at the end of the Second World War. The Aliança used to be one of the great literary and cultural centres of the Algarve."

"So how did it get into the state it's in?"

"Illegal works carried out inside. Floors put in without adequate support. The authorities found out and refused to issue a licence to put seating outside in case the building came down. Yet they leave plenty of other dangers untouched when it suits them. It's not just the Aliança, the whole city is falling apart. Holes in the roads. Tortuous bureaucracy. Missing funds. We all think things will improve but instead we get more of the same. Hence the protests."

Rylands paused for breath. It was an all-too-familiar story. I had written it many times in different guises.

"But it was a popular decision to allow this place to reopen," he went on. "People have a need to reassure themselves that life hasn't changed out of all recognition, don't you think? There used to be other emblematic venues here, all with evocative names: the Atlantico, the Brazilian café, where people gathered to talk and play board games and study. All gone now. Faro used to be a wonderful place to live—even as recently as ten years ago. You could park anywhere you wanted. Not everything was about money. Now, we're taxed to oblivion and everyone thinks the city politicians are all in it together to make sure we keep paying through the nose."

There was a pause, during which he seemed to register that politics was a tricky subject between strangers. He picked up the carafe and distributed the last few inches of wine between our glasses. "How about something to eat?" he asked.

Odd, how the choice of words can make the difference. If he'd said, "Would you like to come out to dinner?" I would have said no. But something to eat, that was fine. Everyone had to have something to eat.

It wasn't just politeness. I wanted to carry on the conversation to find out as much as I could.

"I'd be delighted."

We didn't go far, only to the restaurant next door. At a table outside on the cobbles, we had a view of the café's grand façade and the comings and goings in front of it. Over saffron-infused fish stew and another carafe of Vinho Verde, a larger one this time, Rylands seemed relaxed and more than happy to share his knowledge. I found myself warming to him as he expanded a bit on what I knew of Portuguese history: the nation of seafarers and navigators; the decades under the fascist dictator Salazar and the overthrow of his authoritarian rule in the Carnation Revolution of 1974; the shakedown that followed and membership of the European Union. The boom in tourism had brought prosperity for some and destruction for others.

"Places like Horta das Rochas?" I prompted.

"Horta das Rochas was one of the first developments. On rocks above the sea, as the name implies. It had once been a farm and the key to success was the extent of the land that came with it—enough to create a small golf course as well as pools and tennis courts. It was a new idea then, though it caught on in a big way. The atmosphere was relaxed and easygoing, yet all the facilities were on site. Not prohibitively expensive for the owners to run either, or the tourists to stay at. In many ways it was the model for what was to come."

"No allegations of dodgy dealing there?"

Rylands hesitated. "Show me somewhere on the Algarve where mud isn't slung. Some of it sticks, some of it doesn't. I couldn't tell you. As far as I know, Horta das Rochas is clean. It certainly was when it was built."

"But some of these resorts aren't?"

"Wherever there's big money to be made fast, there's a criminal element. Same all over the world, and the resort business is a prime target. Foreign money, foreign guests, who knows what's suspicious and what's normal?"

"What about Vale Navio?"

"That went to the bad."

"Proven?"

"Oh, yes. There were even some prosecutions. Nothing there now, just rows of abandoned buildings, falling down as fast as they were quickly thrown up. Greed and backhanders killed the golden goose. And a lot of life savings lost by small investors."

"Do you know when the rot set in?"

"In the eighties, I'd say."

"And it had only been built ten years previously."

"That's right. Horta das Rochas, on the other hand, started up in the late 1940s. You shouldn't equate the two."

"I'm just—"

He leaned across the table. "Can I ask you, Joanna— what is the reason for your interest?"

I was prepared for this. Keep it impersonal whenever possible and counter with another question with the implication that it offered some kind of answer. "Have you ever heard of a man called Terry Jackson?"

The first bass sounds had begun to pump from the Folk Faro stage, and I felt my heartbeat quicken to their rhythm.

"Terry Jackson." Rylands frowned. "Don't think so. Why?"

"He had a connection to both resorts."

"Anything else?"

"Just that."

I asked him a bit more about other resorts on the coast, then flew a kite. "There have been other disappearances of young children on the Algarve, haven't there, long before the Tilly Stern case that everyone knows about? Kidnap, ransom demands—the murder of a child. Several cases were linked to Vale Navio."

"A touch before my time, I'm afraid. I didn't get here until 2007."

"I haven't managed to check the local newspaper archives yet. Which one is most likely to have covered these stories?"

"Best bet would be the *Algarve Daily News*."

"Thanks. That's what I thought. You wouldn't have the name of a friendly reporter there, would you?"

"Not off the top of my head."

Our plates were cleared and we talked on over glasses of water and coffee. Mainly, he wanted to know more about my former employment in Brussels and what I made of the dire economic news unfurling from all directions across southern Europe.

"Have you ever heard of a writer called Esta Hartford?" he asked.

"No."

"She wrote a novel set in Portugal called *The Alliance*. Published in 1954. An interesting picture of the country during the Second World War, and afterwards."

"British?"

"American. Italian-American to be precise. She arrived here during the war, and never went back. You should read it. *The Alliance.*"

"I'll make a note."

"It's written as a novel but most of it is true, and it explains a lot," he said.

"What is it about?"

"I'm being pedantic. It's all true, in its way. About? It's about the origins of the situation we find ourselves in today."

"Why write it as a novel then?"

He took awhile before answering, as if he was waiting for me to catch up. I wanted to hear it from him, so I kept quiet.

"Because history books are rewritten—novels are not. The thing is, in the past few years it's quietly become quite a cult read here, in Portuguese translation. It was republished by her son a few years back and has caught on by word of mouth."

He stared pointedly up at the wrought-iron balustrade of the neighbouring building, at the pockmarked façade where chunks of plaster had fallen away. "Have you made the connection yet?"

The penny dropped. "The Alliance . . . the Aliança?"

"Bingo."

I had the distinct feeling he wanted to say a great deal more but was holding back.

"You should read it," he repeated.

The waiter interrupted us there with the bill, which I insisted on paying, and Rylands accepted after a gentlemanly show of reluctance. It was only as we stood to leave that I remembered.

"Horta das Rochas," I said. "When you told me the Café Aliança had plenty to do with it, was that just in the abstract, or was there a specific link?"

"There is a link."

He gave a chuckle. It seemed to be a sound he used to denote a private joke. I was never keen on playing games for information, but sometimes there was no way round. I was the one who had made the first move, and so I had to let him draw even.

"Tell you what," he said. "I'll get hold of a copy of Esta Hartford's book and let you have it. Then we can talk again."

iv

Nathan was still distracted when I told him about meeting Ian Rylands. I had to admit I hadn't learned anything new about Terry Jackson, and there didn't seem much more to say.

On the Thursday he didn't turn up for morning class. No one thought it was that surprising. He'd been out on the tiles again. Even he couldn't escape the cumulative effect of too many all-nighters.

It was quiet without him. The others in the class were all right, but the women seemed to have formed a group that didn't automatically include me. Enzo was eager to take me out to dinner, and I was having to find more and more feeble excuses to avoid the inevitable. Tomas the IT man from Berne was pleasant and friendly, but there wasn't the frame of reference and easy humour I shared with Nathan.

When I went into Café Aliança on the Friday morning, I hadn't heard anything more from Ian Rylands. I'd called the *Algarve Daily News*, but the reporter I needed to talk to was on holiday and wouldn't be back until the following week.

I took it as a kind of acceptance that the same tubby barman prepared a coffee for me without being asked. This time the minuscule coffee cup came without chips in the china, and what's more, breakfast was on offer.

"*Tosta?*" he asked.

I now knew that was toast and cheese, and accepted eagerly. We attempted a halting continuation of our exchange. His name was João. It would soon be the weekend, I managed to say, as if that might have been news to him (this is the worst aspect of trying to speak in a new language: it makes you seem stupid), and I had decided to go to the beach.

João nodded encouragingly and asked slowly and clearly if I liked to swim. I did. He told me to have fun but not to fall asleep on the beach; the wind could burn. It wasn't a meeting of minds but it was progress.

As I paid the small bill in coins and picked up my bag to go, João raised a finger and reached under the bar. He brought out a small package, its brown wrapping paper mummified by parcel tape, and held it out to me.

"What is it?" Actually, I think I asked him *how* it was.

"For you."

Sure enough, in the small exposed patch of paper was my name, etched in neat block capitals.

I didn't open the package there and then, mainly because it was bound too tightly to be ripped into, and partly because I've learned the value of a public poker face when confronted with anything unexpected. João delved again under the counter and produced a knife, but I shook my head and slipped the parcel into my bag.

It weighed like lead in the bag over my shoulder until I got to the nearest pharmacy and went in to buy a pair of nail scissors. On a bench on a small square at a junction of cobbled streets, I slit open the tape and extracted the contents. There was no note enclosed, but there was no need for one.

It was a book, an old hardback with a torn dust jacket. *The Alliance* by Esta Hartford.

I hurried on, hoping to find Nathan had used his day off wisely and was now fully restored. But he was not there when we sat down for Caterina's class, and he didn't appear his usual ten minutes in.

None of the other students had heard from him. They seemed to think that if any of us were to have done, I was the most likely—which was true.

"Senhora Davim?" I put my head round the office door on my way out. "Can I ask you—is Nathan not well?"

"We think so, but we don't know." She shrugged, raising painted eyebrows. "I was going to ask you."

"I don't suppose you have his mobile number?"

"He didn't give it to you?"

"It didn't seem necessary. We were here all day in person."

"We are not permitted—"

"Have you tried it?"

Senhora Davim pursed her lips. "I left a message. He has not returned my call."

What was she supposed to do? Not much, she implied with a drumroll of fingernails on the desk. He was a grown man, and it had only been two days. If he chose not to attend each session of a course he had paid for, that was his business. I didn't disagree and exited graciously. If I left it there, she might change her mind about giving me his number if he failed to come in on Monday.

I tried to recall the street Nathan's lodgings were in but I'd never known exactly where he was staying.

Neither could I remember any specific landmarks that might have narrowed it down, except a stork's nest on a lamppost, and I wasn't so desperate that I was willing to tramp all over town searching for that.

But Nathan's absence was all the more frustrating because I was eager to rake over my conversation with Ian Rylands. The way he had left the book for me in the café was odd, even faintly creepy. How did he even know I would return? And there was something else that bothered me, an anomaly that had taken a while to rise to the surface of my consciousness: how was it that Rylands remembered my old colleague Will Venning's name from a one-off approach by telephone—he said they had spoken but not met—yet he couldn't recall the name of any reporters at a local newspaper?

The other students filed out of the language centre in orderly fashion. Some of the women were meeting up later at O Castelo, and promised to look out for Nathan. I told Enzo my long-standing boyfriend was coming for the weekend, and went back alone to my studio.

Later that evening, using the Wi-Fi signal at the bar-bakery in the Rua Dr. Francisco Gomes, I was idly checking my emails and various news sites when I had an idea. I pulled up Facebook and entered Nathan's name in the search bar.

He wasn't on Facebook. Fair enough, it was worth a try. But I rarely give up when I want to know something, so I googled "Nathan Emberlin," wondering whether he was on any other social media sites.

It was a very uncommon name. Only four results came up, not one of them for a British man. The only Nathan Emberlins in the whole world were a couple of old men in the American Midwest, one of them allegedly a hundred and six years old, to be precise. I sat back, shocked. How did a young person, in these days of all-pervasive social networking, not register anywhere online?

I pressed search again, thinking there must have been a glitch. The result was the same.

V

The temperature was climbing. The air was heavy with orange dust from the Sahara that fell like a sprinkling of paprika powder over the town's white sills and ledges. I walked down to the ferry, needing to get out over water to catch some fresh wind. As the boat ploughed through green salt marshes, I did breathe more easily. Saturday morning, and the day was mine. But I was not feeling relaxed.

Heading south to the narrow sand strip of the Ilha da Culatra, where the outer rim of the marshes was exposed to the full strength of the sea, we could see the lighthouse on the horizon marking the Cape of Santa Maria, the southernmost point of continental Portugal.

Fishing activity was all around, most visibly on the smallest scale. Men rowed solo, their boats stacked with rods and other gear. Groups of men and women stood knee-deep in the water with rods and lines; here and there rods stood upright, screwed into the wet silt to allow one person to operate several lines. Clam diggers bent and scraped at the mud, reminding me yet again of Nathan.

There was no getting away from what was now an obstinate unease about him. Our conversation on the ferry to Faro beach took on a significance it hadn't at the time. He'd said he hadn't come by plane but by bus. So where had he come from? Another town on the Algarve? From Spain? If he could afford the not inconsiderable fees for the language course, it surely could not have been a lack of money that made him opt for the bus.

The ferry docked. A man standing on the jetty fished out an octopus to cheers of encouragement.

I followed the other passengers down a sandy path in the direction of the lighthouse. There were plenty of buildings here, of solid Moorish design in white-painted stone with roof terraces and pretty gardens of cacti and other parched-earth plants. They looked like holiday homes. At the beach, walkways of wooden slats led off left and right. It was as well to keep to them; the sand under my flip-flops was too hot to walk on.

The beach was not crowded, and the further I went, the more isolated and exposed it became. I swam in the grey-blue rollers with only a few other bathers in sight, but lasted only half an hour in the raw dazzle of the sun before I returned to a more populated spot where sunshades were available.

The cry of a doughnut vendor against a background of waves collapsing and receding brought Nathan to mind yet again.

The only possible conclusion was that Nathan Emberlin was not his real name. Possibly he had chosen it because it was one of those rare things, a completely blank slate. But why?

The wind picked up and fanned some life back into the coast. By the time I had returned to town, washed the sticky sand out of my hair, and assessed the red burn marks on my shoulders, the temperature had fallen back to a pleasant simmer for the evening.

I wandered down towards the marina. Perhaps I would try a new place to eat that Tomas had recommended. With plenty of time to decide, I had a fizzy water at a waterside kiosk. A couple of guys raised their glasses to me, and I felt good as I strolled towards the maze of cobbled streets. I'd worried sometimes over the past few months that I'd forgotten how to have fun.

A top in one of the clothes shops had caught my eye on the way to class, and I thought I'd go and try it on, might even wear it later to one of the clubs Nathan talked about. It was about time I had a little adventure. I turned the corner into the entrance on the Rua Vasco da Gama.

About thirty metres ahead of me was a tall man with white hair and a loose cotton drill jacket. He looked just like Ian Rylands. I picked up my pace, keeping him in sight. The evening parade packed the street. Casual shoppers stopped dead and changed direction right in front of me. Couples stood reading menus outside restaurants. Children ran swerving arcs through the crowd. I bumped into someone and in the seconds I looked away from the white-haired figure ahead, to apologise, I lost him.

I walked faster towards the junction with a small triangular square where restaurant tables were laid for dinner under some trees. Cars were permitted here, and on the other side of the square the man was waiting to cross the road. I could see his face. It was Ian Rylands. There was no doubt about it. I called out. He appeared not to hear.

I carried on behind him, deciding not to run, just to catch up naturally. Only a few streets to the northwest of the main tourist area, even more businesses were closed, apartment blocks were shabby, and peeling buildings stood empty under À Venda notices. One house, once beautifully dressed in blue and white tiles, was now stripped to patches of terra-cotta and graffiti. Weeds tufted from the gutters.

Rylands was still ahead of me, though not by very far now. I expected him to sense my approach at any moment and look round. But he didn't. He kept up a steady march down unprepossessing side streets.

We emerged into a large square dominated by a church and a modern post office. He headed straight across the cobblestones to the steps of the church. That was when I hung back, feeling as if a line of acceptability had been breached. I'd only wanted to catch up with him to thank him for the book, and possibly to ask him why he'd chosen to leave it at the Aliança without even letting me know it was there. But he had led me so far from where I'd spotted him that I felt too self-conscious. Any approach would now be awkward.

He went into the church.

I wasn't going to follow him. Suppose he was a devout man. That would make me—well, I didn't care to contemplate what that would make me.

Tucked into the side of the square, camouflaged by plane trees, a small bar offered a couple of tables with a view of the church steps. One was taken by a group of older men playing cards. I took the other and ordered a beer.

The waitress didn't know whether there was a church service on Saturday evening. Or, more likely, she couldn't work out what I was trying to ask her, either in Portuguese or in English. I made my bottle of Sagres last as long as I could, but Rylands did not reappear on the church steps. After a while—and the euphoric effect of the beer on an empty stomach may have had a bearing on this—my decision to hang back no longer seemed so vital.

I made a circuit of the square and then gave in to impulse. Beggars held their hands out as I paused at the entrance to the church. A mad shriek from across the square made me jump. Two drunks had started fighting down by the post office, flailing arms beating the dust out of each other's clothes. I went in. The Church of the Third Order of Our Lady of Mount Carmel, I read in English.

The space was more intimate than the exterior had indicated. A soaring arch over an ornate altar and the reredos behind it was embellished by astonishing gold work. Intricate baroque carvings dripped with gilding. In contrast, the wooden pews were plain, in rows over a red carpet. They were empty.

To the right of the altar was an entrance into an antechamber with the air of a dining room in a Tudor house.

"The Chapel of Bones?" asked a middle-aged woman quietly in accented English.

She handed me a printed brochure. I read the word "ossuary" and allowed her to make the sale. For a euro coin, I was granted access to a cramped garden. It might just be possible to claim I was doing my sightseeing at a quiet time when the tourists had gone, so I opened the brochure and looked around.

A short path led to another doorway. This was the mysterious Chapel of Bones. An inscription over the threshold read: "Stop here and think of the fate that will befall you—1816."

At first glance, it seemed to be a shell grotto. I registered the skulls first. Then, I saw it: the inner walls and ceiling were entirely covered with a mosaic of skulls and other human bones, laid out in patterns that were all the more macabre for their intricate orderliness. Some were so small they must have been children's heads.

Ian Rylands wasn't there. But Nathan was.

He stood in the far corner, looking uneasy. I went over to him, unable to hide my surprise. Dark circles under his eyes and the prominent bones of his face made for uncomfortable comparisons with the surroundings.

"Nathan! Bloody hell. What are you doing here? And where have you been?"

He tried and failed to rally his easygoing persona. "Just . . . hanging."

I wasn't in any mood to be messed about. "Where's Rylands?"

"What?"

"Ian Rylands."

"Who?"

I gave him a hard stare.

Nathan wiped his hands through his hair and looked away.

"Don't play games with me, Nathan."

"I'm really not. What the hell are you doing here anyway?"

A standoff ensued. I kept quiet until he cracked.

"OK. I came to meet someone here—but they didn't turn up."

"They?"

"He." Nathan sighed. He looked as if he needed to sleep for a week on a food drip. "Look, shall we get out of here? I've been here for an hour and it's giving me the creeps."

"An hour?"

He led the way back out into the garden. "I was told to be here at seven."

"Who, though? Who were you meeting?" My impatience was increasing.

We nodded at the woman in the Tudor dining room and passed through into the nave without speaking. Still no one in the pews. Nathan reached into the side pocket of his jeans as we went out onto the church steps, and took out a coin, which he gave to the nearest beggar, a toothless woman in black. I looked around for Ian Rylands—down in the square, by the ugly modern post office building, under the trees outside the bar— but he was nowhere to be seen.

We set off towards the marina. Smells of hot oil and garlic and fish funnelled down the narrow streets; clatter and chatter wafted from small dark restaurants.

"Who, Nathan?"

"All right, all right. A bloke called Peter Maitland. I've been doing what you said. I went to Albufeira as it's the nearest big town to Vale Navio and I checked the records. It was easier than I thought. There was a girl on the information desk at the town hall, and she was super-helpful."

"Which records?"

"The electoral roll. If Terry Jackson was registered, there would be an address for him."

"And was he?"

"No."

"Might not be the right place. Or he might not be eligible to vote."

"For sure. But I reckoned Albufeira was a big town and it would cover places all around. I got them to look at the lists of local taxpayers, too, but they still didn't come up with anything. So I'm going down the corridor to leave and this man runs after me and gives me a piece of paper with a name and phone number on it. Peter Maitland. Apparently, this Maitland had been in recently asking to check the records for Terry Jackson, too. And he left his details, saying that if ever anyone else came asking the same question, would they pass them on."

"So you got in touch with him."

"Exactly."

"You spoke to him?"

"Yeah, but not for long. He didn't seem to want to say too much, and neither did I."

"Did you ask why he was interested in Terry Jackson?"

"Didn't get a chance. He told me to meet him at the small chapel at the Largo do Carmo at seven o'clock today. He didn't say it was full of flaming bones—not sure I appreciate his sense of humour."

We passed several unsmiling older men, stepping off the pavement onto the road as they seemed determined not to give way to us. They moved with a compacted strength that might have been borne of aggression, or a barely buried resentment of the tourists who were keeping the town afloat.

"But Peter Maitland never showed up," I said, feeling queasy. "Did you see anyone who you thought might have been him?"

"What do you mean?"

"When you got to the church, was there anyone else there—in particular, a man who you thought might have been this Peter Maitland?"

"There were a few people around in the main part of the church. I didn't really look too closely. I went straight to the little chapel because that's where he said to go. No one came into the bones place except a French couple, and then some women—and then you."

"You didn't notice a tall, white-haired man with a loose, cream cotton jacket?"

"Now you come to mention it . . . perhaps there was someone who looked like that. He was over by one of the gold recesses on the other side of the altar."

"Did he seem to notice you?"

"How would I know? Why do you ask?"

"Because I followed Ian Rylands and I saw him go into the church at about ten to seven. Rylands is the Anglo-Algarve Association guy I met last week," I reminded him. "He couldn't wait to help me out with what I wanted to know. I don't have a good feeling about this."

"It's just a coincidence."

"Perhaps, but . . ." I shook my head. "No. What did this Maitland sound like on the phone? How old did he sound? Did he have any kind of accent?"

Nathan gave a long exhalation. "He sounded . . . older. Quite a posh accent. A bit like yours."

"Or Rylands'."

When we spotted a modest pizzeria close to the junction where I'd almost caught up with Rylands, I steered Nathan into it, fed him a large pizza and limited his alcohol intake to a small beer.

"Now I want to ask you something else," I said. "Is Nathan Emberlin your real name?"

He blinked. "It is for now."

"Care to explain?"

His elbows were on the table and his head went down into his hands. I watched the long brown fingers kneading his scalp through the mop of hair.

Minutes went by.

When he raised his head he looked me straight in the eye. "This is not easy," he said. "And you probably won't even believe me. I don't even know whether I do, actually."

He twisted the buttons at the open neck of his shirt. I noticed for the first time that his fingernails were bitten, or maybe they hadn't been before. I smiled to let him know I was on his side and could wait as long as necessary.

"You know the other day I said I might have found out something about the children who have been snatched down here? That it was nothing new—it's been happening for a long time?"

"Yes."

He paused to change the position of the pepper and the bottle of chili oil, then began to twist his empty beer bottle.

"When I said Terry Jackson was a family friend . . . I thought he was, anyway, but maybe he wasn't. He used to come round once in a while to see my dad when he was still alive. Lung cancer, before you ask. Eight years ago. Too many cigarettes."

The beer bottle was being ground into the table.

"I thought Roy was my dad and all. I didn't know anything until my mum died six months ago. A hit-and-run as she was crossing the road outside where she worked in Bexleyheath. And she wasn't my mum either, it seems. They never said a word about it.

"But when mum—Sue—was in hospital a letter arrived for her. I put it in a pile in the hall and forgot about it. She wasn't in any state to read anything. She was just lying there with tubes and machines bleeping. It was weeks afterwards that I opened the letter. It was from Terry Jackson, sent from Portugal, telling her to stop asking questions and stirring up the past. I had no idea what it was all about, and there was no return address for him. But the tone of it was pretty unpleasant. I'd always known Terry had dealings in Spain and Portugal, and that Roy was a bit of a South London wheeler-dealer, minor league. There were things you didn't ask about, with both of them.

"Then, when I was clearing out the house—I suppose I was looking more carefully for anything that could explain what the letter meant—I found some adoption papers. I couldn't believe it. I was two years old when Roy and Sue became my legal parents. What's more, the papers were in Spanish. I couldn't understand what was going on."

"Any other family that you could ask?"

"We weren't big on family. Roy had fallen out with his family over the company he kept, and hers had never liked him. There wasn't anyone to ask about it. I went mental for a while. I hadn't seen that one coming. I was so angry that they never told me . . . who doesn't tell their child they are adopted? Maybe years and years ago, but not nowadays." He raised his palms in despair.

"So I decided to get myself over to Spain and see if I could find out anything about my real parents. It was all I could think of to do."

His eyes were almost black.

"The address on the adoption papers was an agency in Malaga, but it no longer existed. I went back time after time, asking all the older people I could find in the area whether they had ever heard of it, and no one had. Then, one old dear in the next building told me she used to know someone who worked there, who had been very kind when her cat got injured, took it to the vet, paid for it . . . Anyway, to cut to the chase, she put me in touch with this woman, and I managed to meet her. She was very nervous, but I think she really was a nice woman, and she did want to help. She said she'd left the adoption agency when she found out it wasn't all above the line. Most of it was, but some wasn't.

"I got out the papers and showed them to her. She studied them and went a bit shaky. She said she remembered my case and she hadn't been happy about it. I asked how she could remember one case that far back, and she said it was because it was the first one she had questioned."

"Questioned in what way?"

"She was told to put on the form that my birth parents were Spanish, from a specific village down the coast, but she knew that wasn't true. She'd overheard the agency director talking about the two-year-old boy who had been brought from Portugal. A place was mentioned, somewhere called Horta das Rochas. And she knew that there was some kind of deal brokered with a man called Jackson. She found out later he was a small-time criminal based on the Algarve."

"She didn't contact the police?"

"I think she was scared. She claimed she didn't know Terry Jackson was dodgy until some time after the adoption had gone through. Perhaps she found out other bits and pieces it was better to keep quiet about. Malaga has a reputation, you know. But she definitely felt guilty about it when I came along. Made me swear on my life never to give her name."

I bit my lip. "To rewind a little bit," I said gently. "You said that child abductions have been happening here for a long time. Are you saying what I think you are?"

He nodded.

"It's a bit of a stretch, isn't it?" I said.

"That's what I want to find out. There were several child abductions linked to Vale Navio in the early nineties. There might have been more that never made the news. I knew that was where Terry Jackson worked because I remembered him talking about it when he came to see my dad. He used to go on about it all the time, boasting about the money he was making there. It kind of became a family catchphrase. If anyone did a sweet deal or came into money, we called it 'Vale Navio.'"

"How many other people have you told?"

"No one."

We sat quietly for a while.

"Why 'Nathan Emberlin'?"

"Because that was the name I had when I arrived at the adoption agency in Malaga, the name on the papers when the agency handed me over, supposedly all nice and legal, to Roy and Sue Harris on September 16, 1992. It was on the document."

"Do I still call you Nathan?"

"I quite like it. It's more who I really am than Josh Harris, after all."

I made Nathan put his number in my mobile, and then rang it while he was still there to make sure it was correct, and that he had mine. This time, I wanted to get everything right.

"You should get some sleep," I said. "You'll make yourself ill if you don't."

"Fat chance of that. The girls in my house will be raring for action, and they don't take no for an answer. There'll be too much noise and then everyone'll be off clubbing again. And then . . . look, I don't want you to think I'm losing it or anything, right, but I think my room got broken into. My stuff was messed about, but I couldn't find anything missing. Then one of the girls told me the man who was asking about me had come back and that he gave her the creeps. Now I keep thinking I might have seen him myself, and that he's following me, but there again, I might be getting paranoid. I mean, if he wanted to see me, why doesn't he just knock on the door?"

He seemed so vulnerable, I wanted instinctively to comfort him.

"All right, come back to mine, then." I'd said it before I could stop myself. "That's not an invitation in the way you think it is. I just want to give you a break, that's all."

I thought he would refuse, but he didn't. He had a glass of water and went straight to sleep in the bed; I took the sofa. I did try, but I couldn't get to sleep; my head was full of too many thoughts fighting for attention. The book Ian Rylands had given me was on the shelf where I'd left it, yet another nagging distraction that night. At one o'clock I clicked on the dim lamp on the side table. Nathan didn't stir. He was stone still under the sheet.

I started to read.

PART TWO

Excerpt from *The Alliance* by Esta Hartford, first edition published 1954

i

In Lisbon, flowers cascaded from every balcony. That was what she noticed. He exulted in the lights that blazed through the night and the imported whisky and cigarettes, freely available. In the way of married couples, they saw things differently but together Alva and Michael Barton were the lucky ones.

They had made it to Portugal, blown like seeds in the wind across Europe as the war closed in. In the city's grand baroque avenues the old order prevailed. Twilights fell, with an ache that was half regret and half euphoria, into soft slow evenings.

"The only question is, how long will it last?" asked Ronald as he tamped tobacco into his pipe.

The three of them were sitting in a café on the Praça Dom Pedro IV, an imposing square known as Rossio.

A black-and-white-cobblestone wave pattern rippled across it like a tide stopped in stone. Water splashed from fountains before a grand theater and a railway station with the dimensions and beauty of a cathedral and an advertisement for Porto Sandeman rose high above trees, trams, and cars: a potent flag of commerce larger than any banner of national sovereignty.

"You don't think Portugal can hold out?" Michael spoke in the tone of voice he used when he was working: casual interest, disguising grave concern.

Ronald lit the pipe and made kissing noises at the end of the stem. Smoke released gently from the bowl. "Spain has been primed by the Germans. Between them, they could overrun this country in an evening. Worse than that," he went on, with deadpan cheer that Alva hoped was the famous British sense of humor, "the Germans here boast that it would take one telephone call from Hitler to Salazar to annex Portugal."

"Very funny," she said.

"My dear, you do realize that the chap in charge here is a fascist, too? Dr. Salazar may not strut around shouting, but they call him the Plainclothes Dictator. The place is mined with fifth columnists ready to spring into action when the word is given. No one knows which way it will go. How's the accommodation, by the way?"

It was thanks to Ronald that they had made it at all. Thanks to Ronald, too, that they had an attic room at the Hotel Métropole on Rossio Square in the center of town. In the sudden influx of refugees, rooms were not easy to find.

The Bartons replied simultaneously.

"It's great," said Michael.

"A touch cramped but OK," said Alva.

"The Métropole is expensive and full of Nazis. Just so you know," said Ronald. "But keep hold of the room until you find your feet."

The journey had started in Paris, or in Rome, or in New York, depending on how far back you wanted to go. At the end of 1938, Michael Barton was bureau chief for Associated Press in Rome; thirty-seven years old and considered a safe pair of hands. He was in wire contact every day with reporters who were watching what was happening in Germany and it wasn't good. In newspaper terms, that wasn't necessarily bad, but it meant he needed to get in closer. Leaving Rome was more of a wrench for Alva. For two years she had been cheerful in its sunny chaos, had loved the connection with her Italian blood. But she trusted her husband. When he told her he was transferring to Paris, she didn't question his judgment.

Even after war was declared, there was no sense of panic outside the news agencies. In the capital, the French seemed dismissive of any threat, determined to ignore it with the same disdain they used for oafish tourists. For Americans in Paris not much seemed to change: the bars and bookshops, the theaters and restaurants and dance halls were full; the couture houses were busy. No expense was spared by their French hosts to give sumptuous private parties: fancy dress parties, black and white balls, winter festivals. If you hadn't been there in the spring of 1940, you wouldn't have known that the City of Light lost none of its gaiety and fabled April beauty that year. Plenty of people were still kidding themselves that everything would be all right, and wealthy and well-connected American expatriates knew they could always buy their way out of trouble.

It wasn't until June, when the German army strolled into France with a contempt for the Maginot Line worthy of a Parisian waiter, that Michael told his wife it was time for them to get out.

"Where to?"

"Wherever we can get to."

A million goodbyes were being said. The only talk was of travel plans. No seats were available on trains; the railways were full of troops. There was a private bus going to Bordeaux. Bordeaux was a port. If they got there fast enough there were bound to be ships sailing into safe territory. Someone had a neighbor who had chartered this bus, word had spread, and the Bartons paid double to take the chance, carrying what precious possessions they could, leaving most behind at a hotel where Michael trusted the concierge.

The bus left the Quai Voltaire with not a spare inch between passengers, including many children and several dogs as well as luggage. The air was stifling, even with every window open. There was always one child crying. The smell of warm bread and cheese mingled with engine fumes and dirty diapers was nauseating.

It was just as well they hadn't a child of their own, Alva told herself, and for the first time she felt glad. They had no one but themselves to worry about. At least they had transport. All along the dusty roads was an unending procession of people moving south, carrying all that they could, pushing their possessions in carts and barrows. She found herself watching out for the children, as they sat mutely on sacks or struggled ahead on foot.

At Tours, they stopped in a line of traffic. The driver leaned out, speaking to someone on the road below. "What's up ahead?"

"Troop concentrations."

"What does that mean?"

"That's what we've been told. No one allowed to proceed further."

After an hour going nowhere, Michael extricated himself from his seat and went up to talk to the driver.

"The city was bombed last night, and the damage was pretty bad," he relayed to Alva. "The authorities don't want the news to spread to the wider population and among the refugees. Too demoralizing."

The driver stood at the head of the bus and said he would be taking a detour to Poitiers.

At Poitiers, there was more chaos and crowds, queues to every public door and space, restaurants and cafés full to bursting. People sat on pavement waiting for food from the relief organizations; others prepared to sleep in the parks and squares. The bus went on through without stopping. On the other side of town the driver pulled into a truck stop to take stock of the situation in discussion with the drivers of other vehicles. Rumors abounded. The Germans were at Bordeaux. Roadblocks had already been set up. The files of refugees were being attacked by machine guns from planes.

The passengers were unanimous. Hungry and tired though they were, they would press on, avoiding Bordeaux. Night was falling, but the good driver was willing. It was the right decision. As the bus rattled on through the forests of the Landes, it passed fewer and fewer people and vehicles on the road. They had outrun the mass flight south; it seemed as if peace had miraculously returned.

They made it to Bayonne and then got stuck. Half the world seemed to have had the same idea. The foreign consulates there were under siege from people—like them—who needed papers to go any further. The Bartons were walking wearily toward the Place Gambetta when a car drew up. It was a preposterously large sports car, and at the wheel was Ronald Bagshaw.

Bagshaw was an acquaintance from Paris who often seemed to be present when there was a gathering of journalists or types. Not the smart gatherings in ballrooms and ambassadors' residences, but the ones that started in someone's apartment and went on to nightclubs and supper shows. He was pleasant enough, though Alva had never been quite sure what it was he did. He was British and told her at a party once that he had been a young officer in the army during the Great War and then had something to do with smoothing out the aftermath. He had the reputation of being a fixer, anyway, someone with the connections everyone was looking for. In the circumstances, he was just the man.

His car was open, long and gray, and loaded up with possessions. A steamer trunk sat on a shelf above the rear fender.

"Can I offer you a lift?" he asked, grinning.

"Where are you going?" countered Michael, as if that mattered.

"Lisbon, I thought."

So they accepted.

"Sling your stuff in. We can re-jig it later."

The rear seat was crammed with suitcases and boxes. They climbed into the bench seat up front with him. The leather of the seat—racy red leather—stuck to the back of Alva's bare legs.

"Packard Roadster," said Michael admiringly.

"Best car in the world," said Ronald. "Have to hand it to you chaps. You know how to make a smooth powerful car."

It was, too. With a car like this, they had strength on their side.

Alva realized later that at no time during their flight into the unknown did Michael ask her if she was frightened. Either he expected that she was and saw no point in alluding to it, or he assumed that their accustomed immersion in foreign news stories had insulated them both from taking anything too personally.

He was making notes as they went along, with a view to filing copy. It was not their crisis, he seemed to be saying; they were only witnesses.

But Alva was afraid. It seemed clear enough to her that their foreign status bestowed no immunity from danger. Fear was in the air, electric as a coming storm. Above, small dark enemy fighter planes swooped low over the roads. Mostly for effect, but now and then they would open fire and kill for sport. Alva set her eyes on the horizon and clasped her hands tightly in her lap. She decided to put her trust in Ronald and his calm worldliness. He spoke fluent French and conveyed the impression that he was on home turf wherever he was, and that they could trust him to find a way through. He managed to drive at some speed while proceeding with the utmost care and she had to admit that was re-assuring.

There was time to get one or two things straight, too. It turned out that Ronald had been decorated in the Great War and held government office. He was highly educated and had written several books about politics and travel though he didn't consider himself primarily a writer. A private income from shares in a family-owned bank allowed him to roam and observe and write as the whim took him. He had an ex-wife but no children.

"We'll need papers to cross to Spain," said Ronald. "I'm assuming you haven't got a fistful of exit permits and visas."

They hadn't.

"Not to worry, neither have I. Luckily, I know a man who does."

Within spitting distance of the Spanish border, confusion reigned at His Britannic Majesty's Consulate in Bayonne. The office seemed to be besieged by a mob but the consul was nowhere to be found. No one could leave France without the correct papers. An assortment of naval officers attempted to deal with the crowd, as tempers rose and desperation set in.

"Ah, French intransigence and love of bureaucracy, even in the face of mortal adversity," said Ronald. "Pure obstructionism. I don't think we should wait around, do you?"

He had a word with one of the naval officers. Having ascertained that the consular stamps and the stenographer were still there, Ronald took the Bartons into a side room where he coolly dictated several passes of his own devising and then stamped them with every official seal they could find, signing them himself in a fudged hand.

They stayed the night in a hotel and left the next morning at dawn to drive to the border at Hendaye and on into Spain, trailing a sweet stink of gasoline from the jerry cans Ronald had filled and lashed to the back. The brightness intensified. Ronald put up the car's black-fabric hood to protect them from sunstroke. From anything else that came down from above—planes and gunfire—they had no defense. The elegant vehicle grew a pelt of dust. The suspension groaned and clunked as it tore into potholed tracks that passed for roads.

I am a refugee, thought Alva, repeating it to herself, incredulously, as they bowled along. Before long they had stopped. The road was blocked by a river of humanity, some in vehicles, most on foot. Engine noise was stilled, replaced by the dull tramp of feet, creaking of wooden carts and worse, cries of despair. No, she revised the thought, these poor wretches are the real refugees.

We're special, Michael used to say to her. He set great store by the ways they were unique. He really seemed to believe it, for all his worldliness. Definitely smarter than he looked, with that long face (slightly wolfish, if you didn't know him and receive those widemouthed smiles) and the nose that got broken in a baseball game;

the habit of running his hand through the hair on the back of his head and leaving it sticking up. Even now, at nearly forty, he looked like a regular guy who liked sports, and played it to his advantage, connecting with other men in a way that was so patently genuine that no one could resist. By the time they cottoned on to his technique they were talking, and had already said too much.

The car started up. They began to move. What was the point of giving in to panic? Think positive. It was warm and she never liked the cold—that southern Italian blood again. Wherever the road led, that was where they were going. They had come a long way since New York. Alva was a secretary—well, a typist with big ideas—on the sports desk at the *Times* when she noticed Michael liked to hang around to pick up spare tickets to games. He was a big Dodgers fan in those days. Their first date, he took her to a game, and fed her a hot dog that spilled mustard down her expensive navy jacket. He didn't even notice that, far less remember it. A whole week's pay, that jacket had cost.

Soon they could see the sea border. Then another holdup pinned them down again on the bridge from France to Spain. Ronald lit his pipe and got out of the car to greet some old friends. Between the lines of cars going nowhere over the water, he had somehow bumped into people he knew.

Alva looked around and tried to detach herself like Michael. She felt it too strongly, though: in the course of leaving one life and crossing into another, they had ground to a halt. Who knew if they would ever get across? Too many people kept looking up at the sky, and she worried about an air attack. Michael struck a nonchalant pose as he lit and smoked a cigarette he had been saving.

Hours passed before the traffic moved forward to complete the crossing. Their documentation was examined. Finally, it was stamped. Their transit visa did not allow them to stay any longer than one night in San Sebastian but they had no desire to stay longer than necessary in arid, impoverished Spain, where portraits of General Franco were flanked by smaller likenesses of Hitler and Mussolini. After a night of fitful sleep on itchy straw mattresses in another small hotel, they clambered into the Packard and set their course for neutral Portugal.

Spain gave a good impression of being enemy territory. As foreigners escaping from France, they were permitted to drive along the coast road, past sea and shacks. Under the wide roofs of wooden houses—it rained a great deal here, explained Ronald—hung bunches of maize, some so big they were the size of sacks. It was a tense road trip through hostile territory. Anything might happen to stop them, at any crossroad.

It was important to keep as clean and tidy as possible, Ronald said. Whereas some poor wretches on the road seemed to have given up, he shaved: not only to keep up morale, but because it was easier to bluff with a clean face. Michael followed his advice and Alva tried to keep her hair in check with a scarf.

Again, they were lucky. They covered the ground without hindrance, stopping only to refuel the tank and feed themselves on hard bread bought at a roadside stall. As they covered the last miles to the border crossing into Portugal, Alva prayed for grace. They approached the Spanish border guards. They passed the fake documents with a wave of the hand. Her fingernails dug into the flesh of her palms as they covered the no-man's-land to the Portuguese post at Vilar Formoso. They were greeted by young British men in flannels and tweeds who dispensed tea and eggs and meat stew, a band of brothers from a number of British firms in Porto who had organized a welcome for their own, but who held nothing back from any Americans, nor from the Belgians, Poles, and French who were equally in need. The Portuguese were friendly and hospitable, the atmosphere immediately lighter. They ate gratefully and greedily. They did not even mind the fleas, such was their relief at finding a bed of sorts for the night: another straw mattress on the floor of an outhouse. Ronald slept in the car.

But there was to be more waiting, as soon became clear. The next morning they were herded into the mass of people who needed to pass through the customs house and passport control before they could proceed anywhere. They walked to the railway station and got in line. On the walls, blue and white ceramic tiles told stories in pictures, of cities and travelers, and of the inhabitants of the country into which they had fallen, and there was plenty of time to study them. A train had come in, full of Jewish faces. When the Bartons and Ronald finally got to the head of the line late in the afternoon, their passports were confiscated, despite Ronald's best efforts to negotiate. Lisbon was full to the bursting point, they were told, and they could go only as far as Caldas da Rainha, some ninety kilometers outside the capital, until they could arrange to travel on to another country. The passports would be returned to them in Caldas da Rainha. The police were polite and fair, but it was hard not to feel that they had ended up, after all, being penned into some kind of holding camp.

It wasn't ideal, but they were released to get on the road again. At first the landscape was made up of scrubby yellow fields, just like those they had crossed under the incessant sun of Castile, but after a while they breathed more easily in swelling uplands, where the hills were wooded and green and cut deeply with ravines. Silver-running streams fed orchards. Vineyards flourished. Flowers bloomed.

At Caldas da Rainha, hotel rooms were available, along with generous dinners. Old-established thermal baths were central to the town's identity, and Ronald recommended they use them immediately to alleviate their aches and pains, ignoring the faint odor of rotten eggs in the tepid, sulphurous water. All she wanted to do afterward was to sleep, to allow her mind to calm, catch up with their altered circumstances.

They stayed in Caldas for a week, suspended in clouds of steam and uncertainty. Here, too, the Portuguese were courteous and welcoming. Ronald came and went, eventually returning with permission for them to move on to Lisbon.

The heat grew unbearable as they drove further south. Most of the roads were not tarred, just baked earth sprinkled with gravel. It wasn't wise to travel in the hours after lunch until five o'clock; the heat was suffocating. Dust thrown up by the car wheels obscured the roadside sights: hot, flower-fragranced earth; hillside villages; the medieval walled city of Óbidos, high on a hill scored by a single winding road; pine woods releasing their deep green scent.

Ronald explained in some detail how the war situation was militarily the same as in 1808, when the threat was from Napoleon's dominance of Europe. "Never forget that Portugal is England's oldest ally," he said. "We'll be all right."

They arrived in a city of calm, tree-lined avenues, elegant houses, flowers planted in window boxes and along all the main roads. Now and then there were tantalizing glimpses of the river Tagus, wide as a blue sea at the end of the street.

ii

The attic room at the Hotel Métropole was stuffy and a long way from the bathroom. But the Bartons were used to being thrown back on their own resources. Wasn't that how they had ended up here? They were still the people they were before they lay on these hard twin beds, getting up each morning to eat salty toasted cheese sandwiches for breakfast and lobsters and langoustines for lunch, considered not extravagant but very standard local fare. Scrupulous cleanliness was the norm and they were treated with warmth and cordiality by the Portuguese at the hotel, in the cafés, in the shops.

Like Rome, Lisbon was a city on seven hills. After it was destroyed by the great earthquake of 1755, the architecture that rose from the ruins was bold and uniform in style, the best the eighteenth century could offer. Set back from the Tagus waterfront behind a wide square with a horseman statue was a triumphal arch with colonnaded buildings forming wings to either side, reminiscent of the Rue de Rivoli in Paris. In its way, the city was as self-confident and beguiling as Paris. It even had its Champs Elysée: the magnificent tree-lined Avenida de la Liberdade.

On display in the stores of the Rua Augusta was an abundance of goods and food, much of it imported: McVitie's biscuits from England, Haig whisky from Scotland, German stollen cakes made with marzipan. Newspapers with all the familiar titles, the *Daily Mail* from London, the *Herald* and *France-Soir* from Paris, the *Deutsche Allgemeine Zeitung*, squashed together into the racks in similar proportion to the displaced persons in the cafés. The British Embassy was next to the building that housed the German Legation, which left the Union Jack fluttering with authority only a few hundred yards from the Nazi swastika.

At night, Lisbon possessed a rare beauty. Light danced from shops and houses; churches and palaces were floodlit like stage sets. The streets were full with a sense of happiness until three in the morning. The clubs oozed American dance music. It was all too possible to mistake it for a safe haven, a place of excitement and adventure. When they heard gunfire as they walked through a side street, on the second night, they cowered against a wall but no advance troops appeared. The next day they were told that what they had most likely heard was the beating of carpets. A local law forbade the practice between the hours of nine a.m. and midnight, so those householders who abhorred early rising beat their carpets in the party hours.

In the days after their arrival, the Bartons experienced a peculiar kind of loneliness tinged with possibilities. No one knew who they were. They could be whomsoever they chose. By the same token, there was no shared history with others, no acts of kindness and connection that root a person to a place. Achievements in a former life had no bearing.

Alva wrote in her journal: "Like all the many refugees, we report to the police at regular intervals. We assume no certainty but the continuous threat of deportation. We are vagabonds in a country that, in the friendliest way possible, does not want us. Spain is largely closed to foreigners, with only transit permitted. Portugal—a small, poor country—is the only open door for those many thousands fleeing west who hope to make the final jump across the sea toward the Americas."

Michael put it more succinctly. "We are huddled on the edge of Europe, with nowhere left to run." That was the opening line of the first newspaper piece he sent back to New York.

At first, the big question was how soon they would be able to get home. The length of time it was taking for a visa to be issued or a sea passage to be allocated was getting longer. Every day there were lines outside an office to be endured. You couldn't trust that word of any progress would reach you; you had to go in person, at least three times a week, to the consulate, or the American Export Lines bureau, which was the exit of choice. If you could afford it, that is.

As the city's luminous streets filled with strangers, the star prize was an American visa. The United States Consulate on the Rua Augusta was in a state of siege, and new acquaintances who had excused themselves from café tables would meet sooner than they wanted in the waiting line that snaked down the stairs from the Immigration Section. Everyone knew the name on the door: Mr. Herbert Pell, the United States minister in charge, and "Pelling" soon became shorthand for trying again.

"Here's the deal," said Michael, pulling off his tie on his return from the shipping office on their fifth day in Lisbon.

Alva looked up from a guidebook she was reading, lying on her bed as there was no chair in the room.

"There are three thousand displaced persons wanting berths from the last remaining open port of continental Europe, and more arriving by the day. A ship sails once a week and it can only take one hundred and eighty passengers."

"So . . . months then," she said.

"That's optimistic."

"What about by air?"

"There's the Pan Am Clipper but you'd have to sell your soul to get on that if you're not either extremely wealthy and well-connected, or you work in some kind of official role."

Michael took a couple steps one way at the end of the bed and a couple more back. "I've been thinking."

"Yes?"

"The way to get through this is to work. Not to put too fine a point on it, we need funds. I couldn't withdraw everything from the bank in Paris, and our cash won't last for long. Plus, there are stories playing out here—more than you would believe. Once the AP knows I've pitched up here it shouldn't be too hard for me to get in on the action." Alva didn't disagree with any of it. They had to have money. Michael had a fine track record; he would surely be able to pick up enough work to tide them over.

It didn't take him long to find out where the international press corps drank. After that, he began most of his days at the Café Eva on Rossio Square with the other pressmen. They gathered for a convivial coffee at nine outside under the canvas parasols and swapped information, keeping each other in the loop. He knew Blake Curnow from way back, or knew of him, at any rate. They had ex-colleagues in common back in New York. Blake was saturnine and cynical and worth listening to. He had been in Madrid at the *Herald Tribune* bureau there, and had got himself into some kind of trouble with the Spanish authorities. He was separated from his wife, who was giving him more trouble from New Jersey. In Lisbon, Blake had wangled some post in the information department at the U.S. Embassy and had a boss he called the Propagandist-in-Chief.

Alva was never more grateful that Michael was outgoing and made friends easily, even if that was only on a superficial level. The way he had of acting confident when he was worried worked in his favor, too; with his regular guy smiles and the gray flannels and sports coat, he fit right in.

It wasn't quite as easy to get going as he'd hoped, though. The AP had a full staff, all of whom guarded their positions zealously. What crumbs were offered to Michael were mostly just "a hat full of disappointments." That was a phrase Michael used. Alva never knew where it came from. She never heard anyone else use it. Perhaps it was a local term from the wilds of New Hampshire where his folks were farmers and shopkeepers. But he didn't let anything go, which made him both a great reporter and a spouse with an unforgiving streak. Here in Lisbon he seemed immune from the almost universal setbacks and atmosphere of anxiety.

Alva took her cue from him, as always. But it wasn't so far from her own temperament. Her father's family, the Marinellis, came to the United States from Calabria at the turn of the century. Her mother was only half-Italian, being the daughter of a Neapolitan immigrant and a nice girl from the Bronx. Alva wouldn't have known how to sit around and do nothing. The Marinellis tried not to get involved with disappointment either, by the hatful or otherwise; they just worked harder and trusted that everyone had to get a break sometimes.

Alva decided she, too, should have a useful occupation.

In Rome, Michael had bought a Leica camera when he needed a last-minute illustration for some piece he was sending by AP Wirephoto. There wasn't a story that couldn't be improved by a good picture.

Alva was the one who really took to the Leica. She walked around with it in her bag and learned about light and shutter speed, and how to focus fast to capture a good frame. She'd harbored some thoughts about being a writer but those had been quietly shut down after Michael was less than encouraging. But he had no objections to her becoming a photographer. He even made use of her pictures from time to time when none better were available at short notice.

By 1940, Lisbon was one of the few countries in Europe where you could still point a camera at a port or an airfield, or a factory or government building or hospital. But with the fear of invasion so constant, no one knew how long this freedom would last. It was worth getting what stock shots could be taken. Soon Alva was going out to take photographs, looking for all the world like another bored woman forced to be a tourist as she waited for transit, trying not to think of herself as one of those sad people who were stuck between a past that lay ruined in another country and a future on the other side of an ocean with no means of crossing.

She captured the present moment—the present, that was all any of them had. Focus. Press the shutter button. Rossio Square, the statue of Dom Pedro IV on a column nearly thirty yards high. The bronze fountain. The waves of black and white cobblestones, like the tide coming in, rippling across the square, scene of revolutions and bullfights. In the run-down Alfama district, washing was strung up high on lines above the street like flags flapping, the neutral flags of normality. She photographed barefoot fisherwomen walking with their baskets on their heads; the yellow trams as they cornered like fairground rides past tiled buildings; groups of men staring bemused at the newfangled traffic lights as they changed from green to red.

She went down to the maritime airport at Cabo Ruivo to see the Clipper flying boat terminal. A boat with wings sat buzzing on the water off the end of a long pier. Its nose and tail turned up perkily; the wings were set high on the fuselage like shoulders raised in a sulk; on each wing, two propellers. The Stars and Stripes painted on a cheek below the cockpit was a cheerful wave from the old country. She snapped away as a launch went out to fetch the passengers, delivering them to a pontoon at the end of the pier, steadied by men in sailors' whites; she continued to take photographs as these passengers came ashore—men mostly, in dark suits and overcoats and hats. They carried briefcases, and walked with the air of businessmen arriving at their commuter stop on the way to the office. Several looked down or turned their heads away from her as they passed. Only one person looked pleased and excited to have arrived, a woman who took the arm of the man she was with, and chattered through a beaming smile.

"Who are all these people?" she asked Michael later.

They had wandered down to the port and slipped into a garden restaurant where an elderly couple served clams and green wine to the background music of ships' horns on the river.

"Do they look like businessmen?"

"I guess. And their mistresses, maybe."

"They're politicians and diplomats and journalists—or that's what it says on their papers."

"They're not?"

"They're spies, honey."

"Surely not—not just delivered by the planeload!"

"They'll be what they pretend to be, at least they'll try. Just . . . they have a higher purpose. There are hundreds of new officers at all the embassies here. As we know, they're certainly not all stamping visas." He cocked his head to one side, intimating that everyone knew, except her. "Mostly, they're spies."

They ate in silence for a few minutes.

"Either that, or they're looking to get rich quick," he said. "I just filed a story about the trade in false travel documents. The embassies of several small countries have been quick to spot the commercial opportunities of supplying papers. There was an auction. Bids were taken for new passports with visas to various South American countries. According to the U.S. and British Embassies, these documents are meaningless, but there were still too many willing to take a chance. News spread through the cafés, and people have paid thousands of dollars. They don't want to know that the likelihood is they will be stuck on a boat that never gets permission to dock anywhere."

"When folks are desperate . . ."

"That's right."

"At least we haven't been forced to leave a home where our families have lived for generations to the mercy of an advancing army," said Alva. "It's not so bad here for us, is it?"

"We're doing OK, don't you think?"

"I found a little photography shop today that has very good rates for developing. Their film is cheap, too. We'll see if it's any good."

Later on, one of the magazine photographers Michael knew, a man who was regularly published in *The*

Living Age, let Alva have use of the darkroom he had found, on the understanding that Michael would put in a good word for him with the *New York Times.* That kind of barter was the lifeblood of the Waiting Room, as they had started to call it. The other kind of barter was in information, and given Michael's gift for eliciting that, it didn't take long for the city to sharpen into focus along with her pictures.

Alva went out with renewed hope, and in the evenings she would return with the muscles in her legs aching from walking up and down hills.

iii

There was another oddity that summer in Lisbon. The prelude was a cacophony of pageant processions and fiesta bands that would surge noisily from side streets, stopping the traffic. It took Alva a while to make the connection: the city was host to a great exhibition and trade fair, the Portuguese World Exhibition, a celebration of the country's proud history and, by implication, the glories of the current regime. It was a message to the world, and perhaps more importantly to the Portuguese themselves, that all was well and it was business as usual in this happiest of nations, founded exactly eight hundred years previously. Three hundred years had passed since independence from Spain in 1640. A shiny new road—the "Marginal"—had been built along the coast to Estoril and the fishing village of

Cascais. Fresh water had been supplied to the inner city for the first time. Programs of municipal building were under way. Literacy rates were rapidly improving.

The Portuguese World Exhibition was staged on the banks of the Tagus with the sixteenth-century Jerónimos monastery on the rising hill behind as a dramatic backdrop. A brand-new square had been constructed, complete with a formal garden and fountain. To Alva, as she stood taking it all in, it looked like a film set full of disjointed structures from different movies. Moorish influences jostled up against modernity. Futuristic streets led surprisingly to a drawbridge into medieval chambers where flames burned at the feet of knights in chain mail. The pavilions were self-consciously modern, sending the message that Portugal was looking to the future. On the riverside was the Monument to the Discoveries, a monolithic stone shaped into the prow of a ship on which stone carvings represented the greatest of the nation's seafaring explorers. In pride of place was Prince Henry the Navigator.

Music swelled through the air on a pleasant breeze as she watched a jeweler fashion flowers from silver filigree, and admired a boat he had made using the same technique. A lace maker tatted with a rapid determination that made Alva smile and think of Michael at his typewriter. Hundreds of people were acting parts and showing off their skills in "roads" dedicated to each region of the country. In the Rua do Algarve a man was plaiting grass into rope. When Alva stepped back to get a better picture, she bumped into someone and turned to apologize. It was Ronald Bagshaw.

"Oh, we meet again!" she said. "How are you enjoying all this?"

"It's fascinating. It should never be forgotten, when speaking to the Portuguese, that they are a proud nation that once ruled the seas and led the way in exploring the world beyond their small country on the edge of Europe. History is important here. Come on, let me buy you a coffee."

They found an open café in front of an exhibition stand decked with all the flags of the world. The Stars and Stripes was one away from the Nazi insignia. The Bartons hadn't seen much of Ronald since the week they had arrived. Last they had heard he had moved out of town to Sintra, where he had a room in a palace with a butler at his disposal. Alva got the impression Michael didn't like him all that much, but had put it down to being one of those difficulties due to the great debt they owed him—a reminder of weakness that could not easily be forgiven.

They sat at a small round table. The sun was bright and they both had to squint. He was wearing a suit in a loose cut that made her think he might have had it made up since his arrival, though she didn't ask.

"All these national crafts and heroes—it's rather too close to triumphalism for current tastes, isn't it," said Ronald.

"I'm not sure an exhibition of ships in bottles strikes quite the same terror as a line of tanks, but I take your point."

"You're not still at the Métropole, are you?"

"We are, but we're working on it. We need to find somewhere more reasonable."

"Not that comfortable, the Met."

"It's not that bad."

"I meant the other guests."

"We haven't had any problems."

"It's a German hotel. Half the rooms are let to Nazi agents."

"You told us."

"And the Café Nicola, the Art Deco place—watch out for the Portuguese secret police there. They're all in with the Gestapo, don't forget. Be careful."

"Thanks for the tip, but we're fine. None of this is anything to do with us, don't forget."

The waiter chose that moment to come over.

"A man came to the embassy the other day," Ronald went on after giving their order. "A Jew from Antwerp.

Opened a manila envelope and showed us what was inside. Uncut diamonds, worth an absolute fortune. Wanted fair exchange for a visa."

"Does a bribe like that work?"

"Not that I saw. Maybe it did. What I'm saying is that these are desperate times. There's no one who is uninvolved."

The crowds passed, the women in their bright finery, many in variations of the national costume. "Have you been out to Estoril yet?" he asked.

"Not yet."

"You must. How is Michael getting on? I hear he's fixed up with a job."

"Not exactly. Just freelancing until we can get a berth home. But yes, he's keen to work, he always is. He likes to feel he's doing his bit."

Ronald frowned. "Does he think America should enter the war?"

"That's not what I meant."

"Does he, though?"

"I think he's glad we're not in it—presently, anyhow."

"We'll win, of course," he said. "It's just a question of how long it will take, and at what cost."

They were both silent. Ronald watched a man in a dark suit with shoulder pads stop and consult a leaflet, then linger at a stall selling sweet sticky carob cakes. When he noticed Alva was following his gaze, Ronald sat back in his chair and put his hands behind his head. He might have been relaxing but she noticed that he kept checking back to see if the man was still there as they discussed which way Portugal was swaying.

"Dr. Salazar is a university professor, an economist not a jack-booted soldier," he said. "There's much competing propaganda to show whether the Allied or the Axis powers are most supportive of Portugal—and which are the snakes in the grass, plotting to oust Salazar. As far as the ordinary Portuguese are concerned, the identity of the enemy is still unknown."

"And in the meantime, it's business as usual."

"There are a number of relief associations or war services that need clerical assistance," he said. "If you were interested, I could put in a word."

"That's kind. I'll bear it in mind."

"There's a rather strict Catholic attitude to women in this country. It helps if you have a clearly defined official role."

"What do you mean?"

"You'll find out. In the meantime, be sure to dress respectfully and don't go out by yourself at night. Not that you would have any reason to, I don't suppose."

It was not unusual for a woman to have her bottom pinched in the street, as Alva had discovered and had been learning to accept as a form of flattery. She was going to have to reconsider.

"Peasant women carry an equal load with their men," said Ronald. "If a man is proud, he will let his woman take the burden while he walks beside her unencumbered. But the rules change for middle- and upper-class women. They do not go out alone to a bar or café. They do not even accompany their husbands to such a venue. They do not drink in public and there is nowhere acceptable for women to meet over cups of coffee. They visit each other at home. Children are brought up strictly, and girls are married off very quickly with little experience. It's a very old-fashioned existence."

She wasn't quite sure what he was saying besides showing off his knowledge of the social hierarchy. From what she knew of women in Rome, paying lip service to social etiquette did not mean they lived completely circumscribed lives, only that the organizing of private adventures required a certain amount of planning.

"You need to be careful," he said.

"So you said."

"These are tricky times. There's a lot of capital to be made here from the war. Everyone wants something, from the politicians to the whores down at the docks."

"I know."

"Never forget you are probably being watched. If not by the Germans, then by the local PVDE—the Portuguese have their secret police watching the foreigners."

He continued with similar forthrightness as another band marched past, followed by a troupe of cheerleaders waving gay paper streamers from sticks. "The Gestapo is operating in Lisbon, and the Portuguese police are doing nothing to stop them. They took one anti-Nazi writer from the street last week, and he hasn't been seen since."

"It seems so unreal."

"Damn right it does." He looked hard at her. "What you must not forget, Mrs. Barton, is that the *escudo* is not the only currency in Lisbon. In a country where newspapers and radio are censored by an authoritarian government, the most valuable commodity of all is information."

The band finished playing and stopped by the fountain. The musicians were hardly more than children; they started splashing water over one another, shouting and laughing.

"How are you getting back?" Ronald asked.

The Packard was parked close by, so he gave her a lift back to Rossio Square.

———

A flock of starlings rose into the pink and gold sky over blackened rooftops as Alva came out of the hotel that evening to meet Michael at the Café Eva. She paused to take a glance around. No one was looking at her as she stepped onto the sidewalk. All she saw and sensed were the petals fallen on stone, the luxuriant brightness, the spiced breaths of breeze, but no afternoon conspiracies.

A yellow tram slid past the café. The passing of the last carriage revealed the usual crowd outside. Blake Curnow was there: a tall, thin man with intense eyes magnified by thick-rimmed glasses and very dark wiry hair that was graying at the temples. He was always watchful as he chain-smoked. Frank Ellis, another freelance journalist, was less taciturn, a man whose gangling teenage self still dominated his body. He had a markedly short snub nose, slightly off center. The more Alva got to know him the more she wondered whether that was the result of a punch to the face—he was extremely annoying. And it was hard not to look into the twin tunnels of those round black nostrils when he had the unfortunate habit of tipping his head back.

There were three other men Alva didn't know. They looked up impatiently as she approached. The Café Eva was considered an all-male working environment.

"We'll see you tomorrow," Michael said to the table as he stood and reached for the jacket hanging from the back of his chair. There was no question of her sitting down with them for a drink.

"Why will we see them tomorrow?" she asked when they were out of earshot.

"We're all going to Estoril."

"Why didn't you tell me before?"

"It's only just been fixed up."

She didn't make too much of it. She wanted to see Estoril, after all.

iv

They took the train west out of the city, with the sea beckoning through dusty windows.

It hadn't been easy to find a place to stay for the night, said Michael. The hotels and pensions were full to capacity, the richer refugees finding the most pleasant places in which to continue their lives in the most pleasant circumstances possible. They were booked into a backstreet pension. The main crowd, mostly pressmen and their girlfriends, were driving up; Alva was more than happy on the train. She and Michael had spent little enough time together lately, and the short journey would be a chance to be alone, with the prospect of a weekend break.

At Estoril the brightness almost knocked her off her feet. The wind was dry and hot. Dust swirled in the air. She caught a piece of grit in the eye, which streamed as she tried to blink it away. The beach was unremarkable, long and flat, the waves tinged with gray.

"Where are we meeting the others?" she asked.

"In the bar at the Hotel Palácio. The most glamorous hotel on the coast. Unless you're German, in which case you'd be at the Hotel do Parque."

She reached for his hand as they walked along from the train station, and felt something close to carefree. She wasn't sure she was dressed for the Palácio, in a sprigged cotton dress and local sandals, but who cared?

The hotel was a white mausoleum in a manicured green garden. Palm trees swelled in the breeze. Six square pillars held up the covered entrance, on which flew flags of all nations. Inside were more columns, and chandeliers dripping light from cavernous ceilings. The Bartons had to ask for directions to the Bar Estoril and were shown to a long narrow room, paneled in wood and set with mirrors and French chairs and low tables. They moved like pieces in a game of chess across the black-and-white-checkerboard floor to where Blake Curnow and Frank Ellis were sitting with two women and a man she hadn't met before.

Blake introduced his girl as Mary, and Frank's as Anita. Mary regarded them coolly, eyes intelligent behind tortoiseshell glasses. Anita, in contrast, had a sulky face, with fleshy lips that contorted into exaggerated shapes as she expressed her emphatic delight that they had made it; she was already drunk. The man was a British journalist, David something, who said he wrote for the *London Daily Mirror*. He was pleasant-looking, his manner relaxed, a notch short of languorous even as he spoke of the British bulldog spirit and the evacuation of Dunkirk.

A new round of gin and tonics was ordered.

"How are you liking Lisbon?" the *Mirror* man asked Alva, in a tone that suggested she might have chosen it as part of the itinerary of a world tour.

"It's . . . interesting."

"It certainly is. How's your Portuguese coming along?"

"Slowly, I'm afraid. But I don't think I'll be here long enough to invest in lessons."

He missed her point. "It's not too difficult, you know. Not if you have Latin. Though you have to beware of the pitfalls, the old linguistic *faux amis*. When I arrived one of the first headlines I read stated categorically: *O Sr. Roosevelt está constipado*, which seemed an unwarranted intrusion into the President's private life—until I discovered it meant he had a cold."

"That's funny," said Anita, with another grimace.

"How long have you been here?" Alva asked David.

"Oh, decades—that's what it feels like, at any rate. At least here there's no talk of prison camps or relief committees. It's all money and gambling stakes at the famous casino, though the waiting and watching are the same even for the wealthiest exiles filling empty days with fine food and wine and idle chatter. They get their news about onward transit delivered by telegram on silver trays. This place and the Hotel Inglaterra is Allied territory. The Hotel Atlântico and the Parque belong to the Germans."

"What about the casino?"

"No-man's-land. I've never been so adept at reading upside down and listening in to other people's conversation."

"I'm sure these new skills will stand you in good stead in the future."

"We never stop learning, do we?"

Through the high windows of the bar, the gardens outside were green and inviting. The sun was high in the sky, and here they were huddled around a table in a paneled room.

"Doesn't anyone go to the beach in Estoril?" asked Alva.

"Everyone goes to the beach."

Except us, she thought.

"It's good swimming," went on David, again oblivious to her meaning. "All the languages of Europe can be heard down there. Though our customs are somewhat less welcome. I hope you haven't brought a two-piece bathing costume."

"As a matter of fact, I haven't. Why?"

"The Portuguese are in a moral panic. Two-piece costumes for women, and topless trunks by men are decreed to be tantamount to nudism, and banned by the authorities."

"I'll be sure to remember."

"Do. Flouting the rules is a penal offense and a special force of police has been formed to enforce the ban."

Two hours and too many gin and tonics later, the Bartons staggered down to the beach and fell asleep in their clothes on beds laid out for sunbathers.

They awoke, out of sorts, to the scent of sardines grilling on charcoal fires on the beachfront. After several wrong turns, Michael succeeded in finding the small pension where he had booked a room for the night, and they bathed and changed into clean clothes.

An argument ensued about whether they would join the others for dinner as arranged. Michael wanted to; Alva did not. In the end, she prevailed, on the grounds that she had too often lately trailed after him as he went right ahead doing just what he wanted. For once, she said, she wanted them to do what *she* wanted.

And they did. They went to an inexpensive restaurant with a view of the sea, but somehow the accusations continued. Alva didn't know what possessed her, but she brought up the baby issue again—why did the worst fights, the ones you normally treated like unexploded bombs, blow up at the very time when you were supposed to be relaxing and enjoying yourself? The barbs from both sides snagged deep. They hardly tasted their food, and the skirmishes continued until Alva wept.

"I'm going to the casino," said Michael, his tone dangerously even. "I wanted you to come, but now you won't, will you?"

The casino was a low modern structure at the far end of a formal garden that sloped down to the sea. For the first time on Michael's arm, Alva felt unaccountably alone as they swept through the portico under neon letters that spelled out where they were; Michael seemed unaware, as was usual now, of her inner qualms. She had to skitter under her long dress to keep up with his forthright stride.

In the foyer, he seemed to check himself, which caught her feet in a tangle. Then he raised his head and pushed off again, like an actor making a stage entrance.

She didn't rate a glance. It was the interior of the fabled casino he had come to see.

The glamour of the gaming room—the men in black tie, the women ostentatiously decked in jewels—was incidental to the green baize tables. A hubbub of conversation rose and fell against a ticktack of the ball in the roulette wheel and betting chips jostling under the croupier's rake. Wealthy refugees of all nationalities watched each other and the games in a joyless dance.

The Bartons made a tour of the room, Michael still gripping her arm stiffly. She was propelled past a card table where Blake Curnow and Mary were standing over David the British journalist. David sat behind a pile of chips; to his right a well-upholstered Jew wearing a large diamond ring on his pinkie; to his left, a shark-eyed man whose black uniform announced his status as a Nazi SS officer. Michael nodded toward Blake and Mary, but they did not linger.

Their circuit completed, Michael bought some gaming chips. Alva refrained from asking whether they could afford to lose them.

At a roulette table under a crystal chandelier, they watched the croupier swoop over the numbers, the turning of the wheel and the white fire of diamonds under the light. Alva could only guess who the players were: aristocratic women in silk, businessmen with too much to lose by staying where they came from, perhaps even members of royal families unknown to her. Others watched, slightly bored. Among the players were several more Nazi officers. Despite their everyday proximity in Lisbon, this was the first time Alma had been this close to them in a social setting. One of them, pork-faced and bulky, was losing consistently, huffing and puffing; in defiance of his express orders, black refused to come up.

Michael gave her three roulette chips.

"Next game, put them on number twenty-nine," he whispered.

"I'll choose for myself."

"No, you won't. Do it."

The table was cleared. Alva hesitated.

She put the three chips on twenty-nine.

Twenty-nine lost. She knew it would.

Alva excused herself. "I have something in my eye again. I'm going to fix it in the ladies' room."

She went out into the foyer and looked around, blinking, for a sign to the restrooms.

"A moment, please."

Alva started.

The man had a curiously pale and featureless face. Even his eyes were a pale muddy gray with barely any lashes. The accent was impossible to place. "Tell your husband to make it less obvious next time."

"I beg your pardon?"

"Just tell him."

He leaned forward and spoke into her ear. "If he's going to get you involved, he has to be serious. Tell him he's been warned."

She was about to tell him he was mistaken, when he clamped a hand on her upper arm. "No questions," he said.

She had some questions all right, but they weren't for him.

In the days that followed, Michael brushed aside her concerns, claiming she must have been mistaken for someone else. Alva grew more adept at observing who was there and exactly what they were doing. She was no longer an innocent. *We'll be out of it soon,* she told herself.

It was October before it became clear that they weren't going anywhere.

"I thought you had our names on the Export Lines list," she said, careful to control the anger that welled up.

"I thought about it, and decided we needed to stay."

"Needed to stay? Needed, in what sense?"

"Alva, you just don't get it, do you? Look around for Christ's sake! It's all going on here—if I can't make this work and get back into a senior position with the AP in Lisbon now, I'll be finished as a reporter. Rome, fled. Paris, fled. I can't leave again. This is my last chance!"

From a newsman's point of view, she could see that. At the time, she had seen their flights to safety in purely personal terms. "You should have discussed it with me, not just decided. I'm involved, too! But no, you just left me expecting we were going to get a departure date sooner or later. You said you'd been going to the Pan Am office!"

"Sending pieces back to New York, not booking our passage."

"What?"

He gave her that look that said he was going to explain it very simply. "Because Portugal is neutral, the censors will not permit publication of anything that might be offensive to either side, or more pertinently, to their own government. So what we do is this—we give copy to the air passengers taking the Pan Am clipper to New York. They deliver it for us, for a small fee, usually, though some may do it for love and liberty."

She shook her head slowly.

"I thought you understood," he said.

Alva caught the expression on his face, the one that husbands give their wives, or vice versa: bewilderment that what had once been affection had turned to such hatred. She had seen it between other people, and noticed it often here, where long waits made for short tempers within couples. She had never thought it would happen to them.

"Of course I understand," she said quietly.

He pulled off his tie and hung it over the back of the chair. Turning his back to her, he went over to the washstand, and spoke to her reflection in the mirror. "You do want to stay here, don't you?"

"Sure. Do we have another option?"

"It's a fascinating place." He was able to say it as if they were on the outside looking in, or watching a movie of the place as it gradually revealed its story. Not as active participants in tragic events.

She looked at the lines outside the shipping offices differently after that; they were not made up of people like them, after all. Michael was doing what he loved, and they were staying in Lisbon.

PART THREE

Faro—August 2014

i

Nathan's hair was wet from the shower and his shirt was on inside out. The sight of him in the little studio, as I let myself in, was oddly disconcerting.

"How did you sleep?" I asked, knowing he had been out for the count for at least ten hours. I shut the door behind me with an elbow and put my bags down on the table. "I went out to get some bread and ham and fruit and stuff for breakfast."

"That's a lot of shopping."

"I didn't know what you'd want."

He rubbed his face. "Thanks, Jo—really, thanks a lot. You OK?"

"Fine. I sat up reading for too long but apart from that, all good."

I felt pretty bleary, to tell the truth. After my night reading Esta Hartford's book, immersed in a different time and situation, the present had a jagged, unreal edge to it. The feeling was compounded by the sight of Nathan pulling apart a pack of biscuits and flopping into a decadent pose in the room's only chair. I forced myself to concentrate on the reasons he was here, and the questions that disturbed me as much as the puddles of his clothes on the floor. More questions than before, not the least being how Esta Hartford's supposedly true story could possibly have a bearing on the here and now.

"What day is it?" he asked.

"Sunday."

"Thought so. Just wasn't, you know, sure."

I made us both some instant coffee, which he took with two teaspoons of the sugar I'd just bought, guessing that it would be needed.

"I need to go to Vale Navio," he said, between mouthfuls. "Then on to Horta das Rochas. I've been putting it off because I wanted to find out as much as I could beforehand."

"What can you do there?"

He shrugged. "Ask around about Terry Jackson. See if I can get a handle on where he is now. Better than sitting here doing nothing."

"But I thought Vale Navio was derelict now." I'd looked it up online when he'd first mentioned the place to me. Google images had shown the hotel complex deserted and shaggy with scrubby weeds. "Will there be anyone there to ask? Even if it was a good idea to ask around openly about Terry Jackson, which, incidentally, I don't think it is."

"There's no more I can do anywhere else. So that's where I'm going."

"Hang on a minute. Let's think this through. How are you going to get there?"

"Train? Buses? It can't be that hard."

I shook my head. "Better to hire a car. I'm coming with you."

"You don't have to."

The way he said it, turning to me so the deep blue of his eyes lasered mine, was probably as close as he would get to saying that he wanted me along.

"I know I don't have to. But I am."

He didn't argue.

"Do you want to go back to your room, get a change of clothes, or something?"

"I've got a few things in my bag."

"Just one thing before we leave then," I said, not wanting to ask why, exactly, he carried spare clothes in his rucksack. "You might want to put your shirt on the right way out."

The heat was still uncomfortable, like hot breath on the skin. Within ten minutes my forehead was wet and irritated under the band of my straw hat.

We had decided to hire the car from the airport; the rental places there would be able to let us have one immediately and more discreetly than anywhere in town. I wanted us to be as anonymous as possible, just in case.

The easiest way to the airport was by bus. At the bus shelter, a woman of about forty—an old, careworn forty—sat on the plastic bench and poured bottled water on a deformed leg. Her heel stuck out at an angle; it must have been hard to walk on. I watched, unable to stop myself, as she washed both feet, both legs, with slow, methodical relief, then tipped her head back against the bus shelter, eyes closed, the black hairs on her shins slicked and gleaming. Nathan watched her and I could see he was wondering whether he could help her in some way, but in the end decided there was nothing he could offer. She remained seated as our bus arrived and filled.

The passengers on this route were an unusual mix. The bus to the airport went on to Faro beach, meaning that those with suitcases jostled for seats with people in flip-flops carrying swimming bags: the air travellers, steeled for delays and inconveniences; and the relaxed, enjoying the prospect of a few aimless hours of splashing and sunbathing; each of us, in our differing ways, suspending normal life.

At the entrance to the airport, the bus took a rolling surge past the monolithic Soviet-style statues of sturdy people gazing up at planes in the sky. We alighted by the line of taxis; Nathan went to buy the most detailed street map of the Albufeira region available while I hired a basic white Seat Leon for a week.

Forty minutes later we were heading west. I drove and Nathan held the map open on his knees, with no macho posturing about already knowing the way.

"If you don't mind taking the toll road, it won't be much more than half an hour," he said.

"Let's do it."

We could see the dual carriageway carving away from the hills behind Faro and into low scrub, orchards, and sun-baked grass. The traffic was light, but the reason became clear as soon as we drove up and tried to pay the toll. It accepted only prepaid electronic tickets and there was nowhere to pay by coin or bank card.

"Looks like it's the back roads for us, then." I turned the car around.

"Someone was telling me about the chaos the Portuguese have made of their *estradas* since they decided to try and raise money by charging to use the motorways that used to be free. They've spent more money making these half-baked tolls than they've raised in revenue, and hardly anyone uses them. Meanwhile, the other roads are being overused and need more repairs. Leaving everyone out of pocket and angry. It's been a complete cock-up."

"Did that come from your bus driver mate?"

"Yeah, think it might have been. OK, then, we take the second exit off this roundabout onto the N125."

It wasn't hard to find Vale Navio as we approached on the Estrada de Vilamoura. We passed well-kept properties with gleaming white walls and palms growing in neat gardens and long low villas. It all gave a pleasant impression of the suburban dream fulfilled in the sun.

Nathan reached down into his bag and removed something I couldn't see.

"What's that?"

"Wire cutters."

I thought better of asking where he'd got them, or even making some smart comment.

Vale Navio was only a few hundred metres off the main road and, rather unexpectedly, I drove straight in. There were no rusty gates or padlocks to be broken.

"It's the middle of nowhere," said Nathan, craning round in his seat. "Why would you come out here when you could be in a resort by the sea or closer to all the action in Albufeira?"

Why indeed? We followed the drive through grey-streaked apartment blocks constructed in a style that gave equal nods to the Moorish and the package holiday market with its expectation of private balconies. It was a ghost village. Weeds were rampant. Scrubby bushes pushed through the walls of the grounds and the concrete pathways; overgrown plants reached up to the higher storeys and hung weeds from the balconies.

The main buildings had once been elegant colonnades, low and curving under a red roof. Now the white masonry paint was a dirty, pitted grey, as if smudged and shaded in a charcoal drawing. Here and there on walls patched with rain stains were scribbles of graffiti.

"Looks completely empty," said Nathan.

"It may not be. There are probably squatters somewhere."

I pulled up and parked discreetly behind a bank of bushes that would soon be small trees.

Nathan sprang out of the car and marched off without a word.

I followed him more slowly up the path towards what looked like the main building. Spikes of tough grass that sprang from cracks scratched my legs. In what was once the landscaped approach, the shallow saucer of a water feature held grass and rubble. The atmosphere was a long way from a holiday welcome; as I walked, shoulders back and doing my best impression of an innocently curious tourist, I was aware that someone could very well be watching us from any one of hundreds of black windows.

"It's all open," said Nathan as I caught up.

He was right. There seemed to be no doors or windows remaining; they must have been stolen and recycled years ago. The structure looked sound enough, though. Inside, a reception area was a shock of bright, vapid colours and builders' debris on the floor. The walls were painted with thick stripes of daffodil yellow and orange. On one side of a garish turquoise archway was a cartoonish mural of a shapely woman in a red dress and a man in a Mexican hat kneeling to kiss her hand.

"It looks like something out of Disneyland," said Nathan. "Not that I've ever been."

"Extraordinary."

"Someone's come and hacked off all the tiles over there."

"And the floor, too."

We crunched through shards of broken terra-cotta and broken plastic and screwed-up paper and through to a large open room decorated in the same style. It was like walking into an animated film set in Mexico.

"All that's missing is the spray of bullet holes," said Nathan.

"Don't joke."

"I wasn't."

I bent down to pick up a pad of bills I'd kicked. "This was the restaurant," I said. "The 'Mexiko,' look."

"Very original."

"That must have been the kitchen through there, though everything's been ripped out."

Nathan wandered back to the reception counter and started looking behind it. I went into an office. On the floor under a sagging shelf were thick ring binder files spewing their contents. I picked up a handful of papers. Many of them were in English, complaints from guests about the cleanliness of the accommodation, the quality of the food, and general unhelpfulness of the staff, issues that could reasonably have been solved; and others, mostly about the distance from the sea, which could not. I noted the dates (2001 to 2003) and flipped through the other files but found nothing of interest.

"Not sure I'd want to come here alone at night," I said.

"Some of the damage could have been done by sledge-hammer."

I started. "What was that?"

"What?"

"Shh . . ."

We waited.

"I thought I heard rustling," I said.

"Can't hear anything. Maybe a rat."

It could have been, or perhaps some far larger feral creature had us in its sights. "Let's go, there's nothing here." I didn't want to tell Nathan how scared I'd been for those few seconds.

Outside, the ragged palm trees were a reminder of sunshine breaks and better times.

"Not too many people around to ask about Terry Jackson," I said.

"Looks like it's been a while, doesn't it? He used to drink at The Lucky Horseshoe. Always mentioned it. He spent a lot of time there, and it was where he did some of the business that we didn't ask about."

"We could try the riding centre," I said, scrolling through a saved email I'd sent myself with notes about this sad outpost of the Algarve.

Nathan narrowed his eyes, as if he couldn't believe anyone could be that stupid. "The Lucky Horseshoe. It's a pub—or a bar, anyway."

I mirrored his expression. "Well, yes it is. But it doesn't seem to be here, does it. And the riding centre is one of the few parts of Vale Navio that is still up and running, and perhaps the name of the bar implies the riding centre was quite close by."

His face changed, lit by a smile, and he pointed a finger at me. "I like the way you're thinking."

We got back into the car and tried to drive a little further around the complex to find The Lucky Horseshoe. First one road, then another ended in a mound of compacted earth deliberately placed across the tarmac to make a dead end. It took me a nine-point turn by the filthy hole of a swimming pool to turn around.

There was no sign of any building that might once have been Terry Jackson's local.

"Vale Navio used to be really lively—it was lovely."

The riding stables were small and friendly. A small group of children were just leaving the well-kept yard on leading reins. Horses in the paddock were sleek and well-muscled. The slim, middle-aged Englishwoman who introduced herself as the owner—"Call me Pip, everyone else does"—was clearly used to questions about the timeshare resort, though her diplomacy was too ingrained to let much slip. No amount of jaunty yellow and white paint on the low stable buildings could mask the unavoidable reality that they were hard up against the abandoned resort, however. It was an eerie outlook onto Vale Navio's weed-tufted apartments.

"Once you get out into the countryside, it's gorgeous here," she assured us. "There are fig and banana and cork trees to hack through. Lots of lovely wildlife. It's really unspoilt, a taste of the old Algarve."

"Business looks good, here. Lots of lovely write-ups online," I said.

"We're doing fine. What is it that you want to know, exactly?"

"Can you remember when the complex closed down?" asked Nathan.

"You'd be amazed how many times I'm asked that," said Pip. "It was in 2003. By all accounts, everyone got too greedy: the developers, the investors—and the criminal gangs who were rumoured to have taken over the timeshare operation. But the rot set in long before then. Around 1992 or 1993, someone involved in the resort did a runner with a wodge of cash from sales of new apartments that were going to be built. After that the place gradually went bankrupt. The hotel went downhill and the tourists stopped coming. The owners of the timeshares had lawyers on the case for years but never got anywhere. Their deeds weren't worth the paper they were printed on. The banks foreclosed on their investments. But some of the private villas on the complex are still lived in."

I tried to imagine how dreadful that must be, surrounded by a derelict resort. "What about squatters?"

"Oh, there are squatters. And drug users and glue sniffers. I wouldn't advise you to wander around there at night."

"The money must have gone into other pockets," said Nathan.

"Sure. But I have no knowledge of any of that. In my position, I don't pry."

"No. Quite," I said.

Nathan looked around casually. "Don't suppose The Lucky Horseshoe is still going?"

"That's a blast from the past. No, that got closed down while the rest of Vale Navio was still going. It was just over there."

"Ever have a drink there yourself?" he asked.

Pip shook her head. "The odd one, but I wasn't a regular. I'm not a big drinker. And it was mainly the holidaymakers in there, you know. They had entertainment and quizzes, that sort of thing."

"Mainly? You wouldn't happen to know anyone who was a regular, who still lives down here?"

She thought for a moment, while I willed Nathan not to mention Terry Jackson by name, just to exercise a bit of subtlety.

"It used to be owned by a British man called Terry," said Pip.

"Can you remember his surname?" I asked.

"Not sure I can . . ."

"It wasn't Jackson, was it?" prompted Nathan.

"Yes . . . now you say it, perhaps it was."

Between Albufeira and Portimão, heading west towards Horta das Rochas, we stopped for a cold drink and a sandwich and the chance to take stock.

From the terrace of the café we could see orange-gold and tawny brown cliffs crumbling like ancient walls above the beach. Teetering columns of rough-hewn rock stood out in the sea, giving a desolate grandeur to the shore, like the flooded ruins of a mediaeval cathedral.

Across a blue-and-white-tiled table, Nathan jiggled one knee and drummed his fingers on the scrap of paper Pip had given us, on which he had scrawled what she recalled of his family's old friend Terry Jackson. It wasn't much, but it was some traction at last.

"That would make sense, wouldn't it, that he was the owner of the bar," said Nathan. He drained a glass of Coca-Cola and rattled the ice. "It would explain why he was so involved with Vale Navio, and also that it was somewhere he could meet his dodgy mates and feel sure he wasn't treading on anyone else's toes."

"It's definitely a start," I said cautiously. "And it's interesting that Pip remembers him having other business interests over this side of Albufeira. But I'm not sure where we go from here, except to have a look at Horta das Rochas."

That's what we'd decided as soon as we left the stables. It wasn't much further west and Nathan's blood was up for the chase. Not for the first time that day, I had to check myself and question what I thought I was doing. Whether it was really such a good idea to get involved. But then, as I looked at his eager, determined face and absolute conviction that he had to do this, I couldn't help feeling a spark of excitement. I tried to tell myself this was down to the potential story, and the story alone, but that wasn't the truth. I was equally fascinated by Nathan.

"Still nothing from this Ian Rylands?" he asked.

"No. I've left several messages. Any more and it starts to look desperate. What about your 'Peter Maitland'?"

"Same."

When Nathan went off to pay the bill, insisting this was his shout, I pulled out my phone and made another call.

"Will Venning."

"Will, it's Jo Millard."

"Hi, Jo—how are things?"

"Not too bad, thanks. I'll come straight to the point. I'm in Portugal and I was wondering whether you had

a contact number, or even better, an address for someone here. I gather he helped you out on a story some
time ago."

"I'll do my best." He didn't ask what I needed it for.
We'd always trusted each other.

"A man called Ian Rylands who runs the Anglo-
Algarve Association."

"Spelled R-I-lands?"

"No, with a 'Y.' "

"Leave it with me. I'll get back to you when I get
home. I'm at a barbecue and cricket match with the
kids—no, put that back, please, Sam—sorry. Better
go—we'll speak later, yes?"

"Thanks, Will. Appreciate it."

"What was that about?" asked Nathan.

"A long shot. Guy I work with—used to work with.
When I met Rylands that time he told me that their
paths had crossed. It's worth asking. Journalists tend
to keep a record of the contacts they make. If he finds
anything, he'll get back to me."

Back in the hire car—it was small but surprisingly
comfortable, though I found the gear changes a bit
sticky—we pushed on through acres of modern whitewashed houses, standard Mediterranean developments fringing the golf courses and tennis courts that

brought the sportier tourists and retirees to the region. Prices in some areas had fallen by an eye-watering forty percent recently, though, according to the *Algarve Daily News*. Plenty of people were selling up as overdevelopment bumped up against the continuing financial squeeze.

Horta das Rochas was announced on a sleek black plate, gold lettering, set in a stone gatepost. The entrance was open. Though I couldn't see security cameras, I was sure there were plenty. The driveway snaked through well-tended gardens of umbrella pines and lawn. It was as quiet as Vale Navio, for entirely different reasons. We drove in silence, too, as the red roofs and white walls of holiday villas began to appear, set discreetly in the improbably green landscape. There were signs to tennis courts and the golf course. The main hotel was another modern Moorish design, elegantly accomplished to meet the expectations of visitors used to high-end international resorts. I pulled up and parked easily in a space trimmed by oleander and palms.

Again, Nathan sprang out of the car, already ten metres ahead of me as I leaned in to pull out my bag.

"Let's just take it easy," I said as I caught up with him at the steps of the entrance. "Don't start putting Jackson's name out here yet. We're on holiday, OK? We have all the time in the world to have a late lunch and look around. If anyone wants to know, we thought long and hard about booking to stay here—and wanted to see what we were missing, right?"

He nodded.

I went over to the reception desk, my low-heeled sandals clicking on the polished marble floor, and asked for directions to the beach restaurant.

"How did you know there was a beach restaurant?" Nathan asked as we emerged onto a flower-banked path the other side of the building.

"The wonders of the Internet. I looked this place up."

We followed the path down towards the shore through gardens shaded by pines and emerged at a chic wooden structure concocted mainly of decking and canvas. An enticing barbecue smell rose.

"I bet you're still hungry."

He was. He demolished a dish of piri-piri chicken recommended by the pretty waitress while I picked at the inevitable plate of olives and pale cheese and gazed at the beach with its archipelago of boulders stretching into the sea. Close up, the cliffs looked as if a giant shovel had gouged part of the structure away, leaving an unstable pile of reddish sand. On the higher reaches, pine trees clutched at this unstable seawall, but I could see patches where a frizz of roots held nothing but air.

Perhaps it was my call to Will, bringing back as it did the mental picture of the old newsroom and all the associations that went with it—my old self, in other words—but I felt a bit unsteady, too.

In Brussels I was always wondering if a snippet I heard could be the basis of a story; people came to me with observations and off-cuts of conversation and laid it out like half-sewn patchwork for me to assemble. I'd call Eurobots and bankers and politicians for their reactions, and no one would give me an authentic, illuminating reply, just an automated response spewing standard lines from the machine. In Faro, now here, with Nathan, I was on an authentic trail, destination unknown. I hadn't had this frisson of excitement on a story in years.

I smiled across at him. He pushed his long hair out of his eyes, and I couldn't help but notice he didn't look tired anymore.

My phone rang from the depths of my bag. It had its own special pocket inside but I must have chucked it into the sedimentary layer of old papers and other detritus.

"Don't know how you find anything in that granny sack," said Nathan as I delved in.

"Shut up and hold this." I handed him the exhumed remains of our first picnic on the beach, which he held up between two fingers with wary amusement. "All journalists have big bags they can't find anything in. It's a badge of honour."

I pulled the phone out and answered it just in time. "Hi Will, that was quick. Any luck with Ian Rylands?"

"I have got something, yes. What are you up to over there, by the way?"

"I will tell you, but not right now."

A slight pause at the other end of the line. "All right. I have his number and email, and I've managed to find some old notes, too."

"Will, you're a star."

"The Anglo-Algarve Association, is that what he told you?"

"I got his name from their website."

There was another pause, during which I knew Will was going to tell me something that he knew he shouldn't.

"You know he's ex–Foreign Office?"

"He said he'd been in the civil service, but much happier with early retirement and the pension."

"He played it down then. Some postings to far-flung places early on in his career—Kinshasa, Santiago, Hong Kong—but he ended up a European specialist. Brussels, of course. Bonn in the early nineties, and after the Maastrict Treaty was signed in '92 he kept tabs on the whole European Union project, the political side, from Luxembourg. He would only be quoted anonymously, and I described him as 'a disillusioned former Brussels hand, with nebulous links to the intelligence services.'"

"A spook?"

"Not quite a spook, no. I wouldn't go that far."

"What was your story—the one he was helping you with?"

"It was about the rise of disillusionment across Europe with the EU, and especially with German economic dominance."

"And was he helpful?"

"Let's say he has some pretty contentious views and a few axes to grind. He has some theory about the Nazis after 1945, and the dream that wouldn't die."

"Blimey. Bit of a nutter, then?"

Will exhaled in a way that expressed that was exactly what he thought. He gave me the contact details though, and urged me to keep him in the loop, whatever it was I was up to. We chatted a bit more about old colleagues and then said goodbye knowing there was plenty more to be said but now was not the time or place.

"This is definitely getting weirder," I told Nathan.

I rang the number Will had given me, and after a moment's indecision, left a message for the elusive Ian Rylands.

After we'd eaten, we walked along the pretty beach and through the impressive gardens of the resort. Luggage—and in one case, guests—were delivered and collected from villas in the grounds by golf buggy. The heat was softened by well-spaced trees. Horta das Rochas was secluded and expensive; all was quiet, well-mannered, and offered no insights whatsoever.

Back in Faro I found a parking spot that didn't seem to have any restrictions and we walked back through a small square set with a modern sculpture of a stork. On one bench a couple of middle-aged drunks were kissing like teenagers, their bottles at their feet. An ebony-black man, with an air of loneliness but also under the influence, looked on.

"Don't know about you but I wouldn't mind a proper drink," said Nathan.

"Why not?"

I was longing for a glass of wine after a long hot day on the road punctuated by too many Cokes.

The Bar Verde promised cool green shade but was stifling. Refrigerated displays of fish made you wish you were in there with them, and the smell of cooking faintly sickening. A breeze struggled to get in but went away disappointed.

"This may have been a bad choice," I said. "Let's have this drink and go."

"We could find somewhere where we can sit outside for another one."

"Not for me. I'm going to have an early night." Although I'd been fine all day, buoyed up by the excitement of the quest, I was suddenly feeling the effects of my night sitting up reading.

"I'll walk you back," said Nathan.

On the edge of the marina, crowds were milling around the Folk Faro stage, claiming standing room behind the metal barriers for a free view of the show. Final sound checks boomed. Groups of dancers made bright clusters dressed in national costumes: French Basque, Argentinian, Bulgarian, Macedonian, Hungarian. Above the scene, international flags drooped from their fixings on the rooftop terrace of the Hotel Faro while the starred circle of the EU fluttered on video screens placed either side of the stage.

The night market in the Jardim Manuel Bivar had opened, and, greedy as children, we couldn't resist buying sticky slabs of carob and honey-and-almond cake to share. We ended up strolling slowly through the Old Town gates and into the cathedral square, and over to the steps of the cathedral, where we sat down to open our package. The wide cobbled space, the elegance of its low whitewashed buildings, and the border of orange trees revived my energy level.

"Built on the remains of the Roman forum," he said. "Two thousand years ago. Isn't that amazing?"

"Yes. It is."

We let the night fall around us as we ate, cooled by a welcome breeze, then wandered back to the red door on Rua da Misericórdia.

"You'll be all right going back to yours tonight?" I asked.

"Sure."

"Night in for you, too?"

I had no idea how long it would take him to realise that might be a good idea, but I thought better of prompting him any further. I had to accept that it was up to him.

I'd just had a long, blissful shower when my mobile rang: number unknown. I had a lurch of certainty that this, finally, was Rylands.

"Hello?" I said, professional smile in my tone.

"Hello, Joanna."

I gave a silent curse. "Marc."

"I couldn't leave it like this. We owe each other an explanation, at least. And when you're avoiding my calls . . ."

"So you've called me from someone else's phone?"

He didn't deny it. "Why did you block me?"

"Sorry, it wasn't . . ." But of course it was, and I had no excuses. I rubbed my eyes with a clenched fist in frustration. I was dog-tired from the driving on strange roads and the sun; my eyes stung and my limbs were heavy. I couldn't take another session of emotional recrimination. If he wanted to make that my fault, then he could. I was hard to live with, I would admit to that. I knew how he felt: sometimes it was hard enough living with myself. What I didn't realise until it was too late was what a control freak he was. I felt hemmed in.

"Count yourself lucky," he said.

"Oh?"

"I'm giving you one last chance. I'm going to forgive you for running out on me. For the things you said."

I sighed. "You see me as you want me to be, not what I am, Marc." My body temperature spiked again. I went and stood at the open window from where I had a clear view of the night market. Intermittent whiffs of rich chocolate and orange bakery came my way.

"We can all become whatever we want to be," he replied. "Why can't you just go with it?"

I wondered how well we really knew each other, and couldn't help thinking how it had been only an hour ago with Nathan. The easy company and understanding between us. Even the shorthand in our conversation. Trying to behave with Marc as I had with Nathan was impossible.

"I'm going to come to Faro, we can talk face to face."

"No, don't! Don't come—please."

"But why?"

I didn't reply.

"We have such a good life together," he said.

"No, we don't, Marc. Not really."

"What? Great jobs, interesting places, the money to enjoy ourselves and travel . . . I won't believe you if you say you haven't enjoyed it."

"I don't think we believe in the same things anymore." Silence. I squeezed my eyes tightly closed. "I've met someone else."

"What?"

"I've fallen in love with someone else."

"What the hell are you doing in Portugal on your own then?" It was a fair point. I could tell he didn't believe me.

"I wanted to be sure," I said.

Warm air was closing in.

"And are you sure?"

I was lying to Marc, but instinctively, awkwardly, a picture formed in my mind of Nathan grinning at me across the room that morning, his shirt inside out. I did my best to dispose of it but didn't actually succeed.

"Yes. Very sure," I said. "I'm sorry."

He ended the call. I remained standing by the window. From the far side of the Jardim Manuel Bivar, a folk dance reached crescendo in a frenzy of music, stamping feet, and applause.

ii

Next morning the garden lay cool and green, the cake stalls shuttered. I followed the path across it and heard the scream of aircraft coming in to land on the far side of the lagoon.

At the marina I paused to watch a man in a yellow T-shirt jump into a small boat, start up the outboard motor, and putter off, standing up to hold the tiller. He slipped confidently under the rail bridge without ducking and out of the harbour towards the marshes.

I felt only relief that I was finally free from Marc.

An explosion of engine noise made me jump. It was right next to me so I had no time to do anything but react instinctively. I stepped away. But something jerked at my shoulder, a strong pull, and I felt a sharp punch to my arm. It was from someone riding pillion on a motorcycle and this passenger was pulling on the strap of my bag. His hands knocked into mine. I twisted around, away from my attacker. I clenched my fist around the chunky leather strap. It was broad daylight and I was keeping my bag.

"Hey!" I shouted as loudly as I could.

The traffic in the marina woke up. Other shouts came from the water. The engine roared, and then the motorcycle shot off.

It seemed longer afterwards, but it was all over in seconds.

It was just an attempted bag snatch," I told Nathan when we met up at the Aliança about half an hour later. To his credit, he came running as soon as he got my text. "These things happen everywhere."

The incident had shaken me more than I wanted to admit but I saw nothing to be gained by making a fuss.

"I've still got my bag. That's all that matters. I probably looked like a prime target, standing there daydreaming at the marina."

Nathan pulled a disbelieving face. His concern was rather sweet.

"Let's just forget it," I said.

"But what if it wasn't random? It might have been intended to scare you off. Or, if they had got your bag, to see whether there was anything inside it to show what we're doing."

"You may be getting a bit ahead of yourself there. It's much more likely to be something and nothing."

"I don't want you worrying."

"I'm not worried!"

Both of us had misgivings, it seemed.

Nathan drained his coffee. "I never wanted to put you in danger, Jo. You've been so brilliant, helping me and all. But if this is going to be more dangerous than I thought, then I don't want you involved."

"But I am involved now."

"You can stop, though."

"I don't want to stop." I pressed a finger into the crumbs on my plate and put it in my mouth. "You asked for my help and I'm giving it. Talking of which, I still haven't heard anything back from Ian Rylands."

"You going to try again on the number your mate gave you?"

"I have done."

"Remind me how you left things with him—Rylands?"

"He said to me: 'I'll let you have a copy of Esta Hartford's book. Then we can talk again.' He left the book here for me, under the counter, with João. I got, I read it, and now I'm waiting to talk again."

That's what Rylands had said. There was no ambiguity about it.

"Bit odd," agreed Nathan.

"But it was before you almost met him at the Chapel of Bones," I reminded him. "For all I know he had seen us together."

"What difference does that make?"

"I don't know. It just might, that's all. Think hard—do you think you might have seen him around town here, after that evening when you thought you saw him in the church?"

Nathan gave it a few minutes, then shook his head. "The trouble is, he wasn't exactly memorable, physically. He faded into the background."

He was absolutely right there. I had to admit I could remember few details of his face; with concentration, it almost swam into focus but then receded into an impression only of quietness, of resolve and intelligence. "A man in his seventies with white hair," I said. "A fair height and a hint of military bearing. Sun damage on his face and some kind of black pigment, a mole, maybe worse, on the back of his hand."

I didn't mention the bulging pockets filled with who knew what. The civil service career he had admitted to but clearly had downplayed when I'd asked. I had so many more questions now. He was retired, but I hadn't asked what from. My head had been fuddled with wine when he told me about Esta Hartford and her book. Was there something in his phrasing that I should have taken as a subtle warning?

"He said that behind the sea, the heat, and the lovely Moorish buildings, Faro has a seedy underbelly. A murky ocean of political and economic interests. Not his exact words, but something like that."

Nathan looked up, but not at me. An argument had broken out by the bar, two men shouting and waving their arms and pointing aggressively. I couldn't understand what they were saying, but he could.

"Just politics," he said. "A difference of opinion about central government."

"Quite heartening, really."

The shouting match was joined by a short middle-aged man in a russet jacket. He began to speak in a measured tone at a lower than normal volume so that they had to stop yelling to hear. He looked vaguely familiar, but I couldn't work out why.

It was only as we left the café that I realised that his was the face on the poster plastered inside the café and at strategic locations all across town.

Nathan didn't arrive at class on the Tuesday morning, which concerned me. I'd sent him a text, to which the reply had been decidedly ambiguous. I suspected he was taking more risks, and had decided to keep me out of it, whether I liked it or not. My reaction to that was complicated. I wanted to help him, and I enjoyed spending time with him. After Marc's call, I realised how close Nathan and I had become, without even trying.

The language course ground on, one day leaving me feeling as if I would never get to grips with these new and complex rules and patterns of words, the next that it was beginning to catch fire. Like the familiar paths across the town, I was finding a way through.

After three days' absence, Nathan was waiting for me at the corner of the Jardim as I arrived back at the studio in the afternoon.

"Where have you been?" I asked.

"Not important. But I have got some news."

"Come up."

He paced around as I boiled water in a saucepan to make some tea.

"This morning, right, my phone rings. I answer it, and this bloke says, 'Terry Jackson has heard you're looking for him. Well, now you've found him. He wants to meet you.'"

"Who did he say he was, the man on the phone?"

"He didn't say."

"You're not going on your own," I told him.

"I have to."

"And I'm telling you I am coming, too. Where and when does he want to meet you?"

"On the ferry to Barreta Island. Tomorrow morning at ten."

"I don't like the sound of this. Why the ferry—why the island? It's a bit odd, isn't it?"

Nathan shrugged. "At least there will be other people around."

"All right. You go and meet Terry Jackson, but I'm coming, too. Not with you. Just taking the trip and keeping an eye on what's going on. OK?"

He nodded, then exhaled deeply.

I arrived at the ferry jetty before Nathan. In line to buy my ticket to Barreta Island, I looked around as guilelessly as I could, playing the tourist. There was a brief misunderstanding at the kiosk window when I didn't realise that Barreta was also known as the Ilha Deserta. The Deserted Island, its tourist name.

There didn't seem to be any obvious candidates as far as Terry Jackson was concerned. To be fair, Nathan hadn't been able to furnish much of a description from memory. As a child he'd been more interested in the comics or sweets Terry had once lobbed his way than in details of his appearance. He hadn't been noticeably tall, or fat, or possessed of any odd features that might stick in a boy's mind, apart from an impression that may or may not have been accurate, of reddish hair. ("Not bright red or ginger, just a bit red. But I might be wrong.")

There were a few men waiting, but they were all with wives or partners or children. Nathan sauntered up, avoiding any contact with me, and stood in the queue. Anyone who saw him that day would have assumed he was perfectly relaxed, a good-looking young man sure of himself and his advantages. The woman in the kiosk handed him his ticket with a smile several inches wider than the one she was giving everyone else.

He was starting to get agitated, though. The hands were drumming on the wall, though his posture was elaborately calm. I kept him in the corner of my eye, feeling nervous enough myself.

A small child having a tantrum provided a brief distraction. When I next looked surreptitiously at Nathan, a man had appeared in my line of sight. This man had his back to me, but the height and bearing made my heart lurch.

I hadn't seen that coming. And yet somehow, I felt I should have known. I just wasn't thinking quickly enough. Ian Rylands wasn't close enough to Nathan for them to speak, but I could see Rylands was watching him. Hanging back, pretending to look for something in the depths of my bag, wondering whether Rylands had noticed me or whether all his attention was focused on Nathan, I fiddled around with my phone, reading old texts. Then I held it up to take a discreet photo.

Nathan walked confidently down to the boat and Rylands followed. I hung back until both of them were on board. Most of the trippers went through to the open deck at the front but Nathan went for the interior seats. I could see his reasoning. If anyone wanted to talk, they could find relative privacy where he had chosen. I waited until I saw Rylands sit down opposite him, and only then did I go down to the embarkation pontoon and onto the boat. I waited on deck until the ferry had moved off from the quay, then slipped into the seat next to Nathan.

"Morning, Ian—nice to see you again," I said brightly.

He smiled. "Very good to see you again, Joanna. I was wondering when you would join us."

The old city walls receded across the water and we began to plough through the green marshlands. The sea was grey, and the clam diggers were few and far between.

"There is always a price to be paid when man plays with nature," said Rylands.

Neither of us replied. Nathan started tapping against the steel of the open window. I waited to see where this was leading.

"In order to secure the access to the ports of Faro and Olhão, the inlet known as Barra Nova had to be artificially fixed," said Rylands. "But the stability of the barrier islands has now been undermined. The sands don't stop shifting—the sands of Culatra Island, of the entire coast. The waters of the lagoon are tamed, but no one can control the ocean on the other side. Same cause, different effect."

The message seemed to be that he wasn't going to discuss anything important where we could be overheard.

He carried on speaking in an avuncular manner, as if the three of us were on a family outing. Nathan sat impassively, lacking his characteristic engagement with a stranger. He didn't even smile.

"Fixing the barrage, making the permanent reliable entrance to Faro docks from the salt marsh waterways has destabilised the sand spit islands further out in the unforgiving Atlantic. The sea drift is strong, constantly bullying the islands into new positions, redrawing the coastal maps."

"I didn't come out for a geography lesson," said Nathan. His South London accent was rougher than usual.

Rylands was unperturbed. "Plenty of time when we get there," he said in the same reasonable tone. I was glad of the information Will Venning had passed on; this was exactly how an ex–Foreign Office man would conduct himself while holding his cards close to his chest. What killed me was that Nathan and I had made no plan for this, and had no chance to formulate a strategy; Rylands was the one who had us pinned down.

So we sat in awkward silence as the ferry made progress south towards the island. Nathan and I didn't look at each other, but his leg was jammed against mine as we sat wedged together on the bench seat. I pressed back.

The island jetty, when it eventually came in sight, was a primitive structure, joined to a long wooden walkway up to the one architectural feature: a futuristic restaurant with solar panels to the rear. Most of our fellow passengers headed towards a line of rattan sunshades on the beach.

"We'll go the other way," said Rylands. Another wooden path led through dunes and tough maritime shrubs.

"Why the Ilha Deserta?" asked Nathan. "To make sure I can't do a runner?"

Rylands raised his hands. "I want to find out the truth as much as you do."

Nathan made a noncommittal sound and we exchanged a glance, reassuring each other. Without a word we followed our mysterious guide past a row of small wooden beach huts, five painted blue and one white. Gulls cawed noisily overhead.

We didn't go far, only to a point on the white sand where we were alone, and it really did seem as if we had made landfall on a deserted island, flat and wide and at one with the horizon. Grey-blue Atlantic rollers rose and unfurled on shell-strewn sand. White seabirds gathered at the foamy edge of the water.

"Right, let's have it then," said Nathan. "You're obviously not Terry Jackson. It was you who called me, wasn't it? And are you also the Peter Maitland who told me to meet him the other week in the church?"

"Ah, that. A name I use sometimes. I have to be careful."

I shook my head, hoping to convey my cynicism. It was ridiculously cloak and dagger. Perhaps the old man was a bit touched in the head, and we were wasting our time on a wild-goose chase.

Nathan was impatient. "I'm not playing games, whoever you are. What do you know about Terry Jackson, and why did you use his name to get me here?"

"Let's keep walking," said Rylands. "It looks odd for us to be standing here having a conference."

Ours were the only human footprints in the fine sand; the only other markings had been made by birds. Looking northwards we could still see the high-rise buildings of Faro and the hills behind, yet it felt a world apart. To the south there was nothing, a blue line that led to Africa.

"Terry Jackson," Nathan prompted brusquely. "Do you know him?"

"I have never met Mr. Jackson. I know of him."

"Go on."

I held back from interrupting, waiting to hear what Rylands had to say.

"What most people know of Terry Jackson is that he is the owner of various businesses in and around Albufeira, none of which have ever been more than moderately successful. Several have gone under. There is a suspicion that none of this matters very much as these businesses are not all they seem. I take it you understand my meaning?"

"Just spell it out, Ian," I said, irritated. "And by the way, Nathan, this is not what he told me the night we met." I turned to Rylands and looked him straight in the eye. "I asked you then if you knew anything about Terry Jackson, and you said you didn't think so. Those were your words. And you asked me why I was interested. I told you that I knew he had a connection to Horta das Rochas and Vale Navio, and you wanted to know what else I knew about him."

I stopped there. I wasn't sure, but I had a sinking feeling that I might have provided Rylands with an answer—an answer I had no appreciation, at the time, of its importance.

Rylands smiled. "You're right. Time for some straight talking—from each of us."

"You first," said Nathan.

"Terry Jackson has criminal connections. We know that. Not just the connections—he's been on the inside of some pretty big stuff," said Rylands. "You don't go around the Algarve asking questions about him without word getting back."

I shivered, despite the heat. When Rylands had spoken about being watched, I'd assumed he meant by the authorities. I surmised now that he was far more worried about the criminal element.

"So what's your involvement?" I asked him.

"It started with the Stern case. A couple of years ago I was asked by Leo and Karen Stern to conduct my own investigation into what happened to their little girl. Tilly was only three when she vanished and they kept her in the news, made her the highest-profile missing child in the world, and still there were no answers. All official lines of inquiry were running out of steam and they thought I might be able to look at all angles. I was on the spot. I knew how the Euro-authorities worked. The Anglo-Algarve Association made a pretty good front for ferreting around. The Sterns still pay me a modest retainer."

"The Association doesn't really exist?"

"No, it does. Let's just say . . . it doesn't do much and I personally am only interested in certain aspects of expat life here. I'm sorry to say that I have never managed to uncover any tangible new evidence for the Sterns. God knows, I have tried. But that is how I first came across Esta Hartford's book."

Nathan fidgeted impatiently. "What the hell's that book got to do with any of this—the Stern girl, Terry Jackson? It's just some wartime love story!"

Rylands silenced him with a glacial glare. "Joanna asked me the evening we met about the collapse of Vale Navio and the cases of child murder and abduction in the region that have never been resolved. She also mentioned Terry Jackson. So that tells me something—that you are on the same trail as I am.

Terry Jackson is central to something that happened after Esta Hartford's story ends—but one step at a time. What I need to know is why are you two so interested?"

I struggled to regain my composure. "It's a story. I'm a journalist."

"That might just have been believable, Joanna, if our friend here hadn't been so clearly involved."

"He's my researcher."

Rylands seemed to be about to challenge that, then decided to leave it. "I can only say again: we must speak frankly if I am to help you. Or rather, if we are to help each other."

"And I'm sure you will understand why we are reluctant to trust you with any of our insights, Ian. Given your lack of candour with us so far." I said it as much with the intention of warning Nathan against total openness as making the point to Rylands. "Why did you lie about knowing who Terry Jackson was?"

"Because I had no proof you were who you said you were! You could have been sent to set me up by an associate of Jackson's or one of the other players here. By anyone who wanted to know how much I knew, and how close to the truth I was getting!"

Nathan was clearly as startled as I was by this outburst, and the contrast to the usual measured Foreign

Office tone. "Why are you so interested in Terry Jackson?"

It lasted a fraction of a second, but Ryland's hesitation was not reassuring. "He's the link between the past and the present."

"Come again?" said Nathan. I could see that had rattled him.

Rylands turned to me. "Have you read the book?"

"Yes."

"Have you made the connection?"

I stared at him, not wanting to admit that I hadn't quite, beyond the obvious. Esta Hartford's novel was as far removed from a dodgy wheeler-dealer from South London as it was possible to imagine, but there was one name that had leapt out, towards the end.

"Horta das Rochas," I said. "Terry Jackson had some kind of association there and with the tourist industry here." I didn't want to say too much.

"He was also the owner of a bar at Vale Navio, The Lucky Horseshoe," said Rylands. "Before it closed down, it was the place he used for meeting contacts and a bit of light money laundering. Plenty of strangers wandering in and out to camouflage the hard-core regulars. He has an apartment in Albufeira, but he's not often there. These days he is only occasionally involved in money laundering, but he is protected by powerful contacts and corrupt policemen. There's a lot of that around here." He spoke lightly, but the warning was implicit.

"There's a lot of corruption, full stop," he went on. "And if you know anything of the history of the place, you can't ignore the way a great deal of the . . . unpleasantness joins up to give one big unpleasant picture."

Rylands looked from one of us to the other. "I have reason to think that Terry Jackson played a part in the kidnapping of a two-year-old boy."

Nathan swayed. I pretended to stumble, caught his arm and squeezed tightly. I was still not sure how far we could trust Ian Rylands and I wanted to prevent Nathan from saying anything he might regret. "A bit more serious than money laundering," I said, exhaling a note of surprise.

Nathan seemed to understand. "That is not good," he said.

"But you knew that about Jackson," said Rylands. "That first evening, you asked me whether his name had ever come up in reports of the child abduction cases."

I tried to recall exactly what I had said to him. I thought I'd been more careful than that. We had reached a small red-and-white-striped lighthouse set on an embankment of rocks. The question was, how far could we trust Rylands?

Nathan must have been wondering about that, too. "Why did you try to trick me into meeting you at the Chapel of Bones and then not show up?"

"I wanted to take a look at you, to see who I was dealing with."

It sounded like an honest answer. On the other hand . . . no. I decided Rylands couldn't possibly have made the link between the child and Nathan.

Nathan kicked a piece of driftwood. "Back to Terry Jackson. Are you saying that you found out about him when you were asking questions about Tilly Stern?"

"Yes. I researched as many old cases as I could of children going missing on the Algarve. There were several that happened in and around Vale Navio. His name came up, more than once, when I asked around.

"Look," he went on, "there are the cases like Tilly Stern: a small child on holiday, an opportunist crime. I think it must have been a mistake to take her, unless the parents had some connection that we cannot find."

"That's how some of their nastier critics see it," I said, thinking of the abuse her parents had received for keeping the case in the news, hoping against hope for a breakthrough. "They think the parents were involved somehow."

"For the record, I have found nothing to cast doubt on the parents' integrity. What I am saying is that in

cases of child abduction, there is almost always a logical reason for it. The crime may be heinous, but it is
rational."

He paused.

"There is also the possibility, when a child disap-
pears, that the child has been taken for sexual purposes."

Another pause.

"This is a very distasteful area indeed. Sometimes
the abuse of children in this vile way is about power
and retaining power. The abusers are either black-
mailed as a means of control, or a group engaged together in disgusting activities are bound in loyalty to
each other."

"You saying what I think you are?" asked Nathan.
"Paedos and all that, like they reckon went on with
some of the political scum at Westminster? Powerful
men who thought they were untouchable? Kids in care
who didn't have anyone to look out for them?"

"It wasn't only happening in Britain," said Rylands.
"You should research Belgium in the 1990s."

Was he being sarcastic? I couldn't call it.

"Do you know about this because of your former
employment?" I asked. How was it Will Venning had
described him? *A disillusioned former Brussels hand,
with nebulous links to the intelligence services.* If that

was the case, he might have some very useful, if distasteful, information.

He dodged the question. "I get angry when I read the newspapers. I think more and more people feel the same. Something dark is happening. The old order is vanishing, and with it the old checks and balances. It's worse than anyone can imagine."

"Including child abduction and abuse?"

"This is the way the evidence points, that is all I am saying."

We walked across a bank of gold and white clamshells, all as hollow as any possible response.

"You can dismiss what I say, but don't forget that it was you who came to me, not the other way round."

Nathan and I said nothing.

"Now, do you still want to speak to Terry Jackson?"

Nathan butted in. "You're saying you know for certain he's involved . . . in this? Have you spoken to him yourself?"

"Not personally, though I have suggested several times to the police that they question Jackson."

"And?"

"Nothing has ever come of it." Rylands remained implacable but his features hardened. "So, it's over to you. Do you want to speak to Terry Jackson?"

"I certainly do," said Nathan.

"Well, I have a number for him and I would be very interested to know what happens if you call it." Rylands produced a piece of paper from the breast pocket of his linen jacket and handed it over. "Will you keep me posted?"

Nathan gave a barely perceptible dip of the head.

"If you are going to get involved, you must be prepared to . . ." Rylands hesitated, seeming to change his mind about what he was going to say before he addressed it to me. "Have an open mind, and be careful. Make sure you read the last part of Esta Hartford's book, and if you still want to know more, I suggest you contact a man called Eduardo Walde. You know the name, I assume?"

Nathan and I exchanged glances, shook our heads.

"Who is he?" I said, feeling ever more like a student who had been caught out trying to wing an important topic after an hour's cursory reading.

"Eduardo Walde is someone who has seen what we have been discussing from the heart of the matter. He lives in Lisbon, and he is Esta Hartford's son. Don't take it from me. Find out what happened to his family for yourselves. It shouldn't be hard."

"Why don't you just tell us?" asked Nathan rancorously.

Rylands screwed up his face against the brightness, reconfiguring the dark patterns of sun damage. A fishing boat passed close to the beach, belching smoke as the engine stuttered. "For Mayer, read Walde."

"What's that supposed to mean?" Nathan took an aggressive step towards him. "I've had it with your fun and games, mate. If you've got something to say, just come out and fucking say it!"

"Nathan . . ." I put a hand up to tell him to calm down.

"No, I've had enough! Well, then, come on!"

Rylands was unmoved. "Oh, I tried saying it, believe me. There is more going on, all around us, than you will ever know."

Nathan fidgeted by my side. "Right, that's it. I have had it with this." He started walking away.

"I also know the significance of the name Emberlin," Rylands said calmly, loud enough to stop Nathan in his tracks. "The question is, do you?"

Without waiting for a response, he, too, walked away, in the opposite direction.

"Ian! Come back, you can't leave it there!" I called after him.

"What the—?" Nathan was a coiled spring. "That's right, you just fuck off, mate!"

Rylands pulled his shoulders square and did just that with some elderly dignity.

"What did he mean by that?" asked Nathan. "By any of it?"

"What did you do that for?" I countered. It was hard to know which of them to be angrier with.

"It was just getting stupid."

I couldn't disagree. But as we watched Rylands' back recede up the wooden pathway and disappear, I was torn. Perhaps I should have run after him then, but Nathan moved off down the empty beach and I went with him. Waves broke on the shore and sprackled our arms and faces with sea spray. There were no beach loungers and rattan parasols here. The sun glistered. We sat on the sand, squinting.

"You think he knows who I am?"

"He knows something about you," I said bleakly.

"What about this Eduardo Walde—ever heard of him?" he asked.

"Nope."

Nathan was quiet for a while. I think we were both processing the mental grenades Rylands had thrown. *For Mayer read Walde.* I didn't want to say anything until I could think it through.

Nathan pinched the bridge of his nose and scrunched his eyes tightly closed. "Why did he have to say that . . . about the paedophiles and the child abuse?"

I knew full well why. "Unfortunately, it's one of those issues that isn't unmentionable anymore. It's been pulled out of the shadows, especially where it involves powerful, well-known men. Every newspaper in London is waiting for more to come out and no one dares to discount it anymore."

"I mean, did that happen to me?"

So that was why he had reacted as he did. I should have realised sooner. "I can't give you complete reassurance, Nate, but I think . . . that you would know, deep down, if anything like that had happened to you."

"But it could have done."

"And there are many other reasons why kids are taken. For money. For revenge. To hurt a family. Don't assume."

"You do understand, though?"

I put my arm around him, feeling that the back of his shirt was soaked with sweat. "Of course, I do."

He leaned in and rested his head on my shoulder. He was a boy again. A beautiful broken boy. "And what the hell did he mean about knowing the name Emberlin?"

That, I have to admit, was the part that worried me most. "If you hadn't gone off on one, we might have found out."

"He could just be saying it."

"Maybe." I wasn't convinced though.

"Shit. We have to ask him," said Nathan.

"I think so."

We ran up the wooden walkway. I didn't think we'd come as far as we had. The next ferry back to the mainland was due within the hour. Nathan flew past me, with a smooth, athletic stride. I came around the other side of the restaurant where the raised path to the ferry jetty jinked off at an angle. The boat was there. Nathan hurled himself down the walkway, which bounced under his steps. I had to stop to get my breath back. A stitch in my side jabbed painfully. Was that Rylands on board? Nathan was waving in the direction of the ferry, but he was too late. It pulled away as Rylands watched from the deck rail, ramrod straight, expressionless.

That afternoon on the beach on the Ilha Deserta—it would be four hours until the ferry returned, so we sat on the sand, burning in the sun—I realised something about Nathan. He had courage, more than anyone I had ever known. I've always tried very hard not to appear vulnerable, and it occurred to me that I could learn a lot from him.

Nathan was already at O Castelo when I arrived at nine that night. He had a prime seat on a sofa with a view over the old city walls across the water to the marshlands.

"I called Terry Jackson at the number Rylands gave us."

"That was quick." To tell the truth, I had my doubts the number would work. "Did you speak to him?"

"Yep."

"What did he say?"

"That he heard I'd been looking for him, and how was I, after all these years?"

"How did he sound?"

"Normal. Quite friendly, full of bullshit. He asked me if I wanted to meet for a drink. Not a word that he might have come to my house, done my room over, and had me beaten up, naturally."

Best not to contradict him. "OK . . . so now what?"

"I meet him for a drink, of course."

"I'm not sure that's such a good idea, Nathan."

"What, so I've come all this way and I'm going to bottle it now?"

"No, but—oh, I don't know."

"He wants to meet me at Horta das Rochas."

"When?"

"Tomorrow night."

At least it was in a public place, somewhere that was above the line. I wasn't going to say anything more about it, not now. We had a couple of drinks and ate dinner mostly in silence. Ritzy-reggae on the sound system grated on my nerves. Nathan seemed just out of reach, preoccupied. When he did speak, it was about the past.

"It wasn't a terrible childhood. I can't say that. It was all a bit rough-and-tumble, but I thought I was normal, you know? And now I want to have it out with the people who called themselves my mum and dad but never told me the truth. I want to rage at them. Only they're not here anymore, and so I'm raging at myself . . . for, for not knowing somehow."

"You can't do that. It's not your fault."

I thought he was going to explode. I felt the tension ratchet in him from across the table. But he held it back.

"I was always disruptive as a child, rebellious. But you grow up, don't you? You grow into yourself. You think you understand what you need, what you are. And then . . . you find out you're not yourself. You're someone else, and maybe the . . . shadow of that was always there, even though you didn't know what to call it, or how to live with it. What if that angry child knew all along, but the knowledge got covered over, and over, until it was forgotten?"

"You're still the same person."

"It doesn't feel like it."

I put my hand on his arm and left it there. "We don't know anything for certain yet," I said gently.

"There were . . . incidents. Words. Overheard bits of argument. I put it down to my . . . parents having a complicated relationship. But for a start I should have seen I didn't even look like them."

"But if you weren't looking to see difference, you wouldn't have seen it."

He was a beautiful broken boy, I repeated to myself. In the candlelight, his hair shone as it flopped over his cheekbones. The sadness in his expression was deeper than I had ever seen. I knew if I reached out, he would take any comfort, and validation, I offered. But it was all to do with need, and not desire, I told myself. Perhaps we were equally guilty of sending mixed messages.

I was unsettled as we walked across the lamplit cobbles of the old town, the white bulk of the cathedral rising like a liner from the darkness. Clatter of dishes from restaurants and a tinny note of music from a radio. We were almost through the Largo da Sé when he stopped.

"Actually . . . there's something I want to do." The overly casual way he said it implied some solo mission I suspected I wouldn't want to know about.

"Oh?"

But he surprised me. "You can come with me if you want."

"Where are you going?"

"I'll show you."

Against my better judgement, it has to be said, I wheeled around and trotted alongside him back the way we'd come, past O Castelo and along the lane that led out of the Old Town. We passed no one.

We emerged close to the shore, where the old fortress walls had a crumbly texture from the worst of the sea winds. On stone like nibbled biscuit, a sentinel cactus grew.

"Up here," said Nathan. He started to scramble up, making for the cactus. When I hesitated, unsure the soles of my sandals would offer any grip, he held out a hand to me.

"What the—?"

"You'll see."

I let him pull me up behind him, and we felt as much as saw our way up until we were standing on top of the old walls.

"It's just along here."

The ancient stones were shaggy with sea grasses. We made our way carefully along until we reached a structure. It was a centuries-old lookout point or sentry post. Stretching out before us, the dark sea and marshes.

Immediately my suspicions resurfaced. "This isn't some kind of dodgy hangout at night, is it?" I pulled back.

"Come on!"

All was quiet. I couldn't hear anyone else up here.

Nathan balanced on the outside ledge of the stone hut. "This way round. Be careful of the drop," he said. He gripped my hand tighter. "Whatever happens, don't let go. Now, look inside," he said, in a whisper. "Can you see?"

A coil of while feathers. It was a huge storks' nest.

"Beautiful, aren't they. I just wanted to check they were all right."

We walked back to the Rua da Misericórdia, and said good night. He touched my arm lightly, and was gone.

iii

The following evening we left at seven to give ourselves plenty of time. I wasn't sure if there was an
Algarve rush hour. It went without saying this time that
I was driving him to Horta das Rochas. The plan was
for me to drop him off, wait in the car park for fifteen
minutes, then to wander into the bar, where Terry had
asked Nathan to meet him.

"I'll try taking a photo on my phone, but it may not
be possible."

"Don't start letting the flash off, for God's sake."

"Have faith. I'll think of something. I could always
ask the waiter to take one of me at the table, making
sure he was in the background. There's always a way."

Nathan looked doubtful.

"I won't do anything silly. Don't worry."

———

Nathan left. His saunter might have been convincing had I not got to know him. His shoulders were stiff and the laid-back confidence was lacking. I waited out the quarter of an hour in a corner of the car park screened by oleanders, listening to a music station and straining to pick out words I could understand in the adverts for hypermarkets and insurance. A retouch of my makeup—I wanted to look plausible as a woman out on her own who might be up for a chat with a stranger, or at least who might want a stranger to take a photo of her—and I set off.

The reception area was more crowded than when we'd come that afternoon and eaten at the beach bar. Clumps of suitcases and a couple of groups in travel clothes indicated that the front desk was busy. I went on past and looked for a sign to the bar.

It was a cheery hubbub of noise and clinking glasses. I claimed a table where I could sit with my back to the wall with the bar, the entrance, and the rest of the room all visible. No Nathan, but I wasn't too concerned. It would be typical of him to have decided to take another look around and to keep Terry Jackson waiting. Perhaps Nathan had come into the bar and decided he didn't want to be the one waiting.

A waitress caught my eye, and I ordered a small glass of Vinho Verde. I had no intention of drinking more than a few sips. Still I waited. A man came over and asked if he could sit with me. I sent him away and took a book, a serious literary book, from my bag and pretended to read it while failing to drink my wine. Without Nathan and Terry Jackson in the bar, I needed to give out a different vibe.

After three quarters of an hour, feeling increasingly concerned, I paid my bill and went back across the foyer. I lingered for five minutes, thought about texting Nathan but held back, and then ostentatiously looked at my watch before walking quickly down the steps and back outside. For want of any other idea, I went back to the car.

As I approached, a shadow moved.

I was ready to run—feeling a sense of being followed, remembering the attempted bag snatch—but the assailant hissed, "Jo!"

Nathan grabbed my arm.

"You scared the life out of me! What's going on?"

He pulled me along. We were walking down one of the paths to the small villas in the trees.

"Have you seen Jackson?" I asked.

"No."

"And you weren't in the bar."

"I was, first of all. I went and sat at the bar, but as soon as I did, I got a text asking me to go to Villa Eleven."

"From Jackson?"

"That's the name that came up. I suppose so."

"That's where he wants to see you—Villa Eleven?"

"Yep."

"And that's where we're heading now?" I was distinctly uneasy.

"I don't know what else to do, Jo. I wanted to do this in public, but it doesn't seem like I have a choice. I just thought I shouldn't go without telling you where I was."

"OK. No, you're right. Good thinking."

"It's here."

We were outside a single villa. It was set apart from the others we had passed, which had been in rows of four. This must have been a superior version. The front door was slightly open. Through a window, we could see a couple of lamps burning, but all was quiet.

"I'll stay outside, then. I'll just be over there." I indicated a palm with a thick trunk flanked by bushes, feeling a bit silly.

Nathan knocked at the door. After a minute or so, he pushed the door open and went in. I waited, self-consciously ridiculous in the darkness. I couldn't hear any voices.

Then Nathan emerged. He held me by the arm and I could feel his hand trembling.

"What is it?" I asked, knowing immediately that something was wrong.

"There's no one there—well, there *was*," he whispered.

"What the—?"

"I want you to see this. Then we can tell someone. Don't touch anything."

"Nathan—?" Dread was uncoiling in my stomach.

"Don't say anything."

He led me inside the villa and into the main room. By sliding doors, slightly open, was a sitting area. The only light was cast by a lamp on a side table.

Ian Rylands was sitting in a high-backed armchair. At first glance he looked as if he was sleeping. The glass by his hand had been knocked over.

"Don't go any closer," said Nathan. "He's dead. And my fingerprints are on his neck where I checked for a pulse."

"I don't suppose it was natural causes?"

"I'm no expert, but I wouldn't have thought so."

I don't know where I got the cold-bloodedness from but somehow I knew it could be important. I swiped my phone onto camera, and took three photos of the scene as we had stumbled into it.

iv

As the first witnesses on the scene, we were also ob-vious suspects. I knew that was inevitable, and I could only hope Nathan did, too.

"Tell me again, why did you go to Villa Eleven," said a bald plainclothes detective with a deep blue shadow over his jaw. He had a way of narrowing his eyes in-tently to make sure his prey knew he possessed greater powers. I hadn't caught his name, which was unlike me. An indication of how wrong-footed I was, perhaps.

There was, of course, an obvious response: to tell the truth. Which was that Nathan and I were trying to find a British man called Terry Jackson, and that we thought we had finally succeeded when he asked Nathan to meet him at the hotel. We had to assume that Jackson had also invited the dead man. But as soon as either of us mentioned Terry Jackson, everything we had found out and done so far would be made public and subject to official investigation. I didn't know whether that would be a good or a bad thing. In the end, of course, it was illusory to think there was a choice. In these situations, fudging the truth is never a good idea. I'd covered enough news stories to know that the truth always comes out, and when it does it's the lying to cover it up that causes the most trouble.

"I went to Villa Eleven when my friend came and found me in the car park, and said that the person he had come to the resort to meet had asked him to go there."

The detective—Gamboa? Gameiro?—nodded inscrutably after I stopped speaking, letting the pause lengthen, until it became so awkward that I would be tempted to say something—anything. I knew the technique. Journalists use it all the time. In a small faraway part of my brain, I thought, this is going to be interesting, being on the other side of the questions, standing in the shoes of a suspect being interviewed by the police, seeing close up how the Portuguese authorities conducted themselves when dealing with foreign nationals. Their reputation wasn't good. Guilty until

proven innocent was their usual line. I stopped disso-
ciating myself from the situation and allowed myself to
worry as I waited for him to break the silence.

"Who is this person?"

"A man called Terry Jackson."

"Do you know this man?"

"I have never met him."

"But your friend Joshua knows him."

Joshua? That caught me off-balance. I must have
looked puzzled for the second or two it took me to register that Nathan had given the police his real name,
or rather the name that would be on his passport, the
name he had gone by until he came to Portugal. At
least he was still thinking straight while being interviewed by the police. What was his surname? Think,
think . . . *Harris,* that was it. *"It's more who I am than
Josh Harris."* In sheer relief, I gave myself a mental pat
on the back.

"Did you not know that?"

"I'm sorry?"

"Did you not know that Joshua was here to meet
a man called Terry Jackson? The man he claims to
know?"

"I did know that. Sorry, I misunderstood."

"Where does Mr. Jackson live?"

"Here in Portugal, I believe."

"Where, exactly? Do you have an address?"

"No, I don't know that."

"When did Joshua last see Mr. Jackson alive?"

"I don't know. You'll have to ask him."

"But recently?"

"No, I think it was some years ago."

"Why did they decide to meet now?"

"Terry Jackson was an old friend of . . . Josh's parents. Sadly both his mother and father have died, but while Josh was in Portugal he thought he would try to contact Mr. Jackson. I'm not sure, but I think that he wanted to pass on the sad news." I was playing the innocent as much as I could. I didn't want to complicate matters any more than necessary, though I had no idea how much Nathan was telling them.

We went round and round the same information several times. They asked me how well I knew Joshua. I was waiting nervously for the question that would draw us in closer to the crime. The one question the detective didn't ask: whether the victim had been known to us. Was he waiting for me to volunteer the information? My thoughts were small cars veering from lane to lane on a crowded motorway, trying to judge distances and speeds, and constantly aware of the danger from larger vehicles capable of surprising acceleration.

"OK, you can go now."

It was too late. I simply didn't know how best to say it.

At two o'clock in the morning, I was drinking mineral water in the manager's office. The manager, another person whose full name hadn't registered during a formal introduction, was called Jaime according to his name badge: a stocky man with a thick moustache. He was quiet, but perfectly genial as he made a valiant effort to pretend all was normal. But under the low-energy light, he was crumpled and grey. He sat at his desk in front of a laptop where he might have been surfing the net (Google: *what to do + murder + business premises*), or he might have been playing solitaire; I couldn't see the screen. A uniformed policeman with a marine's stance was outside the door.

I was wondering whether news had spread through the resort or if the pampered guests were sleeping through, undisturbed and unaware of the drama. Part of me, the detached, callously professional part, wanted to take notes and call the night news desk at the *Independent* in London. But I couldn't, of course I couldn't. It turned out I wasn't much of a risk-taker after all, despite my bravado.

Rylands must have been, though, whatever it was that he had taken on. The picture of him in life lingered, queasily: the old-fashioned upright bearing; a man who was puzzled by the modern world, and regarded it with painful bemusement. The other picture of him, as we found him, made me feel nauseous.

Tiredness and shock were taking their toll. I wasn't able to think coherently. I should have said that I knew the identity of the dead man. Did the police know who he was? Was it possible he could have been killed for reasons completely separate from what we'd discussed with him? He had been so careful to cover his tracks . . .

The door opened and the detective showed Nathan in. Then he left us alone.

It occurred to me that the security camera overhead was recording, and that anything Nathan and I had to say to each other would be instantly relayed to the investigation.

"You all right?" he asked me.

I nodded. "You?"

"I'll have some of that water," he said, reaching over for the bottle.

Neither of us said anything else. I needn't have worried. Nathan was sharp. The manager ticktacked his keyboard like a pianist finishing a breezy solo.

It was a while later that the detective—Gambóias; I checked—returned and gave the manager permission to take us to some overnight accommodation.

Once again Nathan's good looks had worked in his favour. Several young women on the staff had noticed him wandering through the gardens down to the beach and back; everything he said he'd done since arriving at the resort checked out. My movements too had been timed and captured on CCTV cameras pointing at the car park.

Preliminary postmortem findings were in, too. Ian Rylands had died of poisoning. Suicide could not be discounted, though murder was a stronger probability. The possibility that finding the body was intended as a terrible warning to us was as yet unexplored. Nor were we told anything about the person who must have booked the villa.

"Come with me, please."

We obeyed, following in close formation out into the grounds and towards a small terrace of guest villas, not as large and well-appointed as the one we had visited earlier. The hotel manager showed us into a pleasantly spacious, predominantly white sitting room with stairs leading to an upper floor. "You can stay here until the morning. The detectives will want to speak to you again."

It was heartening that we were allowed to be together. The arrangement suggested we were in the clear.

The manager left without giving us a key, though.

Nathan took his shoes off and wedged the door open with a Converse sneaker. "I need a smoke," he said, and headed outside again.

I joined him on the dark grass as the smell of the cigarette curled through the night air.

He exhaled deeply. "Shit."

Neither of us said anything for a few minutes.

"Did they ask you anything about Rylands?" I ventured.

"No."

"Terry Jackson?"

"What about Terry Jackson?" said Nathan.

Oh, hell, had he not mentioned him? "That you'd gone to meet him."

"Yeah, that. Nothing else."

Relief.

"They seemed more interested that I went down to the beach first. That was what they kept on about."

"Why?"

Nathan sucked in the smoke. "I saw a dealer down there."

"A dealer? What . . . a drug dealer?" *No*, I was thinking, *not that, too.* "Please tell me you didn't—"

"It's not what you think."

"No?"

"I've seen quite a lot of dealers, one way and another since I've been down here. Don't look at me like that."

"You can't see me. It's too dark."

"Believe me, I know what your face is doing. Look, dealers have contacts with people like Terry Jackson. OK, I'm not saying I'm a saint. Sometimes I had to score, sometimes more than once, just to make it look authentic, and yes, sometimes, I took some stuff— because . . . because I'm messed up right now, you know? But nothing much, I promise you. I left a lot more in nightclubs than I ever took. Nice little present for someone. I'm telling you straight up."

I thought back to the mornings he never turned up at class. It was only what everyone had suspected anyway. "All those long nights," I said.

"Yeah. But not because I was clubbing that late but because I couldn't get back from Albufeira or Vilamoura. I had to sleep sitting up on the beach till the trains started running again in the morning. And not because I was necessarily in a crap state."

"What else haven't you told me, Nathan?" I was really worried now. "I can't help you if you—"

"Calm down, it's all right. I didn't buy anything down on the beach because the guy wasn't there. I just heard he was sometimes, and it was too good a chance to miss, this being a high-roller kind of place that Terry Jackson used. That's the way it works. There's nothing else."

"Bloody dangerous," I muttered. It was the closest we had come to an argument. This wasn't interesting and fun anymore. The smell of smoke filled the black space between us. Not a joint. No scent other than the normal acrid tar and tobacco of a Portuguese cigarette.

"Anyway," he said. "It was a good thing I did go down there to look. Someone saw me, and backed up what I told the police. And if they can track us through the resort, then with any luck, they can track Jackson."

"If it was him. If he was even here. He probably got someone else to do the dirty work."

We both needed to try to get some sleep but that wasn't going to happen until my mind calmed. "What else should I know, Nathan?"

"What do you mean?"

"What else haven't you told me? It's important, for both of us."

"You know everything now. You know more than I've told anyone."

I waited. "Where did you go when you didn't come to class for three days, just after I nearly had my bag snatched?"

"My bus driver mate offered me a free ride to Lagos to go and check out the records there. I reckoned if there was nothing on Jackson in Albufeira, I should look a bit further along the coast. But I didn't find anything, even though I thought I had a lead—a T. Jackson who turned out to be a woman called Tina."

"OK . . . and what else?"

"All right, the girls I said I met in the clubs. There weren't any girls—apart from one, one night, but that was it, I swear. It was just easier to let it seem like I was Jack the Lad, out every night. No one was going to ask for details of what I was getting up to, they could imagine only too well."

"Right." I don't know why but the information made me feel weary. But I wasn't going to ask why he'd let me buy into the Jack the Lad persona, too. Perhaps the reason was just too mortifying to think about.

"This is not just a story for you to dig into. It's my life," said Nathan.

"I'm sorry. I didn't mean—" I hesitated. "Hasn't the time come to get help? Tell the police exactly what you're doing?"

It seemed to me that this was the only way forward, but even as I said it I was wondering how far we could trust the Portuguese police, and Rylands' warnings were ringing in my ears.

We went upstairs, peeling off into separate rooms at the top without even looking inside them first. It was nearly four o'clock when my head went down on the pillow to chase some sleep that wouldn't come, and quarter to five when I next looked at my watch. Not much longer after that, Nathan padded into my room, and saying nothing, curled up beside me. Animal warmth came off him, like a child. He slept; I still couldn't. At around six thirty, I got up and went downstairs noiselessly on the tiled steps.

There was a TV in the living area and I switched it on. Breaking news of Rylands' death was a ticker tape at the bottom of the screen (*"Expatriado britânico encontrado morto no hotel"*). A still photo of the resort was up on the screen. No doubt the TV cameras were on their way.

I wandered over to the kitchenette area. A sparkling clean kettle stood on the worktop but no sign of any coffee or tea. I filled it and set it to boil, then sipped at a mug of hot water, letting the steam soothe my dry eyes.

When I returned to the television screen, a reporter was speaking to the camera by the entrance to the resort. I had to concentrate hard. Even though I knew the subject matter I only got about half the words. A British man. Seventy years old. House in Vilamoura. A description of the hotel and its guest villas. Then I jolted forward, spilling scalding splashes of water over my bare knees. I wasn't sure I had understood correctly. The reporter was a doll with dyed red hair and glossy lips—it was hard to believe news was actually her forte—but I went over what I thought I had just heard, picking out the words that sounded familiar. Walde family. Controversy and tragedy. Connected to the Horta das Rochas hotel. The abduction of a child.

I put the mug on the low table in front of me, and stood up. I had to tell Nathan—then decided not to. Best to wait. Best to find out what more I could. Reports on rolling news changed all the time, for all kinds of reasons—what if this was the only time this was mentioned? I stood closer, increasing the volume. But that was it. Now the setting was being described. The camera panned to show police vehicles blocking the entrance to the resort. The picture cut to show an aerial shot: red cliffs at the edge of the sea, the discreet villas nestled like shy animals in the green pines, now scored through by the headlines moving across the bottom of the screen.

I wasn't sure that I had heard right, that my mind wasn't mixing and matching sounds to the track already playing in my head. Better to let Nathan sleep on while I waited to see whether the information would be repeated.

Curled up on the sofa, I flipped between local channels. The pictures from Horta das Rochas were coming round on a loop. I thought I heard Ian Rylands' name but I wasn't a hundred percent sure. There was no further mention of the Walde family or child abduction.

A knock at the door startled me. I ran my hands through my hair and got up to answer it, heart pounding. Which would it be, hotel staff or the police? It was a young woman, uniformed and holding a large tray covered in a white cloth.

"Breakfast, compliments of the manager," she said. She came in, set it on a table by the window, shook out the cloth to reveal coffee, rolls, and a plate of ham and cheese, nodded and was gone before I could think about finding some money for a tip.

The coffee didn't help my anxiety, and I had to force myself to chew some bread. It occurred to me that simply by mentioning Terry Jackson and his invitation to Nathan to meet him here we had effectively set wheels in motion. The police wouldn't leave it there. It was already done. If Jackson was involved in Rylands' murder, and it certainly looked that way, then Nathan's story was bound to come out, one way or another.

When Nathan finally mooched downstairs, the story was still being broadcast from the entrance gate, the reporters continuing to speak over stock pictures taken inside the grounds and main buildings.

He looked dazed.

"Story's broken," I said.

The room phone rang, and we both jumped.

"This is the manager's office," said a female voice, in English. "I am calling to tell you that the police will be coming to see you soon. Please do not leave the room."

The first thing I said to Nathan was "We have to tell them we knew Rylands. It will come out somehow that we've been seen with him. And then there'll be all sorts of repercussions."

I didn't have long if I was going to tell him about what I thought I'd heard about the Walde family but I decided against it. I wasn't sure enough. At this stage that was a complication we could probably do without.

We took turns to try to shower some life into ourselves and make the best of yesterday's limp clothes.

The police—in the form of Detective Aloisio Gambóias, face now as close-shaven as his head was bald, and a woman police officer called Inez Something— arrived on the doorstep at around eleven.

This time Nathan and I were interviewed together. Gambóias took the lead, while Inez, her aggressively dyed blond hair bobbing, wrote copious notes. The same questions as the previous night. What we both did from the time we arrived at the resort. We both told the same truth as before. I sensed a softening in tone. Though still wary, I took the chance as soon as I could.

"The television news," I said, looking over to the screen still playing with the sound turned down. "The victim has been named as a British man. Ian Rylands."

"They have named him?" Gambóias looked predatory.

"One of the channels said it earlier."

"They shouldn't have done that."

The ticker tape headlines still read "A British expatriate." Male expatriate. No name.

"The thing is, when we found . . . the victim, I thought he looked familiar but I wasn't sure. It was half-light by the lamp, his face was in an odd position, his mouth was open . . ." I didn't want to overdo it. "If it is Ian Rylands, then I should tell you that I have met him. In Faro."

A leap of faith in justice.

Gambóias was impassive. I maintained steady eye contact.

"When did you meet him?"

"A couple of weeks ago."

"How did you meet him?"

"I made contact through the Anglo-Algarve Association."

"Why?"

"Something that interested me. I'm a journalist. I was thinking about maybe writing a feature—"

"Feature?"

"A long article, perhaps for a magazine."

"You did not say this last night."

"Last night I was in shock. I saw a man's body. I wasn't thinking about a man I hardly knew."

"You met this Ian Rylands only once?"

I noted he wasn't confirming or denying the victim's identity. The truth, as near as possible to the whole truth. "Nathan and I took a boat trip to the Ilha Deserta a few days ago. By chance, Ian Rylands was on the ferry, too. We sat with him, and then he walked awhile with us on the island. He is—was?—an interesting man. He was generous with his knowledge."

"What did you talk about?"

"He was explaining the geography of the barrier islands, mostly, as we went through the salt marshes. About how two of the islands were fixed to preserve the port entrances, but that there had been consequences for the outer islands, with the strong sea drift moving the sand." That was all anyone could have overheard.

"And you?" he turned to Nathan, who was sitting uncharacteristically quietly. "You remember this?"

"Yeah . . . sure. He seemed a nice old bloke . . . man."

"But?"

"Bit boring, if I'm totally honest. I wasn't quite as interested as Jo in the geography lesson. I was quite pleased when he wandered off and left us to it."

"You didn't recognise him last night either?"

Nathan shook his head slowly. He did a good job of looking utterly baffled and slightly queasy at the implications. Which wasn't really so far from the truth anyway.

Gambóias rubbed his chin. The silence became oppressive but he was looking at the TV. Inez picked up the remote control from the coffee table in front of us and put the sound up. To the visible annoyance of both of them, the red-haired woman reporter was now broadcasting from inside the grounds. A row of holiday villas stretched behind her, though whether it included Villa Eleven, I couldn't have said. The detectives exchanged glances and Gambóias reached for his phone. He tapped out a text.

I held my breath, as if that would make it easier to hear what the TV reporter was saying. No doubt the glossy hair and lips had persuaded someone to open a door.

Then she said it, distinctively, as if she wanted to get the pronounciation correct. "Ian Rylands."

Gambóias stood up. He took some heavy paces away from us and started shouting into his phone. Nathan looked at the floor and I didn't dare catch Inez's gaze. I fixed on the television screen and offered the reporter my silent thanks. I was coming round to her. She was sharper than she looked.

I spent the afternoon on my own with Gambóias and Inez in a meeting room in the main hotel complex, a business venue kind of room that was designed to make anyone long to be outside in the lush garden beyond the tall windows. Now I had admitted to knowing Rylands, they were drilling down to test what I knew of him. It was more, I suspected, than they did. I was still nervous, but took heart from the fact that they had told us that we were witnesses, not suspects. It simply wasn't possible for us to have killed the man, and I had to draw strength from that. Coincidences happened. We were not suspects.

At one stage, Gambóias asked Inez whether she had heard anything from Faro, and her reply seemed to be that the ferry pilot had indeed noticed the three of us on his boat. That we had sat where I said we had sat. Above the engine noise, it wasn't possible to confirm what we discussed, but we walked up the jetty on the Ilha Deserta together, in a friendly manner.

When there were no more questions they hadn't asked three times already, I was free to go. They told me to wait for Nathan in the main lobby of the hotel. Nathan arrived there half an hour later. His jaw was tight but he said he was fine.

In the car before we set off back to Faro at last, I called Will Venning again. "Have you seen the reports of Ian Rylands' murder?" I asked, cutting to the chase.

"I'm not sure we're going to cover it, Jo. Couple of pars, max. Not for us."

His clipped tone took me aback. "I wasn't calling to file copy, though actually, it is a good story. Just tell me, in all his crazy theories . . . did Rylands ever say anything to you about the authorities having been complicit in child abductions?"

"Listen, Jo . . . let's go for a drink when you get back to Brussels, eh? It would be good to catch up."

"I won't be back for a while. Can't you tell me now?"

Now he sounded awkward. "Bit difficult. Even then, I'm not sure I can help."

Face to face, I would have been better able to judge, but I thought there was an element of embarrassment in his tone. "What are you not telling me, Will?"

A pause.

"Will?"

"You don't want to get involved in conspiracy theories, Jo. It just makes you look a fool."

"Is that what you're saying this is?"

"Believe me, Jo, it's not worth it."

"OK. Message received and understood," I said. "I'll buy you a beer at Les Brasseurs when I get back—and thanks."

I sat staring beyond the windscreen without seeing when the call ended. Before it, I'd been sceptical about Rylands' far-fetched theories. Now . . . perhaps it just wasn't wise to discuss them on the phone where anything might be overheard or even recorded. What was worse, was that Nathan and I had very few options as to what we did next.

"We have to find Eduardo Walde," I said.

"Why?"

"Well . . . we have precious little to go on that doesn't involve Terry Jackson—a man who is definitely in the frame as the killer of Ian Rylands, and whom I suggest it would be wise to avoid as far as possible. And I have a horrible feeling this is rather more relevant than we thought." I reached into my capacious bag and pulled out Esta Hartford's book. "You need to read this."

PART FOUR

Excerpt from *The Alliance* by Esta Hartford, first edition 1954

i

In Lisbon, fall faded into winter. Sea mists rose from the stately estuary and dropped gray furs over the shoulders of the statues of saints and horsemen. In the city's wide avenues yellow trams emerged like lamps from clouded valleys.

Alva navigated her way on foot by the smell of fish and the desolate flap of washed garments strung out overhead. During the day, when Michael was working—he had a corner of the AP office now, even if he wasn't fully on staff—Alva went out with her camera. Her ear was becoming accustomed to the strange sounds of the Portuguese language, with its words that looked intelligible on the page but turned impenetrably Slavic when spoken. Words like *praia* and *mare*, beach and sea. *Peixe*, fish. *Pão*, bread.

A marriage could survive anything so long as there was goodwill and both parties wanted it to survive. At least, that was what Alva told herself. Having counted her blessings, she should try harder to be a good wife while Michael pursued the stories of those unhappy refugees far worse off than they were. The Barton luck had held. They moved out of the Hotel Métropole when Michael met someone who knew someone else who had got on a boat and vacated a two-room apartment in a dingy house behind the Rua Augusta. It was small: one room furnished with a cheap table and a two-seater sofa, and a counter that functioned as a kitchen; the other room filled with a double bed that still left them feeling short-changed as they tried to sleep. But the rent was a third of the price of the hotel, and there was a shower room off the landing with pleasurably strong water pressure. A central location, too; a short stroll to the Café Eva where the foreign correspondents hung out.

Alva quickened her pace, ignoring the inevitable propositions she received as men passed. It was later than she'd thought. After hours pleasantly lost in the gauzy vapors of the river, composing street scenes of figures materializing, she needed to buy food. And to make sure Michael ate it before he headed out again, as he inevitably did, to rejoin his colleagues. His preferred diet of whisky and wine was doing neither of them any favors.

She gave him a dinner of omelette that presented as scrambled eggs, and he pulled on his jacket as soon as he had finished it.

"You going out again?"

There was a pause, in which several stages of the argument were processed but skipped.

"I'm not saying 'don't come,' just that there probably won't be much in it for you," said Michael.

Alva wondered when exactly it had started, this feeling of separation from him. Was it on the journey into Portugal, or had it been earlier? When was the last time they had set out together for an amusing evening on their own? "You go," she said.

"Why do you say it like that?"

She sighed, unwilling to say it again.

"Because you don't like the guys. I know. Well, honey, I have news for you: without these guys, we don't eat."

"It's mainly just him—Curnow."

Michael didn't seem to understand that she found Blake Curnow unnerving. The intense eyes magnified by thick-rimmed glasses, watching her with disinterested pity as he chain-smoked.

"He likes arguing. That's the kind of guy he is."

"It doesn't mean anything, then?"

"It might—or it might not."

Michael held out his hands in mock supplication. Neither of them wanted to open that argument again. There had been too many pointless spats lately.

"So have you decided, do you want to come to Estoril this time, or do you want to stay here?"

"You're going anyway, you mean?"

Of course that's what Michael meant. She was just making him spell it out. Had he always disregarded her wishes? Why couldn't it be like before? The questions were fast forming, like a overflowing river, whirling and eddying. How long had it been like this? Maybe longer than she allowed herself to admit.

"I'm asking my wife if she wants to come to Estoril with me. Is that unreasonable? You'd think I was being unreasonable, the way you look at me."

Another argument neither of them wanted to open. Needless to say, there had been no discussion about having a baby for some time. He went out again, promising he wouldn't be too late. She said goodbye knowing that he would be.

His footsteps receded down the tiled passage, quickened almost joyfully on the stone stairs, and then all was quiet. The cramped living room was dingy under a dim electric bulb. Michael's possessions were strewn about where he had dropped them. In the past she might have seen in them a wry reassurance that he had everything covered, that she (still feeling affectionate) would never change him. Now she took in the discarded tie on the back of a dining chair, one of a mismatched pair, and the inevitable crumpled newspapers, and felt only irritation.

The city, along with Michael, was changing by the day, in ways that were not due solely to increasing familiarity or the turn of the seasons. The streets and cafés looked different—sounded different. More and more foreigners were crowding in, bewildered and frightened, relieved to have made it this far but anxious to move on. It was almost impossible to find a hotel room. Women stood at bars that had previously been the preserve of men only. The polyglot newcomers spoke in low voices. Boredom and tension showed in the slump of their shoulders as they read the same old newspapers in the cafés. Strangers listened eagerly to conversations at neighboring tables, if only for the relief of hearing new thoughts.

Michael, after their initial uncertainties, had landed on his feet. There was a spring in his step as he realized that being in Lisbon was better than watching the war in Paris or Rome. He was optimistic about his prospects in a way that he hadn't been since they first arrived in Rome. Alva's perceptions were rather different. After a while she had grown unnerved by the unstoppable tides of refugees, and bored by the same old conversations, the same questions about whether visa applications had been approved, or tickets confirmed, or bank wires received. The situation became like the weather forecasts in the newspapers: only interesting if there was a specific reason for wanting reassurance. Meanwhile they were all stuck, even those who refused to admit it.

True, there were so many worse places they could have washed up. Only bread was rationed. The beaches were not mined. The Portuguese were friendly, and if rather venal, understandably so. They had not asked for this raggle-taggle invasion, and it was surprising how resiliently welcoming they were. Living costs were extremely reasonable, and the Salazar dictatorship could be explained or excused by the superficial well-being of the people. Above all, Lisbon was alluring, rising above the great river like the steps of a wedding cake, clean and rose-pink at sunset. The sun and the colors masked the poverty of its hidden areas. It was noisy and eager and charming. The bulls were never killed in its bullfights. There was dried cod in abundance to eat, and octopus, and sea bass and sardines. The citizens wept during the mournful *fado* songs, self-indulgently, in a way that allowed a luxurious dimension to tragedy, and named this state *saudade*, for which there was no easy translation; it meant a kind of nostalgia for the present moment, a strange feeling that was both a sad acceptance of destiny and yet celebratory.

The foreigners, the black marketeers, and the art and gem dealers scurried about their business. The British came off planes at Portella airfield in Lisbon wearing homburg hats and carrying umbrellas. Fishwives carried baskets on their heads; barefoot, despite a new law that demanded that all vendors wore shoes; quite often their rope shoes sat atop the sardines.

Would she go with him to Estoril this time? She hadn't decided. After that first trip up the coast, Michael had almost told her something important, she was sure of it. 'I'm not stupid! Please tell me what is going on!' she had shouted. But he hadn't.

Alva shut the door on the emptiness of the apartment and, disregarding Ronald Bagshaw's advice for respectable women, went out alone to the cinema on the Rua dos Sapateiros. There she tried to concentrate on an imported movie and then watched the news reels until she felt repulsed by the black-and-white images from across Europe and to the east: the tank formations and lines of men marching to triumphant music, arms extended in salutes to madness.

She didn't bother to switch on the electric light when she returned to the apartment. When Michael crept in at two in the morning, stinking of Scotch, she was still sitting, thinking, by the open window.

"Where have you been?" she asked.

"Just . . . you know . . ."

"Well, that's just it, Mike. I don't. I don't know what is going on here."

"There's nothing going on."

"Don't lie to me! I can't stand it when you lie to me." She stood and moved toward him, began to press her hands into his chest; he pushed her away. She heard the words come out of her mouth before she had even thought them, knew at the same time he did that she had lost. "It's not fair!"

He started yelling at her then, and she fled to the bedroom and locked the door with his fury reverberating in her ears.

"It's for your own protection," he said through the door.

"You talk of protection?" she said. "What have I got left to protect? What is there left of the person who has already had one life replaced by another, and then another and another? I don't want to stay here, Mike. I want to go home."

"You have to trust me," he said. "No, you *need* to trust me."

"Don't go out every night then. Stay here with me."

"I can't."

"Tell me then."

She unlocked the door. He didn't push it open immediately. When he did, she realized he wasn't as drunk as he was worried. He sat down on the bed and told her about the Canadian reporter.

Jim Kosek was a correspondent for the *Toronto Globe and Mail*, posted to Lisbon not long after the outbreak of war, Canada being in from the start, with its ties to Great Britain. "Last seen going into a *fado* club on the Rua do Capelão in Mouraria close to the castle. He'd told Frank Ellis that he was going to meet a contact, that he had a promise of information that could be a game-changer. He even asked Frank if he would come in and watch them from across the room. But Frank had heard it all before. The information was never as good as promised. And he couldn't abide the wailing, said *fado* took the enamel off his teeth, even if it was a national passion. So Frank said good night to him outside and came on back to the Café Eva."

"Who was the Canadian guy going to meet?" asked Alva.

"All he said to Frank was that he could be on to something big."

"And all newspapermen say that."

"We live in hope."

Alva said nothing.

"Jim Kosek never came out of that club. Blake Curnow and I went back there the next night, but they couldn't even find anyone who would admit to seeing Jim in there. No one. From the manager down. Not even the hatcheck girl—and we were offering a generous tip for her trouble."

"Did you find out what he was on to, who he was meeting there?"

"Turns out, according to one of the other Canadians, he was only supposed to be meeting a guy who works at the airport and keeps an eye on the movements of Axis flights. It's a regular thing that he hands the schedules to the Canadian Embassy."

"And what has any of that to do with Frank?"

"He gets the schedules from Jim and gives them to our guys—at our embassy. All information is useful, even if it does seem small beer at times."

"But Frank is a journalist. Journalists break stories in newspapers, they don't gather information and not use it."

"Sure they do. But Frank's a special case. He wasn't always a reporter. Maybe he's not much of one now. He's a government employee. In the Foreign Service. Everyone's using what they can, see?"

"I see." Alva narrowed her eyes, knowing from the flip tone of her husband's voice that there was more.

"Don't look at me like that. It's enough that the Germans and the Portuguese are watching my every move. I have to contend with you, too?"

"You don't do stuff like that."

"Sure I do. We all do. Jim did it too obviously, in the wrong place, that's the only difference."

Alva leaned against the windowsill, trying to look nonchalant.

"Should you be telling me this?"

"Don't be a fool, Alva."

No, she wasn't. The person in front of her looked just like Michael, raking back his hair with a hand as was his habit when he wanted to appear more relaxed than he felt, but she wasn't sure she knew him at all. Had she ever? And if not, did that make her a fool after all?

"This is only because of the war, though, isn't it? You didn't do stuff like this in Rome?"

"Not all that much."

Silence.

"Why didn't you say?"

In his hesitation was a world of disappointment and frustration.

"I didn't know," said Alva. "In Paris—?"

"It started getting serious. France was preparing for all-out war. Troops were massing. Information was the most important currency there was. No less important for us, even if Uncle Sam wasn't directly involved."

"But that's not quite what you told me three months ago, is it, Mike? When we got out of France, I asked why we didn't just go home to New York, when we could have, and you said you had to make this work and get back into a senior position with the AP. If you didn't make it in Lisbon, you'd be finished as a reporter. That we'd left Rome, left Paris; you couldn't leave again, this was your last chance to hack it. Remember?" She was amazed to hear her own voice sounding so reasonable. She didn't feel reasonable. "To hack it *as a reporter*, Mike, no mention of any of this."

He shrugged, like a boy. "I guess I felt that you would have worried. First rule: keep quiet, the fewer people who know, the better. It's not as if I'm not work-ing for the wire service. I *do* have to prove myself here.

I'm a foreign correspondent, for God's sake. Trouble is what we do."

"So . . ." Alva wanted to make sure she had this right. "We are staying because you have to prove yourself, not because you want to. And not at all because you're excited to be part of some spy games?"

"I wouldn't put it exactly like that, but—why not? It's exciting. It feels like I'm doing my part. It felt like I just couldn't get a break, and then I could."

"But it's dangerous, as Jim Kosek found out!"

"Yeah, well. Any way you want to play it, the war is on here despite what anyone says about neutrality. It's fierce and it's all the more deadly because it's running in secret."

"We're Americans—it's nothing to do with us."

She read the pity in his face, that he thought her so stupid he had no idea where to begin to explain.

"But we will be part of it, Alva. Sooner or later, just like last time."

So now she knew. A good number of the journalists were working as spies. Mostly, they were stringers for the British newspapers, but the Canadians and the Americans were involved, too. In this city teetering on the Atlantic, at the edge of Europe, little was quite what it seemed. It wasn't only the hundreds of staff at every embassy, far more than could ever have been put to work as second secretaries and visa assistants; plenty of others were engaged in observation, incitement, and economic warfare.

Perhaps that was why she sometimes felt as if she was being watched even as she walked innocently down the street. The photography could also be interpreted in an entirely new light, especially her forays down to the quay where the flying boats docked and the studies of the shipping traffic.

As if he read her mind, Michael said, "I've been asked to tell you to stop wandering around with that camera. It draws attention and we don't want that."

"We?"

"Enough, Alva. You need to stop."

She had attributed the feeling of being observed to the codes of behavior expected of women in Portugal. Beyond Ronald's warnings, she had made her own observations. A Portuguese man did not take out a married woman alone. A woman would not usually go to a party without her husband. However, the husband would enjoy evenings out without his wife, leaving her at home as a matter of course. (Though this created the ideal opportunity for her to slip away to an assignation under cover of darkness.) Now she wondered who exactly had been watching her, and why.

If Michael hadn't told her this, she would probably have stayed in Lisbon and did as she pleased while he went to Estoril that weekend. But now she felt uneasy.

ii

I t occurred to Alva that the rich in the palace hotels of Estoril, bathing and dressing and drinking cocktails in the warm summer evenings, were doing very much what they would have been doing in other circumstances. The Bartons were, too, as they walked to the neon-lit casino from their backstreet pension.

When they arrived Michael spent five minutes talking to a man, then giving a note to a cigarette girl. It might have meant something, or not. When she asked, he said, "Word is that the Duke and Duchess of Windsor are in town."

"The English king?"

"Who gave up his throne for the American divorcee who looks like a wooden peg doll."

Alva questioned this with a tilt of the head.

"The girl said we missed them," said Michael. "They've gone again." He usually looked uncomfortable in a tuxedo, but tonight the formal attire seemed to accentuate the keenness in his expression, the liveliness of his eyes, when he was onto a story. Intelligence agents from all sides were mingling among the international clientele, and he could now confide in his wife. "The Nazi intelligence chief is Albert von Karsthof. He's a regular at the casino. Just another superior thug. Women, gambling, drinking, as pleasant a war as can be found. Some of the German women, especially the beautiful ones, will pose as neutral Swiss nationals in order to seduce Allied service personnel. Some of them pass messages by placing chips on certain numbers on the roulette table. It might be a code number, or just as easily a room number."

"It must be a very expensive method," said Alva. "Black twenty-nine," she reminded him. "What did it mean?"

"That wasn't anything—I was just muddying the waters to see what happened."

"You shouldn't have involved me."

"No, I shouldn't have."

Alva watched a young woman with a voluptuous figure and a lascivious face painted with bright lipstick, too bright. Two men in suits came up on either side of her, nodded without smiling, and led her away. What was that about? An old woman, with a lined, leathered face leaned in to talk to a man but looked over his shoulder as she did so, with one large unblinking eye, like a reptile biding its time. Alva thought she saw Ronald Bagshaw, but she might have been mistaken.

Under the dazzle of the chandeliers, she sensed foreign dust, shaken from clothes and baggage, remnants of thousands of lost places thickening the air. The glazed expressions of the men and women standing around the tables never varied whether they won or lost, their fortunes resting elsewhere, in visas and scraps of documents on the cusp of expiration.

Clack, clack, clacketty: the ball rolled in the roulette wheel.

"Yet the players pray to the Holy Ghost," said Alva.

"What?"

"I overheard someone. *Espírito Santo.*"

Michael laughed. "They talk about him all the time here. Doesn't mean what you think."

"No?" There didn't seem that much room for doubt.

"Espírito Santo? Many of them also call him Ricardo, and they rely on him all right. Ricardo Espírito Santo is a banker. A very powerful man, the most influential in Portugal. He has the ear of Salazar, and the money of many more countries. He is . . . facilitating the access of all these people to their funds . . . Let's say, he's having a very good war so far. Ah, there are the others."

He led her to the table where Blake and Frank were sitting with Mary and Anita.

It was Anita, Frank Ellis' girl with the squashy mouth, who told her. Perhaps Frank's close call with Jim Kosek at the *fado* club had got to her, or perhaps she just liked to drink; either way she had knocked back too many martinis and her nose had bled, in a spontaneous rush that dropped wet roses in her yellow silk lap. Alva dutifully went with her to the ladies' powder room, though she got no gratitude.

"I don't know how you can stand it," murmured Anita, pinching her nose, head tilted back against the mirror by the washbasin.

"Here, take this," said Alva. She handed Anita her own handkerchief dampened with cold water. "Do you want me to try to do something about your skirt before it dries?"

"I don't care. If you want to. I said, I don't know how you stand for it."

Alva stared at her. "Stand what?"

"You husband running around town with another woman."

Alva had to steady herself against the vanity unit.

"That . . . Otávia. Her name's Otávia. I'm not married to Frank, but I'd give him hell if he did such a thing."

Alva shivered. In the mirror she glimpsed her reflection, a pinched white face. "Pardon me?"

"Why do you . . . oh, hell, I'm going to throw up . . ."

Still Alva stayed to help her, turning on the faucet and letting the water run, hoping the attendant would not come in at that moment. Yet another grubby, stinking secret to come out in a place where trust was lost, even among those who knew each other well. She left Anita, moaning, head lolling and almost asleep in a chair in the washroom, put a tip in the attendant's saucer and emerged, wound tight, into the foyer.

Alva walked shakily back into the gaming room. Michael was playing blackjack. "Hey, honey, where have you been?" he said, hardly taking his eyes from the cards being dealt, brazening out his broken promise not to risk losing any of their scarce resources.

"I want to talk to you. Now."

"Cut me some slack," said Michael. "I'm going swell here." It was always the same; when Curnow was around, the old Mike upped and left to be replaced by this selfish facsimile. Too many whiskies tossed back too quickly in her absence gave his face a wet sheen.

"Why doesn't it look that way, then?" She didn't dare contemplate how much he was down.

"I want to speak with you," she repeated.

"We can't talk now, can we?"

"I could start, if I had to. You might want to think about what might be overheard, though. You will find me outside. As soon as you like, Mike."

He ignored her, far more interested in his cards on the baize in front of him.

She turned away, heart pounding. Beyond the portico of the main entrance, the garden was pleasantly cool. A scent of jasmine hung under the palms. She breathed in the sweet air, deeply and slowly, trying to rid herself of the sick perfume of vomit and betrayal. The realization hit like one of those winter raindrops that bursts icy sleet on your face, letting you know that snow is on the way. She had always trusted Michael: trusted in their marriage and in his loyalty. Sure, he could be unthinking and bound up in his job; what man was perfect? But he had never been a liar. But as the weeks had passed in Portugal, she had realized that was no longer true. He lied even when he pretended he was telling her the truth at last.

Otávia. Her name's Otávia. Was he about to leave her? Leave her alone in a foreign country with no means of getting home?

A shadow shifted and came toward her. Instinctively she turned her back, sure that it was Michael. She had no idea how she was going to begin until she said it.

"Otávia," she said. "I want to know what the hell you are playing at, and I want it straight." She swung round to see how he took it.

It wasn't Michael.

"Cigarette?" The accent was German.

"No, thank you."

"I saw you leave," said the stranger.

She tensed as a struck match lit the outline of cheekbones and bulky shoulders.

"I'm waiting for someone," she said tersely.

"He is not coming. The cards are more important."

She shook her head. "Please leave me alone."

"I'm not a German, if that is what worries you. I am a Swiss businessman."

Alva made a move back toward the brightly lit entrance. "Good night."

Feeling even more uncomfortable, she waited in the foyer for a while, then returned to the card table where she stood with arms crossed as Michael lost another two rounds. Finally he acknowledged her. He rose unsteadily from his chair, and she smelled the alcohol on his breath as he stumbled against her. He put his arm over her shoulders, a gesture that could have looked romantic, but she knew to be insolent, and they made an attempt at dignity as they made their exit. Palm fronds rustled in the wind as they covered the path down to the road in silence.

"Who's the girl, Mike?"

He had never been able to lie when he was drunk. She braced herself for what she was going to hear.

"What girl?"

Drunk or not, he wasn't going to make this easy.

"The one you go out on the town with. Otávia."

"Who told you about Otávia?"

"It doesn't matter. The point is, I know."

"She's a contact. I asked her to do something for us, and she did. It's not what it looks like."

"What does it look like, Mike?"

"Convincing. I admit it's supposed to be convincing, that she and I . . . you know. But that's all. It's an act. This woman has a friend who is seeing a German officer, they talk, and she passes on any useful information to me. That's all."

"And which side is she really on?"

"She's Portuguese—how would we know? Everyone's tried to recruit the Portuguese locals working around the foreigners. They bend with the wind, according to which side is looking strongest and how much cash is on the table."

"But why? Why get yourself mixed up in this?"

"One of the Nazi intelligence officers here—in Lisbon, rather—has been trying to insin . . . insinuate himself with our side, with the guys at the embassy. We wanted to feed him a barium meal."

She had no idea what he was talking about. "Is he sick?"

"A 'barium meal' is information. Or it pretends to be information . . . but it's untrue, an invention. You feed it in, you wait to see where it comes out."

"And did it . . . come out?"

"We're still waiting. But it will."

"And there's a story in this, or—?" Or is it an excuse for a few cheap thrills, she thought.

Michael threw his shoulders back, playing the big man. "It hardly matters, my dear. Sometimes we don't report the facts at all. Facts are not required. I'm catching up with that custom here, too. The British are way ahead of us on that one. The foreign editions of their papers are almost all misinformation for enemy consumption in the international newspapers on the stands in Lisbon."

Alva stared at the man she thought she knew so well. "Don't patronize me, Mike. I thought we promised we would be honest with each other? Wasn't that what we always said?"

"You think that's important now?"

As a matter of fact, she did.

Michael was sleeping off his hangover the next morning as Alva slipped out of the hotel room. At the beach she found a quiet spot and concentrated on the feel of the wind and the sea on her skin as she watched the waves break.

"Are you feeling better today?"

She turned around. The man was blond and tanned, muscular. He spoke in a formal manner, with a clipped accent that fell toward a British pronunciation.

"I don't know what you mean," she said.

"I saw you at the casino, last night. Then you ran outside."

"You must be mistaking me for someone else. I am perfectly fine, thank you."

"You were upset. A German claiming to be a Swiss businessman approached you in the grounds. He is not a nice man, and you did the right thing—you didn't believe him."

Alva stared but said nothing.

"You don't have your camera today, Mrs. Barton. Yet it would be a beautiful day for photography, don't you think?"

She started, alert suddenly to all the different languages she could hear spoken, including German. It was no longer shocking to find German agents and Nazi officers in the same places as their Allied equivalents. At Lisbon airport, British and U.S. commercial flights landed alongside planes painted in Nazi livery. On the beaches between Estoril and Cascais, the enemies sunbathed together and strolled the same walkways.

"Who are you?"

"My name is Klaus Mayer."

"And you're actually Swiss, are you?"

He gave a short humorless laugh. "Most Germans here claim to be. Especially when they want something. But no, I am not Swiss."

"Why do they lie?"

"Because everyone does. Just like your husband."

She turned her back.

"I did not want to scare you," he said. "That was not my intention."

"What exactly do you want from me, Herr Mayer?"

"I want to help you. The truth is, we could help each other."

"I doubt that."

"You want to know who Otávia is, don't you?"

"How do you—?"

"I heard you asking."

The sounds of the beach, the crashing of the waves and the shrieks of bathers, the hubbub of conversation and cries from the vendors of broiled sardines, seemed to recede.

"I know exactly who you are," said the German. "And your friends, too. Frank Ellis is fooling no one as a reporter. He is too obviously ineffective. Blake Curnow is an excellent journalist and information officer, but it comes too easily to him—he's not as clever as he thinks, he is too casual. But he enjoys the duplicity—whereas your husband is troubled by it, especially as he has realized too late that he is losing you because of this duplicity."

"Please stop this. I am not interested in discussing my husband like this with someone who makes such ridiculous assumptions."

He waited for her to say more. He was obdurate, a solid wall of a man.

"So you know everything, do you—about what he is doing?" It was supposed to be sarcasm, but it came out almost as a plea for information.

"I would say, and I am sorry to be the bearer of bad news, that his worst sins are toward you." A long pause. "Another woman might slap my face and leave now."

She met his eyes, expecting to have to counter the challenge she found there. Instead, there was only kindness in his expression.

Be careful, she told herself, this is how men like this win. "I wouldn't betray him that easily."

"Betrayal is the ultimate form of self-expression. We live in brutal times."

Again, he made it hard for her to make a response. She didn't disagree.

"When you return to the city, if you want my help, you can find me at the Hotel Métropole," he said. "Whatever you think you know, I am sincere."

Was that a casual insult, given the common knowledge that the place was effectively a German SS stronghold?

"When hell freezes over," she muttered.

He didn't seem to notice. Perhaps he was used to it. She wouldn't ask about the woman.

She walked away, down to the sea.

"He knows exactly who we all are. And he's been watching me, too," Alva told Michael. He looked rested, far better than he deserved.

"Klaus Mayer, you said?" Michael had not reacted at all in the way she had expected. He was delighted, couldn't have been happier. He had pulled on yesterday's crumpled shirt and left the three top buttons open. She wanted to slap him.

"He's an Abwehr officer, Alva. The German intelligence agency."

"I know what it is."

"I think you should string him along. It's a game of cat and mouse, of course, but this could be just the break I need. If you were the one to throw the stone and run away . . ."

"Whatever do you mean?"

Michael was pacing with excitement. "Agree to meet him. Hear him out and see what he wants. Hope to gain more than he does. Feed him some barium, see where it gets dumped."

He didn't appear to have any sense of how frightened she had been. He was too enraptured by the intrigue.

"What do you think he wants?"

"That's what we have to find out."

"But Mike—"

All the way along he had kept her at arm's length from what he was doing, and now he was asking her to become actively involved. She didn't know how to react: was she to be pleased that he thought her useful now, or appalled that he was so blithe about the poten-

tial risks she would be taking? But maybe he wasn't the
only one who was changing. On balance she was more
angry with Michael than upset. He refused to say anything more about Otávia. Alva could barely look him
in the eye, perhaps not wanting to see more shame or
deception there, as she listened to his schemes.

iii

In Lisbon at that time, rumors flew ever more wildly: Germany planned to occupy Portugal within seven days; the partisan Spanish were planning their own invasion; someone had seen Nazi stormtroopers in the Avenida de la Liberdade. Innocents were arrested by the Portuguese police.

At dawn one morning a great black crow blundered through the open window and into the bedroom of the cramped apartment. The curtains swelled then released the intruder. The room shrank as blue-black wings flapped and became violent. The thought of the poisonous-looking beak that could slice into skin, or an eye, made Alva pull the sheet around her and over her head. "It won't go out on its own, Mike. Get it out!"

Reluctantly, he sat up and reached for the towel he had dropped over the washstand. She peeked out as he held up the towel and advanced on the bird as it knocked into her toiletries on the top of the chest of drawers and scattered them on the floor.

"Flying vermin," he said. "I don't want to touch it."

He shook the towel ineffectually. Alva squirmed.

Michael lunged for the curtain and threw the window as wide as it would go. She heard him moving heavily, and the crow's wings beating, and then the window was slammed shut.

A minor incident, except that when Alva closed her eyes again, all she could see was the crow. Cruelty embedded in the ordinary that seemed to warn of evil. She had never been superstitious, but this shook her. The room had closed around a threat that she had not the courage to confront.

Alva passed the Hotel Métropole and carried on along the Praça Dom Pedro IV. According to Michael, a diamond dealer had been found shot in his room there the previous day. ("Probably doing rather too well out of the general desperation.") Even people who owned valuable gems were worried that they were running out of money, that they had not been able to bring enough, that their hastily arranged affairs were left open to theft and fraud.

She found the bookstore and went inside. She had been browsing awhile in the English language section, when she felt a tap on the shoulder.

"Mrs. Barton, always a pleasure to meet again," said Ronald Bagshaw. "Have you managed to find anything to your liking despite the lamentable quality of the selection on offer?"

"Hello, Ronald. I'm not sure—perhaps you could help me. I was hoping to find a book about the history and customs of this country. But there seem to be very few guidebooks to Portugal in any language. The best I can find is a travel guide to Spain with a few pages tacked on the end about Portugal."

"Fairly typical, I think you'll find. Portugal has never been on any main itinerary. A closed-in country—what is known as a 'hidden gem'—and all the better for it, in my opinion."

"Is there any publication you can recommend?"

"You'll have to wait for it. An intrepid Englishwoman of my acquaintance has recently set off to the south, intending to write a travelogue."

There was a hint of mockery in the way he said it that made her rise to the challenge.

"Interesting. How is she traveling?"

"She drives her own little car. Rather badly, as it happens, but she hasn't come a cropper yet. There is a great deal less traffic on the roads down south so I expect all will be well and she'll reach Faro without mishap."

"Faro?"

"A town on the Algarve coast, rather charming."

"Will she be safe traveling on her own?"

"I don't see why not. The coastline is beautiful and rather wild, but the people are delighted to receive visitors. Faro is no backwater. She is chasing after pink flamingos."

"I beg your pardon?"

"All kinds of birds can be found on the sea marshes, and she has heard that pink flamingos can be spotted. So she is off, in the grand tradition of English eccentricity."

Alva replaced the unsatisfactory book. "That makes this sound very dull indeed."

"A cup of coffee?" he offered.

"Thank you, but no, not this time. I am expected somewhere." It was a lie, but she noted the flicker of interest it raised.

Bagshaw stepped back and raised his hat. "Another time, then. Goodbye, Alva."

"Goodbye. And thank you for your advice."

"You're welcome. Though I hardly gave any."

She smiled sweetly. "And I am most grateful for that."

"Ronald set me thinking."

Michael looked up.

"I want to make the most of being here," she said. "I should take advantage of all there is to see in this closed-off country."

"Well sure . . ."

Positive and optimistic, that's what he wanted to see, so she would give it to him. "I'm going to take a trip south."

She watched him gauge the advantages. It would be easier for both of them if she wasn't there waiting and wondering what he was doing. He would be able to do what the hell he liked at night, too. "I guess if Bagshaw is taking you—"

She shook her head. "There's an Englishwoman who has set off to write a travelogue on her own. That's what I want to do. Have an adventure. Take pictures of a part of the country hardly any foreigners know beyond Lisbon and Porto—do it while this edge of Europe still survives outside the war. I want to go on my own."

That was when the argument started. "You will not."

"I want to do this trip from a woman's perspective. It can be done. Imagine the copy! That could make something special for a magazine, couldn't it! We are in the business of taking risks. That's what you said."

"But this is different!"

"No, it is not, Mike."

After the standoff, which lasted the best part of a week, a compromise was reached. A couple they knew, John and Betty Andrews—he was U.S. Embassy staff and due a week off in February—happened to tell Michael they were taking a vacation. Their plan was to drive to the Algarve in the south of the country and spend their time exploring the wild coast full of caves and spectacular rock formations. Even in winter, there were days of warm sunshine.

"Why don't you go with them?" he asked Alva.

"I couldn't possibly! They won't want me tagging along."

"Sure, they wouldn't mind. He owes me a favor."

She wasn't going to ask what that was. Better to take what was offered, then play it her own way when she was beyond his control. So she agreed. Michael was letting her go, and she supposed she should appreciate it. It did occur to her that he might have had reasons of his own; he had never given an entirely satisfactory explanation for Otávia.

Betty and John Andrews were as straightforward as their names. She was petite and brunette, a neat-waisted creature with kind but dull conversation. He was pale, clearly exhausted, but maintained a bluff can-do attitude worthy of his Wisconsin origins. Alva assumed Michael had met him through his new trade and that part of the deal was that John Andrews kept a close watch on her. He was Diplomatic Corps accredited, which meant he was the closest thing to travel insurance she was likely to be offered.

Alva sat in the back of their sedan, a hat pulled down deep over her forehead. She was excited, yes, but there was another feeling that she had not yet identified: it might have been freedom, or relief. Either way, she put it down to the open road, the rush of wind as they bowled along. It would do Michael and her good to spend a little time apart. Watching John and Betty, their mild bickering over which route to take, the flatness of their voices, the air of resignation, she wondered whether the same might not have been true for them, too, and that perhaps, far from feeling that a third party was an intrusion, they had welcomed the ballast of a passenger.

The only way across the Tagus was by steamer ferry crossing, the first bridge being over eighty kilometers from the mouth of the estuary. Alva observed the city, the buildings encrusting the hills, its high castles and venerable churches diminishing across the wide river. The water simmered with shipping crafts, from primitive canoes and sailing yachts to warships of the United States Navy in close proximity to those of the Japanese. The sky was azure, far from the gray of a New York February. It was an electric morning, or that may have been her nerves crackling. What awaited her? The country could swallow her up, and there would be barely a trace left that she had ever been there. At that moment, she didn't care. She was free, heading south into the blue.

As soon as they reached the landing stage at Cacilhas, the landscape felt different. In Lisbon and Estoril they had gotten used to the sight of large American cars, the latest models, on the roads. Either the Portuguese drove those, or they had no car. Away from the main routes, all was quiet, except for the occasional rusting French vehicle, but the side roads were rough going, and the shaking and pitching soon led them to abandon the scenic backwoods, dense with umbrella pines.

The town of Setúbal, on the Rio Sado, was set on a fine harbor. They stopped at a junction. Child beggars ran up to them and John dropped a few pennies. He had heard there was disapproval if foreigners ignored beggars.

Leaving the town, the road continued through shady pine woods for some time until the soil became poorer and the countryside uncultivated. Soon the view was of endless scrublands, rolling out toward ragged, barren hills and desolation. It felt remote already. Villages were shuttered, and the dusty locals stared glumly as they passed through. Mules drew carts piled with cabbages and potatoes.

They stopped to picnic in an olive grove. Betty spread a tablecloth on spiky ground and unwrapped packages of bread and cheese and cold roast chicken and oranges. They had a few glasses of wine to toast their vacation and John spoke of how he had been posted to Lisbon as a consular officer two years previously, which meant he was midway through his tour. He had learned plenty about the country and was keen to know more.

They were now in the Alentejo region, John explained. It was a vast province, almost desertlike in parts, and said to have no shade except during the hours of darkness. Away from the main towns, there was a sense that the villages were self-contained worlds with their own ways and histories. Betty seemed content to listen to him talking, without adding any of her own thoughts.

They pushed on quickly, eager to make the coast before nightfall. They planned to stay the night at Quarteira, where the Andrewses had been assured the winter climate was warm and settled. The sea was heated by the beneficent Gulf Stream, and the hotel justifiably called Bella Vista. By the afternoon the road was bordered with vineyards and fruit orchards. Both men and women tilled the fields barefoot, stooped over the earth in bright costumes of scarlet and orange, yellow and blue. Carts pulled by oxen lumbered past loaded with dried maize. When they stopped for a break to stretch their legs, Alva bought some preserved figs from a peasant woman in a straw sombrero who only reluctantly accepted payment, and insisted that they also take six plump oranges. John resumed his commentary about the explorers of the Middle Ages, the desolate points from which they set sail, and Alva allowed her eyes to close.

It was dark when they arrived at Quarteira, and none of its anticipated beauties were visible. They were shown to spotlessly clean plain rooms and a spicy fish dish was provided for their supper.

At breakfast the next morning, in a room filled with light and a view of the sea, Alva said to the Andrewses,

"I'll leave you to enjoy your day here," she said. "I am going to take a train trip."

John straightened his glasses. "I'm not sure, Alva. I promised Michael I would be responsible for you."

"And I appreciate that, John. Very much. But my mind is quite made up."

"But you can't!" said Betty. "However can you, on your own?"

"The same as anyone else. I walk to the rail station and I take a train. I want to see the flamingos."

"Flamingos?" repeated Betty.

"Did Michael not tell you? I have wanted to see the wild flamingos on the salt marshes ever since I arrived in Portugal."

"We'll have to come with you, won't we, John?"

"No," said Alva. "You really don't. I'll tell you all about it when I get back, now if you don't mind, I must hurry to catch the coast train."

She left them to their breakfast, suppressing the urge to pop a piece of toast into Betty's open mouth.

iv

At Faro, she walked out of the station and was immediately surrounded by children offering to carry her luggage.

Alva gave them a few coins but toted her own bags along the main street to the harbor. A year ago, she thought, she would have been nervously aware of being alone in a strange place, but through all that had happened since leaving Rome, she had toughened up. She was conscious that she was testing herself, and she thought that might have something to do with Michael, but chose not to dwell on that. *Whatever I find here, I can handle myself,* she repeated to the beat of her steps. If an Englishwoman who is a terrible driver can travel alone, so can I.

The walkway along the seawall was softened by short palm trees shaped like upended shaving brushes. A row of shops sold fishing equipment, ropes, and parts for boat repairs. Beyond were grander buildings, and ancient walls. A raised bandstand stood proud on a patch of grass ringed by public benches. Alva caught a few curious glances in return as she went by, but she did not elicit much interest.

She hesitated, wondering which was the best way to find somewhere to stay, and then turned left up a street marked in painted tiles as Rua Dr. Francisco Gomes. Not far along the street was the kind of grand cosmopolitan café she was familiar with from Paris and now Lisbon. She would be able to order a decent lunch there.

The Hotel Sol was a good find: cheap, clean, and within a five-minute walk of the café down a quiet side street. A yellow plaster façade was held together by a long wrought-iron balcony, and there must have been few other visitors as she was shown a room with long windows that opened out onto it. It was as well she had her rudimentary grasp of Portuguese, as the owner and his wife were a couple in late middle age who spoke no English. Senhor Cardoso dressed his hair with scented pomade; his formal suit was worn to a shine, but his courteous manner showed quiet pride in their establishment. Senhora Cardoso had a plump, unlined face and wore a hand-knitted sweater with a cardigan over her shoulders; whenever she sat down, at the desk, or in the corner room off the entrance foyer, she would take out her knitting needles and continue with whatever new garment she was creating. She even knitted standing up, pulling wool from a ball in her pocket.

It was a nice, family-run hotel, a thoughtful recommendation for a woman on her own. Alva unpacked her sparse belongings, and rested awhile before going out again.

Through the ornate gatehouse, the Arco da Vila, she discovered a wide piazza around a cathedral, caught in a web of narrow cobbled streets. Orange trees around the edge of the square held glowing lamps of fruit. She went into the cathedral, sat for a while, then lit a candle.

The sun was burning a hole in the horizon when she arrived back at the harbor where a crowd had gathered. Two couples danced to an accordion and a drum on the quayside, the men in black and the women dressed in regional costume. She watched as the dancers worked through patterns of intricate movements. Out on the water, bright bunting garlanded the masts of the fishing boats at anchor.

She raised her camera and focused carefully, hoping the light would hold for a while.

A marching file of boys in blue uniforms arrived from the direction of the customs house, and then a wide banner hove into view followed by children dressed as angels with wings made of paper. She hardly had time to wonder what was taking place when a procession formed behind a statue carried on a table by eight men in robes. As the statue wobbled past—the effigy of a saint, Alva deduced—the men and women in the crowd bowed and crossed themselves. It was followed by more children in costume, brocaded cloaks and embroidered dresses, and more trestles bearing images of Christ and the Blessed Virgin. All moved in silence toward the fishing boats.

The sky seemed to explode. Sirens blared from trawlers outside the harbor walls, horns were sounded, and fireworks screamed into the sunset leaving trails of sparks and burst into flower with loud bangs. A pall of smoke unfurled across the water bringing the scent of gunpowder, the convulsions above illuminating the figures and the procession. A priest brought up the rear, walking slowly under a canopy held by six bearers, giving the Sacrament. Again the crowd dropped at the knee as he faced the boats and blessed them.

Alva watched for a while longer as the procession broke up and children were claimed by their families, small groups formed and dispersed, and the crowd thinned.

Night fell. Faro was darker than Lisbon. In place of the capital's gaudy light shows, carbine lamps moved across the harbor as night fishermen prepared their boats and set off. Soon the lamps were so few that it was possible to see them being extinguished, one by one, like rooms in a distant house.

The crucifix above the bed and the crude light on the ceiling confused her. For a few seconds, after a deep sleep without waking, she thought she was still in the cramped apartment in Lisbon, and reached out for Michael. The bed was narrow and she was the only occupant.

Sun gilded the windowsill but the iron of the bedstead was freezing cold. Alva stretched and then padded over to the washstand. If she was going to give the right impression in a town like this she had to be proper in all respects. A plain skirt and coat. Blouse with collar. Sensible shoes. She brushed her hair and applied some lipstick, took a handkerchief, clean and pressed into a triangle, from her suitcase and placed it in her purse. A dab of verbena cologne on the inside of her wrists, and she was presentable.

When she went out she had the sensation that the cobbled pavement was wobbling under her feet. The morning was not as bright today. The harbor water reflected clouds. You got so used to being saturated by light in this country that overcast skies seemed weighty and depressing. She supposed she ought to let Michael know she was okay. The Café Eva had a telephone booth; it was highly probable that the Aliança would, too. When she next went in, she would ask about making a call. For now, she walked in the other direction, through the Old Town with its defensive walls and out to the embankment where the sea lapped.

For so long, Michael had been her anchor. Now she was adrift—she had cut herself adrift. The events of the past few years had put so many relationships under strain. It was just the war, people said. But they were different, surely? There must have been a moment when it started. Was it in the bus down from Paris, when he could not bear the children's crying? If one of those babies had been his own, he would have felt differently. Or so she had thought; she might have been wrong. Was it in Ronald Bagshaw's car, when Michael felt small and beholden instead of plain lucky? Was it in the visceral light and poisoned normality of Lisbon where no one knew what to believe, or the hedonistic unreality of Estoril?

The same Atlantic water joined the two of them but the more Alva stood contemplating it, the more the way back seemed un-navigable. Waves churned and chopped the surface into scribbles made by the wind, like messages she wished she could read.

After one of her old school friends had separated from her husband, Alva saw the man once with a new woman friend in a line for the movies at Loew's 175th Street Theater. How strange that had been. All those evenings spent bowling and eating meatball dinners on cheap furniture; the life they had all joked would get better, and maybe it did, just not in ways any of them had imagined. For a moment she wanted to have it all back. If she thought hard enough she could still be that person again, with the red dress she saved up for from Bloomingdale's and the pure happiness that Mike was there by her side.

She shivered. Any glimmers of sunshine had been snuffed out. It was a swirling winter morning, damp with mist. A fresh wind pushed at her, a powerful hand on her back. She could always go back to Lisbon. But not while she was trying to process this new person, unrecognizable person, she was becoming—wanting to become, despite her fears. Surely she still carried the kernel of the girl who once went to Catholic church and helped in the store after school, who polished the eggplants till they gleamed and arranged the green peppers and smiled at customers in a way that left them in no doubt that the family was genuinely pleased they had decided to shop for their groceries at Marinelli's? She felt wetness on her cheeks. It was impossible to tell whether it was caused by the sharp breeze, or by unhappiness.

She found shelter in the lee of ancient stones salted white by winter winds and gave in to her feelings. She was furious with Michael. Not sad, not wistful, not hollowed out by loss, but howling inside with anger. She wanted to scream. If he was here right now she would beat her fists against his chest, railing in her outrage against his insulting calm.

At the growl of a small airplane above, she tensed instinctively. She had thought that she would be less fearful further away from the savagery of the war. But she had brought the ugly reminders with her.

The streets of the Old Town felt almost uninhabited. A man in a dusty black suit stared as she passed. She put her head down, resigned to being more cautious than in the capital city where the influx of strangers had relaxed the rules and the curiosity value of foreign women. For the first time she wondered if she had made a mistake in coming to this unfamiliar place where the streets made waves under your feet and the wind pushed the breath out of you.

She came out of the old gate on the Rua da Misericórdia and crossed the road into the public garden. At first she told herself she was just imagining things. But as she exited the garden and turned north into a street of shops and other businesses she was not so sure. It was the sensor they had all developed in Lisbon where the Portuguese secret police watched the Americans and the British watched the Germans, and observed the Germans returning the favor. When eyes were on you, it felt as real as a hand reaching out to tap halfway between the back of the neck and the top of the right arm.

She stopped as if to look in a shop window. At a certain angle, she could see back up the street behind her. The man was wearing a black homberg hat, pulled down low. The coat that swung from broad shoulders and self-confident bearing gave the lie to any assumption he was a local fisherman or peasant. He also stopped and feigned interest in some display. She set off, and repeated the maneuver; he did the same. Instantaneously, she quickened her pace.

Think this through, she reminded herself, forcing herself to slow down. The police would know by now that she was an American visitor; she had filled in a form with her passport number when she checked into the hotel. She was doing nothing wrong. She felt the tension in her shoulders ease, all the while stiffening her resolve not to let down her guard. Another glance back—it bothered her that there was something she needed to recall, but couldn't—and she walked on toward a public place. She would go to a café, have a cup of coffee, act normally. She tried not to hurry toward the Café Aliança. However mad she was at him, she ought to make that telephone call to Michael. Close to lunchtime, he would most likely be at the Café Eva. She had a quick coffee for form's sake and to ask how to place a long-distance national call. Ten minutes later, a waiter came over to her table, and showed her to the booth.

She spoke clearly, in a phrase she knew, into the heavy Bakelite receiver. "Is Senhor Michael Barton with you, please?"

In her mind she could see the Lisbon café: the shiny brown wood of the bar, the globe lights glowing around the walls, the cigarette smoke, the clatter of bottle and glasses, cups and saucers. Michael would be at the usual table, leaning in to hear what was being said, that frown of concentration when he was memorizing what he was being told, not wanting to spoil an illusory confidence by reaching into his breast pocket for that small notebook.

"He's not here."

"Do you have any idea where I might find him?"

There was a silence, during which her panic drew sweat to her hairline.

"No, senhora."

And that was that. That was the moment. Would it have been different if Michael had come to the telephone, a little the worse for rough brandy, a little belligerent maybe, at being called to account, but none the less there? She would never know. Somewhere in the sea mists of Lisbon he had disappeared into a world where she did not exist. She put down the receiver knowing only that she had lost him. Perhaps it had happened much earlier, but it had only just registered. She shut the door of the booth. Her feet on the polished checkerboard floor seemed unreal, as if they did not belong to her, that she was not actually in this place but could break out of it like waking from a bad dream.

She sensed rather than saw the figure planted in black shoes that blocked her path. She stopped and looked up. The man in the homberg and the well-cut coat was waiting for her. He removed the hat and nodded a curt greeting.

It was Klaus Mayer.

She tried to sidestep him, but he grabbed hold of her arm. "Please don't make a fuss, Mrs. Barton. That would be most regrettable," he said. "Just accept that I am here and that I would be most grateful to have a conversation with you."

None of the waiters or even any of the customers took any notice of her as she tried to signal that she was leaving under duress. The café was busy and lunch was being served with bustling efficiency. Mayer steered her out of the Café Aliança, north into a maze of streets.

As they crossed a triangular road intersection, she thought she saw another man make eye contact with the German. His strength propelled her along, not roughly but carrying the message that she would do what he asked, whether she wanted to or not. She stumbled and he pulled her upright as easily as if she were a child.

"Are you all right?" It didn't sound like a threat.

"I'm fine. Where are you taking me?"

He didn't answer but kept her moving.

"What do you want with me?"

This was serious. She had started by wanting to show Michael that she was not just his little woman, sitting alone while he engaged in his war games, that she was as strong as he was, if not more so. But it was a foolish game.

Mayer led her up some steps. It was only when they entered the building that she realized it was a church. He propelled her into a side chapel watched over by a statue of the Virgin Mary, her hand stretched out as if in benefaction. They sat on simple wooden chairs.

Silence.

She stared ahead, tensed for whatever would fall. Instinctively, she began a mute prayer.

"Thank you," he said at last.

Still she would not acknowledge him.

Mayer shifted in his seat. It was too small for such a big man. "It was brave of you to come. I did not think you would."

"You gave me no choice."

"I mean, that you came to Faro."

She twisted round at that. "I came to the Algarve to get away from Lisbon—and Estoril, for that matter. I am here of my own choosing. Whatever you seem to think, you are mistaken if you believe this has anything whatsoever to do with you, Herr Mayer."

"That is very interesting."

Alva stood up. "I have no idea why that should be. I am going to leave now, if you have no reason to detain me." She made for the carved wooden screen that separated the chapel from the nave.

He didn't get up or try to stop her. "You really don't know?" he asked.

"Know what?"

"I have been trying to get the British in Lisbon to trust me. For entirely understandable reasons, they do not. So I tried the Canadians, but their man was a liability. So the only way to prove myself was through the amateurs. You understand what I am saying?"

"Really, I do not, Herr Mayer. Why should you be so surprised that the British don't trust a German in Lisbon?"

"A German may have Nazi connections, and not be a Nazi."

"Too many games are being played."

"Indeed there are, Mrs. Barton."

"But I don't want to play, Herr Mayer." She turned to go.

"Yet you have been outplayed—and you don't even know it."

Again, she was pinned down on the point of leaving. "I beg your pardon?"

"Why do you think you came to Faro?"

"I came because it sounded like an interesting place where a woman might travel alone."

"And who told you about it?"

"A friend in Lisbon."

He shook his head, giving a disconcerting smile. "Interesting choice of words. A friend."

"I wish you would stop speaking in riddles."

"That's how the British refer to their intelligence officers: as 'friends.' It wouldn't have been a man called Bagshaw who cleverly suggested Faro as a destination, would it?"

She said nothing.

"And how did you travel to the Algarve? Would it have been made easy for you in some way to make the journey south?"

"My husband didn't want me to make the trip," she said more firmly than she felt.

"And yet he arranged for some more acquaintances to facilitate it. You did not come on the train because too many of the conductors on the trains out of Lisbon are in the pay of the Abwehr and can be relied upon to report the movements of any foreign nationals. Tell me, Mrs. Barton, do they have diplomatic connections, the people you came with? Can you be absolutely sure that your husband did not want you to make this trip?"

She was speechless.

"He has been very clever. If a little . . ."

Sneaky, that was the word, thought Alva. Michael knew her so well. He had used her determination and turned it against her. Oh, he had been clever, all right.

"It sounds as if you know a great deal, Herr Mayer. Unfortunately for you, this is where it ends, because I do not. I have nothing to do with whatever my husband might be involved in, and I know nothing that could be remotely of consequence to you. So there we have it. A wasted journey on both our parts."

"Far from it, Mrs. Barton. Lies and expectations. They work best when they conform. I am an officer of the German Abwehr, that is true. I work very diligently and I believe I am respected by my fellow officers in Lisbon and Berlin. But then, not all of us are Nazis." He paused, and then repeated it slowly and softly, this time holding her stare. "Not all of us are Nazis."

"Why are you telling me?"

"Because I have to prove it. I have to prove it to you. A person who really doesn't have any preconceptions or any interest in the games being played."

Alva clenched her hands together. "What if I'm a fool, though? Someone who believes everything she is told?"

"No one, least of all your husband, thinks you are a fool, Mrs. Barton."

They sat in silence for a while. Faint remnants of incense floated on the cool air.

"The British are suspicious," Mayer went on. "They are right to be. They have been bitten already by infiltrators claiming to be agents working against the Third Reich. The Americans and Canadians take the same view, though they at least threw me to their amateurs and collectors of rumor in the press corps. Which is how I had the pleasure to be acquainted with your husband."

"Don't tell me anymore. I want no part in this."

He rose, and bowed his head. "Any evening, you can find me at the Café Aliança at six o'clock. If you change your mind, if you decide that I am to be trusted—or if you need help, of any kind . . ."

The heels of her sensible shoes echoed from the aisle as she took her leave.

Somehow she found her way out of the maze of streets. Then she kept on walking until she could hear the applause of the sea pounding the pebbly shore.

A stork waded into the shallows, picking up its spindly legs delicately as a prudish maiden aunt, and with the same distaste for show. With a dipping motion of its head it pulled up some delicacy from the flooded grass. There were no flamingos.

Out where the breakers formed, there was land; in the near distance, fields of white snow at the edge of the ocean. Nothing was what it should be. Michael had used her. The lucky ones no more. For miles, she walked through wind and tears toward the snowfields. She reached the intense white brilliance as it started to glow in a beam of sunlight from the strange mauve-black sky. A solitary man straightened his back from raking the white flakes.

They were the only two people in sight. She raised her arm in feeble greeting and he returned the gesture.

"What is it?" she asked, pointing to the snow crystals.

The man did not seem to understand.

She pointed again, and looked puzzled.

He bent over and put a pinch in his palm, then offered it, pointing at his tongue. When she hesitated he put a flake in his mouth. She did the same. It was salt. He was a salt-panner. Salt of the earth—that was one of her father's favorite phrases, the greatest compliment he could give.

The man fluttered his hands, trying another mime. He pointed at her, and the town along the coast. Then he blew out a great gust of air and looked to the scudding clouds.

She nodded. She could feel the wind getting stronger. Go back, go back, he motioned, but with a toothless grin. It was good advice, and she took it.

The waves were getting higher with each crash against the seawall, and the wind was pulling the sea and the sky out of shape by the time she made it.

She was exhausted when she reached the hotel, nauseous with anger at Michael and Ronald Bagshaw. Mostly Michael.

So who am I, she wondered, now that I am no longer Michael Barton's unquestioning wife? I am the descendant of fishermen and ropemakers and sailors and carpenters, and women who were lace-tatters and cheesemakers and vegetable-growers and mothers in the old country; the daughter of merchants in the New World.

Nonna Alva, her grandmother, saved the money she made by raising goats and making cheese, and kept it in a china box decorated with flowers. Then her grandfather found it and drank it all away when the carpentry business did badly. After a while, Nonna Alva stopped making cheese. That was the only choice women had then, to refuse to go on. It was different for Alva; she was an American. But she couldn't get back home. We cannot go back to what we once were, she thought, none of us can.

V

The next day the wind was violent. Clouds clustered like purple grapes.

In the breakfast room at the hotel, a stout businessman from Porto spoke to her in English and showed her the morning newspaper.

"Lisbon has declared a state of emergency. There is great destruction in the north where the storm broke."

"My husband is in Lisbon. I must telephone," she said automatically.

"The telephone here is not working. Maybe the wires are down."

"I didn't know there was one here."

"There's one in the office, but as I say, it's not working. I have tried."

"Will it get bad here, too?"

"The storm is coming. At low tide this morning the sea was already risen to the top of the seawall when it would normally have been forty meters out."

"I should go now, then."

"Be careful. Would you like me to come with you?"

"I'll be fine—thank you."

When Alva ventured out she was pushed back immediately into a doorway. The force of the storm was horizontal, sweeping rain and seawater through roiling streets.

Church bells were tolling, hardly audible above the howling gale.

A man flapped his hands at her. "Go back!" he shouted. "It's dangerous close to the sea."

But it was not far to the Aliança. She had reached the top of the Rua Dr. Francisco Gomes when a flowerpot fell from a balcony and smashed in front of her on the road. The wind was funnelling due north from the sea.

"Perigoso! Perigoso!" yelled a man who was helping to haul a fishing boat up into the streets for safety. Dangerous. "Go back!" he motioned.

Through driving rain she saw more boats upended and secured behind the houses in the lanes that ran east to west. Under her feet, the pavement was flooding. Waves were reaching further up into the town, smearing wet sand over cobbles and doorsteps. The sea was pushing at the cracks under doors and windows.

Alva stopped to catch her breath, gulping in saltwater as the wind almost knocked her off her feet. She turned back, and felt as if she was picked up and thrown in the direction she had come.

That night there was no electricity supply. The Cardosos fetched smoky tallow candles and lit a fire in the main room. They all huddled around it, Senhora Cardoso gripping the beads of her rosary and her lips moving in silent incantation.

It wasn't calm enough to venture out until lunchtime the next day. The businessman from Porto—his name was Senhor Ferraz—donned an English tweed coat and insisted on accompanying her to the Aliança. Alva did not dissuade him on the basis that she might be grateful for his translation skills. The newspaper headlines carried words she could understand, though, alongside photographs of wrecked boats and fallen trees: *"Um Ciclone sobre Lisboa," "Grandes Desastres,""Tragicos."*

At least a hundred and thirty people had died in the storm. There were always more casualties during a daytime storm. More people were outside when debris was falling from roofs and chimneys, and trees were uprooted, and loose objects were bowled along flat ground by ferocious winds. There was still no telephone connection to the north; too many telegraph lines were down, the manager informed her. How urgent was it that she place her call?

"My husband is in Lisbon."

He did all he could, which was to bring her a coffee on the house.

The café was filled with survivors and heroes. The checkerboard floor was wet with mud marched in on men's boots. The local news was bad, too. Whole fishing fleets along the coast had been sunk or badly damaged; men had died trying to rescue their boats. A four-thousand-ton Greek freighter, the *Mimosa,* had flashed an SOS at the height of the storm but was now believed lost. Its cargo of cork was starting to wash up on shore.

Ferraz passed on what he heard. Some of the beaches had assumed completely different shapes. Praia de Faro on Ancão peninsula and Culatra village were flooded. The houses there were destroyed—the waves had helped themselves to the foundations—and precious contents had floated out to sea. About a hundred people on the Ihla de Farol had waited, standing on the beach, for rescue to come: twelve hours without food and water in the wind and the rain. Boats were reduced to driftwood. The tuna fishing camp on Barreta Island at Cape Santa

Maria was decimated by the waves. A new inlet had been carved at Ancão, gouged by the elements; Cabanas Island had completely disappeared. Other channels had vanished. But there was nearly a riot when one man said loudly that everyone knew the islands were not sensible places to live. Even inland, olive and fruit trees had been felled and stripped of their branches. A quarter of the cropping trees had been lost in Moncarapacho, Pechão, Fuzeta, and Tavira.

Alva stared beyond the window into the mist. Three men emerged from the whiteout. Two looked like fishermen, bringing the brackish scent of the sea in with them on damp, stained clothes as they came inside and brushed past her. They struck up an urgent conversation with a man in the far corner, and they all looked toward the revolving door.

The next man in was Klaus Mayer.

Alva pulled herself back behind the crowd and watched as the German pushed his way to the bar. He was as bedraggled as any of the men who had been battling the sea. The barman nodded and poured him a brandy. No money changed hands. Something in the manner of both men told her that they were well acquainted.

Alva stayed where she was, tracking Mayer across the room to the table in the corner. He sat without waiting to be invited, then reached inside his coat and extracted a package the size of a book, which he placed on the table in front of the original occupant. The later arrivals seemed to gather closer to Mayer as the wrapping was pulled away. An arm patted Mayer's shoulder. A toast was raised. The conversation continued in a closer huddle.

Was he to be believed when he said he had offered his services to the British and Canadians and been turned down? What exactly was he doing here? He was clearly known by these men, was obviously involved in some local activity. But there was no one with whom she could discuss any of it.

"Excuse me, Senhora."

The waiter startled her. "Yes?"

"The man over there. He ask you to go to his table."

Klaus Mayer raised a hand in half-greeting.

"Please to follow."

The other men were introduced as two fishermen, and a man who ran the trades in the local market. She didn't catch the names.

"Is this a social event, Herr Mayer?"

"It is not. It is a lucky chance for me that you happen to be here. I want you to see what I have brought these good fellows." He was serious.

The other men seemed to await her reaction as Mayer flipped up the brown paper wrapping on the item she had seen him pass over, briefly held it open, tapped it, then covered it again. It was not a book. The material was a hard dull yellow. It looked like gold, a bar of gold.

She looked at him quizzically, waiting for him to confirm it. He did not. "I assume you know about the trade in gold for wolfram, Mrs. Barton?"

"I'm afraid I don't even know what wolfram is."

One of the men, who clearly understood English, gave a snort of derision, and uttered what sounded like a curse or two in Portuguese, as if he could not understand why Mayer had brought this woman over into their private cabal. Alva felt increasingly discomfited as Mayer placated him.

Then he spoke to her in a bright tone that she suspected was intended to be insulting. "Wolfram is another name for the chemical element tungsten. It is used in weapons manufacture. Portugal happens to have some of the most extensive deposits and mines in the world. There is a great deal of competition for this product between the Allies and the Axis powers. In order to secure it, the German gold arrives in diplomatic bags, on planes, in trucks arriving through Spain, and by sea. Paper currency is not much trusted anymore, after so much that the Third Reich was sending proved to be counterfeit."

She tried to spot Ferraz, hoping he would linger in the café. She would feel more confident if he would.

"Please try to concentrate, Mrs. Barton," Mayer said more pleasantly than the words were intended. He seemed nervous, and she wondered what justification he had given the men for speaking to her in front of them.

"Last night these men and I tried and failed to rescue the crew of a trawler boat bringing gold from Germany via Spain. But this gold was not brought in to buy Portuguese wolfram. The Third Reich also needs food and other commodities to keep its expanding territories supplied. There is a powerful black market in operation. Southern Portugal is one of the best suppliers. This"—he indicated the gold—"is for almonds and fish and oranges to sell in Paris and Berlin at the kind of inflated prices that will line the pockets of the middlemen for life. German, French, Italian businessmen are making a killing on these goods—and some of the worst profiteers are officers of the Gestapo.

"Every month a Nazi officer meets this trawler to oversee the secure transfer of the gold and its conversion into fruit and fish from the Algarve. This time, I came. I intended to take a sample of the gold and give it to the British along with the names of several high-ranking Nazis in Paris who were ripe for blackmail over their racketeering. But now you are here, and the storm did its worst, my plans have changed. I don't have to take the gold to prove anything."

"I don't understand."

"I have sent a message to Berlin to say that regrettably the vessel went down in the storm, that the crew and the gold were lost. Though as you can see, the gold is not lost. The gold will stay here, with these men. A scheme will be implemented with the local bank to dispense the funds through the Café Aliança stock exchange, to be distributed where local need is greatest."

"And what do you want me for?"

"You are a witness to the fact."

"How do you know you can trust me?" asked Alva.

"May we speak alone?"

"If you must."

She spotted Ferraz trying to read a newspaper while being jostled by the swelling crowd. So long as he was here she felt safe.

"There might be a table free in the back."

When she did not refuse, he led her to a more quiet room beyond the bar. They had to push through a throng of customers around the telephone booth. Alva wondered whether the lines had been repaired and she ought to try again to speak to Michael.

"Here," said Mayer.

A waiter pulled out a chair for her and she was face-to-face with the German across a small table.

"Do I scare you, Mrs. Barton? You must not be scared, I give you my word I mean you no harm. All you have to do is to listen to what I have to say."

"Go on, then."

Mayer spoke rapidly to the waiter and then gave her his full attention. "In normal circumstances, we tend to be able to make judgments based on the evidence we can see before us, and our own experience. Here, at this time, life is not normal. Many aspects are misleading, deliberately so. It is hard to know what the truth is, and what to do with it if we find it, but I am not what you think. I am an intelligence officer in the German Abwehr, that may be true, but I am no Nazi. I subscribe to no absolutes, no belief system that demands acceptance of a complete set of ideas, only what seems honest and fair in its own circumstances. Some have thought me left-wing as I am able to argue convincingly for some of Marx's theories. Others conclude that I must naturally be a fascist. Neither is the case. For me, there can be no rigid doctrine. If I have hatred for anything, I hate ideology and those who follow one blind to the human cost. That way lies madness—and inhumanity."

His manner was courteously formal, the voice measured and low. His hands remained steady, lightly clasped on the table. "I know. It is hard for you to know what to believe."

There were no outside references, no Mike to act as a sounding board. She nodded for him to continue.

"If you say nothing, it is astonishing how often people will assume your views are their own."

As she allowed herself to look at him properly for the first time she saw that Klaus Mayer had blue eyes and sandy blond hair. He was an older version (what was he, in his early thirties?) of one of those jocks at high school she had never dared speak to but had admired from a distance, or through lowered lashes as they strutted between classes and the football field or track. His shoulders were broad. His skin was not good, or it hadn't been when he was younger and the marks of the struggle remained. But the chin was firm and the cheekbones high.

He continued gravely. "I studied English at the University of Heidelberg and as part of my studies I spent a year at Oxford. When I returned to Germany in 1934 for my final year, Nazism had begun to spread through the institutions. Several of my professors had been dismissed. One, who had been a mentor to me, had been deported for the crime of having Jewish antecedents. It was profoundly shocking. The university seemed to have embraced Nazism without question. The new authorities were vandals, anti-intellectuals. I was no longer one of them."

"And yet you *are* one of them." She couldn't help herself. It had to be said. "You work for German intelligence."

Silence.

"No one was surprised when I was approached by the Gestapo at the start of the war. My command of the English language was exemplary. I was chosen to play a vital role: as an interpreter of Allied communications. I was sent to Lisbon."

"As a spy. Yet another spy in Lisbon."

"A good one."

Alva was grateful that the waiter chose that second to place a carafe of wine and two glasses, a basket of bread and some cheese on the table. She was still not sure how many layers of subtlety she was supposed to understand.

"Berlin is keeping the Lisbon escape hatch open for the people of Europe. They could close it at any time, but the reason the borders remain open is that there is some gain for the Third Reich. The Abwehr is very active. Its officers are like fishermen waiting with nets to pull out any of the arrivals who might be of interest: desperate people, who need money and will do almost anything to get it; adventurers with dangerous pasts and useful skills; businessmen, deal-makers who understand that their future prosperity depends on how quickly normal economic activity resumes in Europe when the war has ended; they have no allegiance to countries, or sides, only to their own success.

"All these can be turned to the Führer's service against the enemy. I have seen it happening. I know who they are. And all I have been able to do so far is send misleading information back to Berlin. Half-rumor, half-reality. The very obviousness of my position gives me a certain . . . freedom. My instructions were to watch the British and the Americans, to speak to you if possible, to find out what those on the periphery of the war effort were doing, the armies of so-called diplomats and newspaper reporters. So, among others, I watched your husband and his fellow writers."

"They know."

"Of course. After a while I approached them. Blake Curnow is a very thirsty man. That was a long night with a man I don't like or trust."

Alva fidgeted with a piece of bread, but didn't eat it. "You are taking a big risk telling me this, Herr Mayer."

"Perhaps. But I have already told it to the British in Lisbon. The problem is that they don't believe me. Or they are too cautious to believe me. They suspect a trap, and I cannot blame them for that. I went to the Canadians next, but got the same response. But they did decide to tip off one of their roving amateurs, a journalist."

"Jim Kosek?"

Alva drank some wine, hoping to calm her nerves. Her heart was pumping fast.

"The Gestapo took him. It was a harsh punishment for mere incompetence and the suspicion that he had Polish connections. And I am left in a very difficult position. Sooner rather than later I will be exposed. Somehow I have to get protection from the British and their allies. I have to use someone who is a maverick player. So I let Ronald Bagshaw find out that a consignment of gold is coming into Faro to buy black market supplies for the Third Reich. Meanwhile I volunteer to meet it and oversee the payment while I am scouting for more Nazi informers in the south. Now I need a witness to what I will do next. It is arranged, most delicately . . ."

"But you can't have known I would come to Faro," said Alva, reasonably enough. "Why didn't Bagshaw just come himself?"

Mayer shook his head. "Too dangerous. He is known, and one never knows who is watching."

"And if I hadn't come?"

"I would have had to find some other way."

"But . . . how do I know this is not a setup?"

"I will have to persuade you that it is not."

Alva shifted in her seat. An argument had broken out among the men waiting around the telephone booth. It was impossible to tell whether it was because lines had been restored or because calls still could not be made.

"Tell me," she said. "The crew of the boat that brought the gold. Were they Germans?"

"Germans and Spanish."

"Did you try to save them?"

"We did. I swear we did, Palhares and his men and I. I know what you are thinking, but we had the gold. It had been handed over. We were in Palhares' ketch, alongside their boat of a similar size. We could never have got close enough to the trawler that night, so they sent two men in a launch from Tavira. They had pulled away when a series of huge waves crashed down on all of us. The water overwhelmed the launch, but we were lucky. Palhares is a fisherman. He knows these seas well. With him as skipper we seemed to rise up the steep waves and remain upright. But the two men in the launch—they were swept away. We couldn't even see where they were. We shone lights on the water, we circled as best we could, but they had gone. There was nothing we could do but try to save ourselves. What kind of man do you think I am?"

"I don't know," she said in a whisper. "I don't know anything anymore."

Not even myself, she thought. They were all telling stories. The reporters told stories. The refugees arrived telling versions of their lives that seemed fantastical. The spies spun their tales. The Portuguese pretended to be on whichever side paid more or seemed to have the advantage. Husbands and wives became experienced practitioners of deception.

How did Mayer know that she had thrown away so many casual assumptions, that she was now a stranger to herself? That girl going to the newspaper office in New York, nervously sipping a coffee she didn't really want because she was thrilled to be sitting on a red leather seat in a diner with the loose-limbed reporter who used to run up the stairs smiling in that way that made her stomach jitter; later, the newlywed whirling around Rome in a daze of excitement and happiness:

that person no longer seemed to be her. Klaus Mayer was looking at her all the time she was thinking this, waiting. After a while, his gaze softened. She realized with some embarrassment that she had been staring into his eyes, never breaking the connection between them.

"I think you believe me."

She gave nothing away.

"I have several agents and informants here in Faro. Some give me information to pass on; the most trusted send back their own reports to Berlin. The Abwehr in Lisbon is delighted with my progress and the information these carefully cultivated agents provide. It is most useful when they corroborate each other's facts, and they almost always do, as I made them all up. They don't exist. I invent all their stories for the abasement of the Third Reich."

"You keep calling it the Third Reich. You don't call it Germany," said Alva.

"It is not Germany. The Germany I once knew has gone."

Like the Michael Barton she once knew had gone.

Mayer reached into a pocket, extracting a crumpled piece of paper. It looked like a typewritten letter with brown handwriting between the lines. He spoke fast, as if he thought she might get up and leave.

"This came into the Abwehr station in Lisbon a few days ago from a Serbian posing as Portuguese who exports raw materials to Britain and reports back to us. He's a terrible rogue, but one finds oneself liking him. All he wants is money. I give him a list of questions about what is being supplied to the British and what else they want and why, and he finds a way of answering them.

"I found out quite by chance that his methods involved popping round to the British MI6 station a few streets away and handing over the sheet for them to fill in. All completely misleadingly, of course, but with enough seeds of truth and verisimilitude to be most convincing. I know exactly what he's been doing. He is working for the British while pretending to work for the Germans. And now I am pretending to believe him. The ink used between the lines in the letter is made from a Pyramidon tablet, usually taken for a headache, dissolved in pure white gin. You fill a fountain pen with it, just like ink. Then more alcohol is applied to the paper at its destination to reveal the invisible writing. I want you to take this back to Lisbon, go straight to the American Embassy and ask for Hayward, the chief intelligence officer. Tell him what I have told you and hand over the paper. He will inform his British counterpart. That's all I ask."

What he was telling her, with such urgency, was either desperate or calculated.

"What would happen if it became known that you were . . . helping the other side . . . ?"

"I would be executed by the Abwehr."

She had a rush of light-headedness, which must have been the wine on an empty stomach. Neither of them had eaten any of the food on the table between them.

vi

"Allow me to introduce Senhor Calixto Tagaio, who is the manager of the Faro cooperative bank. Senhor, I present Mrs. Alva Barton of New York and Lisbon who is here as an independent witness to the proceedings," said Mayer.

A small man with horn-rimmed glasses and slicked-back hair was sitting in front of him removing various items from a briefcase. Several substantial ledgers were open on a table and three strongboxes.

They shook hands.

"What would you like me to do?" Alva asked.

"Please be seated at the back of the room so you can see everyone in it. Make notes if you wish. Have you brought your camera?"

She nodded.

"Good. You may take any pictures you choose, though we will not pose officially. I will not dictate any terms. You shall be the judge of what you see."

Alva looked down at the coral-and-white-checkerboard floor as she walked across it, feeling like a chess piece being dropped into position for a risky move. The café was filling up, mainly with men. The atmosphere was serious. The fisherman Palhares was there, dressed in a patched Sunday suit. She thought she recognized another of the men who had been with Mayer the previous day. Many wore gaily-patterned blankets draped over their shoulders. Others were dressed in sheepskin pants.

The Café Aliança was often used as the venue for an unofficial local exchange, she had learned, where goods and money and even services could change hands with no interference, or taxes, from outside authorities; salt and fish, carob and dried fruit might be bartered for seasoned wood or boat repairs.

The room went quiet as the fisherman addressed the gathering. He introduced Mayer and said a few words in the direction of the two other men who had been on Palhares' boat. There were gasps as gold bars were unwrapped from what looked like pieces of tarpaulin and handed over to the bank manager, who exchanged them for paper bills. Then, one by one, men were called to the table, holding black hats tight to the stomach in both hands. They were fishermen, salt-panners, farmers, chandlers, boat builders, and fruit growers who came first, in a hierarchy of need. They spoke, the committee listened, a record was made, and money changed hands. Then came the poor and the dispossessed who had lost the roofs from their houses, and those who were facing doctors' bills for injuries.

It was evening by the time the money from the strongboxes had been dispersed and replaced by the gold. At the end, a woman dressed all in black except for a red shawl came in and sang. All shades of emotion seemed to be contained within the sound of her song: comfort, longing, nostalgia, regret, sadness, and hope for the future.

Palhares the fisherman spoke a little English. He invited them to eat in his home, which was a great honor, Mayer explained. "You cannot refuse. It would be an insult."

They walked the few lanes to Palhares' house, where his wife cooked white fish with preserved pimento and potato. It was good. Much wine was consumed in a seemingly endless round of toasts.

Mayer offered to show her back to her hotel.

"That was quite something, what you did today," said Alva. It sounded trite, but she meant it. "Will they be OK, those people, now?"

"For most of them, the money will help. But others . . . it's not so easy. The fishermen who live out on the islands, for instance. The salt-panners. The clam-diggers. The shape of the land has been changed, the beaches where they worked have disappeared. Some of them have lost everything."

They walked on, contemplating that.

"Good night, Herr Mayer," she said, outside the Hotel Sol.

"Klaus," he said. "From now on, I am Klaus—to you."

"Alva, then—to you."

"How are you getting back to Lisbon?"

"I am supposed to be traveling back with the couple I drove down with, but I won't. I'm too mad at them."

"So, how then? By train?"

"I guess."

"You don't have to take the train all the way. I have to go back, too. You can come with me in my car, and I will set you down at a station not too far from Lisbon. We might even have a little sunshine along the way, what do you think?"

"I think that sunshine has been in rather short supply of late."

He held out a hand. She could hardly breathe as she moved forward to take it. The flesh of his palm was rough.

"Burned by ropes in the storm," he said, apologizing.

It was such a fragile understanding it was possible it did not exist at all. Klaus Mayer claimed to be on the side of the angels, and the men of Faro believed him. Sitting beside him, in the passenger seat of his powerful gunmetal gray car, Alva felt strangely safe. She was riding a sleek, purring tiger as they headed west along the coast under a china blue sky.

There was a brittle edge to the air that was all that remained of the storm. Alva looked out to sea, then back at his profile as if she couldn't quite believe who she was trusting behind the wheel. He met her glance and smiled. She noted the laughter creases around his blue eyes and thought that yet again, she would have to reevaluate what she had learned and experienced in the past year.

"All good?" he asked.

"Yes."

The light, the color, the sounds: today everything was like a movie flickering to life. She could hear words on the wind and see what was written on the water. Life was not always what it seemed on the surface.

By noon heat had returned to the sun. They stopped at a deserted beach where rocks tumbled into the water to breathe in the air. If this was winter, what would it be like in summer? The ocean glittered like the lights of a fiesta. The sea breeze that ruffled the hem of her skirt felt intimate, sensual. Klaus produced a pomegranate and opened it with a Swiss army knife to expose the ruby seeds; the juice from these jewels ran down her chin. He stopped a drip with his finger and laughed.

They hardly spoke except to agree that they wanted more: more of the sea and the sky and the sun.

At sunset they approached a small inn. It was closed until spring, but the man who answered their knock on the door offered a small boy on a bicycle to show them the way to a house where they could be put up for the night. It was hard to find, said the man, but he was sure it would please them. The boy pedaled off at a great pace and they followed, bumping on ruts in a rapidly deteriorating road, as he led them into a pine forest that grew thicker and more fragrant as they burrowed further into its heart away from the sea. The twilight thickened.

Then progress was blocked by a monumental gate hung from stone pillars. But the boy jumped off his bicycle, unlatched the gate, and pushed the fancy iron grilles open to allow the car to pass. He then waved them through, surprised and uncertain whether to accept when Klaus put a large coin in his hand.

The route led through the forest for a mile or so before they arrived at a wide courtyard in the center of which was a splashing fountain topped by a stone mermaid. Lamps were lit in the gathering darkness, as if the inhabitants of the house were expecting visitors, although there had seemed no possible way for them to have been warned of any impending arrival.

The house was enormous: grand and elegant with an aristocratic air. Lit windows cast pools of light at their feet. The fortresslike front door opened and two servants hastened out to greet them and help with their baggage.

Alva smoothed down her skirt and hoped her travel-crumpled clothes would pass muster as she and Klaus were shown into a lofty hall that bristled with antlers. Perhaps it was an old hunting lodge. A fine array of heraldic shields fixed high on the walls intimated a glorious history.

In a large and sumptuous sitting room they were greeted warmly by an elderly lady and an even older man in a black robe. She spoke in French, the international language of diplomacy. "I am Maria de Saldanha Oliveira, and this is Monseignor de Matos, my private chaplain."

Alva thought fast, working out what best to say. It would be unwise, for all kinds of reasons, to introduce themselves as a German officer and an American woman. As an American, she was a neutral. She took the woman's offered hand and said firmly in English, "Alva and Michael Barton. From the United States of America."

"How delightful." She spoke in a cultured, international accent. "I hope you will stay with us tonight, Mr. and Mrs. Barton. I can offer you a room and dinner."

A fire crackled under a marble mantel and gave an agreeable glow to the room, which might otherwise have seemed overwhelming.

"It is we who are charmed and delighted," said Klaus.

I didn't know you could do an American accent," said Alva, trying not to giggle.

"I am a master of disguise."

"What a place!" She whirled around, giddy from her daring as much as the motion. The room they had been given was lined in silk brocade of rich forest green. The curtains of the four-poster bed were intricately embroidered with tendrils and flowers. "It's like stepping back into bygone times—a magical place in the middle of the forest!"

"Not real life," said Klaus.

They looked at each other and knew they both had the same thought. It was just the day they had had, out on the road, by the sea, in the seering light. The pretense that life was gentle and safe. He was going to kiss her, she knew it, and wanted him to, so much.

But he didn't. "We have to be very careful what we say in front of the other guests."

"Of course."

But when they went downstairs to be taken across a gallery murmuring with ancestral portraits to a grand dining room, it was clear from the place settings that they were the only guests. They were treated to an exquisite dinner of many small courses and many glasses of velvety Portuguese wine, all served as if they were visiting royalty. The noblewoman Maria de Saldanha Oliveira was a graceful hostess. She was a widow who had lived in Paris and sought reassurance that all was not lost of the old world. The priest, she, and her late husband had met in Paris. He was an unusual man of the church in that he did not mention religion but imparted a sense of profound peace. Conversation was not of the war, but of art and philosophy and music, of which Klaus showed himself impressively knowledgeable, and of the history of the region. Their hostess told the charming tale of an Arab lord who planted thousands of almond trees to blossom white in spring for his wife who dreamed of seeing snow. She was enchanted by Alva's interest in photography.

She asked no personal questions. It was only in the months and years after the event that Alva understood this was a deliberate tactic on the part of a worldly and perceptive woman.

In their shared room, Klaus gave her his hand and she put it to her collarbone. Then she waited as he trailed a finger down the exposed skin below her neck, and into the low line of her dress. It began. His mouth on hers was expressively questioning at first, then generous and exciting.

His touch was warm and sure. Was the thrill of it because it was not her husband's, part of the eroticism a very private satisfaction that she was a woman who could take her pleasures with the duplicity of a man? She had claimed him as her husband and nodded her thanks to the footman who had shown them into the room with the curtained double bed.

In unseen ways, her world was shattering. Knowing it was wrong, she was falling, fleeing normality for a fantastical interlude outside real life, laughing and playing at love because they could. The smoothness of his body was so different from . . . no, she could not think it. After the storm, they had washed up on this foreign shore. The night was real, and yet it was not real. They were in a house in a perfumed pine forest. Behind brocade curtains they were in a new country. She wanted him, wanted the physical act, more than she had ever imagined possible.

Afterward, the feather mattress seemed to hold them like a cloud, high above the floor, as the night vanished, over all too soon, she had a sudden painful understanding of the meaning of the mysterious word *saudade*— the yearning for past happiness. She was both joyful and unbearably sad. Perhaps they would wake from the dream to find themselves outside in the forest, huddled in the roots of a tree.

The next morning liveried retainers brought a hip bath into the adjoining room, then filled it with steaming water from copper pans and laid out a mountain of soft white towels. For breakfast they were offered coffee and eggs, oranges, honey, dried figs, and blanched almonds and a basket of food for their journey: bread and cheese, custard cakes and more fruit, with wine and a homemade cherry liqueur.

Maria de Saldanha Oliveira would not hear of taking any kind of payment. "Go well, be valiant!" she said.

Alva wanted to ask if she could take a photograph of her, but was wary of giving offense. Not even of the house, for the footman was waiting, and it was impossible to ask permission without seeming gauche.

Again their hostess wished them well, and they were off.

Through a landscape of cork trees, the enchantment receded, lost mile by mile. Men in white collarless shirts and black waistcoats and pants stopped their labors by the roadside to watch the car stir up red dust as it went past, a car still a rarity in these parts. Quarteira was passed in an instant. She recalled nothing of the earlier visit, only her longing to be elsewhere. At Setúbal, they had lunch at a restaurant overlooking the fine harbor. Farther along, a rough fisherman's beach was dominated by the canning factory. Lines of men helped pull in the boats.

Alva was astounded at how differently she saw it now. She watched with soaring heart the way the sea sparkled so intensely; the white of the houses was dazzling above the gay colors of the boats packed tightly against the quay. It was an excitement she had last felt a lifetime ago when the lucky ones left New York on the steamer for England, and then on across Europe by train to Rome, their honeymoon trip. She wanted to whirl herself around in this otherness, this heady weightlessness in air and light.

Then, longing to hold fast to exultation even as it was wrenched away, they were at the railway station. They found the platform. Too soon came the farewell kiss and the promise, and the train to Lisbon.

It was only when she arrived in the city that Alva remembered—with a dart to the heart—what she carried in her handbag. Only a month ago, she would have shown it to Michael first, allowed him to make the decision. But she was no longer that person. For security, Alva took a cab to the American Embassy and asked to speak to the chief intelligence officer. Then she handed over the letter from the Serbian double agent, with the writing between the lines clearly visible, just as Klaus had asked.

vii

Alva returned to Michael. He seemed pleased to see her. But he was delighted—gleefully, outrageously delighted—to hear that she had made contact with Klaus Mayer.

Two nights later, she went with her husband to an apartment in a nondescript building in Cais do Sodre where Ronald Bagshaw was waiting with a bottle of brandy. Two other men were present; they were introduced as Mr. Jones of the British Embassy and Mr. Miller of the American. She answered their questions and explained in close detail what she had witnessed in Faro. The letter had been examined by both sides and pronounced authentic. Alva recounted what she had witnessed of the distribution of the gold, showed the photographs she had developed. She passed on the information Mayer had revealed in order to be believed and lied only by omission, when she was asked how he had behaved toward her. "He behaved like a perfect gentleman," she said.

So now they were all pretending. I am now a liar and a cheat, too, thought Alva, thinking unrepentantly of her husband. We know where we stand then.

To everyone who knew them, Michael and Alva had had their difficulties, but these had apparently been resolved. Alva wrote optimistic letters home and was careful not to include anything that could imply otherwise.

In December, everything changed. The Japanese bombed Pearl Harbor and the United States was officially at war. Michael and Alva were no longer neutrals.

The AP office grew more crowded, and more rooms were rented. There was still a party every night of the week. They began to forfeit the Café Eva to spend evenings at the Nina Bar nightclub with other inveterate talkers and rumormongers. "Dedicating our livers to the Allied cause," said Michael cheerfully, and now Alva had proved her mettle, she was one of them.

At the Nina all nationalities gathered, watched over by its Austrian owner and ringmaster, a sleek young man named Danielski. Freddy Danielski hated the Germans, but he let them in to dance and shout over a Cossack band with all the rest. He had a girlfriend, a merry Scottish-American blond named Marjorie, who seemed to enjoy her work as a go-between who passed disinformation to journalists and other listeners.

Alva was initiated into the world of "sibs" and "midweek specials"—short for "sibilant," these were false pieces of "information" whispered into the right ears. She even began to enjoy coffee at the Café Eva, where she would chat and laugh with the vivacious Marjorie, whom she liked. They might have been better friends but Marjorie was always so busy. After twenty minutes, when she stood up to go, Alva would carelessly leave her copy of a newspaper, always the Portuguese *O Seculo,* which Marjorie would pick up, equally carelessly. Inside was a sheet of flimsy paper containing the notes for stories to be disseminated that night.

For Freddy Danielski was a magician with a piece of gossip. Around all the tables at the Nina Bar he went, having been briefed exactly which fiction should be dropped into which willing ear. Freddy Danielski worked so hard he had black rings under his eyes, so marked that he looked like a panda.

With the blessing of her husband, Alva met Klaus Mayer once a week at a small nightclub on the edge of the rundown Alfama district, well away from the river where the sailors and the foreign visitors went. Unknown to Michael, when she danced closely with Klaus, it was no act. The Latin rhythms insinuated into her body and a kind of elation filled her, slow and sensuous. They danced to the music of North Africa, to jazz, and shuffled close to the slow ululations of a *fado* singer as they exchanged information carefully crafted to mislead the Third Reich and corroborate other fictions.

"What if one of your people sees us?" Alva asked the first time. She was more frightened now, but it was for him, not herself.

"If they did, it wouldn't necessarily be a bad thing. As far as von Kartshof is concerned, you are the one who is betraying your country and I am the clever operative. You are a valuable asset, and like me, you will be protected because you are helping to deliver him a safe yet productive war waged from flower-filled villas in the sun, nights at the casino, and drunken parties with willing women."

As the weeks and months went by in Lisbon, the night at Maria de Saldanha Oliveira's house had taken on a dream quality. Had it even happened? The touch of his hand as he led her to the tiny dance floor told her it had. Until I met Klaus I experienced life but I did not feel it, thought Alva.

On the nights when she was not expected to meet Klaus, she remembered Ronald Bagshaw's explanation of how Portuguese married women conducted their affairs while their husbands were out for the evening, and found it most useful.

During the day, Alva found work with the American Joint Distribution Committee in Rua do Áurea helping Jewish refugees, supporting those in need and finding routes out of Europe to sanctuary. What the world did not see until after the war was known from the beginning in Lisbon. The city took in people who had run west for their lives, and heard their accounts of harrowing train journeys and unexpected stops and trucks that were equipped with hissing poison showers. Most of them knew it might take years for them to reach their destinations. Meanwhile they attempted to trace loved ones left behind in the horror.

Wherever he could, Klaus provided any information he could to rebalance the cruel demonstrations of power that had halted their progress.

From time to time, Ronald Bagshaw would question her about Klaus Mayer's motives and whether she was certain of his continuing sincerity. Alva would reply that he seemed to have a genuine abhorrence of Hitler and the Nazi party. He had feared what they could achieve in the event of a German victory in Europe.

But what assurances could there be? They were all making judgments about each other's honesty, all the time; doubting, then deciding to trust but always wary, the dealers in loyalty and love no better that the traders in lethal arms and diamonds, platinum and leathers, carob and oranges. They were all slippery opportunists, in their way.

Then, in 1944, as the tide turned in the Allies' favor, a sober assessment by Nazi intelligence concluded that its Abwehr station in Lisbon was dangerously immoral and lazy. Their building on the Rua Buenos Aires was a den of vice. It was discovered that several high-ranking officers were behind foreign currency scams that allowed them to live high on the hog. Von Kartshof himself, whose judgment had been impaired by an affair with a French *vicomtesse*, was sent to the Eastern front. The rope was tightening.

One night in April, Klaus didn't show up for their assignation at the nightclub.

Michael was also fully occupied. In his head he was preparing a book he was going to write after the war.

With the end in sight, pressure in Portugal eased. No one seemed to be worried about Klaus Mayer; it appeared their side had no more need of him. Observant as he was when driven by his own needs, Michael did not guess his wife's true feelings, that, worried raw, Alva feared the worst for Klaus. No one had heard from him, and it seemed impossible to find out what had happened.

When Michael finally booked them a passage home, Alva refused to go.

He was incredulous. "Alva, I need to get you home, back to New York. You're coming home. That's what you want!"

She shook her head so rapidly it was more like a quiver. "Not anymore. Too late, Mike. I need to find out—"

"Alva—our berths on the ship are booked."

He looked her up and down, as if he was checking she was actually the same woman he had brought with him to Portugal.

"Don't do that," she said. She went over to the window. Rain streaked down the glass, leaving a watery cracked mirror.

Michael was an indistinct reflection behind her. It occurred to her that she was standing in the doorway between two lives, a Janus, the double-headed Roman god of beginnings and endings; as if she had never stood in the Catholic church in Washington Heights and promised to love, honor, and obey Michael, till death did they part; as if he had never promised to care for her for the rest of their lives.

"I can't do it, Mike, and I won't."

"Are you crazy?"

"Maybe I am."

"I did the best I could for us, Alva. You know that."

She knew that was the truth, however painful. "You did, Mike. But it still worked out wrong for us."

"And so now—what?" He was losing his temper. "You stay on here—still complaining I don't look after you?"

They went round in circles, in generalizations. It was such a truism to say that the war had changed people. So self-evident it would have been crass to put it into words; Michael, the wordsmith, simply opened his shoulders and made a gesture with his hands that was half helpless, half as if he was releasing her. Then he cried, great gulping sobs. And she watched him, unable to offer the slightest comfort. Neither did she quite tell him the truth.

"It was just the war," she said.

The Bartons were far from unique, after all. Of course she felt guilt and embarrassment. It occurred to her that the way Michael had behaved toward her might also have been born of those two tormenting emotions. But it was done now. In the end, it was agreed. She would sail back across the Atlantic with him, and while he would do his best to persuade her otherwise, if he did not succeed in changing her mind, they would see a divorce lawyer in New York and she could return.

The letter to Alva arrived, via Freddy Danielski and Marjorie, two days before they were due to sail. It was post-marked Faro.

viii

Klaus always said it was the happiest day of his life when Alva arrived at the railway station in Faro.

When he saw how close he was to being discovered in Lisbon, he had run to the one place he felt safe. One by one his imaginary group of agents went silent. He sat out the rest of the war working alongside the fisherman Palhares, accepting the help and protection that was freely offered in the town. A Gestapo officer who came to investigate why the town's suppliers of the Nazi black market were no longer willing to cooperate was mysteriously shot. Subsequently no witnesses could be found, even to the German's presence in the town. Word was he had been asking whether anyone had seen Klaus Mayer.

Klaus had hidden the letter he wrote to Alva for several weeks while deciding whether to risk sending it. He had seen the Germans who remained in Lisbon, those who had not fled to South America, becoming not less but more dangerous. They called themselves the Iron Nazis, making a pact to keep alive their vision for German dominance in Europe. The Lisbon Pact was sealed as Berlin was reduced to ashes and rubble.

All this was forgotten as Alva stepped from the train.

The day they saw Horta das Rochas for the first time, they had set out to find Maria de Saldanha Oliveira's house again. No limousine this time, only a third-hand Peugeot to rattle them over the rutted roads. So many of the paths into the pine forests looked the same. When they finally stumbled across it, the gates were locked and there was no other entry to the grounds. At the inn where more than four years previously they had been sent to the estate led by the boy on the bicycle, they found the same boy, ever helpful, and now a youth with an incipient moustache. The noble old lady had died, he told them.

"The estate is being sold," he said. "You can buy the house if you want!"

They all laughed at the absurdity.

"We could go look at it, just to see it again," said Alva.

"Darling, could we?"

"I suppose so."

That afternoon, accompanied by a land agent, they went and stood in the courtyard. The coach house and the stables were empty. Looking up at the magical place that had brought them together, they caught hands. Alva gave silent thanks once again to their late benefactress (could she have known what she was doing?). Then they were shown to the less imposing corners of the estate.

One of the abandoned farms, full of olive groves and orchards, could have been made viable. Another was close to dereliction. Its name was simply the Garden of Rocks, Horta das Rochas. The land was no good for agriculture; it was rocky and too close to the shore. It was barely sufficient for the raising of goats and the keeping of bees, which had been the tenant's last failed venture. Pine woods grew thickly over this outpost of the estate, giving way abruptly to red cliffs above the ocean.

Torches of cynara lit the way in electric blue, down the sea path. A carpet of pine needles cushioned their steps down to the beach.

On the high ground, a thick-walled farmhouse was smothered by the weight of oleander blossoms on trees that grew too close. But the air inside was cool, and when they opened the windows upstairs they framed a sea of lapis lazuli.

PART FIVE

Faro—September 2014

i

If the police were making progress finding Terry Jackson there was no hint of it in any of the news reports of Rylands' murder. Detective Gambóias was now certain it was murder. The booking for Villa Eleven at Horta das Rochas had been made using a stolen credit card. A car with false registration plates had arrived at five o'clock on the day Rylands died. The public was asked for information regarding the movements of the car, but nothing else. No mention was made of the throwaway mobile phone used to send Nathan a text, apparently from Jackson.

After a few days, the story slipped down the schedules as fresh tragedies, wars, and epidemics pushed it from public consciousness. We were allowed to return to Faro, so long as the local police knew exactly where to find us.

I went back to the language course. There didn't seem anything else I could do, especially as I had told the police that that was my reason for being in Portugal. Sometimes Nathan was in class, too; sometimes he wasn't; without him, the atmosphere would become oppressively businesslike. I found it hard to concentrate. My thoughts wandered incessantly, and though I smiled politely at the others and took coffee with them in the breaks, the early sense of student camaraderie had gone. Even Enzo the jolly Italian shoe salesman had became earnest and somewhat disapproving when Nathan deigned to join us, telling him, on more than one occasion, that he thought Nathan should take his studies more seriously.

"You read the book?" I asked Nathan on one of the days he did come in.

We were walking back to the centre of town, just the two of us. He was remote, as he'd been for most of the week. He'd either rushed away or made it clear he didn't want company—my company, at least. That hurt, as it seemed to suggest that all he had wanted from me was my journalistic expertise. I'd thought I meant more to him than that. Though, to be fair, on the days when I didn't see him I had often checked in with a text and he always replied. This felt like the first chance I'd had for a while to have a serious conversation with him.

"I read it."

We passed a bar on the Rua de Santo António. He went in, no discussion, and he ordered a couple of vodka shots. I declined. He threw back both, with ostentatious defiance.

"I called the PR office at Holz-Rocha, the company that owns Horta das Rochas," I said.

I reckoned that in the days after official confirmation that the death of Ian Rylands was murder not suicide, it was routine stuff for a journalist to call the resort's spokeswoman and ask about the history of the hotel.

"I mentioned the name Walde casually, as an established fact. No one denied it. The woman I spoke to confirmed that the company grew out of the hotel founded in an old farmhouse on the land there by a German called Karl Walde in 1947. Apparently the Walde family no longer runs the resort on a day-to-day basis, though they retain a controlling interest in the company. They've diversified into transport and property."

I watched Nathan assessing the empty shot glasses and waited to see whether he would meet me halfway. "For Mayer, read Walde," I said.

"That's what Rylands said."

"Yes." I was relieved not to have to labour the point.

"What about this Eduardo Walde he told us to contact? Does he even exist?"

I nodded. "He's the company chairman: head of the Walde family."

Nathan gave me a sideways look.

"I asked about Karl Walde's wife, but didn't get anywhere with a name. But that doesn't mean much. Only that the notes given to the PR woman don't mention her. She might well not know anything beyond the version that goes on the brochures. The important part is that the name Walde is right."

"Anything else?"

"I held fire on mentioning child abduction, if that's what you mean. One step at a time. I've tried the Internet but there's not much there—1992 is just a bit too early to find newspaper coverage online. The name Walde does link to a few Portuguese entries that seem to concern the disappearance of children—I was using Google Translate—but only as a reference, no details. Other than that, from what I can see this so-called quiet cult that has grown up around Esta Hartford's novel was probably an exaggeration by Rylands. It wasn't mentioned in any reports that I could find in the newspapers."

Nathan raised a palm to get the barman's attention.

"So what we need to find out," I said, with an irritated edge in my tone, "is how far the characters in the book were an accurate depiction of real life. We're working on the assumption that Karl Walde is portrayed in the novel as Klaus Mayer, and Esta herself as Alva, but we only have Rylands' word for it."

"So far, we have Horta das Rochas—and what else?"

The barman hovered a hand over the vodka bottle, but I was relieved to see Nathan shake his head. "Orange juice, please."

"Well, we know why Rylands was interested in the place, and why he so wanted Klaus Mayer's story to be true, don't we?" I said, less tensely. This was the hardest part to square, the most frustrating part of Esta's novel, in which too much information was covered in a few paragraphs. "At the end of the war, Alva leaves Michael and goes to the Algarve to be with Klaus. They're happy, really happy, and they find Horta das Rochas. But they are watching their backs. He's still worried about the former Nazis who stay in Lisbon and what they might do. He thinks they are dangerous people."

"He was probably right."

I frowned and shook my head. "This Lisbon Pact business needs to be treated with caution. Clearly, Rylands lapped it up and used it to put some air under his conspiracy theories. All we know for certain is that

Klaus Mayer—Karl Walde—moved to the Algarve after the war and went into the nascent tourist industry. And he has a son called Eduardo who inherited his business."

"They weren't whiter than white though, were they, Klaus and Alva?" said Nathan. "She didn't go looking for an affair but they had one and obviously kept it going when they got back to Lisbon. And it's not put out there in words, but where did they get the money to buy Horta das Rochas?"

It was a good question.

"Surely the banking systems in Europe were still in meltdown in 1945 . . . how did two foreign nationals get the funds across the borders? Unless . . ."

"I see what you mean," I said. "There might have been something put aside for him in the bank in Faro after the gold was distributed. Perhaps it was never all distributed in one go. It would have been more sensible to keep some back to use as a contingency fund."

"But he ran to Faro when he left Lisbon. He knew he had friends here. Klaus—Karl, whatever—got help from the friends he made in Faro, didn't he? And after the war he wouldn't have been able to stay in the Algarve and set up a business if he hadn't had good relations with the locals."

Not only had he read the book, he had read it carefully. Yet again, I was left thinking there was a lot more to Nathan Emberlin (or Josh Harris) than was immediately apparent.

I could probably have approached Eduardo Walde plausibly enough as yet another hack wanting background information to the murder of Ian Rylands. However, from what I deduced from reading the news reports, the closest anyone was getting to him was a statement from the same PR woman I'd spoken to. There was no doubt that the story was bad for the Horta das Rochas brand, and from the point of view of the company, the sooner the tragedy faded in the public imagination, the better.

If Nathan and I wanted to chase the story, we were better off not drawing attention to ourselves or acting suspiciously in any way. Going through the obvious channels to get to Eduardo Walde would be like putting our hands up in public. We had to find a way in below the line—to think laterally and to pick away at the details of any available sources of information.

It was easy to find confirmation online of the great storm described by Esta Hartford. It was the worst natural catastrophe in the Iberian peninsula for almost two hundred years. The storm broke in the afternoon of February 14, 1941, a Friday, with a direct strike on Lisbon. By the afternoon of fifteenth, it was one of the five fiercest windstorms across the whole of Europe in the twentieth century. The wind speeds at Lisbon were almost eighty miles an hour; on the Algarve coast, they reached a hundred and fifty miles an hour at Portimão. In San Sebastian in Spain, winds a hundred and eighty miles an hour were recorded.

There was major disruption of road and rail links, and electricity and telephone lines. On Sunday, February 16, all communication was lost between Lisbon and the rest of the country. A storm surge up the Tagus estuary, huge waves driven by southwesterly winds, sank a hundred and fifty boats moored close to the city. The peak of the cyclone coincided with high tide. Water was thrown up over the river's banks and protective walls, and flooded into the streets. The steamboat station was flooded, and the waves reached twenty metres high.

On the railway between Cascais and Lisbon, where the train ran along the coast on a small cliff, the retaining wall crumbled. Another seawall protecting the casino at Estoril was destroyed and the two-hundred-year-old cedars between the Hotel do Parque and the Hotel Estoril were drowned in sea water.

In the south, most of the recorded damage concerned the olive groves, where thousands of trees were blown down, and the devastation of the coastal area.

I had talked to everyone I could about the storm: the owner of the language school and her secretary; João the barman at the Aliança; the helpful man behind the desk at the tourist information office; even the elderly man selling tickets to enter the cathedral—but drew a succession of blanks. It was as if, unlike almost everywhere else in Europe, events during the Second World War had hardly figured in the lives of their parents and grandparents.

Nathan actually threw the word "obsessed" at me, before realising, as we both started to laugh, that it was equally applicable to him.

We wandered aimlessly towards Faro railway station. It was early evening and we were having half-thoughts about getting on a train to Tavira for a change of scene. The train that we might or might not get didn't leave for another half an hour, so we paused outside the old carob bean factory, now a community art space. I liked the name: Fábrica dos Sentidos (Factory of the Senses). Nathan was taken by the notion that the space was open to anyone with a new idea, from art to business. Craftsmen and women could work, exhibit, and network for a symbolic nominal rent and the emphasis was on reusing and recycling materials. Everything was built lovingly with discarded items, including wood from the town's old library.

A living statue, all Victoriana and gothic lace, still and sinister, sat outside on the cobbled pavement, any expression on her face hidden behind a gold mask.

"It's not a woman," said Nathan as we strolled up. "It's a man."

I looked closer. He was right. At the edge of the golden face were wisps of sideburn. Nothing was what it seemed.

"Watch out!" Nathan grabbed my arm.

I sprang back, ready to protect myself from the figure in front of me. But Nathan had seen the real danger. The wheels of a car seemed to scuff my heels as he pulled me out of its path.

"Shit!" he said. "What the hell just happened?"

Heart pumping, legs shaking, I stared at the car, now screaming away down the narrow street. It was an ordinary-looking car, very similar to the Seat I'd rented. I was still clinging on to Nathan, with a horrible feeling that the near-miss had been deliberate, wondering how I was going to say it without freaking him out. He had put his arms around me as I looked around in a panic, checking that the car wasn't coming back from any other direction. I was just about to say something when I saw the poster on the building opposite.

It was one of the election posters: a head shot of the candidate and a tagline I could now understand: "One hundred days without ideas, one hundred days without action, one hundred days without history."

The words dried in my mouth. "That poster. The candidate," I managed to get out. "Look at the name."

"Nuno Palhares."

"The maverick political candidate who got the café reopened. Who is standing on a ticket of tradition and localism. Don't you recognise the name?"

Nathan frowned.

"Palhares was the fisherman who brought the Nazi gold in. Who worked with Klaus Mayer to distribute the funds according to local need."

"You think it might be the same family?"

"If the book is true, I'd bet the house on it."

"Hang on, though—the author changed the names of the characters, she didn't use their real names."

"Not for herself and Karl, but all the Portuguese places are given their real names. She could have done that for some of the people, too."

"Not convinced. What the—? Where are you going now?"

I was almost running, my legs burning adrenaline, Nathan reluctantly keeping pace. The Café Aliança was within sight. A few customers were gathered around the outside tables, taking advantage of another perfect day of sunshine. I pushed the revolving door and went over to João at the bar.

"Nuno Palhares . . . is he here?" I asked, not bothering with any chat about how the local electioneering was going.

"Not yet."

I turned to Nathan. "Shall we wait?"

Nathan shrugged. We waited, over a few desultory beers, but Palhares didn't show.

"Tomorrow morning, perhaps," said João as we left.

We walked back across the public garden. Nathan was quiet, as he had been all evening at the café. I wondered whether I had hurt or offended him by taking the initiative, or more likely, annoyed him with my focus on Esta Hartford's book when all he wanted to do was to find out about the child abductions.

I felt him bump against me, and then his hand caught mine. We walked through the dark garden without speaking, his hand warm in mine, neither of us daring to mention it. Streetlights cast glittering ladders across the water of the marina. Our footsteps padded over the cobbles. I wondered if he could hear my breathing.

At the door to my studio I stopped to get out my key. He pushed the red door and it swung back, open as usual. Perhaps that should have worried me more than it did but my mind was full of other things. Nathan stood at the dark entrance, holding the door wide for me and still saying nothing.

"Okay, I'll see you in the morning, then," I said.

He had let go of my hand so I reached out to touch his upper arm, intending it as reassurance that we were still as one on what had to be done. We'd go back to the café for breakfast, and we'd speak to Nuno Palhares. There was nothing else to be done until then.

He leaned in and I felt his arm come around my waist. I gave him the hug I thought he needed. His mouth was by my ear, and he gave a tiny sigh. Then I felt his lips touch mine, but only a brush.

"Can I come up?" he whispered.

The studio looked a bit messier than I remembered leaving it, but I wasn't really concentrating on the room. Nathan reached for me as soon as I'd shut the door.

I let him pull me closer. For all our banter and mild flirtation I hadn't considered this a possibility. I was curious, and flattered, but it was more than that—far more. By the time both his arms were around me, and he dipped his head to kiss me, the physical attraction between us was overwhelming.

Neither of us spoke.

He ran a finger lightly down the opening of my blouse, and waited, barely touching my skin until he saw me smile. It felt good.

Nathan was gentle and playful in bed compared to Marc—more gentle than anyone I'd ever been with, yet imaginatively so. His touch was electric. That was a surprise, too. What can I say? It was fun, very sensual, and I enjoyed every moment. I thought it was probably a one-off event. I didn't mind too much about that. It was worth it, not only to sate my curiosity about him but because, as I let myself go, moving on top of him, feeling his silky muscles responding beneath me, I had such a profound sense of release and reconnection with my younger self, by which I mean the person who could simply be, without complication. I was glad it had happened.

The next morning he looked into my eyes and gave me such a heart-flippingly lovely grin that I relaxed completely.

We went down to the street and along to the Café Aliança for breakfast together.

João was behind the bar wiping glasses. He nodded as we walked across the checkerboard floor. We ordered coffee and *tostas*. He brought them over to a table under an old photograph of fishermen mending nets, followed not long afterwards by the political candidate. In the flesh, Nuno Palhares had a buttery complexion, a smooth plump face and dark bearlike eyes.

"He is happy to speak to anyone, if they have—or not—a vote in Faro," said João by way of introduction as we exchanged names.

"You can tell the people you meet here that I am a good guy!" Palhares said in American-accented English. His professional handshake was warm and firm. It was clear from the start that his English was vastly superior to Nathan's command of local slang and my halting Portuguese. He was of medium height, but broad shoulders and a distinct presence made him seem larger. The smile seemed sincere, and exposed teeth that surely had received the attentions of an expensive cosmetic dentist.

He accepted our offer of coffee and sat down, all geniality and openness. "So, you are interested in my campaign?"

"It was your name that made me stop and think," I said.

Palhares did a pantomimed double take.

"I have recently read a book," I opened. "I don't know if it's true in every respect, but it concerns events here during the Second World War."

"Here—in Faro?"

"Yes. Right here in this café, too. It was written by a woman who came here in the 1940s." I knew I had struck a chord because Palhares leaned in, his brown button eyes engaged. I watched them carefully. "The book is called *The Alliance*."

Palhares blinked. We had him; I knew it then.

"You know that book?" he asked.

A pause.

"What do you want to know?" he asked.

Nathan jumped straight in. "Is it a true story?" he asked. His bluntness could easily have backfired, but our luck held.

"As much as I know, it is true," said the man cautiously but with a degree of interest that encouraged me to push on.

"In the book, the fisherman—was he a relative?"

"No."

My shoulders slumped involuntarily. I had been so sure. "So . . . was there no connection, Esta Hartford just happened to give your name to one of the characters?"

"Ah . . . she switched the names around a bit."

I sat up. "So—?"

"My father, Calixto Palhares, was the manager of the bank."

I tried not to let my excitement show. "And the good German, Klaus Mayer? He was also based on a real person?"

"Oh, yes. He was real, but that wasn't his real name."

"What was his name?"

Palhares went to lift his coffee cup, and then replaced it. He seemed to know how important this was, and he played it as a true professional. "His real name was Karl Walde."

"Do you remember your father speaking of him?" I asked.

"Of course. This was a story he loved to tell. I grew up with it. Karl stayed in Portugal with the woman he met during the war, and my father and he became close friends."

"You remember meeting him then?"

"Very well."

"A good man?" asked Nathan.

"A good man, yes. He and his wife—Esta, who wrote the book—they made a great success of a hotel the other side of Albufeira. One of the first to bring the tourists to the Algarve from the cold north of Europe. They got warm; we got prosperity!"

"This hotel—it grew into the Horta das Rochas resort, is that correct?"

"That is correct."

"And he and your father remained close friends after that, or—?"

"Karl Walde was a big man. He never changed, even when he became rich. Compared to many here, he became very rich. But what you read in the book about how he helped the poor Portuguese on the Algarve was also true. He did many good works for the people here.

"I was not expecting to be talking about this with you." He looked genuinely touched. "But it's good. I am glad to tell the story. It was because of my father and Karl Walde that I became a local politician."

I have met enough politicians in my time to be deeply cynical. Most of them are opportunists and narcissists, more concerned with how their contribution will be judged rather than fighting for what might work best across party boundaries. Either Nuno Palhares was a terrific actor, or he was the most heartfelt candidate I had ever met.

"How did it really happen, when your father and Karl Walde met—was it during the storm in 1941 as it is in the book?"

Palhares settled in his plastic chair, which gave a loud crack. "That night, it felt like the end of the world. That is what my father always said."

"And the fishermen and Karl Walde brought the gold back here?"

"Yes. They tried to save the men who drowned, but they could not. They brought the gold to the bank and my father helped to distribute the funds to help repair the damage, and to recompense the farmers and fishermen and salt-panners and boatmen who had lost so much. All true."

I looked around at the café's crumbling grandeur, trying to picture the scene.

"It was the work of a great humanitarian," went on Palhares. "Other men were digging and clearing, doing what they could with nothing. The gold was Karl Walde's tool and he gave it to us. What happened in 1941 was not unique. These events are natural phenomena. They occur randomly."

For a moment I thought he was talking about war, not storms.

"In the long run, coastal engineering actually weakens the natural coastal defences in the event of storm surges. We live in a time of false confidence. We also believe that our science will predict and save, when nature unleashes her worst. But the truth is that the population is not prepared to deal with these forgotten calamities. We live in an everlasting present, with our governments and our media—when we should be looking to the past and reading the warnings there.

"Every time some disaster happens, the authorities say that lessons will be learned. But with reconstruction comes forgetting. Each time, the catastrophe seems unique. But terrible events are not unique; they are recurrent. There is such faith in technology to keep us safe, touching really, but misguided. Never forgetting, that is the only insurance policy worth having. Memories and experience are undervalued. Who remembers the Great Storm of 1941 now?"

It was hard to disagree.

"What happened to Karl Walde afterwards?" asked Nathan.

"He and Esta had two children. Eduardo was born in 1948, the year before me. His sister Carolina came soon after."

"A happy marriage?"

"It seemed to be."

"They can't still be alive, can they?"

"No. Though Esta made it to her late eighties. Karl died much earlier. A heart attack, I think."

"That was when his son, Eduardo, took over at Horta das Rochas, is that right?"

Palhares considered this. "It wasn't too long, certainly, before Eduardo became the boss."

"Were you ever friendly with him?" I was imagining two sons of two friends. It had to be worth the question.

"As boys we were friends, yes. Later, it was harder."

"Was there a reason for that, or was it—?"

"When Eduardo took over as the hotel manager he had the idea to develop the resort into what it is today. But he had a hard time. Crime and corruption were growing. By the 1980s, organised crime had moved into the Algarve resorts."

"Did that affect the Walde family?" asked Nathan.

Palhares stared at him, for the first time seeming to calculate how much he ought to say. "You don't know?"

"Know what?"

"About what happened to the Walde family?"

Silence. A vein pulsed in Nathan's neck. I wanted to reach out to him and dared not.

"In 1992, Carolina's husband was murdered and her child was taken from the garden of the family house—no ransom demand was made, so the family never knew whether it was a failed extortion racket, a deal gone wrong, or a lesson being taught. It was a time when several children were abducted, one found murdered, none returned. The gangsters who killed Luiz Vicente, Carolina's husband, were never brought to justice. The two-year-old boy was never seen again."

We walked away dazed, but with the one prize we wanted. Palhares had given us an office telephone number and a message for Eduardo Walde; I was to say immediately that we had spoken to him.

At one point, Palhares had given Nathan a long glance that made me wonder whether he had guessed why we were so insistent on talking about the Walde family, but he said nothing.

Nathan dropped an arm over my shoulders. "So what do we tell Eduardo Walde? Where do we start?"

"We tell him we have a confidential matter to discuss."

"That just sounds dodgy."

"That we were the ones who found Rylands?"

"I think we have to."

"We tell him the truth, or as close to the truth as we can. That Rylands gave me the book. Where it led. Our suspicions that we may have some information about the boy who was kidnapped. See what his reaction is. Or we could go to the police or the British Consul with this and let the authorities handle it."

A silence. The implications of allowing officialdom to intercede grew and settled.

"Bloody great, isn't it? Not just organised crime, but Nazis, too."

"Not a Nazi. A good German."

"Go on, do it."

We walked to a bench in the Jardim Manuel Bivar and I rang the number for Eduardo Walde.

We spoke in English—his English was extremely good—but even so it was impossible on the telephone to gauge his reaction to my request for a meeting, even when I explained that we were the ones who had discovered Ian Rylands' body. That was understandable. As far as he knew, we were a couple of ghouls who wanted to milk the situation for all it was worth. In his position I would probably have thought the same.

He suggested a public space: the embankment of the Tagus, by the Monument to the Discoveries.

"Lisbon?" asked Nathan, one knee jiggling with impatience.

I nodded. "The monument where Alva ran into Ronald Bagshaw, in the book, when she was finding her feet in Portugal," I reminded him.

If he thought that was interesting or otherwise, he didn't say.

"When?"

"Tomorrow at noon."

We went to the beach that afternoon, the one close to the airport. Taking the ferry was a way of passing the time, of relaxing before whatever was to come. Back in town we had dinner in a tourist café and went back to my studio. It was only then, when I couldn't find my phone charger, that I remembered the feeling I'd had the previous evening when I'd opened the door.

"I think someone was in here yesterday," I said.

"Er, that would be us?"

"Very funny. No . . . there was something not quite right."

"Stuff missing?"

"No, just not where I left it."

"You're sure—really sure?"

I still couldn't find the charger, which was annoying. But maybe he was right; we'd messed up the studio ourselves. Nathan put his arms around me and my physical reaction to his touch was even stronger now I knew how good we were together. He didn't speak much and I was glad about that. I didn't want him to tell me he was grateful for what I'd done for him, much less have it confirmed that that was the reason he was making love to me so tenderly. But compared to the previous night, when my self-absorption had been a form of self-defence, I wanted to give more than ever.

ii

According to the online route-finder, it would take three and a quarter hours to cover the two hundred and seventy-eight kilometres between Faro and Lisbon, almost all by motorway. I asked Nathan if he wanted to drive, but he was happy to let me. That suited me. It wouldn't be a scenic route through the Alentejo region, just the fastest way.

The next morning we were up and drinking coffee by seven and left my studio before half past. The car didn't seem to be quite where I thought I'd left it, but even so, by eight we had managed to buy a motorway toll card at the airport. Nathan was in reflective mode, but navigating with helpful amounts of notice before turnings were expected. We were a good team.

We followed the signs for Norte e Oeste A22-Loulé-Centro and began the swoop down towards the unmanned tollbooth.

"This had better work," I muttered.

"Police car over there. At least there's someone to ask if it doesn't."

I drew up at the booth and leaned out of the open window to read the instructions on the machine. "Seems fairly straightforward."

"Looks like we've got help anyway," said Nathan.

Two police officers appeared. One bent down to speak to me.

"Would you mind getting out of the car, please?" He spoke in English, which was an immediate tip-off that all was not well. How did he know which language to address us in?

I gave them a professional smile to show we had nothing to hide. The officers did not reciprocate. Their faces were in deep shadow under the peaks of their caps, features barely visible.

"Both of you—out."

Nathan swore under his breath. I wasn't sure whether they heard.

"Take it easy," I said softly. "We've done nothing wrong."

The lead officer motioned us to stand away from the car and to raise our hands. The other twisted his cheek into his shoulder and spoke into the radio fixed to his shirt. Nathan and I were separated and patted down.

"Your names?"

We gave them in turn. Once again, Nathan reverted to Josh.

Then the other officer pulled Nathan's hands behind his back. As he did so, the first said: "Joshua Harris. You are being arrested. You must return to Faro police headquarters."

"Arrested—on what grounds?" I said shakily.

"We will speak to you again about the death of Ian Rylands."

"What?" At last Nathan seemed to have woken up to what was happening.

"I'm coming with you," I said. "Don't worry."

"No," said the other officer, speaking to us for the first time. "Joshua comes alone. He comes now."

"That can't be right," I said. "He hasn't done anything. We've told the investigation everything we know!"

They were already walking Nathan away. He tried to pull round to look at me, but they manhandled him roughly between them to keep him moving in the direction they wanted.

I reached for my phone, but couldn't think who to call. By this stage Nathan was being pushed into the back of the police car. "We'll get this sorted. Hang in there!" I shouted.

I panicked. Who was there to call for help? The owner of the language school? Nuno Palhares? The British Consulate in Lisbon? I had to get him a lawyer, but how to go about finding a good one?

The police car was moving, pulling out and accelerating fast. It passed me and I caught a blur of Nathan looking dazed in the back. I had to calm down and think fast. I needed to contact someone who had connections, who knew from the inside how the Portuguese justice system worked, and in my turmoil I realised I already had the meeting set up. Eduardo Walde. He was our best chance, and it would be easier to explain face-to-face. If necessary, he would be able to call his old friend, the political candidate.

I put my phone in my bag and got back behind the wheel. If the toll card didn't work, to hell with it, let them fine me. But it did. I slipped onto the motorway and headed north, foot down on the accelerator as hard as I dared.

At a service station I stopped to check how I was going to get to the northern bank of the Tagus estuary and the Padrão dos Descobrimentos, the Monument of the Discoveries. I found a guidebook in English and bought it and a bottle of cold water and some chocolate, which I ate quickly in the car as I flipped the pages.

The monument was across the river from the Jerónimos Monastery, I skim-read. There was a photo of the three-sailed ship's prow in stone, frozen in the act of setting out to explore new worlds, the nation's famed explorers joined by mapmakers and monks and cosmographers among the figures scanning the horizon. It could be reached via an underpass from the monastery gardens, though I imagined the river would be wide there. That could be a backup plan, but only if I couldn't park any closer.

I decided to make for the Avenida Brasilia. From the picture in the guidebook there was a small marina to the left with what looked like a car park. I snapped the guidebook shut and restarted the engine. Not too far now: the A2 motorway crossed the Tagus on the Ponte 25 de Abril bridge, then I needed to take the first exit that allowed me access to the road along the northern embankment.

Not far from the monument, I spotted an Italian restaurant with a car park. I pulled in feeling slightly sweaty and infinitely relieved. Traffic on the main road roared in my ears. I took a sip of water and let myself lean back in my seat. I closed my eyes, hoping I had done the right thing. It was twenty minutes before Eduardo Walde was due.

With ten minutes to go I got out and locked the car, and walked towards the dark blue river. As I drew nearer, the pavement became a mosaic depicting a giant compass with charts of the routes taken by the adventurous Portuguese in the fifteenth and sixteenth centuries. Symmetrical black and white waves rippled across the cobbles, the same motif as in Faro of the sea creeping over the city. I waded across to the monument.

It was a spectacular piece of art: a ship's prow jutting over the water, stone wind in swelling stone sails, soaring upwards to a viewing platform. On board, rising behind the lead figure of Prince Henry the Navigator, the dream crew was depicted in intricate stone carvings. A welcome gust of fresh cool air from the west brought a seagull in to perch cheekily on the Navigator's hat.

Multicoloured flags fluttered around the base of the white stone sculpture. It was hard not to stare at any men who arrived on their own. I tried to imagine Alva Barton—or Esta Hartford, rather—standing on this very spot; tried to picture flying boats landing on the estuary, and could not. I was too wound up, questioning my judgement in coming to Lisbon when I should have followed Nathan and the police back to Faro.

My mobile rang. The name flashed up: Eduardo Walde.

"Are you the young woman in the black and white dress?" asked the voice.

I looked around cautiously, feeling wrong-footed. Time had moved on from the days when strangers had to make awkward personal approaches. Several men had phones pressed to an ear. Most were talking rapidly. Only one was not moving, holding up a hand in general greeting.

"I see you," I said.

We walked towards each other.

He was a man with a presence. You couldn't help but notice his height; he must have been six three at least. He moved with a sense of purpose. The jacket was held over the shoulder with a hooked finger. A beautifully laundered white shirt and pressed casual trousers held up by a leather belt. Thick pepper-and-salt hair. A smooth and tanned face with no deep creases spoke of good genes as well as money.

We shook hands. His eyes were pale blue, with grey flecks.

"You came alone?" he asked. His accent was a light American.

I nodded, wondering whether he had, too.

"I thought there would be two of you."

"Senhor Palhares called you, didn't he?"

"He did."

It was a stilted exchange. We were testing each other.

"Shall we walk?" he said, establishing who was in charge. "I can't spare too much time out of the office at present, so I intend to take my exercise while you tell me why you needed to see me."

He must have been in his sixties, but I could well believe that exercise was important to him. Eduardo Walde had the air of a keen golfer or sailor, a man who enjoyed healthy outdoor pursuits and could afford to indulge in the best when he was not enjoying success in other spheres. He set off briskly along the river walk, and I fell in with his pace.

I had rehearsed how to begin.

"Senhor Walde . . . as you know, I was one of the visitors who found the body of Ian Rylands. I may have some new information about the case but before I go on, I want to ask you if you believe in pure coincidence."

He didn't miss a beat as he strode forward. "Coincidences happen."

"And then another coincidence—and another?" I pressed on without waiting for a reply. "You see, beyond the first one, I don't. I start to ask questions."

"Go on."

"I came here to ask you about some of them, but first I want to tell you something in good faith." I turned to watch his reaction. "I met Ian Rylands before my friend and I found him in the villa. About two weeks before. He told me about Esta Hartford's book and he gave me a copy to read."

Walde stopped and we faced each other. "You're talking about *The Alliance*?" His tone was still neutral.

"Yes."

"And that is your strange coincidence?"

"It's the first one," I said. "Ian Rylands told me you were Esta Hartford's son and that the book is essentially a true story. It was because I recognised his family name in it that I spoke to Nuno Palhares in Faro, and he confirmed it."

"I'm not sure where this is leading."

"Senhor Walde, did you know Ian Rylands—or know of him, at least, before he was murdered?"

A breeze ran over the estuary, making crepe of the surface. "I understand that you are a journalist, Miss Millard. Tell me, will this conversation appear as an insider's account of the crime for a newspaper?"

"No, that's absolutely not the reason I'm here. I give you my word. I need your help," I said. "Urgently. Not for myself, but for Nathan—I mean, Josh, the friend who was with me that night. He's been arrested. That's why he's not here."

A long pause.

"I knew of Ian Rylands," he said at last. "But I never met him."

"But he tried to speak to you?"

"A few times."

"About the book?"

"It seemed to be some kind of obsession with him. I saw the articles he was putting online for his expat association. But there was nothing to gain by getting involved with him. I had to think of the Horta das Rochas image. It was better to leave it."

"Did he ever let you know that he had any kind of information that went beyond the book?"

"What do you mean?"

"When I came into contact with Ian Rylands—I was the one who initiated our meeting by calling the Anglo-Algarve Association—it was because I had been asked . . . to find out about the seedy side of Vale Navio." I kept it vague, carefully fixing on his pale blue eyes, trying to show my sincerity as well as search for reciprocity. "When we met, we ended up talking about circumstantial evidence that linked . . . to cases of child abduction, going back many years."

He blinked first.

"I have very little to go on here," I went on, pressing home my tiny advantage, "but both Rylands—and Nuno Palhares, when I found him—hinted that your family knew something about this."

"Be very careful what you say . . ."

"There is a very serious reason I ask."

I could feel him evaluating whether or not he could trust me, and whether any information he shared would suit his purposes. It didn't occur to me—at least not for longer than a few rapid heartbeats—that I might not be able to trust him.

He started to walk again, moving briskly.

"And the biggest coincidence of all," I said as I plunged on after him, "that now seems to be nothing of the kind, is that my friend Nathan—that's what he's been calling himself since he's been here, not Josh Harris—should be the one to find Ian Rylands at Horta das Rochas, of all places."

"Where is this leading . . . what do you want from me, Miss Millard?"

I took a deep breath. "Have you seen a photograph of Nathan?"

"What?"

"Some of the reports named us. Maybe the newspapers managed to find a picture, I don't know. I didn't see them."

"I don't recall seeing any pictures of either of you. As far as I am aware you were witnesses not suspects. Unless you are about to tell me differently."

I was in free fall. It was all coming out in a rush of instinct. "I may regret doing this. And I may be wrong. But please would you look at this."

I reached into my bag for my phone. I swiped the screen and held out a photo of Nathan at the beach on the Ilha Deserta. Part of me felt as if I might have lost my mind.

"Nice-looking young man. I can see why you want to save him."

"What else do you see, Senhor? Or do you honestly see nothing?"

He took the phone and assessed it.

"Nathan Emberlin," I said. "Adopted aged two, rubber stamped by a barely legal agency in Malaga in 1992. Brought up in London by known associates of a man called Terry Jackson, an old friend of the family. Terry Jackson was the man Nathan came to meet at Horta das Rochas. Who left a message telling him to go to Villa Eleven, where he found Ian Rylands dead."

"He was two years old in 1992?"

"Correct."

There was a long silence, then, "Nathan Emberlin. That is his name?"

"The name on his adoption papers, yes."

"He was coming here with you, today?"

"Until we were pulled over at the motorway toll-booth leaving Faro. Nathan was arrested."

"Show me another photo."

I found one taken at O Castelo that did justice to his smile.

"Where is he now?"

"Faro police headquarters, I assume. The police said they wanted to interview him again about Ian Rylands' death. But if they say they have evidence, they are lying."

"Did they declare him *arguido*?"

"Not in front of me. But maybe when they had him pinned down in the car." I felt a jolt of fear. *Arguido* was a word known to anyone who had followed the Tilly Stern child abduction case. It meant "a formal suspect," and it had been applied by the Portuguese investigating authorities to the little girl's distraught parents. If Nathan was now an *arguido* in the Rylands case, he needed help even more urgently.

"Okay . . . we don't know that yet. The first thing he needs is a lawyer."

Nothing had been said, but I could tell that everything had changed.

We took Eduardo Walde's car, a chauffeur-driven Mercedes, into the centre of town. He called someone on his mobile. The brief conversation sounded clipped. From the comfort of the limousine, the red suspension bridge over the Tagus loomed, giving a sense of grandeur to the estuary, then we turned away and left it behind.

"This is the Lapa district," said Walde. "Quiet and safe, near the foreign embassies."

Perhaps I should have been more wary of getting into his car. I knew nothing about him beyond what I had read and assumed. This was no small, barely consequential risk I was taking. This was a serious gamble. If I had called it wrong, the consequences could be disastrous, not only for me but for Nathan, too.

We passed several imposing properties with flags and ornate polished plaques before the Mercedes pulled up outside a modest yellow building with green shutters. It had a plain, modern façade with a Juliet balcony on the upper storey. The only other people in the immediate vicinity were the guards standing outside the diplomatic missions.

The chauffeur opened the car doors and Walde led me inside. He put his head round the door to an office, and said something to the person inside, then we followed a passage to a room with the air of a gentleman's library. "Take a seat," he told me. "This is where I work when I'm in town. We'll have a coffee and then my lawyer will join us."

Walde came round the desk and stood in front of the leather chair where he had placed me. I shifted uneasily. "Nathan Emberlin," he said. "Did it occur to you it was a strange name?"

"I didn't think so . . . at first."

"A name with a message, no?"

"I worked out that it was a false name."

"But not what it meant?"

I could hear the echo of Ian Rylands saying, "I know the significance of the name Emberlin. The question is, do you?"—his words carried away with the squeal of gulls on the wind.

Walde went over to one of the bookshelves and ran a finger across a line of office files. "Nathan—from the root word meaning born. Emberlin—a German name. Berlin."

"What is the importance of the name?"

"I will tell you, but first I want you to tell me as much as you know about the man you call Nathan Emberlin."

As succinctly as I could, forcing myself to keep my voice even, I explained how Nathan had come to confide in me, how he had arrived on the Algarve looking for answers to what he had found in his adoptive mother's possessions. How from the moment he started asking about Terry Jackson, one incident had led to another.

"And you believe what he says."

"At first—to be honest—no, I didn't. Not really. It seemed like an incredible story. Perhaps one that he wanted to believe. But as I got to know him better, and became more involved in the story myself . . . it began to seem more plausible," I concluded carefully.

Noises in the passage gave way to footsteps. A slight man, a blade of grass next to Eduardo's solidity, entered the room. The two greeted each other as old friends. "This is Fausto Ribeiro. Our family lawyer."

He and I shook hands and exchanged guarded looks.

"We are going to speak in English," said Eduardo. "I don't want any misunderstandings among us. First, I want you to tell Fausto, slowly and clearly, what you have just told me."

I did so, looking from one to the other, trying to read their expressions. As was only to be expected, the lawyer returned the favour with interest, and then bent his head to write in a notebook. I understood, of course I did. They were right to be cynical. For all they knew this could all be a cruel and elaborate ruse designed to extract money, or to cause more pain.

"Have you ever heard of Terry Jackson?" I asked, looking from one to the other.

The pause gave it away.

"Jackson was a small-time fixer used as a middle man by . . . certain elements in Albufeira," said Ribeiro.

"Would you consider him dangerous?"

"Not really."

"Are you sure?"

Walde cleared his throat. "What exactly do you know about Terry Jackson?"

"Only what I have already told you. He was involved in the deal that saw Nathan—let's call him Nathan—adopted by the Harris family in South London. Jackson may or may not have been involved in the abduction of the child. He was certainly the middle man. The boy was delivered to an agency in Malaga and Jackson arranged for friends of his to adopt him. He saw the boy from time to time as he was growing up. The boy knew him as a friend of the family.

"But now Nathan is an adult. His adoptive parents have passed away and he has come looking for Jackson, for an explanation of the adoption papers he has found. Perhaps the papers should have been destroyed long ago—who knows? But Jackson knows that Nathan wants to see him. He even spoke to Nathan—a phone

call, and Nathan is as sure as he can be that it was him—
the day before we went to Horta das Rochas. Nathan
went there expecting to meet him."

I hesitated. "Jackson told him to go to Villa Eleven
and that's when we found Rylands dead."

"I see."

"The police didn't tell you that?"

Eduardo extracted a large white handkerchief and
wiped it over his forehead. "No."

The link kept coming back to Terry Jackson, the one
person Nathan knew. I thought of the sequence of unpleasant events, starting with the attempted bag snatch.
"I think someone has been inside the studio where I've
been staying, and there was a half-arsed attempt to run
me down with a car the other day."

"You are sure? This was deliberate?" asked Eduardo.

"Who can tell? Now I'm wondering, is Terry Jackson well-connected enough to have police contacts who
could have set Nathan up?"

"Jackson keeps a very low profile. He used to own
a bar, like a classic expat, though it's gone now. It had
a reputation for trafficking North African immigrants,
though nothing was ever proved, of course. Money
laundering and fixing behind the scenes for his associates, too. He must have some useful police connections."

Ribeiro asked only one question. "Have you told the police any of this?"

"No. Rylands' warnings about corruption and the way the parents of Tilly Stern were treated made me wary of them."

The two men seemed silently to exchange thoughts. Had I said too much?

"Good," said Eduardo. "Now show Fausto the photographs you showed me."

As I swiped to find them again on my phone, Eduardo went to the far side of the desk and unlocked a drawer. He pulled out a folder, went through it, and removed some of its contents. "Look at this, and tell me what your first reaction is."

It was a colour photo of a lovely young woman with olive skin. The smile, the set of the lips and the shape of the face were disconcertingly familiar.

"Who is she?"

"That is Carolina, my sister. And these," he held out a clutch of photocopies, "are pages from the original manuscript of my mother's book that were not published in the 1954 edition."

PART SIX

Excerpt from *The Alliance* by Esta Hartford, pages excised from the 1954 edition

i

A few careless minutes in a blood-orange sunset, that was all it took to lose a child.

As shadows stretched from the rocks across the sand, the sea and sky merged into shimmering copper and red; it was hard to tell if she was flying above the water, or standing on air. Behind her, the path up led through the rubble of rocks to the garden at Horta das Rochas, to the wildflower meadows and bee orchids.

Alva shouldn't have allowed herself to linger in this dream state, but she treasured these moments of otherworldliness, needed to feel them and give thanks. The accidental nature of being caught behind a certain border at a certain time underpinned Alva's understanding of the world and her life with Klaus. In Portugal, one of the few places in Europe where their relationship could be understood, they had become opportunists—and optimists.

She could smell the eucalyptus and warm resinous pine sap, could taste the juice of the first apricots they had planted. It hadn't always been easy, but they had done it. They had built a life here from nothing, a home and a business. They were good people, the Portuguese. Many of the older generation were quite uneducated. If they had to stop to ask the way, a village elder would have to find a child to read the name of the town as shown on the map. But they were unfailingly kind and courteous, and seemingly unperturbed that they had no part in a world increasingly governed by strange symbols on pages and signs.

The younger generation, who had toiled with them in the early months at Horta das Rochas, had proved loyal as well as hardworking. The old farmhouse was now extended, with twelve large suites and a breakfast room. Corrugated roofs had been replaced by tiles. Another courtyard had been added, with bougainvillea flowing over the walls, orange trees, and flower troughs. Modern iron gates graced the entrance.

She had made a leap of faith, and had been rewarded. One era had slipped over into the next, war gave way to peace, a marriage was lost and a new one gained: a second chance, a different life, the luck of the navigator who beached upon a new continent.

Alva called the children before she turned around. Within a few seconds, she felt a sticky hand on her leg, and glanced down to see her two-year-old daughter gazing out to sea, equally transfixed. She felt another lift to the heart.

"Time to go back," she said.

The boy, older by a year, was over by the rock pool where he lay for hours staring at minute stirrings. It was only a few yards away. Not more than a few steps from where she'd been standing. But he wasn't there now.

"Where's Tico?" she asked, using his Portuguese baby name.

"Gone," said the girl.

"He can't be!" Alva called his name again, starting to run over toward the caves. They both called again. No answer. She had been stupidly oblivious, when she should have felt the prickle of danger.

"Tico!"

"Tico!"

In the beginning, she had used her skills constantly: patience and observation, subtlety and guile. She had needed them, they both had. Vigilance was vital. When had she stopped being vigilant? How could she have forgotten?

They shouted across the beach, but he had vanished.

"Come on, Cara," she said urgently, swooping back to take the girl's hand.

The wind-carved caves were dark and damp. Their voices echoed as they called.

This can't be happening, she thought. He wasn't in the water; she would have seen him, the cove was so small, so private. He couldn't have been taken; they had seen no one else all afternoon. She turned on herself, tearing into her own stupidity and carelessness.

The sunset reddened as she hauled the plump toddler up the cliff path, stumbling in her fear and haste, still calling the boy's name. Shadows twisted in the wind. Up the rocky steps to the garden, across the drift of gold coin daisies, mocking in their gaiety, legs heavy with dread. "Klaus!"

No sign of him either.

"Klaus?"

Was anyone here? The house was drained of life. She spun around in panic, was about to run out into the grounds when she heard a groan. She stood still, trying to listen. In a scullery room off the kitchen, Klaus lay on the floor, clutching his stomach.

"What's happened?" cried Alva. "And where's Tico? Have you seen Tico?"

"The guests—I thought they were guests . . ."

"What?"

Klaus was gasping for breath. He clutched at his chest and stomach.

"Who—what have they done to you?"

"Beat me . . . two of them . . . I didn't recognize at first . . ."

How to tell him she had failed in her most important job, to keep the children safe? She felt sick and scared, as if she, too, had taken a punch to the stomach.

"Go after . . . go to him . . ."

"Where—?"

Neither of them was making any sense.

Klaus hauled himself up on his elbows. "Call Dinis . . . ! We have to stop them. They have Edmundo!"

"Stay with Pappi," cried Alva, pushing Carolina toward him. She ran outside, calling for the groundsman, running in the only logical direction, towards the path leading to the Albufeira road.

Dusk was closing in. Her sandals slipped on the stony track. Past sentinel stalks and seedheads summer-bleached to shades of bone.

"Tico! Dinis!"

Gasping and lurching like a drunkard, she blundered on. What if she was heading in the wrong direction? Where was her boy now? Images shuffled into her consciousness: the inlets cut from the rocks by pounding waves, leaving secret caves and beaches; the sinister holes gouged from the edge of the land where the sea was a white rim of churned foam, waves roaring. The winds were unpredictable. The quick sea could change in an instant, from apparent calm to violent wave patterns crisscrossing and overwhelming the undertow. Not far away was the inlet known as the Cauldron, a deep noisy chasm clawed by the furious sea.

She turned around, called again wildly, and began to haul herself back into a run. Who were these people who had done this? What did they want? Or was it cruelty for sick pleasure?

"Dinis! Are you there?"

But it was her fault, too. She should never have taken her eyes off the children, not even for a minute. She couldn't move fast enough. It was as though she was weighted down. Her son. How she had longed for a child when she was married to Michael, and how the war had denied her the choice. When they left Rome she thought she might be expecting, only to find when they pitched up at the hotel in Paris that she wasn't. The joy, the elation, when her newborn son was placed in her arms, Klaus at her side. She could feel that joy still, pulling up through her body. She could not let this be the terrible, wave-throwing, wind-howling dead end.

"Tico! Dinis!"

Silence, roaring in her ears.

It felt like hours before she heard an answering shout. Dinis emerged slowly from the pines. At first she thought the groundsman was alone; but as he came closer she saw that he had the boy in his arms. He carried him so tenderly that Alva understood immediately. A mother knew. Her son was no longer alive.

She fell forward, feeling her face contort.

"He was left by the gate . . . like a foundling child . . ." said Dinis. He was a large man, a woodcutter in a fairy tale. His lilting Portuguese should have reassured her, but it could not.

Hands shaking, Alva scrabbled to touch her son, to take him in her own arms. He was still warm. "Tico! My Tico!"

Then, the miracle. The boy stirred. He was wriggling against her. She could hardly see him in the matte darkness but she could feel the life of him.

"We have to tell the police." Alva still shook. Edmundo, elfin face ribbed with tears, clung to her.

Klaus seemed too still. "We carry on as normal. We have to."

She loved him for his steadiness and stubborn practicality, but this was too much. "We must tell the police what's happened."

"There's no point."

"What do you mean, no point? What happened today?"

Klaus seemed diminished. "They have found us."

"Who have?"

"This was a warning."

"Who?"

"It was only a matter of time."

Alva tried to console him. "They've gone now."

"Dinis is sure?"

"He saw them off with his pitchfork."

Klaus gave a short, savage laugh. "That won't protect us."

"What is this?"

He looked at her steadily, as if judging how much to say. "We thought it was, but the war is not yet over."

He had been so practical, so resourceful. So lonely in his growing fear, wanting to protect her. It was a shock to discover he had kept this to himself. The menace was not over; it lurked not in shadows, but in the sunshine. It was the mark of the man that he took it so quietly, covering his despair with hard work and faith that the world allowed for justice.

With Dinis standing watch over the children, they went out into the newly fallen night. The spiky artichoke thistles scratched her bare arm. Goat bells sang with the waves below but the sounds belonged to a simpler time. Klaus looked anemic against the yellow walls and abundant pink oleander.

"Do you remember you were once approached by a man outside the casino in Estoril who claimed to be a Swiss businessman?"

She opened her mouth to speak.

He touched her shoulder gently. "Don't say anything. You know I was watching you, even then."

Sweat trickled unpleasantly down her spine. Nothing felt solid anymore.

"His name was Manfred Himmelreich. He was an intelligence staff member of the German Embassy."

"It was the night before you approached me on the esplanade while Michael slept off his hangover," she said, remembering her fury.

"I despised Himmelreich," said Klaus. "His trafficking of black market goods back to Germany, his cut of every transaction. The dislike was mutual, I need hardly say. When I had to leave Lisbon in a hurry, Himmelreich already suspected I knew more than I claimed about how the Nazi black market buying operation went wrong in Faro. He sent one of his associates, a man called Axel Emberlin, to hunt me down there in 1944. I shot him dead."

He paused, as if waiting for her reaction. She said nothing.

"If I hadn't, I would have been dead myself."

"I understand."

Klaus pulled himself up taller. "It turned out Himmelreich was keeping it all in the family. Emberlin was a cousin. Equally vicious. The officer sent from Berlin to investigate Emberlin's death was Gerd, Himmelreich's younger brother. Each of them fanatical Nazis, well aware of the advantages of being in Portugal with the war turning against the Nazis.

"By 1944 the Germans were transferring all the assets they could to their embassies in neutral countries: looted gold, stolen art, securities, gems. Manfred Himmelreich has access to the deposits in Lisbon banks that need to be well hidden. They managed that, all right. It's quite a family business. They are very clever, Himmelreich and his brother, though they never managed to prove I was responsible for Emberlin's demise.

"Both brothers will escape trial for war crimes as Salazar continually blocks negotiations with the Allies who demand that Nazis in Portugal be returned to them. Hundreds of Nazis remain free to go about their everyday lives in Portugal."

"But what has any of this to do with what happened today?" asked Alva.

Klaus considered, then seemed to overcome some reluctance. "Even before the war ended, the Allies' military intelligence warned it was possible that, with the large amounts of assets available to these Germans, there was a danger they would attempt to keep the objectives of the Third Reich alive. They also seemed to have the protection of Portuguese sympathizers and the State's secret police. But nothing was done. They called themselves the 'Iron Nazis' and the Himmelreich brothers became leading members. They made what they termed the Lisbon Pact to remain loyal to one another and the wider objective of rebuilding German power in Europe. It would be achieved not by military means, but economically, using German assets of dubious origin. Much of it was looted from occupied countries, from national banks and businesses as well as property seized from the Jews. They used it to build up their business in Portugal as well as subvert trade and local politics. During the war they controlled the supply of black market goods out of Portugal and into

Germany; afterwards, they subverted ordinary controls of trade across borders.

"Manfred and Gerd were so rich they took up permanent residence in the Hotel Métropole, from where they started buying up businesses, many of those with export potential. It was only a matter of time before they turned to the travel industry, especially on the undeveloped Algarve coast. Three hundred days of sun a year to be exploited."

"And now they've found us."

She waited for him to say something but he remained silent. "Are they just bullies? Will they go away if we don't react?" Their boy was safe. The relief made Alva believe anything was possible.

"And we live every day wondering what they will try next?"

"There's nothing we can offer them. That's what we tell them."

Klaus shook his head. "They are ruthless, believe me: rich in assets; bankrupt of morals. But that is what has made the Himmelreichs so powerful. This was not a serious attempt to take our Tico. This was a threat. Nothing more or less. A threat to show what they could do if they wanted. To take what we value most. Believe me, I know the way their minds work."

She wasn't going to argue.

The world outside their carefully idealized landscape was still rotten. In her happiness, she had allowed herself to forget that life could be tawdry and violent.

"Is it money they want?"

"There's always that. But no, I don't think that's what they want most of all."

"What then?"

"They want me, as a German, to accept the Lisbon Pact. To be part of it. To pay their tariffs and accept their trade rules. That's what they call it. We would say blackmail."

"Buying a quiet life."

"Maybe."

Silence.

"So they have been in contact with you—before today?"

"Yes."

A breeze brushed her skin, soft as chiffon, and it seemed to mock her. She would not berate him, not now. "You don't play by their rules. You never have."

"Exactly."

"So what do we do?"

"We don't do anything," he said. "You must leave this to me." As if an unseen chain of command still existed, though there was no other side to thank and reward Klaus now, no one to call on for help.

Dried blood. That was the shade of the rocks at daybreak. After a sleepless night, Alva stood, feeling disembodied, at the top of the cliff path. The tide was looking for the best angle of attack. The boulders in the sea were pockmarked islands, prized from gaping wounds in the cliff. Nothing was stable. Not the sand displaced by crabs and insects and the waves. Not the sea's weave worked and reworked by the wind. Not the ever-fluctuating dark shapes beneath the surface, the sunken cities of stones and sea grass.

She shivered. The children were safe. Klaus was safe. She tried to reassure herself. Although she had risen innumerable times in the night to creep along the corridor for confirmation, it had been impossible to set her mind at rest.

It took her awhile to decide what she was going to do.

Her passport was about to expire. The trip to Lisbon to renew it had already been discussed. She and Klaus had agreed she would go on her own, that there was no need for him to leave the hotel. Now it was clear that one of them had to be with the children at all times. She persuaded him, with the greatest difficulty, to allow her to go as planned.

At the United States Embassy in Lisbon the consular official was an enthusiastic young man with a feeble mustache. If it had been grown to lend gravitas befitting his position, it had only the effect of underlining his youth. Alva's was the first appointment of the day, and he seemed a little bleary, still trying to reconcile the administrative demands of the U.S. government with Iberian hours. After the papers and headshot photographs were presented, taken, and signed, Alva asked what protection was afforded to American citizens in Portugal.

"Depends what you do, lady."

"I mean, if a U.S. citizen was threatened."

"This embassy is considered to be the United States. Our territory. There is no one can harm you here. Does that help?"

"I guess so."

"Come back at the end of the day. Your new passport should be ready for you then."

"One more thing . . ."

"Yes, ma'am?"

"Do the foreign correspondents still meet at the Café Eva?"

It obviously didn't mean anything to him. "You could go see."

Alva thought about asking at the British Embassy for Ronald Bagshaw, but quickly discounted that. He wouldn't be there now. No one she used to know was still here.

The Café Eva was unchanged, except for the clientele. The ghosts of Michael, Frank Ellis, and Blake Curnow lingered in a smoke-filled corner, but she walked on by without regret, only a passing wonder at the person she used to be.

She had been so sure that she could rely on nothing but her own guile that she had booked a hairdressing appointment at the salon at the Hotel Métropole for the latest short cut with permanent wave. The style would flatter her, she thought, and hint that she was no docile country wife. On the way to the salon, she went into a dress shop and spent some money she had saved on a midnight blue creation à la mode with a wide flowing skirt.

She emerged from the salon newly shorn, unused to the air on her neck, and having successfully achieved the real aim of her visit. It was the same the world over: hairdressers loved to gossip. She now knew that Manfred Himmelreich did indeed maintain a suite at the hotel, and that the hairdressing bills of several women had been charged to his account. In the ladies' restroom, she changed into her new dress and applied a little eyeliner and lipstick. Now she was confident she looked the part.

Alva crossed the hotel foyer to the reception desk. Once again she was ambushed by the past, as she remembered standing, waiting nervously, in this very spot, the day she arrived in the city with Michael. She was stronger now, in every way, she told herself sternly.

"I should like to leave a message for one of your guests, Herr Manfred Himmelreich." She handed over a sealed envelope to the concièrge. "Will you see that he gets it as soon as possible, please?"

A courteous nod.

She made her exit conscious of his eyes on her. "I am an American citizen in a neutral country; I have nothing to fear," she repeated to herself as she slowed her pace along the Praça Dom Pedro IV.

An hour and a half later, having allowed ample time for her message to be delivered, she entered the neighborhood fish restaurant down by the waterside where she and Michael had once regularly sat in the garden. It was the only place she could think of where she would feel safe, and she hoped it hadn't changed too much in a decade.

First impressions were that it had not. She glanced around. Lunchtime service was almost over, and customers were drinking coffee or squeezing out the last drops of wine in carafes. She told the waiter she was expecting a guest and was shown to a table for two.

Now all she could do was wait. According to the chatty coiffeuse, Himmelreich was a large man with a several chins; the inference being that ready cash rather than physical charms provided the attraction for the women he sent to be crimped and permed. His clothes would be expensive, and she should expect a cigar clamped in his teeth.

The only possibility was a man of about sixty who slid a lascivious look over her. She had the impression that Himmelreich was younger, but this man was alone at his table, raising a thin cigar to slack fleshy lips. Alva watched discreetly. After about five minutes, he was joined by another man, younger, with a pencil mustache. This one took off a baggy, belted raincoat, splashed with mud (the weather was fine; where had he been?). Both looked her way and then away again.

Minutes passed. Alva waved away the waiter apologetically, saying she would wait until her friend arrived, then thought better of it and ordered a glass of watered wine. The reality of what she had done was beginning to bite. She took a deep breath. She would be pleasant and she would stand her ground and say what she wanted to say to this man. Horta das Rochas was an independent business. The war was over. The Nazis had been defeated. She was an American and he could do nothing to her that would not see him pay a worse price himself. You had to stand up to bullies, that was the only way.

Again she found herself thinking of Michael, that she could almost hear him saying it. Where was he now? She hoped he was happy. She had a lot to thank him for, one way and another. It turned out after the divorce that her family hadn't thought much of Michael. They were even less well-disposed to an ex–German officer, as it turned out, and resistant to any explanation she could offer. She still wrote her parents, trying to explain what it was to know true contentment. Sometimes she heard back, sometimes not.

"Frau Mayer?"

The man wore a suit that hung admirably well over an obese body. He narrowed his eyes; the lenses of his round glasses were smeared, so that he seemed to squint from behind smutty portholes. From the way he mopped sweat from his brow and chins, it was evident that he was acutely uncomfortable in the heat.

"Herr Himmelreich. Thank you for coming," she said pleasantly. "I believe we have met before. Do sit down."

Alva wondered if she could discern any resemblance to the man who spoke to her in the garden at Estoril now that he had run to fat, his features swollen by too many fish-and-potato dishes served in oil. She could not.

He clicked his fingers at the waiter and asked for French brandy, speaking in Portuguese with a pronounced German accent. He took the chair opposite her, overflowing the seat. So far he had not spoken to her beyond ascertaining her identity. She felt the air deaden around him, now that it was too late to back away.

"I assume you know why I have asked to meet with you," said Alva.

"I can guess—from your name. I do not know you." He looked around. He was still sweating profusely. "I must say, I'm surprised you know this place."

"I used to come here during the war."

"I see."

"I want to explain to you in person why I am not intimidated by you and your associates, Herr Himmelreich."

Alva watched closely as he scanned the room. Considering the importance of this conversation, it was highly irritating not to have his full attention. Was it possible he was nervous? She waited for him to turn back to her and said nothing more as another woman came into the restaurant on her own and was shown to a table. A diamond brooch winked from her lapel, and she wore a wide-brimmed hat low on her brow. Himmelreich was still staring as she took off the hat to reveal half-moon eyebrows drawn by pencil.

"The reason you cannot intimidate me is—"

He held up a chubby finger. "Excuse me."

"I would like you to hear me out, please."

But he had pulled himself upright, with some effort. "Just one moment."

Alva sat back in her seat. Her heart was beating uncomfortably fast with the effort of maintaining the veneer of calmness and confidence that she had decided was crucial. A person had to stand up for what they knew was right. If they hadn't learned that from the sacrifices of war, they hadn't learned anything.

Himmelreich jerked his unwieldy belly between the tables and out the entrance. Through the window she could see him out on the street, jabbing his finger at a young man. From side on, he was balder than she thought, with a large bruise above one ear. Was this shambling wreck truly a cruel opportunist who had evaded war crimes?

The waiter brought her glass of watered wine. Alva smiled; he did not. As he bent down to place it on the table, he leaned in and spoke directly into the ear. "Go now. Get out. Quickly." At least she thought that was what he was saying. Then, in a normal voice, pointing, "Yes, Senhora, the toilet is in the back."

She hesitated.

"It's all right, someone will show you."

Alva picked up her bag and rose. She was halfway to the kitchen when unseen arms grabbed her and she stumbled forward as she was dragged into a side room. Her squeak of protest was capped by a hand over her mouth. The door closed on her.

From the main room came shouting, then a woman screamed. Several gunshots were followed by the sound of boots on the wooden floor. The crash of falling furniture. Alva waited, listening, her back rigid against the wall of the tiny room. She could hear a man's voice, pleading, in Portuguese. Cutlery clattered onto a hard surface. Dishes smashed and the noise continued to ring, as if a plate was spinning on the hardwood floor. Then the sounds died away, and all she could hear was her own breathing. She didn't dare emerge.

Minutes passed.

A soft knock on the door. "Senhora? It is OK."

Alva stepped out unsteadily. "What happened?"

"Don't look," the waiter was saying. "You must not look."

"But I—oh—"

She saw the blood on the tablecloth first, scarlet poppies across the white linen. Then she saw the woman: the woman with the painted half-moon eyebrows who had caught Himmelreich's attention. She was slumped sideways over the banquette where she had been sitting. A corsage of blood flowered on her chest.

"What's happened? Who is she?" asked Alva, her voice shaky.

"Best not to ask."

A man in a pinstripe suit materialized at her side. His accent was unmistakably British. "I'd get out of here if I were you."

He reminded her of Ronald Bagshaw, though it wasn't him. This Englishman had a pointed nose and a sharp parting, but the same air of bemused detachment. Lord only knew what he was doing there.

"But—"

"The police will be here any minute, and you won't want to get caught up."

She hardly had time to register anything more about the man before he propelled her outside onto the street.

There was no sign of Himmelreich, nor the man she had seen him speaking to. "Do you know a man named Himmelreich?"

He reassessed her. She could see him calculating. "You should count yourself lucky. Very lucky indeed."

"What do you mean?"

"That could have been you."

"How—why do you say that?"

"A woman on her own, easily mistaken if the gunman doesn't know precisely what his intended victim looks like."

"But—"

"Stop asking questions and go now, while you can."

"Who are you?"

A crowd was gathering, and she was jostled. When she looked back, the man had gone. Alva pushed her way through, feeling more frightened now that the immediate danger had passed. She used every scrap of her strength to walk back toward the center of town, looking for a taxi cab. Was it really possible that she could have been the intended victim? That she had recklessly put herself in the line of fire, because the Himmelreichs were just as ruthless as Klaus had said? Who had saved her—the waiter, the British man, or someone else who remained in the shadows? Part of her didn't want to know the answer.

She finally found a cab, gave the name of the modest business hotel where she had stayed the previous night and left her overnight bag, and sat rigidly upright in the deep seat, watching the familiar landmarks slide by.

How much worse had she made the situation? She had assumed this was a fair fight. She found herself mentally overlaying the grand Lisbon avenue with the cathedral square in Faro. She and Klaus hadn't long bought Horta das Rochas when they took a trip along the coast to Faro to see his friends. Palhares had shown them how to read the stories told by the cathedral's *azulejos*, tales of history and faith, then they climbed up a narrow winding stairway to the *miradouro*, the bell tower, and gazed out over the grassy marshes and mud flats.

"For centuries few people have dared to live out there on these sandy uncertainties," said Klaus. "But the fisherman will take the risk. The sand moves. The shore creeps to the east even as his feet seem to be standing firm. But all he wants is a house with a bamboo ceiling, a reliable boat, his tools, and the great wide sea full of fish."

"You are an idealist."

"Does that appeal to you?"

"Yes."

"Then you are a free spirit, Alva. I like that."

She had laughed. "My father used to call me a free spirit, but you know something? I wasn't. Not really. I acted the part because it was expected, but I was always a worrier, though I took pains to disguise it because worriers never seemed like too much fun. But don't you worry. I promise I will never give you cause to worry."

A few hours later, she collected her new passport from the embassy, and took the train south.

PART SEVEN
Lisbon—September 2014

i

The silver Mercedes accelerated. Eduardo Walde and I were in the back, Ribeiro in the passenger seat. As we headed for the motorway and Faro, I wondered what I was going to do about the rental car parked at the Italian restaurant, but I put it out of my mind.

"I gather that you recently reissued your mother's book," I said.

"I did."

"Were the excised pages included?"

"Yes, though not in quite that form."

I hesitated, unsure whether I was ready to believe whatever he was going to tell me. "What Esta wrote about the other Germans who stayed on here—was any of that actually true, or was it just a dramatic twist to her story?"

Eduardo took his time, then looked me in the eye. "It was true. Many of the ex-Nazis who spent the war in Lisbon and Estoril escaped to South America to avoid the trials in Nuremberg. Others remained, becoming more confident as the British and Americans failed to get them repatriated."

"And the Lisbon Pact?"

"There were always rumours that the so-called Iron Nazis remained in Portugal to keep their ideology alive. But Karl and Esta wanted nothing to do with these people. They chose to live in the south, where life is simpler. Soon they have children: me and my sister Carolina. But still the difficulty doesn't entirely go away. The problem is, people like the Himmelreichs have access to great wealth in a very poor country. The money makes it easy for them to influence the way business is done. They change the rules. They control trade."

He was watching for my reaction.

"Maybe you should have spoken to Ian Rylands after all," I said.

"Maybe that is precisely why I didn't."

I was uneasy, yet fascinated at the same time. "Why did you republish it?"

Walde exhaled, and looked away. "Because nothing has changed."

I waited for him to explain further but he did not.

"If the story is true, was it you—the boy who was snatched from the beach?"

"That's what my mother told me, when . . ." He stopped. "I can't remember it happening."

"And her confrontation with Himmelreich?"

"She was a brave woman. She kept that to herself for years afterwards."

"What about the man who warned her off, after the shooting at the restaurant?"

"Who knows? Obviously, as in many places in the decades after the war, there were quiet watchers who never left."

"So why did Esta write the book, then? Because she was very brave, or because she was scared?"

"A little of both, maybe. Maybe she just wanted their position on record, that her husband was no Nazi. In the end, even when it was published by a small New York imprint, hardly anyone bought it, or even knew about it. It was too soon after the war. No one wanted to read books about it. Everyone had their own story, and too much was raw."

"But now they do." I thought of the demonstrations in Faro, the fiercely fought local elections and the way everyone was looking to blame others. I wondered what Walde's motives were in publishing the unexpurgated version in Portuguese.

"The original manuscript of *The Alliance* was in a safe-deposit box in a Lisbon bank. 'If I should die in suspicious circumstances,' my mother had written, in her handwriting, not typewritten, on the papers. I found it about five years ago, realised parts of this manuscript had never seen the light of day. We must assume that she cut them on the grounds of personal safety or perhaps the publishing house would not take the risk of printing them."

"There are all kinds of reasons why it would have been hard to publish. But you included it in your edition?"

"A carefully edited version, as I said. The name Himmelreich doesn't feature."

"That was a real name?"

"Yes."

"What happened after the end of the book?"

He paused before responding. "Life was complicated. Karl and Esta stayed in Portugal because this is a country that did not judge their relationship. They waited a long time for her divorce. The Salazar dictatorship was still in place. The press was censored, and the bulk of the rural populace was still illiterate in any case. The ordinary people of Portugal were poor, yet—thanks to the economist Salazar, the country had made a very impressive profit from the war. Portugal's gold reserves had increased tenfold. There was controversy about Portugal's Nazi gold but Salazar argued that it was legitimate payment. The dispute would never really be resolved."

We had reached the red suspension bridge over the river I had crossed earlier.

"Until 1974—April twenty-fifth—this was known as the Salazar bridge."

"The date of the revolution?"

"The Carnation Revolution. The popular overthrow of Salazar's Estado Novo—his authoritarian New State," said Walde. "The military sent to restore order put flowers in the barrels of their weapons to show they would not fire. It was wonderful."

We sat in silence for a few moments.

"But in the south, Karl and Esta worked hard," I prompted. "Why did they choose the hotel trade?"

"When he graduated from university, my father was offered a position with a National Socialist organisation named Kraft Durch Freude—strength through joy. It was known as KdF. If one thinks of a Nazi organisation, one automatically assumes it will be very unpleasant, but such was not the case with this one. It was intended to provide leisure activities and travel for ordinary German workers, especially those who had never previously had the opportunity—or the means—to go abroad. Under the system, the workers had a right to paid holidays and a certain amount of time for leisure each year, even the temporary and other casual workers. In its way, it was most enlightened. Egalitarian, too: the berths on the cruise ships were allocated by ballot despite the fact that all classes were on board.

"Before the war, the KdF had a fleet of ships and river cruisers, and the trips it offered were easily affordable by even the lowliest factory worker. The worst one could say is that as its ultimate aim was to keep the workforce in good health and spirits, it was contributing to the grand project. Of course there was an element of propaganda . . . not only were the workers grateful, but it broadcast a clear message of confident success to other countries.

"Millions of people took the opportunity it offered, and before the war it was the largest tourism industry in the world. The KdF built an enormous spa and hotel complex on the island of Rügen. You might have heard about that."

"Yes, I think I do remember seeing pictures of it once. A television documentary perhaps." In my mind's eye I could see the monolithic ruins, rows of Soviet-style blocks facing the North Sea.

"Then the concept was expanded across Europe, beginning with boat trips around the Baltic Sea, and the coast of Norway. But soon the voyages were more ambitious, to the sunny south. Spain, Italy—and Portugal.

"My father was involved in the planning of the routes before the war. I think he took the job to tread water while he waited to see how the political situation would develop. When war came, not only did he have contacts in other countries but he was also a linguist. He made the perfect intelligence agent."

Sitting in the limousine with Eduardo Walde and his lawyer, I had to assume that the book was not completely disingenuous and that his father really had worked against the Nazi machine. I was uncomfortably aware that I couldn't count on it, though. I couldn't count on anything.

"When the KdF ship the *Wilhelm Gustav* came to Lisbon in 1938, my father was on board. She sailed from Hamburg and went on to Madeira. A lovely ship. Carried fifteen hundred passengers. She even had a Musikhalle—a ballroom with orchestra. She was sunk in the Baltic Sea in 1945 by a Soviet torpedo with more than nine thousand refugees on board, half of them children, while it was evacuating German civilians and officials and military from Poland as the Red Army closed in."

I looked away, involuntarily. Beyond the car window, scrubby, nondescript hills rose and fell away as the smooth carriageway of the A2 unspooled. The powerful engine of the car seemed to float above the tarmac as it covered the kilometres. I would have bet anything that European Union money had built this road. It was a far cry from the journey Esta detailed in the book, of her journey south when the dust and heat made driving unbearable during the hot afternoons. I was covering the whole distance twice in one day.

Eduardo steered the discussion back on track. "My father knew about travel and vacations, how to provide everything in one place—if not on a ship, then on a rocky piece of coastland. The hotel at Horta das Rochas became a successful business. Other resort developments on the Algarve coast copied their model. But it was not, as my parents hoped, a world away from postwar politics. The threat from the Himmelreichs seemed to recede, but where there is big money, big crime follows. Bribery for building contracts. Blackmail of officials. Timeshare scandals."

"Organised crime," I said, thinking of Vale Navio.

"The trouble is," Eduardo went on, "that those who shape the world have a vested interest in pretending that parts of the same story can be kept separate. Nothing is ever completely separate, Joanna."

In the use of my name, Walde sounded both sad and almost avuncular.

"What exactly are we talking about, Senhor Walde?"

"Call me, Eduardo, for God's sake. If we are talking about this, all formality is over. In more than one unpleasant instance when the chancers and criminals moved in, differences were resolved by violence. More than once, a child was kidnapped and held to ransom.

"But we wanted no part of any get-rich-quick schemes. Why would we want to get involved in time-share scams? We held firm when pressure was put on us. My sister Carolina's Portuguese husband Luiz Vicente went to the police with what we knew about the criminal element infiltrating the leisure developments.

"For his trouble, Luiz was attacked and their child was taken. It all happened in the garden of the family house on the edge of Horta das Rochas, very quickly, one Sunday afternoon. Who takes a child? It's either someone with a problem—a woman, usually, in those cases—or it's someone with a grudge, someone who wants leverage, or someone who wants money. There were reasons it could have been any of those. We waited for a ransom demand, but it never came. Then we had to assume this was more personal than a simple kidnap-and-ransom-demand like the other cases. We could not ignore the warning we had been given many years before. When Luiz died of his injuries two months later, it became a murder case, too."

"I'm so sorry."

"For years, the Himmelreichs had let us be, though one of their companies had expanded into the vacation business, mainly cheap hotels. They tried to undercut us, but they had little understanding of our market. Unfortunately, by then, they were players in the trade organisations who made the rules. Government officials, the planning and tax authorities . . . they could all be persuaded to support the Himmelreichs' business ventures. There was a growing grey area of official-dom controlled by money from organised crime. The pressures on us grew. When we resisted, they proved ruthless."

"You think it was them?"

"We know it was. It was dressed up as part of the timeshare chicanery of the 1980s and early 1990s, but the abduction of Carolina's son was an act of revenge."

"For not joining the Lisbon Pact?" I couldn't keep the incredulity out of my tone.

"No, a dish served much colder than that. This was for the Himmelreichs' cousin, Axel Emberlin." Eduardo watched me carefully. "Perhaps the name was used on your friend's birth certificate as a nasty little reminder, if the paperwork was ever traced, that they knew Karl Walde shot Emberlin in Faro. But it is also proof of the connection. You will note the perpetrators have no fear of what might happen if it is understood. They are too well protected."

It seemed incredible that the story could be true. Maybe part of me hadn't been expecting that.

"My family paid a terrible price. Carolina suffered terribly after the loss of both her child and her husband. She could no longer work. All she could do was look for Rafael."

Rafael. A third name. If he was this boy, Nathan was changing yet again into a different person.

"But the police investigation drew a blank. The authorities, the police, the social workers, they asked the same questions again and again. We could give no different answers. There were no answers. The borders into Spain were not closed quickly enough to check those leaving the country. We knew the perpetrators could have slipped away leaving no trace."

"Did they find out who killed Carolina's husband?"

"No. The police made a few useless arrests, but it was all for show. They got nowhere. The perpetrators had powerful allies."

I wondered whether the same would be true for the Rylands case.

"We were at a dead end," he said.

The word hung awkwardly, but he shrugged. That was what it was. "Thoughts of our boy were with us all the hours in the day and night. Not to know whether he was alive or dead, or how he suffered—it was with us every minute of every day. But there was never an answer."

"And Carolina, now?" I hardly dared ask. "Is she—?"

"She was brave as a lioness. With no proof to the contrary, you must believe that your child might still be alive, that one day they might be found. For months, she kept her dignity while we did whatever we could. We hired private detectives. We befriended the police detectives. We pulled strings, any connections we had. But nothing worked. Then came the suicide attempts."

I could hardly bear to hear it. None of us had proof that this had anything at all to do with Nathan and his improbable story, I told myself. Yet all my instincts were pointing in one direction and it was clear that Eduardo's were, too. Or was that desperation? A stab of anxiety hit me. What if Nathan had been making it all up? Was I an idiot for believing him, and worse, had I inflicted more pain on the Walde family with a cock-and-bull story? I almost didn't want to hear any more.

But then I thought about the time I'd spent with Nathan. His sweet nature and generosity and willingness to trust in strangers could now be seen as extraordinary courage. To have managed to retain those qualities was a mark of the man he had become.

"But this Terry Jackson," Eduardo went on. "When Fausto told you he worked as a fixer for 'certain elements' he was being cautious. Jackson is a known associate of the Himmelreich family."

I was digesting that when Ribeiro's mobile rang.

The lawyer spoke only a few succinct words before ending the call. "Palhares has also been arrested and is at Faro police station."

Walde swore in Portuguese.

It couldn't be another coincidence, surely.

We sped along the soulless autoroute, the driver making easy work of the ground I had covered with less power and comfort only that morning. I had managed what I had set out to do, although I had no real sense of what was going to happen next. If Nathan really was his nephew, and it was obvious that Eduardo had decided that was a possibility, then it followed that he would do all it took to get him released and to speak to him.

"Do you know why Nuno Palhares has been arrested, too?" I asked. "Is it because Nathan was seen speaking to him at the Café Aliança?"

"They are not saying. It might be political, though. They are saying he, too, has links to the murder of Ian Rylands," said Ribeiro.

"They probably spoke in the café, too," I suggested. "Rylands was fascinated by the place."

"I have been told," said Walde, "that in the regional elections, some of the candidates are openly quoting from Esta Hartford's book. One of them is my old friend Nuno Palhares. When it seems Palhares is gaining too much support, especially after he negotiated the reopening of the Café Aliança for political meetings, he is charged with a crime, which of course he did not commit. But do the voters understand that? No, they just think there must be something suspicious about him."

"But Portugal is no third-world country. That kind of electoral manipulation doesn't happen in Europe."

Eduardo made a sceptical face. "If you say so."

By now we were on the outskirts of Faro negotiating the tentacles of the road feeding the airport, heading towards the shabby apartment blocks that rose from heat-baked ground. The Jardim Manuel Bivar, the marina, the gate to the Old Town, all were subtly changed by my view through the window of the Walde limousine. We headed straight to the Polícia Judiciária. The chauffeur dropped us outside the Old Town gateway and we walked up the narrow cobbled Rua Municipio to an unassuming white-rendered building with a green outer door. The Directoria de Faro was announced unobtrusively on a tiled plate to the left of the door.

Ribeiro led the way. "They are expecting us."

I couldn't help but remember the television reports of the Tilly Stern case, the pinched faces of the parents as they were captured walking this same route, entering this doorway to the baying of the press pack gathered outside. We slipped through the entrance heralded only by another burst of low-key ringtone from Ribeiro's mobile.

ii

It was an interminable wait, on hard plastic seating. In the unsettling acoustics of the police headquarters, part cold stone building, part institutional bubble, I fretted away the hours with cups of strong coffee. Would I be interviewed again if the detectives were serious about linking Nathan to Rylands' death? I was left to stew.

It was almost midnight when Walde and Ribeiro reappeared. Both looked drained. They were closely followed by Nuno Palhares, surrounded by a group of furious men, some flinging what sounded like angry recriminations to the officers accompanying them.

I stood up.

"Released without charge," said Walde.

"And Nathan?"

Walde nodded in the direction they had come. I thought he meant that Nathan was still being held, but a few seconds later, he emerged. I didn't stop to think how it would look. I hurled myself at him and he wrapped his arms around me. I closed my eyes, perilously close to tears.

Then there were more arms around the two of us. They seemed to belong to Eduardo Walde.

I had no chance to ask what had transpired between them, as we all made a rapid exit into the narrow cobbled street. Walde, still with an arm around Nathan, began speaking into his phone.

"Carolina," he said urgently. "It's me."

He nodded at me, and strode away to speak privately.

"Are you OK?" I asked Nathan.

"Thanks to you. Come here." He pulled me closer and hugged me again, awkwardly.

"Do you think—has Eduardo spoken to you?" I didn't know where to start.

"He has, he has . . . but how did you do it? I can't believe . . . you are amazing, you know that . . ." He was almost incoherent.

"Shhh, it's all right. There will be plenty of time to explain. Take it easy."

It felt like comforting a child, the child he had once been.

"I told Eduardo I would take a DNA test, but then he showed a ph-photo of her . . . and said he would show me photographs of himself in his early twenties—that I would be astonished to see the likeness . . ."

The relief gave way to a wave of profound exhaustion.

"He said she was in Cascais."

"His sister?" I assumed that was who he meant.

Nathan rubbed his forehead. He did not seem to hear.

Eduardo returned, his face deeply shadowed by the dim light of the streetlamp beside the entrance where we were still waiting, like wreckage caught between rocks.

"We are going to Cascais," he said.

"Now?" asked Nathan.

"Why not? It's only one more sleepless night."

In the car heading north—I assume the chauffeur had rested during the hours we were at the police station—Nathan and I sat in the back with Eduardo. Nathan held my hand tightly. I dropped my head on his shoulder and I think we both slept for a while. A bend in the road brought me round from a vivid dream (a door unlocking and a missed train) not knowing where

I was. For one blissful moment I thought we were curled up in my little studio.

As I struggled to regain consciousness I wondered what Eduardo and his lawyer made of our relationship. Any conclusions they came to were likely to be wrong, unless they had a greater instinctive understanding of him than I did. If they assumed anything from our shy closeness, they made no comment. Whatever it was, that night it was incommunicable to anyone else.

I was blearily awake as we slid into Estoril and along the grand seafront avenue at first light. Sea and sky were the same muted blue-grey.

"Not far now," said Eduardo.

At Cascais, the palms were less majestic than at Estoril, the town smaller and prettier. On the other side of the bay, the light was golden yet we emerged from the car into dusky shadow. Brick steps led up to an imposing house that grew out of a seawall shaggy with wind-blown plants. From an upper storey, an Italianate loggia overlooked the beach.

Eduardo asked Nathan if he was ready. He said he was, though he looked daunted. They ascended the steps, followed by Ribeiro. As Nathan went into the house without a glance back the thought sliced through my sleep-deprived head that this was the moment he ceased to be Nathan, ceased to be Josh Harris, and had the chance to reclaim his identity as Rafael.

I was left with the chauffeur, whose name turned out to be Tiago. I don't think anyone had given a thought to us, which was entirely understandable. If there had been a café open, I would have suggested breakfast but it was still too early. Tiago stretched his legs for a few minutes then got back into the driver's seat, miming that he intended to snatch some sleep while he was parked. He had earned his rest, so I left him to it and wandered down to the beach.

Waves curled onto coarse sand that granulated the froth. It looked like crystallised ginger. I watched for a while, hoping to calm myself, then turned to stare up at the house, noting how many of the windows were shuttered, and tried to guess how the story was reaching its climax within.

How would, or could, the severed ties be rejoined? Was it possible Carolina would recognise her child? A mother who had suffered the loss of her only child, whose love was frozen in time like the statues of leaping dolphins and stately warriors on horseback, impervious to change. A fossil love, deeply embedded. And the dread niggle: what if I was wrong, and Nathan was not their lost boy?

I took off my sandals and walked into the edge of the water. It was freezing cold, like needles under my feet. I almost lost my balance as small sharp stones threaded more pain across my soles.

Nathan. Josh. Rafael. Which one was he?

iii

At the western end of Cascais, the yellow fort sat on a long rock, jutting out from the beach into the sea like a run-aground battleship. Brown ridged cliffs rose up beyond, dunes behind. Nowadays the Fortaleza do Guincho, cannons at the entrance, is a luxury hotel at the western end of Cascais, and this was where Eduardo arranged a room for me that day, to try to catch some sleep while the family conducted its business.

I was shown through an interior courtyard to a fine room, seventeenth-century according to the booklet on the desk, with a wide view of the rollers crashing below as the tide came in. And there I waited. I showered. I had a long bath. I rinsed out my underwear and sent my dress to the hotel laundry for a two-hour service—the same dress I had been wearing since I drove to Lisbon to meet Eduardo by the Monument to the Discoveries the previous day. It felt like much longer.

But I was too pent-up to rest properly. I considered making inroads into the minibar but resisted, taking the sensible option of ordering some food from room service. Even though I was hungry, I couldn't eat much. My phone was either in my hand or by my side at all times. I desperately wanted to call Nathan but knew that I had to hold off, to let him contact me when he was ready. It remained silent. Not even the jaunty whistle of a text arriving.

It was early evening before I heard anything.

"We are coming over to you," said Eduardo. "Dinner at eight in the restaurant."

He sounded strained. "Is everything all right?"

"Yes . . . yes, of course."

"Just . . . an emotional day . . ."

"Yes. Extremely so."

I hoped that was all it was.

At least my dress felt fresh as I pulled it on. I brushed my hair and did a scratch job on my face with the old cosmetics that floated loose at the bottom of my bag.

The dining room at the Fortaleza do Guincho might as well have been on an ocean liner, surrounded by the sea and sky. The others, minus the lawyer, were there when I arrived, installed at a table in one corner by the panoramic window. Eduardo and Nathan stood—was this awkward for Nathan?—and I was introduced to a slim, well-preserved woman in late middle age. Carolina would have been lovely once, I could tell, before suffering etched deep lines on her face. Her eyes watered.

I held out my hand, not knowing what else to do, but she got up and gave me an encouraging smile, and then a shaky hug. Nathan took my hand and held on to it when I sat down next to him. "All right?" I mouthed to him. He nodded, also teary.

Carolina was scarcely able to look away from him, transfixed by his every movement.

"Thank you," she said to me, over and over in a light American accent, voice slightly husky. I could see that Nathan was taken with her. Conversation was forced, the usual social niceties inappropriate.

"How long have you known each other?" she asked me. If she had any misgivings about the age difference between her son and me, she did not allow them to show.

"Not all that long," I replied.

"A lifetime," said Nathan.

I thought I knew what he meant. At least I hoped I did. I had known him, as Nathan Emberlin, for as long as he had existed. I gave his hand a squeeze under the table though it made me feel sad.

"Do I still call you Nathan?" I asked.

"To us, he is Rafael," said Carolina. "Healing from God—that is what his name means, and it has never been more true."

The question of whether he was who the Waldes hoped he was seemed resolved. Food and wine was ordered. Family history was exchanged. I supposed this was an extension of the conversations they had been having all day.

"For two decades I prayed to a deity who did not seem to be listening. I should have had more faith," said Carolina. "There was a statue of the Virgin Mary on the hall table in my mother's house. She was tall, half a metre high, with family rosaries draped over her shoulders. My mother told me that when she was a child she once saw oily tears rolling down the Virgin's cheeks. When she touched her she was warm, warm as my mother's skin. I have the statue still. She has never cried again. Her blessings remained dammed behind that smooth, knowing face."

She was giving vent to a stream of pent-up emotion. "When the snatch happened, the hours and minutes before did not seem important. I was not taking notice of them. It was only afterwards that they became the most crucial moments of my life. I picked my memories clean until they were sterile but there was nothing more. I detached from life, barren of expectation. But now he is here, and it is a miracle." She gave him a hesitantly broad smile, perhaps one that she had not used for more than twenty years. "My child, returned to me as a man."

It hardly needed to be said that there was still a delicate puzzle to be resolved, that there were parts of him that were forever lost to her, that she could never know or understand. Perhaps, for now, it was enough just to know that such a long period of suffering had concluded.

There was a sense of history, of stories converging. Nathan gave them a picture of his boyhood in South London, fleshing out the bones of the story he must already have told them.

"What is so strange is that it's only recently that I found out that what I thought belonged to me there, didn't. Not the family, the relatives, the memories they shared with me. There was no connection, except that I was there. It's like a bomb has hit the house, the garden, the streets around and now it's just a wasteland. I can't explain it any better than that. Like I said,

I'm not the person I thought I was. The only link was with Terry Jackson."

I looked at Nathan fondly, then at the other two. "You have to admire this man's tenacity and courage," I said.

Eduardo nodded. Carolina seemed about to cry.

"What about Terry?" asked Nathan. "We need to get hold of him."

"Let's get our house in order first."

I assumed Eduardo was referring to an official DNA test. They would certainly need it to build the case from the bottom up.

"There are a few things I want to say to Terry Jackson," said Nathan.

"Don't worry, we're working on it."

Over a succession of delicate fish dishes, the conversation was more positive. Justice would be served, they had no doubt of that. The family had money and an excellent lawyer, as well as media contacts. The possibility was discussed that Nathan might become involved in the various Walde businesses. Not only had Nathan been reunited with his family, but with them had come new opportunities in Portugal he had never even considered.

"It's a good country," said Eduardo. "Not perfect, but where is?"

It was as if the past twenty-four hours had revitalised his faith in human nature. Optimism had replaced cynicism.

At the end of the evening, the three of them departed for Carolina's house. Carolina asked if I wanted to come back with them for the night, but I judged it better to stay where I was. The last thing I wanted was to crowd Nathan and his mother.

He gave me a peck on the lips as we said good night.

"You didn't tell me," I said softly. "What name?"

A fingertip landed tenderly on the end of my nose. "For now, to you, Nathan. I like the way you say it."

I wasn't sure what to make of that, but I smiled, and said, "Sleep tight."

"See you tomorrow. I'll pick you up."

At ten o'clock the next morning the concièrge rang up to tell me a limousine was waiting. I assumed the chauffeur had come alone to provide a taxi service, but when I got down to reception, Nathan was there. He bounded over, fizzing with all his old energy and more.

It wasn't far back to Cascais, but Nathan asked Tiago to take the coast road and then drop us at Praia da Rainha. I sat back and let him take charge. He didn't stop talking—about Carolina, about Eduardo and Eduardo's children, his cousins; what he had been told about his father Luiz's family—until we reached the town and the small beach in town where I'd sat early the previous morning.

I saw more now, beyond the rocks strewn across the sand and the needle-cold water: the way the buildings perched on rocks at the edge of the sea at in the centre, the shape of the beach that would once have been used only by fishermen. A tower shaped like a church steeple rose and stabbed the sky from an aristocratic house on the eastern end of the small bay. A restaurant called Fim do Mundo, the end of the world.

The past bore down heavily. What made someone leave one life and strike out for another, like Esta, or Karl—or Nathan? How could a person cope who discovered they were not who they thought they were? Were they the lucky ones, those who could step out of a shed skin and move forward? I had found it hard enough to escape my own, mundane past.

"We're getting the DNA test done this afternoon, at some private clinic in Lisbon," he said.

"Good," I said, because I wanted him, wanted them all, to have peace of mind. "The sooner the better."

Nathan held my hand again as we walked along the beach. I could already feel that our relationship was reverting to the comfort of friendship, and I didn't mind, not really. I was happy to have shared what we had. It had never been a realistic prospect, the two of us—but fun while it lasted.

"What are you going to do now?" I asked, after a while.

He was silent for a long minute, then he leaned in and kissed me, slowly and beautifully. It might have been for the last time—or maybe not. Who knew?

iv

I went with them to Lisbon and picked up the rental car I'd abandoned. Eduardo insisted that he would deal with it, get it returned to a Hertz office in the capital for me, but I thanked him and declined. After the past few days, I wanted some independent thinking time, and an undemanding drive to Faro, on an underused toll road with nothing to hurry back for, was just what I needed.

I took it easy, listening to music on the radio, which gave way to a current affairs hour. It was all the same old: public anger, scandals, cover-ups, the ever rising cost of living, unemployment, declining living and social conditions, discontent and distrust of the political elite. My Portuguese was good enough now to get the gist. I switched it off.

It was mid-afternoon by the time I dropped the car at the airport. I couldn't think of any reason to keep hold of it now. The bus into Faro centre was almost empty except for a few travellers with luggage and some people returning early from the beach. The sky had gradually become overcast. I went straight back to the studio. I felt a few drops of rain on my face, as I fumbled for the keys. The red main door on the Rua da Misericórdia swung open as usual. My footsteps echoed on the stone stairs. It seemed a long time since I was last here.

A cup of tea, that's what I wanted. I remember imagining the comfort of its taste and steam as I put the key into the lock and pushed open the door. The studio looked a lot more untidy than it should have been. This time there was no room for doubt.

"You took your time."

The voice came from the wall behind the door. I froze. I should have slammed the door and run back down the stairs but I wasn't quick enough. The door was kicked shut behind me and a small man with receding red hair stood in front of me.

"Who the hell are you?" I asked.

He gave a smirk. "I think you know who I am."

"I really don't. I want you to get out, whoever you are."

He remained stock-still. The threat was real. He may not have been all that tall but he was strong and wiry. The rolled-up shirtsleeves showed the muscles on his forearms.

Another offensive smirk. "You've been trying to find me. Now you have."

Terry Jackson sprang forward, knocking the breath out of me. I was up against the wall with his hand around my throat. His white, freckled face was close to mine. "You have no idea who you are dealing with. I have got some very bad friends, you know what I'm saying? Unlike me, they have no manners. And they really don't know when to stop."

He released his hand, though I still felt the finger marks on my neck.

"Where's the boy?" he asked.

I shook my head.

"The police had to let him go the other night, but he's not at his place and he's not here, so where is the little fucker? He wants to see me—well, I'm here now."

I tried staring him out, but when I didn't reply he came back at me, pushing his right forearm into my throat.

"I don't know where he is!" I cried. "He's not here."

"Wrong answer."

"He's in Lisbon."

Jackson released me. "What's he doing there?"

"He's with the Waldes," I said. "He's found his family. You won't get him now."

"Wrong again."

A shrug, as defiant as I dared.

"The Waldes are not his family," he said.

"It's too late now. There's nothing you can say to stop him."

"You believed all that bull, did you? Haven't you worked out yet that bloke of yours is a waste of space?"

I knew I had to stay calm.

Jackson sniffed, looked around and then back at me. "He's not the Walde boy."

"The Waldes think otherwise."

There was a long pause while he took his time lighting a cigarette, then assessing the burning tip. I hoped he wouldn't use it to give me burns.

"He's been lying to you, hasn't he—to you all. Naughty boy. Like 'em younger, do you?"

I let the insult go.

"The Walde boy is dead."

Again, I made no response, though my mind was working overtime.

"He was done away with more than twenty years ago."

Could it be true? Did Jackson know for certain because he was there when it happened?

Jackson took a couple of paces across the room, sucking on his cigarette. The smell of it filled the confined space.

I had to treat this as one of those chess-move interviews: act confidently, as if I knew far more than I did; offer a degree of empathy; appear to give good information of my own in return for answers; show independence, not blind loyalty. And my initial response was genuine enough.

"Seriously—he's been lying about all of this?"

"Pants on fucking fire."

I didn't know what to believe. But I was beginning to understand why Jackson had tracked Nathan down to Faro to find out what kind of threat he posed, and to deal with him, whether the boy had survived after he was taken, or not. The last thing he wanted was for the twenty-year-old Walde case to be stirred up again by the son of an old acquaintance.

Jackson watched me carefully. "I expect you'd like to have a word with him now, eh?"

Too right I would.

"So the boy's in Lisbon. Where in Lisbon?"

I started to walk over to the window, but he pushed me back, hard. I pictured Nathan with Carolina and

Eduardo at the Fortaleza do Guincho and felt sick. We had all so badly wanted his story to be true. Even looking at the photographs, it had been possible to convince ourselves that there was a family resemblance.

"I can tell you," I said, standing my ground. "But first I want to know something. Ian Rylands. Why was he killed?"

"He was way too interested in things that didn't concern him. The resorts, the people who ran them, what went on in the war . . ."

"Who killed him?"

"He killed himself by refusing to give up."

As I thought. Jackson knew. Maybe he did it himself. Up till then I hadn't wanted to admit that Jackson was capable of doing me serious harm. I wondered if I could use my mobile to get help, but there was no chance of making a call.

He must have read some of this on my face. Jackson held out a surprisingly small hand. "Phone. Now."

I blanked him.

"Now!"

My bag was still hanging from my shoulder. I delved inside it, for the pocket where I always kept it to hand. "It always gets lost at the bottom," I said, pretending to rummage. I found my phone and switched it on. I don't know what I thought I could achieve. Sending a text was out of the question. I swiped the screen, pressed the phone log and held my finger on the first contact, the last number dialled. "It always falls to the bottom. Big bag."

Jackson advanced. "Give it here."

"I'm trying to find it!" I shouted. I stopped scrabbling and looked up, hoping my phone had dialled. I couldn't think who it was I had called last, or even if I had pressed the name at the top of the list. "Patience, Mr. Jackson. Nathan is at a private clinic in the Rua da Misericórdia." I assumed there would be a street of that name in Lisbon. It was the best I could think of in the circumstances to try to convey where I was and who was in the studio with me.

"A clinic?"

"For a DNA test. If you're right, he won't get away with it."

Jackson grabbed my bag. I dropped the phone deep inside. He put his hand in but fished up nothing from the deep layer of old receipts, notebooks and pens, bags of nuts and scummy cosmetics.

"I must have lost it," I said. "Flaming hell."

"Right, you're coming with me. In fact, you can drive. Where have you left that heap of tin you hired?"

"Not far from the usual place."

If I could only get out of the studio and onto the street, I reckoned I would be a lot safer. He obviously didn't know the Seat had been returned to the airport.

I pulled the door of the studio shut behind us, noting the lack of damage to the lock. More confirmation I was dealing with a professional. I waited until we were out in public. There were people around, but the ordinary scene seemed too quiet, unfamiliar. Despite the grey clouds, the heat and humidity were oppressive. Palm trees slumped and the boats in the marina were still.

"Was it you driving that car at me, the other day?" I asked. It seemed so obvious now.

"A friendly warning."

"There were other, more polite, ways to tell me."

Jackson held my arm firmly as we walked in light rain towards the Rua Dr. Francisco Gomes. Oleander petals were limp brown curls on the ground.

"What do you want from me?" I asked.

No response.

"I think you're assuming I know more than I do," I said to the well-worn black trainers on Jackson's feet. "I've only just met this guy, and I only know what he told me, and if it's all rubbish anyway—then, what can I help you with?"

"You can get him to come and see me. I don't like people who have no loyalty. I helped his family—I helped him—and what do I get for it? He comes out here and starts accusing me of all sorts. He needs to be told."

"The Café Aliança doesn't look too busy," I said as we passed. I prayed the phone was still on. "I could really do with a coffee before we set out."

"You trying to annoy me?"

"I could do with a coffee—and I think I might have left my phone in there."

"Keep walking."

"Just let me go and ask about my phone. If you want me to get in touch with Nathan, that's the only way I'm going to do it."

Before he could pull me back, I dived towards the revolving door. He stuck with me. At the bar, João was polishing glasses.

I gave him an intense look, darting my eyes sideways to Jackson, and said quickly in English, "When I was in earlier I think I must have left my phone on the table." I flung my hand towards a table where I had never sat. "When I was with Senhor Palhares. Is he still here?" I was counting on João to take the hint.

"I will go and ask. Wait here, please," he said without a flicker of recognition.

Jackson was tense at my side. I could see he could hardly believe I had got him in this position. I could hardly believe it myself. I was getting used to taking stupid risks. "Do you want to get hold of Nathan, or not, Mr. Jackson?" I said.

But Jackson had had enough. I felt a sharp pain in my arm, as if it had been cut with the tip of a knife, and then he wheeled me round roughly and pulled me towards the door.

"Not another word," he said.

My arm felt wet. I had a feeling it was blood but couldn't check because Jackson was holding on to me so closely. We bumped together through the revolving door and out into the street again. He muttered under his breath and marched me towards the street where I used to leave the car.

"Where is it?" he snarled.

"What?"

"Do you want to get hurt? The car!"

"I gave it back. Didn't think I would need it again."

Jackson looked around. Then dug his fingers into my arm where it hurt. "Don't move an inch." I only cried out when I saw the blood spreading.

Within a minute, he had broken into another parked car, yet another anonymous small white vehicle. He made it look so easy. Anyone seeing it done would have thought he had the keys, not a clutch of small metal prongs. He opened the passenger door and pushed me into the seat, locking the door before going round to the other side. The engine gunned and he put his foot down.

"Where are we going?"

"Just shut up, now. I've had enough of you."

We headed west out of Faro, in the direction of the airport but avoiding the main road. I held my arm tightly, hoping the bleeding would stop soon. I felt as if I was outside myself, watching as reality distorted.

The car swerved into a housing estate of high-rise blocks so suddenly that I felt nauseous. We pulled up sharply at a kerb and I expected to be told to get out. Jackson left the engine running as he opened the glove compartment and rummaged through the contents. The only item that interested him was a rag, perhaps for cleaning the windscreen. He shook it out, and said, "Come here. Lean forward. Arms back." Then he tied my wrists together behind my back. "Do you want to go in the fucking boot?" he shouted when I resisted. The material was stiff and scratchy. Then, from his pocket, he produced an eye mask, the kind you get on long-haul flights, and put it on me. "Now put your head to one side and pretend you're asleep."

The car pulled away. After a while the road became uncomfortably pitted, which told me we were keeping to the back routes. He can't have wanted me and my eye mask to be spotted. We bounced around for some time. It felt like forever, and all the time I was trying to work out how to find out where we were and saying it out loud in the fading hope that my phone was still live.

But I didn't know where I was, or where we were heading.

The car stopped. The engine died. I heard Jackson open the driver's door, slam it shut, and then his footsteps around to my side. He wrenched the door open and reached in to get me on my feet.

"Why won't you tell me where we are? I thought you wanted me to help you?"

"When I'm ready."

We stumbled along together, my bag having slipped from my shoulder and swinging from my bound wrists. I made harder work of walking than I needed to, in a vain attempt to make him take the mask off my eyes. Wherever we were, it was very quiet and he can't have been concerned that anyone might see us. Underfoot, the path was uneven. I tripped a couple of times and he stopped me from falling with an iron grip. I tried to register any sounds or smells that might give me a clue to our whereabouts but there was nothing, not even the cry of a seabird.

I bumped into a solid wall, painfully scraping my cheekbone. Jackson laughed. I heard a light metal jangle and what sounded like a lock being released. A door opening. I was pushed inside.

Now I could smell something. The interior was damp. Musty, too. It hadn't been aired for a while. Jackson closed the door behind us. The unmistakable sound followed of bolts being shot, then a scraping sound across the floor.

"Take a seat," said Jackson. He took my shoulders roughly and backed me into a hard chair. "Right, a nice change of scene to help you to focus."

"I never said I wouldn't help you, Mr. Jackson. You didn't need to bring me wherever this is."

"I needed to show you I'm serious."

"Please can you take this mask off my eyes? It's making me feel claustrophobic. I can't think with it on."

Silence.

"Tell you what. I'm going to leave you for a while. To concentrate your mind."

"But what do you want me to do?"

His answer was the door opening and closing again. There didn't seem any way of untying my wrists, which were beginning to hurt as much as the cut in my right arm.

I knew my phone must be losing power, so I had to take the chance. "Please help me," I said aloud. "Terry Jackson has taken me somewhere west of Faro. We came by car on back roads—an hour maybe? I can't be sure. Not very long. It's a musty building. I'm at ground level. I'm blindfolded. My wrists are tied. It's very quiet, no cars or anyone around."

The black silence seemed to engulf me, the worst kind of sleepless night. Minutes stretched into—I don't know how long. Perhaps I did go to sleep after all.

When I came to, I said it all again, several times, even though I was sure it was hopeless. I was just repeating the loop again, wondering whether I was going mad, when I thought I heard something. I stopped to listen, holding my breath. It wasn't Jackson returning. It was further away than that.

"'I think . . . that was a horse neighing."

The penny dropped. "I'm at The Lucky Horseshoe at Vale Navio."

It was a very long night. I assumed it was night because it was cold in the damp building. Jackson had obviously decided to let me stew. The chances of anyone coming past his abandoned business were slim. Even if

I screamed, in the unlikely event of anyone hearing me, they would assume it was one of the Vale Navio squatters or other undesirables, and steer clear.

I was hungry and very thirsty now. Feeling quite weak, too, though spurts of anger cut through my lethargy. I must have been dozing when the locks on the door rattled.

"Terry?" I called. I'd decided I had to behave as if we were friends, and I was going to do whatever it took to get him whatever the hell it was he wanted.

Footsteps came across the floor. It certainly sounded as if the space was big enough for a holiday bar.

"In a more helpful mood today, I hope?"

"Yes."

"I brought you some breakfast." The rustle of a paper wrapping was enough to make me salivate. "But first things first, eh?"

Jackson pulled up a chair.

"Now, I thought we could take another little trip together today. But first I need to make sure your friend is still in Lisbon."

"Please can I take the mask off—and I desperately need to go to the loo—"

"Tut, tut. Very demanding. I thought we were going to have a nice chat before you reverted to type."

"Tell me what you need."

"That's better. As I say, we are going to go up to Lisbon and you are going to show me where our boy is. Understand?"

"Yes."

"You know where you left him?"

"Yes."

"Good. Now we're getting somewhere."

Jackson released my numb hands, which refused even to tingle for a worryingly long time, and then flicked back the eye mask. I forced myself to look him in the eye and thank him.

I was right. We were in the middle of what had once been a bar. Empty bottles stood to attention on shelves. Broken chairs and tables were stacked haphazardly. Windows were boarded up and there was evidence of an alarming leak from the ceiling.

The erstwhile landlord tossed me a custard tart in a paper bag and I was about to eat it when I remembered how Ian Rylands died. "Sorry," I said. "Lactose intolerant. I'll be ill if I eat this."

He stared me down, and then shrugged. "Suit yourself." He snatched it back and ate it himself as my stomach growled.

"Loo, please," I said. "It's either here or in the car."

He had just agreed, when there was a bleep from my bag. My mobile was warning me it needed recharging.

"What's that?" he asked.

I tensed for whatever repercussions were going to follow. Just then, there was an almighty shattering of wood and glass. An explosion of smoke. Shouting figures burst in. I was grabbed from behind, unable to give more than a squeak of protest as the breath was knocked out of me. It was only when I was clutched protectively to a black-clad chest and rushed outside through a side door hanging off its hinges that I realised it was the police.

Two men got out of a police car waiting around the corner and ran towards me. They were Eduardo Walde and Nathan.

"Thank you, thank you . . ." I didn't know what else to say as I fell on them. I felt as if I was going to collapse.

"What's happened to your arm—are you okay?" asked Nathan.

"It's nothing. Looks worse than it was—I think Jackson had a knife, but it's not much more than a scratch. He won't be done for attempted murder," I joked feebly.

"Very brave," said Eduardo.

"Maybe a bit too brave," said Nathan, as I clung to him for support. He held the back of my head and pressed me tightly to him. "Bloody hell, Jo . . ."

"Did it work? Did you get my call? I tried to call one of you but all I could manage was the log—last number dialled . . ."

Nathan nodded. "It came through to me. You cut out quite quickly, but I heard you going along the street talking to him. God, I'm proud of you." He held me tightly.

"And Nuno called me, after you went into the Aliança," said Eduardo. "As soon as the barman gave us a description of the man you were with, we came racing down here. I'm sorry we had to waste time, but we had to get the police on board."

"But if my mobile cut out—how did you know where I was?"

"I knew. I just knew," said Nathan. "The Lucky Horseshoe was always where he hung out."

"Wasn't it too obvious a place to hide me?" I couldn't understand why Jackson had been so unimaginative.

"Only to those who know him of old," said Eduardo grimly.

They both helped me walk to the police car. Jackson was being shoved pretty roughly into another. For once I didn't know quite what to say to Nathan. I was still in shock, still processing the implications of what Jackson had said about the Walde boy being murdered not long after he was abducted.

V

This time when the police took my statement, I had the formidable Fausto Ribeiro at my side to ensure I wasn't kept for longer than necessary. The detectives' focus was now on Jackson and his associates among the Himmelreich family, the murder of Ian Rylands, and the relevance of a child disappearance case that had never been solved.

"Jackson was protected by the Himmelreichs for years, ever since he spirited the Walde child away to Malaga to be adopted in England," said Ribeiro. "But no longer. Ever since the Stern case, when too many questions have been asked about children who have disappeared in this part of Portugal, Jackson has had to protect himself the best he could."

"I hope he has a long and uncomfortable night ahead of him," I said. It seemed only just.

When I was free to go, Eduardo insisted that I come back to Cascais. I accepted. I hadn't been looking forward to going back to the studio on my own.

All I wanted was a bath and a sandwich and to go to bed when we arrived back at Carolina's house. Nathan was gently solicitous and concerned. I assured him I was fine, only exhausted. But for once, I felt uneasy with him. Had Jackson told me the truth about Nathan, or was he trying to confuse me? I couldn't think about it anymore. One thing was certain, I didn't want to be the messenger of bad news. Either way, the results of the DNA test would tell the family. I slept fitfully, waking each time to vivid, absurd dreams. I was amazed to find it was almost eleven when the light warmed me and I looked at my watch. Even then I didn't get up until Nathan put his head round the door.

"How are you?"

"Good, thanks. You?" I didn't really need to ask. He seemed recharged, glowing with happiness, his lovely face no longer carved to the bone, the shadows gone.

He came and sat on the bed. "Relieved. Guilty at what I've put you through."

"It wasn't your fault."

"No, but—"

He reached out to me in a way I now recognised. My physical desire for him was heightened by the knowledge that what we both wanted to do, to make the world recede until it was just the two of us, skin on skin, would have been an impropriety at this moment in his mother's house. He knew that, too, but I was touched by his need to reassure me that nothing had changed between us.

I steeled myself. "Tell me, did you get the DNA results?"

"Yep."

"And?"

"All good."

"Rafael?"

"Yes. It feels . . . I don't know . . . weird. But good."

"Well . . . thank God for that."

"Carolina has been . . . well, you can imagine."

"Yes." I had the strongest feeling I couldn't leave it there, though. Everything we had done so far had been about finding the truth, all of it. "Were you there, when the medics announced the results?"

"No. The clinic called Eduardo. He told me."

"It must have been quite a moment."

"It certainly was." He paused. "What you did . . . with Jackson . . . you are pretty amazing, you know."

"It was the last stupid risk I want to take for a while," I said.

"What?"

"Nothing."

"It will be good to finally know exactly what happened. Now the police have Jackson."

"If he tells them."

"Are you OK, Jo? You sound a bit funny."

"Just . . . processing everything, you know."

He looked hurt, so I gave him a peck on the cheek. He was so very beautiful, with that curious vulnerability, I thought sadly. No wonder the Waldes wanted to claim him, no matter what.

I couldn't shake my downbeat mood even after the best coffee I'd ever tasted. I knew I had to speak to Eduardo. I asked where he was and a maid showed me through dark green shutters to a terrace at the back of the house. It overlooked a courtyard garden prettily planned around a series of Moorish arches. Eduardo was tapping at a laptop on a wrought-iron table.

He stood up and asked how I was. I smiled and said I was fine, thanked him again. All I wanted was to get it over with, to ask what I had to ask, for once and for all.

In the garden below, Carolina and Nathan—I still didn't know what to call him; Rafael made me uncomfortable—were talking, two dark heads close together.

"How are *you* feeling?" I asked Eduardo.

He didn't respond for a while. "As if everything has come right."

"Has it, though—really?"

"What do you mean?"

A deep breath. "Jackson told me the boy . . . didn't survive long after the abduction."

"I see."

The sound of Carolina's laughter reached us.

"She has suffered greatly, and now she is happy," I said, searching his still-handsome face for signs of stress.

"That is true."

Another pause.

"You see, I was wondering whether . . . maybe . . . the DNA result that you all wanted so much was not actually the one that the clinic confirmed . . ."

Eduardo looked out at the luxuriant garden, lost somewhere in the middle distance. Then he shook his head. "Come with me."

He led me into a sitting room.

A pair of antique prints on the wall showed maps of the world dated 1511. I remembered what he said about the Portuguese and their history; perhaps he was now claiming Nathan as the famous navigators had once claimed new territories. And whoever Nathan was, though there was a dead space where his past had once been, he still had a good heart. I couldn't blame him for taking this chance—this lucky chance, perhaps—to change his life. What he had been through could have broken a lesser spirit.

Eduardo went over to a wall table. He picked up a piece of folded white paper and handed it to me. The name and logo of a clinic in Lisbon was embossed on the letterhead.

"I'm not sure whether your Portuguese is good enough to understand the fine print, but," he put a finger on it, "this line is very simple. 'Nathan Emberlin, the given name on adoption papers, is the son of Carolina de Almeida Vicente.'"

I closed my eyes. Relief coursed through my veins. "Jackson was lying, after all."

"He had to try all that he could to stop Rafa—and you—from getting to the truth. The Himmelreichs will be most unhappy for the investigation to be reopened. As it is, let us hope that the consequences for all involved are severe."

I felt slightly ashamed, but said in my defence, "You understand I had to ask?"

"I do." He considered for a moment. "I am glad you think I possess such a ruthless kindness."

He brushed aside any further awkwardness with a hand through the air. "Now, you'll be interested to know that I've just opened an email from Aloisio Gambóias, the detective in charge of the Rylands case. I've heard it said that to find out who has committed a crime, you first have to know how it was committed. And how poor Mr. Rylands died is very interesting indeed."

"I thought they knew he was poisoned."

"Indeed. But it was not administered to him in the glass of whisky found by his side. A puncture point in his back shows it was injected. And it is the type of poison that is so telling." Eduardo paused, enjoying the suspense. "The residues and lactates in his blood were compatible with the hydrocyanic liquids used by the Germans during the Second World War. Cyanide, in other words."

I exhaled. "Another lesson being taught?"

"Very likely."

"So, again, it points to—"

"The Himmelreichs."

"But if nothing has ever stopped them before . . . ?"

"This time I think they have overreached themselves. Perhaps they no longer have their paid influences. Perhaps that is why they were so desperate to stop Rafa and you. This time, it will come out, I think. I hear that Terry Jackson has been singing to the police like a little bird in a cage while he awaits trial.

"And there are new vested interests. With the southern European countries suffering economically, Germany is being asked to play a major role in bailing out Portugal—as well as Greece, and possibly Spain. But if Portugal is still sitting on gold reserves of dubious wartime origins . . . Before now the question of Nazi gold has always been shut down. In 1999 a European Commission report on Portugal's gold reserves found that the country was not liable to pay compensation for looted wartime gold. But the commission was led by a Portuguese ex–prime minister, so . . ."

"Interesting times."

"Very interesting."

"There wouldn't be any of the wartime gold left in the bank in Faro, would there?"

Eduardo laughed. "That all went to good causes a long time ago."

"I did wonder whether . . . maybe some went towards the cost of buying Horta das Rochas after the war?" I had come so far that I might as well ask one more intrusive question.

Eduardo answered straightaway. "I believe Calixto Palhares did lend my father funds for the purchase. But it was not a great deal of money. Horta das Rochas was an unprofitable old farm in a very poor part of the country. No one else wanted it. And the loan was paid back as soon as Karl inherited some money back in Germany. Alva eventually had family money, too, from America."

I felt elated as we went out to join Rafa and his mother down in the courtyard garden. I thought I might be able to call him Rafa; it suited him. He looked dazzling that morning, his face lit by inner radiance. It was mirrored by Carolina's expression as they stood admiring a bronze sculpture of a stork.

"Remember climbing up to the storks' nest on the old fort wall?"

I nodded.

He reached for my hand, and I felt a shiver of excitement.

"Whatever happens," he said, holding tightly, "don't let go."

vi

And so, I haven't. I have written, as he wanted me to, the story of how I met Nathan Emberlin in Faro in August 2014, and how he regained his real identity as Rafael Carlos de Almeida Vicente. It was intended to give hope to other families who have lost a child in similar circumstances. At the beginning I tried to be objective, to give the facts alone, but that proved impossible; I was personally involved. It was easy to understand why Esta Hartford wrote her story as a novel, giving herself the safety net of deniability and flexibility when the facts were too stark.

Because there are always more than just facts, even in a true story. It takes time to evaluate every aspect and angle. Some contradictions can be accepted as nothing more complicated than human nature. Perhaps that was why I allowed myself to fall in love with Nathan, and even to live with him for a while in Lisbon. I still care for him, want the best for him.

But I have doubts.

Parts of the story still make me uneasy. Every aspect Nathan and Carolina endorsed as an obvious truth, I made myself examine dispassionately. I had to be sure. Privately, I couldn't stop wondering whether Nathan really was the boy the Walde family so wanted him to be. When I pressed Eduardo to admit that he was claiming Nathan for pragmatic reasons, he had the papers from the clinic that did the DNA test all ready and waiting for me. But were they genuine? I didn't examine them closely. Even if I had, I reasoned, they would have stood up to scrutiny; Eduardo Walde could well have come to a lucrative arrangement with the clinic behind closed doors no matter what the scientific outcome. He and Nathan had clearly formed a bond, right from the start.

When Terry Jackson told me the boy was long dead, I assumed he would say anything to stop me in my tracks. But did it follow, necessarily, that he was lying? Other children went missing around that time. Was it possible that another boy had been substituted between the kidnap of the Walde boy and the arrival of a child at the Malaga adoption agency? I had started to think that the mention of Horta das Rochas by the woman who used to work there in Nathan's story seemed a little too pat, that perhaps it was designed to mislead. So far Jackson has made no admission that would worsen his situation and it could be years until he can be questioned in court. The judicial process moves slowly in Portugal.

For months, I put my qualms aside and lived in the moment. Lisbon scintillated with light. Nathan and I were gifted the use of an apartment with views over the city's terra-cotta roofs to the river. He began working with Eduardo at the family company, a precious apprentice who charmed wherever he went. We partied with a young rich crowd, but we were equally happy alone together. We laughed a lot. I wondered how faithful Nathan would be, but he proved both loving and loyal. Our miraculous summer extended into winter.

Spring had banished the sea mists by the time I finished my account of our mission. My uneasiness about its resolution remained, though. I had to decide how to live with that, while Nathan had become Rafa all too completely, with no further imperative to question the family's faith in him.

For both of us, in our different ways, my continuing concerns were a form of punishment.

"What about the photographs of my mother when she was young? I look like her," he would say.

"We all see what we want to see."

"But we don't have to think about this anymore."

"Whoever you are, you are extraordinary," I told him. "Nothing can change that."

It made me desperately sad, knowing I was spoiling something so special. But, if I'm honest, our romance no longer had that spark ignited by the excitement of the quest. Perhaps I should have trusted more, accepted good fortune with grace, and conceded that passion, by its very nature, inevitably evolved into a quieter bond. He told me often that he loved me. But his gratitude became hard to bear.

I stayed until June. I will always think of Portugal, and the time we had together, as three hundred days of sun. I'm sure I will never meet anyone as captivating, generous, and courageous as Nathan Emberlin. But in the end, tempting as it was to ride the wave into a life of comfort and loving friendship, I could not find consolation in a beautiful lie.

THE END

Author's Note

The seeds of this novel were sown when I traveled to Faro with my daughter, Maddy, who had booked herself a two-week Portuguese language course there. She was only seventeen at the time, and I felt I couldn't allow her to go alone, though she would have done so quite happily. While she went to class every morning, I wandered around the town with a street map, camera, and my notebook.

I am always inspired to write by the places I visit, and Faro was no exception. I had never been there before, though I knew the name from a hundred airport departure boards as the hub for tourists traveling to the Algarve coast. Maddy and I were charmed from the first evening by its mosaic pavements, by the laid-back atmosphere in the August heat, by the sea and the glimpses of green salt marsh. In the afternoons, we found various ways to get to the beaches and islands—and the first time we went to Praia de Faro we found the sea curiously green and furry, though this is not the usual state of affairs.

It's important to say here that, for all the geographical accuracy of my portrayal of Faro, the town in this book is an imaginary version: certain elements, like the great storm of February 1941 and the reopening of the Café Aliança during the local elections (held, in real life, in 2013), are superficially true, but the story in the book is entirely fictional, from the washed-up whale and the attacks on the storks, to the salvage of wartime gold off the coast here. In particular, I cast no aspersions on any real local politicians or townspeople, or past events. The resort of Horta das Rochas is also completely fictitious, as are the riding stables close to Vale Navio, and though both may have obvious similarities with real-life businesses on the Algarve, this is only in order to give my story the tang of authenticity.

It has been a long time coming, but a big thank you is due to the Portuguese Tourist Board in London. In June 1985, I was lucky enough to be invited on a press trip to Lisbon, Cascais, and Estoril. I was a rookie reporter on the *Kentish Times*, a weekly newspaper based in South London. The trip was an adventure that began with a gathering of six or seven strangers in the departure lounge at Heathrow airport; we were to be escorted by a Portuguese guide with a twinkly smile called João and, in return for writing an article extolling the beauty of this area of Portugal's Atlantic coast, we would be treated to a week of interesting trips and lovely meals.

We had a wonderful time. Everyone seemed to get along, and there was lots of laughter, including a running joke about sardines, though the details of that one have gotten away. We visited Setúbal, Óbidos, Belém, and Sintra, and the *pousadas*, medieval castles and convents that had been transformed into atmospheric hotels. We had dinner one evening at the Fortaleza do Guincho at Cascais, where we drank white port with ice as an aperitif. Unfortunately, when I got back to England and wrote my piece, only four sparse, dull paragraphs made it into print, with no photography. I was so embarrassed that I never went to the trip reunion in London a few months later, not daring to face João again. So if anyone at the Portuguese Tourist Board should find themselves reading this book, may I say *obrigado* and apologize for making you wait so long for some words that do Lisbon and Cascais justice.

During the Second World War, Lisbon must have been a fascinating, yet frightening and desperate, place. As Hitler's armies of occupation swept across Europe, neutral (or supposedly neutral) Portugal became one of the continent's last escape routes; in an image that many will recall, Lisbon was the transit point for Bergman's Ilsa when she was waved off by Bogart's Rick in the classic movie *Casablanca*, made in 1942.

For many of the contemporary details of the era and historical context, I am especially indebted to the following books:

Flight into Portugal by Ronald Bodley. Some details of the Bartons' journey from France—in particular the route they took and Ronald Bagshaw's wonderful sangfroid in obtaining documents allowing onward travel from Bayonne—are adapted from his account, published in 1941 when his observations would still have been fresh.

The Lisbon Route: Entry and Escape in Nazi Europe by Ronald Weber. Not only is this book a treasure trove of fascinating insights, but it's a thrilling read. I have used the name Ronald in the novel in acknowledgment of the invaluable background details this and the previous book provided. It goes without saying that anyone who has been intrigued by the historical background to this story can do no better than read them.

Lisbon: War in the Shadows of the City of Light, 1939–1945 by Neill Lochery. Another highly recommended read, especially for the economic consequences of the war, explanations of the wolfram trade and the importance of "Nazi gold."

Memo to a Firing Squad by Frederick Hazlitt Brennan is an anti-Nazi thriller set in wartime Lisbon and first published in 1943. I read it as part of my research after I had planned the story in detail and started writing this book. In one of those slightly eerie writers' coincidences that seem to occur almost too often to mention, I realized that Hazlitt Brennan had already coined the term "The Lisbon Pact" in relation to Nazi ambitions in Portugal. My first thought was that I should change my text immediately, but in the end—because I enjoy eerie coincidences—I left it, with acknowledgment here that I am not the first to use it.

Simone de Beauvoir's autobiographical *Force of Circumstance* touches on a journey she made to Portugal in February 1945, giving a brief insight into how important black-market supplies of food into France and Germany were. War brought hunger, as the French— and the British, the Dutch, and the Belgians—knew all too well. Any food was at a premium, but fruit and other produce from sunnier places, if available at all, was highly prized, expensive, and, of course, the supply was wide open to corruption. She recognized, from painful recent experience, that many of the poor in southern Portugal were hungry, too.

As ever, I give heartfelt thanks to my wonderful editor, Jennifer Barth, with whom I work so happily, both on the big picture and the small scale, and my equally fabulous literary agent, Stephanie Cabot, whose instincts and advice are second to none.

I'd also like to thank Will Roberts, Erika Storella, and Ellen Goodson at the Gernert Company in New York. Thank you to all involved at HarperCollins, especially Amy Baker, Katherine Beitner, Jonathan Burnham, Cal Morgan, Kathryn Ratcliffe-Lee, Mary Sasso, Jarrod Taylor, Sherry Wasserman, and Erin Wicks. A special thank you to Rebecca Eifion-Jones for insisting, at a difficult time, on being the one to take the author photograph, and doing it superbly.

Finally, but most important, I couldn't have made it through my own difficult time during the writing of this book without the love and support of Rob, Maddy, Helen, Pam, Louise, Felicia, Tanya, Chris, Josine, Charlie, Camilla, Nilufer, Ivan, Sophie, Martin, Sara, Jeremy, Melanie, Liz, John, Tom, all my lovely blog and Facebook friends, and Claire, who found the words that helped so much.

About the Author

D eborah Lawrenson studied English at Cambridge University, and worked in London as a journalist. She is married with a daughter, and lives in Kent, England. Deborah's previous novels include *The Lantern* and *The Sea Garden*.

THE NEW LUXURY IN READING

We hope you enjoyed reading
our new, comfortable print size and found it
an experience you would like to repeat.

Well – you're in luck!

HarperLuxe offers the finest in fiction and
nonfiction books in this same larger print size and
paperback format. Light and easy to read, HarperLuxe
paperbacks are for book lovers who want to see
what they are reading without the strain.

For a full listing of titles and
new releases to come, please visit our website:

www.HarperLuxe.com